BEACH
HOUSE
7

By the Same Author
The Kaligarh Fault

BEACH HOUSE 7

A NOVEL
PAUL ROADARMEL

ST. MARTIN'S PRESS
New York

Design by M. Paul
Copy Editor: Eva Galan Salmieri

Library of Congress Cataloging-in-Publication Data

Roadarmel, Paul.
   Beach House 7.

    I. Title. II. Title: Beach House seven.
PS3568.016B4 1987   813'.54   86-26288
ISBN 0-312-00104-5

"A Joan Kahn Book"

First Edition
10 9 8 7 6 5 4 3 2 1

For my father

A technical solution to a political problem is always seductive.

—THEODORE WHITE

BEACH HOUSE
7

CHAPTER

1

June 1977

The surface of the Gulf of Siam takes on a different character in the breathless summer heat. It's a disturbing change, an apprehensive stillness that settles in when the monsoon is overdue. At times it hardly seems to be water at all, just a sheet of oily glare with massive swells rolling slowly underneath.

Everything had been the same for days now: a cruel limbo of heat and thirst and a growing hopelessness as the little tin pot of a coaster with its cargo of refugees drifted on an open sea. There was a grim irony to their fate; that these wretched souls should have suffered so much and come so far only to be left to bake in this rusting hulk within sight of land. Already they had begun to die—first the very old and then some of the children from dysentery during the night.

The captain was a stubby-legged Chinaman with a flat face and a sweat-stained yachting cap. He wore a permanent scowl and a pair of blackening red suspenders to hook his thumbs from whenever he was strutting around the deck.

The refugees hated him as much as they hated the ones who had driven them from their land. The Communists had taken almost everything they had before allowing them to motor out through the surf to the waiting boat where these foreigners, the captain and his mate, were free to take what the Communists had missed. And for what? For all his promises, for all his boasting, he'd only brought them to this.

He was in it with the rest of them, though. Adrift and helpless with his boat and a hundred or so miserable refugees. When the engine gave out for the last time he'd spent a couple of days below hammering away at it before he finally appeared on deck with his Filipino mate to announce that there was nothing more that could be done. The engine was old, that's all. Worn out. *"Tieu l'guan."* So it goes. And with that he headed for the bridge.

An elderly woman with a little girl tugging at her trousers fell in behind him, scolding him in her old hag's voice and shaking her gnarled fist at his back. He showed no sign that he noticed her and at last she gave it up. Tears streaking down her face, weakened by hunger and the muggy heat, she let the little girl lead her back to her family. The other Vietnamese watched in sullen silence from the shade of the cargo tarpaulins they had draped over the rigging to hide from the blistering sun.

The captain's face was as empty as the face of the sea all around. He was hugging a blunt-barreled AK-47 to his filthy undershirt, his hand wrapped over the trigger guard. The Filipino had a shotgun tossed casually over his shoulder.

The captain shaded his eyes for a moment while he searched the deck below, then he pointed to a soldier who had found a place for himself under a tattered parasol of loose burlap strung up to the rigging over the fo'c'sle.

He was a skinny young man with a hollow face and that haunted look common among the survivors of the new regime's "reeducation" camps. Oddly enough, while most of the refugees sought refuge in their anonymity, this one had gone so far as to smuggle his uniform aboard and change into it shortly after they had put to sea. An act of defiance perhaps, or maybe he was just trying to distinguish himself from the general squalor, as if he could draw upon his military starch to retain his resolute posture. On the deck beside him was a small brown rucksack with the zigzag patch of the 77th Technical Support Unit.

The Filipino regarded him knowingly, shaking his head and making a clucking sound behind his teeth. Another one, eh? Another officer in the late, great Army of the Republic of Vietnam. Aloof from the misery all around him, calm in the face of his plight. He'd seemed poised and alert at first, like the russet-colored gulls of the South China Sea ready to take wing when the time was right, but the endless days at sea had taken their toll. The sharp creases had long since wilted and now his uniform just hung from him, stiff and ringed with dried sweat.

He'd occupied that same spot for days now, watching the

thin smudge of violet to the west where the Malay Peninsula met the sea. The mate knew what the captain was thinking. That soldier was the only passenger aboard now that mattered anymore.

The captain spat a dry string of tobacco juice. He lolled the fat of his jowls through his fingers for a moment, and then gave an order to the mate who replied with a nod, looped the strap of his shotgun over his shoulder and climbed down the iron companion ladder to the deck.

"Trang Van Thep?" he called to the soldier when he'd pushed his way through the litter of people to the foredeck. "You Trang Van Thep, man?" He nudged the young man with the muzzle of his shotgun.

"I am," Thep answered, carefully deflecting the gun with the back of his hand. "What do you want?"

"Cap'n wants to see you." He grinned suddenly, displaying a row of ugly, betel-stained teeth. "Hey, gimme a cigarette?"

Trang Van Thep fished a slender case out of his pocket, selected a cigarette, and gave it to the Filipino. "What is it he wants?" he asked as he hiked himself down to the main deck.

"Cap'n says you know about machines." The Filipino waved his gun in the direction of the engine room hatch. "He thinks maybe you should take a look. What d'you think?"

"I'm a computer systems engineer," Thep told him coldly. "Not a steam fitter."

"Diesel."

"Is that what he wants? He takes my last American dollar and now he expects me to fix his damn boat?"

"Hey, man," the Filipino said. "Hey, cool it, man. He don't know 'bout stuff like that."

Thep stuck a heel against the rail and kicked himself back up to his perch. "So? And what *does* he know about?"

"Well-l-l . . ." The mate was impressed by the soldier's bluster. He took a moment to tamp his cigarette against his wristwatch while he considered how much to tell him. "He knows there's gonna be trouble pretty soon," he admitted. "He knows the currents will have us on the Ko Sua Reefs by tomorrow if your friend doesn't show. And them . . ." He nodded at the nearest of the refugees. "They'll be after our water before that. Look at 'em. They know. They always know, jus' like the cap'n says. He says they've got no gratitude." He giggled at his little joke but saw that it hadn't scored with the soldier.

He straightened, resentfully. "They will kill you, too, if they come. They know you're part of this trouble we're in. An outsider, like the cap'n and me. That's what I'm supposed to tell you. The cap'n says maybe you'd better wait with us up on the bridge, that way we will all be safer."

Thep could see he was right.

"He says maybe you wanna buy one of his guns, too." He struck a match against the bulkhead and lit up while Thep got his rucksack. "*Cuño!*" the mate said, making a face after a couple of quick puffs. "Thought you'd have an American cigarette, man. This thing is awful."

When they reached the bridge the captain scrutinized the young officer while the mate got him an old M-1 from the chart locker.

"How does it work?"

"*Hombre!*" The mate was disgusted. He yanked the rifle away, worked the rusty bolt a few times, and inserted the clip. "Thought you were a soldier, man."

"I was in data processing. Computers. I told you."

"This American who's coming for you, is that what he was in, too? This data stuff?"

Thep took back the rifle and leaned against the rail where he could look out over the miserable refugees sweltering below him on the deck. "That's what everybody was in," he said. "Only they didn't know it."

The captain turned and muttered something in Chinese to the mate, who wiped his nose on his sleeve before translating.

"Cap'n wants to know where your friend is," he said. "He wants to know what makes you so sure he's coming."

"He'll come."

The captain turned and spat over the side. His eyes grew small with suspicion as he bit off another plug of his tar black tobacco. His wet chewing made his grumbling almost unintelligible.

"Listen, man. See, it's not that the cap'n doesn't believe you, y'know what I mean?" the mate said. "It's just that this guy's 'merican. Right? And he says 'mericans only have temporary friends."

"Mm."

"When did'ya see this guy last?"

Thep scowled. "Friendship has nothing to do with it," he replied. "He'll come. He needs something from me. Needs it very badly." He leaned heavily against the bulkhead and let himself slump to the hardwood deck beside his rucksack. He let his blood-shot eyes close and took a few deep breaths. This high off the water there was a slight stirring of fresh air that carried the smell of the crowd off to sea.

He wondered what these vultures would think about their chances if they knew where he'd last seen Peter Voss.

March 17, 1975

It had been late in the evening when they reached the out-skirts of Pleiku and the city was burning. Rearguard action and word that the army was abandoning them had driven the civilian population to the verge of panic. Loudspeakers warned of ap-proaching disaster while elements of the 23rd Division, left be-hind by the ill-fated relief column that had been sent off to relieve the garrison at Buon Ho, were putting the city to the torch.

Mortar fire was working methodically through the outlying districts of the northwest, flattening whole blocks of housing long after resistance had ceased, and terror rockets were falling every-where. Everyone was in flight. These highlands people remem-bered well what had happened when Hue fell during the Tet offensive seven years earlier. Thousands of civilians had been slaughtered there and their bodies tossed into lime pits within sight of the city's ancient citadel. Few doubted that it would happen again.

Three odd rounds came in close enough to throw clods of debris over the truck and taint the air with the bitter smell of cordite. Peter Voss ducked and went for the clutch, ready to brake. He was sweating and shaking, so sure they had him brack-eted that he huddled too low in the seat to see over the dash and had to drive blind through a hundred yards or so of fallen timber and toppled masonry walls before coming up for a look. When he did it was barely in time to swerve away from a gaggle of farmers dragging a cart full of household belongings.

It was a near miss. They seemed shell-shocked and unable to move until he was almost on top of them and then they had to dive out of his way.

The strain was taking its toll on everyone. Voss just wasn't built for an eight-hour stint at the wheel of a big army deuce and a half, he hadn't the beef for it. He was wirey and loose-limbed, built for broken field running, not for this close-in rough stuff. He was desk jockey, not a fighting man and no bones about it.

His dark hair hung in pasted strands. His face was grimy from the red dust of the road, so his squint left dark, chiseled creases in his boyish face. His clenched teeth were gritty and dry from three days on the road. Now and then he would risk taking a hand from the lurching wheel long enough to sweep his matted hair back out of his eyes and sometimes he would hunch forward, peering up at the sky through the windshield as if he could see what was coming next.

Thep had never seen him like this. Captain Voss had his peculiarities, he knew, but physical courage was not among them. And yet he drove on through the shelling and the growing chaos like a madman, determined and grim.

Trang Van Thep, Voss's "Host National Counterpart," crouched low on the seat beside him with his feet braced against the dash to keep himself from banging against the roof of the truck. He was as frightened of Voss as of anything else. In the six years they had worked together at Beach House 7 neither had ever been this close to combat. Now the sight of the city in flames made the point no Ministry of Information news release could deny.

In its last days the Republic of South Vietnam had turned out to be like a great tree that had secretly rotted itself hollow. Standing alone now, it had no chance against a determined storm. When the end came it came so swiftly that even Peter Voss, in spite of all the data his computers were laying out before him, was taken by surprise.

He had known something was up long before the NVA's first feint on Phuoc Binh, of course. Lots of people did. The signs were everywhere: satellite photographs gathered by the big scoop antenna at Pleiku, assembled by the computers at Cam Ranh Bay and relayed through the National Defense Network to the Defense Attache's Office in Saigon showed that the civilian population was being evacuated from Hanoi. The North Vietnamese were taking precautions against any retaliatory air strikes by American B-52s that their planned offensive might provoke.

ACUCID listening devices and seismic counters dropped into the jungles to spy crackled their warnings and the data broadcast throughout the vast reaches of the Electronic Search and Interdiction System. There were enemy troop movements everywhere in the Central Highlands. All of the data pointed to the same thing. There would be no "decent interval," as the Americans preferred to believe were called for by the Paris Accords. These were not isolated skirmishes; they were the beginnings of the final offensive.

In Saigon the brass was busy pretending it wasn't so. A great deal of technological talent was being spent recycling the data that people like Voss were sending in so that it could be reinterpreted in a more positive light. It was through the assurance of these technocrats that Graham Martin, the American ambassador, felt secure enough to leave the country for an extended leave.

At last Voss had figured out what was happening. He'd been part of the war since the early days of the American commitment when the Fisher Proposal introduced the first elements of the "Electronic Battlefield." He knew the difference between data and fact. Garbage in, Garbage out, he told them, but nobody listened. It was a corporate army obsessed with the tools of its trade and it was time for Voss to start packing things up.

One hand for the ship, as sailors say in a storm, and one hand for yourself. He'd have to liquidate the assets of his side business, get whatever he could among the blackmarket bankers in the godowns of Cholon before the Korean caught on. That would be easy enough, these bankers were aware of the power his computers gave him, so when he'd started off he was sure he could do all this and get back to his terminal post at Beach House 7 in time to make his move. All simple enough tasks for someone with Voss's experience but doomed from the start by the crush of events.

"We are in big trouble this time, Captain."

"You bet we are," Voss said without taking his eyes off the road. "And we're gonna be in a lot worse trouble if we don't get to a repeater station in time." The truck bounced into a deep rut and had to grind its way out again.

It was the first time Voss had spoken for more than an hour. Until now he'd been lost in his own dark thoughts, biting at his lower lip and cursing himself for having been such a fool. He pulled a damp cigarette from the packet in his lap and lit it hastily with a monogrammed gold Zippo that went off like a torch. One scam too many, he thought, as the smoke blew back in his face. That's what had gotten him into this mess. This time he had outsmarted himself.

"We should have started for home yesterday," Thep said.

"Yeah, yeah."

"It is true. Or even the day before when we first heard what was happening. Why must we go to Pleiku?" He'd never questioned Voss to his face before, but he had never been so frightened. He'd been in the army for a long time now. He'd come to it a young engineer from a prominent Catholic family in Saigon. He was good at his job. Not very creative, perhaps, but Voss trusted him with most of the mundane details of his operation. When it came down to it, though, when there was the face-to-face dirty stuff to deal with, he was just too middle class. Too Catholic. He hadn't any real aptitude for larceny.

Thep had a reserved, almost aristocratic attitude toward the army because of the extraordinary nature of the technology he was working with. He had become an anomaly within his own culture and he knew it. He had become overqualified for any other place in the leapfrog technocracy that the American war machine had forced upon his country. In effect there was no place for him but the place he held. There was no future for him but the war.

"We must turn north when we get to Highway 7B, Captain," he said. "Away from the fighting. We can go to Da Nang, yes? Use your connections to get a plane to fly us out."

"We won't be much safer in Da Nang, m'friend. Not for long," Voss shouted over the din of the bombardment. "Haven't you figured out what's goin' on? Didn't you understand what that guy back in Quang Tri told us? The blackmarket has switched from goods to services. Forged papers, foreign currency, immigration documents. There's no time to dispose of hard goods, it's all happening too fast."

"He was Chinese, that man," Thep said, reflecting the common prejudice.

Voss went on without listening. "Phuoc Binh City, Buon Ho —both overrun in less than a week. And just yesterday, Ban Me Thuot. The army's pulling out of the highlands, Ace! We're gonna be cut off if we don't hurry—and if that happens I'm gonna lose the whole megillah."

"I do not trust the Chinese."

"Look, just forget 7B, okay? I've got to think up somethin' else, that's all. The word was that Charley's circling around the highway and that's good enough for me. These local blackmarket operators are the only ones who really know what's going on. They get more out of their grapevine in a week than we get out of our surveillance data in a month. If somebody like that tells me it's all over, I believe 'em."

The streets in the southwestern districts were clogged with people trying to join up with the military convoy heading south. They were frightened and angry and less inclined to get out of the way. Voss was operating on raw nerves, beating on the horn as he manhandled the truck sharply through the rubble and the mob. He was sopping with sweat; his Led Zeppelin T-shirt was plastered to his back like Saran Wrap. He was exhausted and sore and still he drove on, fighting his way into the city, barging through crowds and forcing his way around roadblocks.

Some from the mob were trying to climb aboard but he shook them off. Curtains of raw smoke hung low over the streets, stinging his eyes and hiding the way ahead but Voss pushed on like a man possessed. Thep was infected by the fever of the scene. The mob. All around him was the stink of fear and piss and blood. All he had to do was look over at the face behind the wheel, lit by the shelling and the fires all around, to see that Voss was terrified just like everybody else. What could be important enough to him to risk his life like this?

"Please, Captain! Where in hell are we going?" Thep begged. "What are you up to? Just look around, will you? Everybody—*everybody* is running away. Heading for Highway 7B just as I said they would. We must go, too. We *must!* Back to the coast. Back to Da Nang."

Voss swore above the noise. A man with a gaping, toothless mouth and a torn white shirt had come loping out of the dark and scrambled up onto the running board of the truck.

Voss twisted around in his seat to get at him. He stuck the

heel of his hand in the man's chest and shoved hard. The rider made a grunt as if the blow caught him by surprise and fell away. If they were stopped now they'd lose the truck to the mob.

"Captain, please!"

"Don't be stupid," he shouted. "If the rest of 'em want to convoy down 7B, let 'em. They'll be sitting ducks. You stick with me, ace, and we'll not only survive but we'll be the richest damned survivors you ever saw."

"What?"

"You heard me."

"Rich?" Trang Van Thep stared at him in amazement.

Voss laid on the horn as he plowed through a small line of stragglers, some of whom broke from the rest and came running alongside. Others were tossing their bundles and small children into the back. Heedless of Voss's shouts and the direction the truck was heading, they cared only that it was an army truck and that it was moving. They fought each other to get aboard. They kicked and bit and screamed to get aboard.

"What do you mean, 'rich survivor'?" Thep was yelling.

"What's the matter with you?" Voss demanded.

"Rich, that's what you said! Damn you, Captain! This has all been another of your schemes, hasn't it? Another trick."

"Look out, Thep," Voss shouted as a hand snaked in through the window and began groping for the door handle. "Get him off, f'Christ's sake. Get 'm off out of the back. Tell 'em we're not goin' with the others. Tell 'em we're headed for Kontum, that'll get 'em off."

"Kontum? What's in Kontum?" Then he remembered. "The ECHO repeater station? But why, Captain? Why?"

"Because that's where the Tactical Surveillance relay is, dummy. The only on-line system this side of Da Nang. I can use it for a remote."

". . . on . . . on-line . . ."

"Use your head, Ace. Everything I've got, everything *we've* got is tied up in the network's data banks. If I can't get back to Beach House 7 . . ."

"You risked our lives for . . . for . . . ?"

"Jesus Christ, Thep. I can't just skip out on it all. This isn't just another scheme. This is everything we've worked for."

"And maybe we will die here. Maybe this time you have

gotten us killed, do you think of that too?" Trang Van Thep wasn't scared anymore, he was furious. More of the crowd had gotten themselves aboard the truck, swarming over it like insects, but Thep didn't seem to care.

"Look," Voss explained. "I've got to get to the ECHO repeater station to release the transfer program. We'd never get back to Cam Ranh Bay in time. They'll have shut it all down or the Korean will have closed the accounts or something and I'd lose everything. Look, it's not just me. I mean, I've got responsibilities. I've got expenses. Who's gonna take care o' the Kid, huh? Y'know what that's gonna cost?"

"Oh no," Thep shouted. "Oh no. You always use the Kid when it is money you are after. *Money,* that is what this is about. Not the Kid." Tears were running down his face and a thin strand of spittle leaked from his mouth. "And what about me? What if you get me killed, eh? What if the Communists get me? I am supposed to be your friend. . . ."

"Look out, man!" Voss was shoving at somebody who was grabbing through the window. "C'mon, gimme a hand."

". . . I am not just so much data to be used and then dumped."

"Thep, *do* something, f'Christ's sake."

They were all over them now, climbing in the windows, pulling at the doors. Hands and arms were pawing at him from everyplace. The door was torn open. "Thep! Help me! We're gonna lose the truck!"

"Not *we,* Captain Voss," Trang Van Thep said, leaning close so Voss would hear him above the noise. "I'm one of them, remember? And I'm going home."

Voss had lost his grip on the door when it was thrown open, and now he was being pulled from his seat. The heavy truck slowed and then stalled as he grappled with his attackers. There seemed to be hands and arms everywhere, snatching at his hair, catching him by his collar. Arms around his neck wrestling him out from behind the wheel. Fingers stuck into his mouth, hauling at him like a hooked fish. An elbow in the ribs drove the wind out of him and as he doubled over somebody hit him full in the face with a fist.

The blow staggered him. Blood gushed from his nose, lights were going off in his head. He clawed at the wheel weakly but he had lost it. The arm around his throat tightened and finally had him out of the cab and into the mob. Somebody started the engine and swung the high-wheeled truck around. Its disconnected rumble penetrated Voss's daze like a distant beast bearing down on him, and he barely managed to roll out of its way as it drove off into the night.

On the southern edge of town the convoy had already started. Thousands of hysterical townspeople fought their way into its line, swelling its ranks and slowing it to a crawl. It was a madhouse scene full of shouting officers and screaming children. There were sounds of firefights and the regular "crump" of mortar shelling creeping down on them from the darkness.

Anything that could move was turned southward down Highway 7B. Trucks, jeeps, antique Peugeot taxis, Lambretta minicabs, anything that could move was pressed into the flight. Death was at hand. The Convoy of Tears had begun.

June 1977

They saw the yacht from the bridge just before three in the afternoon. The captain grunted something to the mate, who reached down and poked at Trang Van Thep, dozing on the deck beside him.

"That your 'merican friend, man?" the Filipino asked the groggy soldier, pointing to something far off to the northeast.

Thep sprang to his feet, his hunger and doubt forgotten. He rubbed his eyes and braced himself against the hot wooden rail to search the flat sweep of ocean breathlessly. It took him a minute or so to find it, not much more than a white dot suspended in a shimmering mirage just below the horizon. He watched without speaking while the shape grew into the clean white bows of a huge yacht slicing through the glassy surface of the sea as it raced down upon them.

By then the Vietnamese had seen it, too. There was a stirring under the tarps and those who had the strength made their way to the port rail. Someone started a cheer but the others were uncertain and let it die out. Only later as the yacht closed in and they could see what a fine, dashing ship it was did they dare to believe they were saved.

12 . . .

A cheer went up over the noise of grinding motors as one screw worked against the other, pivoting the yacht's high bow slowly along the coaster's midship rail toward the stern. There was a joyful confusion down on the deck. Even those who hadn't the strength to spare joined in the effort of the others to save themselves. Lines were heaved up to the deck of the yacht and somebody managed to get a hawser looped over a passing deck cleat. The men who tried to make it fast were being dragged along the deck of the coaster, tearing up rigging where the hawser crossed the stay lines and ripping a cargo net from its foremast cables.

There were sailors lining the deck of the yacht, bronze-skinned Thais in spotless whites who had left their duties to stare. The refugees were mobbing the rail of the smaller vessel and some of the sailors began shouting and waving them back. The weight of the human cargo above decks had shifted the center of balance so that the crush of people at the port rail had the ancient coaster listing dangerously.

Some of the sailors instinctively began catching the lines that fell near them, tying them off and making grabs at others that missed. One of the refugees had tied off his end of the line and was trying to shimmy across on it. But as the yacht continued coming around the line tightened, stretched, and then snapped behind him, swinging him out to bang against the spotless white hull and drop into the sea.

A woman screamed and another held up her baby for a sailor to take but the bow kept swinging past.

The panic grew. There was something ponderous and inexorable about what was happening and the Vietnamese were helpless before its scale. The first man on the hawser was dragged over a cable stanchion that opened his leg the length of his thigh and left a smear of blood along the deck until he let go. The man behind him wasn't quick enough and went over the side. Some who had begun to suspect the worst began grabbing up the secured lines, testing their weight on them fearfully in case this last chance to stay alive would have to be stolen.

There was a man on the bridge of the yacht issuing orders through an iron-voiced bullhorn. *"Harun Ji Baai?"* he demanded. *"Is this the Harun Ji Baai?"*

There was no expression at all in the man's face, no inflection in his voice. The drama unfolding before him seemed none of his concern, he was here on business. He was a middle-aged oriental man with puffy eyes. He was too large, too pale to be a native of this part of Asia and not dressed for it, either. He seemed weighted down by his shapeless white linen suit and his silk tie was as withered as a dead leaf. His black hair was slicked back, gleaming under a heavy layer of pomade. He was preening at it absently while he waited for a reply.

"Well? Is this the Harun Ji Baai or isn't it?" The commotion aboard the coaster was dwarfed by the booming power of his amplified voice.

"Yes," the captain shouted back. He had other worries right now. The coaster's list was increasing by the minute as sea-water spilled in through uncovered vents, portholes, and other breaches in the ancient hull. And some of the mob below had taken it into their heads to make a try for the yacht's high deck from the coaster's bridge and were pushing their way through the others toward the companion ladder.

"Yes. Yes, this ship *Harun Ji Baai.*"

"Where is Thep? Trang Van Thep?"

The captain didn't reply. He was no longer interested in Thep. It was getting worse on the deck below him. Hysteria was mounting as the water line climbed up the rusty flank of his boat. The slowly passing foredeck of the yacht was festooned with lines and loose cables and even a cargo net that had caught on a forward deck cleat. People were clinging to the lines, now, dragging along the decks or dangling out over the water.

The man with the bullhorn was annoyed. He barked some orders to his crew and he waved peevishly at the would-be boarders. The sailors were taken by surprise, and while some began cutting away the lines the others seemed unsure. They looked around at each other unhappily, not knowing what to do.

A lapse of discipline, but a short one. For at that moment a dark man in a narrow cut suit emerged from the wheelhouse and came swooping down the companionway, the rails sliding through his hands so that his little feet hardly touched the stairs at all. He was a ferret-faced European with black eyes hidden deep in their sockets. As he approached the sailors he pulled a wobbly leather rod from under his jacket, a simple action that sent the reluctant among them scurrying to their task, prying

14 . . .

some of the ropes from their stays and chopping others away with fire axes. They seemed deaf to the cries of those they were dropping into the sea.

"*Trang Van Thep,*" came the call from the bullhorn. "*Captain Voss sent me.*"

"Where is he?" the soldier shouted back. "Where is Peter Voss?"

"*I told you. He sent me after you. Come along, now. I can not wait out here all day.*"

Thep didn't need any encouragement, he was already on his way. He grabbed his rucksack, pushed past the engineer and made his way up the tilting bridge and down to the deck by the cast iron ladder. The starboard rail was clear. Even the dying had somehow managed to drag themselves to the other side. He ran along it and hoisted himself up to the fo'c'sle. It was getting harder to keep his footing on the tilting deck but he managed to find handholds when he needed them and so was able to scramble around until he found a length of rope tied off to a cleat in the bow. He untied it and heaved the end up to the yacht's quarter-deck.

"*Ho! Not so fast there, Thep,*" came the electric voice. "*Have you got it?*"

"Yes, yes," Thep shouted. "It is here." The brown rucksack had slid up against the hand winch at his feet. "Right here, see?" He grabbed it up and waved it for the man in the linen suit to see. Apparently satisfied, the man signaled a sailor on the quarterdeck to secure Thep's line and turned his attention to what was happening forward.

That was the moment the captain choose to make his move. He took a last look at the madhouse around him, climbed over the rail, and made a desperate leap to the passing bow of the yacht. He was only a second ahead of a gang of his passengers who had stormed the open bridge. Pushing the mate ahead of them, they tried to follow the captain but the shift of their weight tipped the coaster so disastrously that they lost their footing and the tilting wing of the bridge struck the teak foredeck of the passing yacht and began ripping up its fine polished planks.

"Arg!" The man with the bullhorn gasped in horror as the rusty steel splintered its way along yard after yard of his fine deck. He turned, waving his arms frantically and shouting a stream of incomprehensible orders at his helmsman, who responded in an equally confused manner, heaving the wheel first one way and then the other.

The growl of the diesels surged and the bow began to pull out and away from the stricken craft. Somebody jumped after it but fell between the hulls as the stern began rotating toward the coaster's bow. The man with the bullhorn was almost frantic. Now they were going to collide at the other end. He was shouting and waving at the helmsman while below the rest of the lines parted, snapping and snaking into the water as that part of the yacht wheeled away, leaving the captain standing alone on the yacht's foredeck, blinking around stupidly with his gun still in his hand and his feet snarled in the arrant cargo net.

"Off!" shouted the man, forgetting his bullhorn. "Get off my boat, you. Get him off my boat." But the curious sailors just gathered to gape at their catch. "Janus," the man yelled. "*Janus, where are you?*"

The man with the leather rod stepped out to where he could be seen from the bridge.

"Well, *do* something, damn you. What do you think I keep you around for, your charm?" And he turned his attention to more pressing matters in the stern.

Janus stiffened under the rebuke. He turned and glowered at the circle of sailors who fell back before him to expose the trespasser in their midst.

The bewildered captain saw him coming and tried to surrender. He had thrown down his weapon and was raising his pudgy hands when all at once Janus seemed to uncoil, to extend his weapon beyond the limits of his reach like a fencer. A lunge. A snap of his leather rod at the side of the captain's skull, a "pop" like a ripe melon and it was over. The Chinaman's face went blank and he sat suddenly down.

Janus hovered over his victim, savoring the moment as blood began dribbling in crooked rivulets from the captain's ear. Then he made a gesture with his thumb. The crewmen gathered around again. Almost gently they lay the captain over onto his side and, starting from the farthest corner, they rolled up the netting and the debris and the captain into a ragged bundle and tossed it over the side into the sea.

In the confusion Trang Van Thep made a fatal mistake. The

stern of the yacht was swinging closer. It was easy to see that it was going to hit the coaster's brittle hull and hit it hard. Panic squeezed at his stomach. He had one chance and only a second to take it so he snatched up his rucksack and, without taking the precaution of securing it, he hauled himself up on his rope and swung out over the churning water.

His timing was perfect. He was out and away just as the yacht's gleaming white hull crushed into the side of the ancient coaster. It reeled under the blow and then gave way to reveal a gash of mangled steelwork a yard wide. It bucked once and settled again as the green sea came rushing in.

Thep's feet hit the polished hull of the yacht at the moment of impact and, with the debris still dropping into the water beneath him, he began his climb toward safety. The man with the bullhorn came running back for a look at the damage. He was leaning over the rail checking things out when the strap slipped from Thep's fingers and the rucksack splashed into the water below.

"Ho?"

Both men watched as it floated there, bobbing with the currents first toward the spinning screws and then toward the hole in the hull of the doomed coaster.

"Why is it floating like that, Trang Van Thep?" he asked almost casually. "That's a good solid piece of computer hardware, isn't it? I should think it would have gone right to the bottom."

"It is small," Thep called up to him. "A little thing, honest. I had it in with my luggage."

"I know the size, Lieutenant. Or at least I can guess. How could I have had dealings with your Peter Voss for so long without learning a few such things? A MAS Unit for such an elaborate system would have to be an independent module, yes?" As he spoke he pulled a penknife from the watch pocket of his suit and opened it with his polished fingernails. "What kind of fool did you and Peter take me for, eh? Did you really think you could buy a ride with a bag of laundry?" And with that he started on the rope, chopping and sawing at it for all he was worth. It was more difficult than he expected, the knife was very dull.

"I could not help it," Thep pleaded. "Please! The Americans must have taken the key when they pulled out, or maybe it was lost or something. I looked everywhere but it was gone. It's not my fault." He tried to shinny up a few more precious inches while the man above him went on hacking at the rope, puffing and sweating until it began to separate strand by strand.

"No. Please!" Thep cried. "Please. There must be another way."

"Oh, I'm sure there is." The man paused. "In fact, I am counting on it." The last few strands of bristling hemp finally snapped. Thep gave a yelp, plunged into the sea and disappeared beneath the foam. He was gone for a long moment and then he broke the surface again, choking and flailing about amid the debris while the yacht swung its churning screws toward him, it's wake already gummy with the coaster's spilling oil.

". . . not my fault!"

But by now the man with the bullhorn had returned to the bridge. Clear of the lines and wreckage, the great yacht swept off toward the northeast, leaving the refugees and their floundering hulk rolling slowly with the swells and currents of the gulf.

CHAPTER

2

Something about the sound of the starboard engine was beginning to disturb Sloane's shallow doze. He was slouched in the jumpseat of an aging DC-3, awake now but not quite ready to move. He kept his eyes shut and just listened for a while as he ran a long list of potential disasters through his mind. After all, it was still his aircraft and would be for another . . . he opened one eye and checked his watch . . . another two, maybe two and a half hours depending on the wind.

There it was again. Some uneven something in the throaty drone of the engines.

He stretched slowly, unfolding into a lanky-legged sprawl. Maybe he'd better go forward and check it out. "Smilin' " Jack Bowers was flying and he wasn't the kind to worry about details until they had developed into serious problems. There'd be a few things said about backseat drivers, but what the hell. Twelve thousand feet over the Gulf of Siam was no place for surprises.

"Alice?" he said as he got to his feet. Her case files were still stacked on a wooden crate where she'd been working on them but she wasn't anywhere in sight. Alice worked for the Relief Services Fund, the operational branch of several cooperating agencies engaged in refugee resettlement that called itself the People Project. She had been transferred from Jakarta to Thailand, where the Cambodian refugees and the Vietnamese boat people were a growing international problem.

"Alice?"

She'd been bumming rides off him for years, cashing in her travel vouchers so she would have some extra money of her own to spend for those emergency needs of her wards that weren't covered by the narrow funding procedures of her agency. She was dedicated and more than a little ruthless in her calling. Her directness was disarming when viewed against the manners practiced in this part of the world, but it wasn't just her method for dealing with the obstructionist mentality that seemed to prevail among the people she had to deal with, it was also her nature. She was born to go barging through life like a bumper car through traffic.

She was lucky, Sloane often thought, having a cause to believe in. It gave her a sense of identity and purpose and the excuse to use whatever and whomever she needed to get her way. But for those few who knew her well, it was hard to tell how much was done for the refugees (*clients,* the People Project liked to call them) and how much out of shear cussedness. That's why they called her Crazy Alice.

Sloane admired the quality and sense of purpose to which she directed her strength, but at the same time she was headstrong and demanding and that was always getting in the way. He had hoped that having her along on this last flight of the last plane of his Inter/Asian Air Service fleet would help him close up shop on the upbeat. A dream as big as this one shouldn't be allowed to get away without a proper send-off. A few laughs at least. Instead they'd ended up in another of their squabbles.

They were often friends and usually lovers, who let each meeting decide the level of their intimacy, both of them free to break it off and pick it up again at some later time in a different guise.

At least that was the understanding. But in practice the relationship hardly ever worked that way. Sometimes it seemed that Alice was more like a perennial affliction than a girlfriend. It was as if they were too close, knew each other too well not to want things from each other they just couldn't have.

They'd been carrying on this de facto romance for almost eight years now, since the days when Sloane was flying for Air America and Alice was earning her nickname for her work with a Quaker relief organization among the Meo tribals in eastern Laos. (Once she had talked him into shuttling a whole village to a safer site. He logged it off as an emergency supply run, which was especially pleasing to Alice because it meant the CIA had to pick up the tab.)

There was a lot to say for those old ways of getting things done. Simple and direct action, not this shadow boxing he'd had to put up with in the cold corporate world he'd been trapped in for the last few years. It seemed now that he'd had a clearer image of himself back then in spite of the war. And besides, he just wasn't the eager young executive type. He preferred a more informal life-style. Even now he was dressed in a ratty old pair of jeans, his favorite, and a light cotton shirt with the sleeves rolled back over his forearms. Already his woolly brown hair needed a trim.

He had to shuffle sideways to squeeze between a pallet of crated machine parts and the galley bulkhead and then duck through a curtain to get into the drafty cockpit. Once there he stopped behind the control deck for a look at the panorama of bright blue sky out ahead.

Smilin' Jack was lying back in his seat with the bill of his baseball cap pulled down over his face. He had one end of a long Filipino cigar under there with him and judging from the length of the smoldering ash he'd been asleep for the last twenty minutes.

"Oh, lord," Sloane said. Crazy Alice was flying his airplane.

She was peering out from behind a few loose locks of honey yellow hair that had fallen over her face, gripping the yoke as if she were locked in a cosmic struggle. Her eyes were riveted to the horizon and her face askew with her remarkable lopsided grin.

"This is fun," she said.

"But . . . but you can't fly!"

"Yeah? What d'ya call this?"

Crazy Alice wasn't crazy, she made other people crazy. Last night, for instance, he had wadded up his best suit and thrown it down the incinerator shaft of the Princess Hotel in Djakarta. Alice had gotten him into another of their "What are you going to do when you grow up" fights and he'd told her about the job offer he had from an old army buddy in Bangkok. "How long do you think you can go on playing 'Terry and the Pirates'?" she'd wanted to know, so he tried to make a point about corporate mentality and the three-piece suit. He was trying to explain his present state of mind and she was trying to tell him that he was too old to just drop out like this and then somebody called the manager, who asked them nicely to quiet down. So the argument wasn't resolved. They never were.

How could she not understand? He'd worked hard and seen the last few years slip by without adding up to anything worthwhile. His hair was thinning, for God's sake. There were lines around his eyes and what was there to show for it? A few airplanes in a company he'd lost. A big corporate job that sucked him dry and gave him no sense of . . . of . . . whatever it was he needed out of life.

It had been a pretty good fight. That stunt with the suit had made its point but he'd regretted it almost at once for it was always best to let Alice score the last point. She was a forgiver of trespassers, was Alice. A seeker of lost sheep. The Lord loveth a repentant sinner and so did Crazy Alice. Even the whiff of conquest was enough to lead to a long night of lovemaking. But there was no penitence in Sloane last night so no rewards for the vanquished. She got the bed and he got the couch.

And as for the suit . . . Well, Sloane never looked quite right in a suit anyhow. For one thing he had the face of a welterweight, with sleepy, hooded eyes and a broken nose he'd suffered some years earlier when he'd overshot the landing strip at a Meo resettlement camp and ended up in the trees. For another, he still had an adolescent's way of carrying himself, as if he'd never gotten used to walking around in a full-sized body. Arms too long for their shirtsleeves, ungainly legs that were always getting in the way. He was at that difficult, in-between age. He was thirty-nine.

"This is easy," Alice said. "Smilin' Jack says the only hard part is getting it up in the air and getting it down again."

"Suppose something happened," Sloane suggested. "And what about the course?"

"Oh, the course. That's . . ." She leaned heavily against the yoke to point at the compass below the control panel and as she did so the nose began to drop. At first she didn't know what was wrong. Then she grabbed at the wheel and that only made things worse: the left wing tucked under. "Oh, m'God."

"Give me that." Sloane reached for the controls but Alice hauled back just in time to forestall the spin they were falling into and had the plane steadied again without him.

Alice blew a lock of hair away from her face. "The course is 280," she said when her confidence had returned.

Three inches of cigar ash dropped onto Smilin' Jack's khaki

jacket and rolled to the floor. An acrid cloud of cigar smoke filled the cockpit. Smilin' Jack had awakened.

"285," he corrected.

"Oh, m'God."

"Now, don't you go worryin' your pretty little head 'bout this, honey," he said. "Just you add ten degrees north to that and I'll catch up when I got it figured." He pulled a map out from under the seat and unfolded it across his lap.

"Did you hear that starboard engine?" Sloane asked him.

"Sure did."

"Sounds funny," Sloane persisted. "Check your tach. It keeps drifting out of sync."

"That's just the ol' governor actin' up again. I'd have put a squawk in the maintenance log but you know how these ol' 'threes' are. You can always squeeze a few more hours out. Want some coffee?"

"Sure."

"Alice, honey?"

"Later." Alice refused to take her eyes from the horizon.

Smilin' Jack poured some coffee from his Thermos into a pair of Styrofoam cups while Sloane pulled a notebook from the navigator's rack and began scribbling through a raft of pink forms.

"What's all that?" Smilin' Jack asked.

"I'm adding the prop synchronizing governor to the OC Transfer forms. Got a couple of other things, too. There's an oil leak . . ."

"Jesus H. Christ, Dave."

"Hm?" Sloane looked up and found Smilin' Jack shaking his head in exasperation. "What's the matter with you?"

"Well, I mean, shit. (Beg pardon, ma'am.)" He nodded to Alice. "I mean, after all the shit they pulled on you and here you are fillin' out all the right forms for them. Dotting all their i's and crossing all their t's just like they was good ol' boys like us. Seems t'me you're being awful damn nice about the whole thing, that's all."

"Skip it, Jack."

"All right. All right." Smilin' Jack turned his attention to the map. "You got robbed, Dave. Or didn't you hear. Five years I've been watching you beg, borrow, and even steal a couple a'times to get this collection of relics whipped into shape. I watched you build yourself a real b'God airline. Twelve planes, wasn't it? Couple of scheduled routes. A goin' operation. And what for? Just so some big Hong Kong syndicate can come along and pull it right out from under you?"

"You're spilling your coffee, Jack."

"Yeah, yeah. You don't want to talk about it, I know."

Sloane was surprised at the outburst. Smilin' Jack was always such an easygoing sort of guy. He was a character out of one of those old adventure movies they used to show on Saturday afternoons at the Bijou with a dozen cartoons. He had a simple, straightforward philosophy: life was funny, that's all. Anything that couldn't be used in a funny story might as well never have happened. Sloane loved these guys and because he loved them he thought he belonged with them. Alice had never understood that.

Why, to hear Smilin' Jack tell it, they'd all practically started the war together. That was in 1960, when "the troubles in Indochina" meant Laos. They had been a bunch of hotshot kids, most of them, with a few leftovers from Korea who'd seen all of this before. Vagabond flyers recruited by a shadow corporation to fly for Air America, the not very secret charter service of the CIA. There was good money in it and an odd sort of glory that nonflyers probably wouldn't understand. They were bush pilots in the insane world of jungle politics, flying C47s and C123s and Caribou STOLS and every other damn thing, swooping in and out of clearings the size of postage stamps, kicking bags of rice over the side at a hundred feet. Medicine, food, ammo—anything.

It was a madhouse—vagrant actions that often made no sense and plans that had nothing to do with the reality of jungle war. Policies constructed in Washington and Moscow were played out to their deadly absurdity and then dropped as the rules changed.

It was a wicked crucible for a thoughtful boy to search for his manhood in, but Sloane had learned early that trying to believe in the war was not the way. All there was to believe in was himself.

They flew from anywhere to anywhere but most of the time they operated on the Plain of Jars supplying the loyalist forces of Prince Souvanna Phouma while the Russians, in their IL14s, did the same for the Pathet Lao—all so the killing could go on.

Smilin' Jack stuck the wet end of his cigar back in his mouth and gave it a chew while he collected his thoughts. It was pretty disgusting by the time he pulled it out again.

"Dammit, Dave. We can't just let it go like this," he said at last. "What this calls for is some sort of a gesture."

"Jack . . ."

"C'mon, Dave. Something big like the good old days."

"Oh, David just loves the good old days," said Alice, brightly.

"Alice . . ."

"What d'you say we take this old bird and just dump it someplace," Smilin' Jack suggested. "Take 'er up to Vientiane and hand 'er over to the Commies."

"No, Jack."

"Dear sirs, you can pick up your new airline F.O.B.—someplace in Southeast Asia. Like the sound a' that?"

"Listen, Jack, just drop it. Okay? You want to do something for me? Good. Take that Pan Am supply job and let me finish what I started in peace."

Everybody wants good guys and bad guys, Sloane thought. You have to win or you have to get even. Well, it just hadn't been that simple. In fact, his whole career in the world of high finance had been a kind of fluke, just another small maneuver in the tangled intrigues of corporate Asia. No heroes, no villains, and not much in the way of passion.

In the end it had all been a matter of cash flow and contractual commitments to what turned out to be several subsidiaries of the same holding company. He had lost the fight a couple of years ago when the holding company began calling the shots. Its contracts made up 80 percent of Inter/Asian revenue so when they "suggested" a merger with New City Credit in Singapore, Sloane took it for a seat on New City's board of directors.

That's all that had happened. That's how David Sloane had gone from fly-boy to conscript in the army of executives that had come to rule postwar Asia. No more dump-or-die landings in some patch of jungle mud. No more long, solitary hours in the sky watching the monsoon thunderheads come looming up over the rim of the world. Now he was a token round-eye in another board room in Singapore. Trapped there until a month ago, when New City Credit decided to concentrate on their long-term prospects and began liquidating their marginal holdings. Inter/Asian Air Service was one of them and when Sloane found out about it he quit.

"I don't know," he'd said, trying to explain his reasoning to Alice the night before the flight. "It just seems that something must have happened while guys like us were stuck in the war. Like the rest of the world shifted gear and took off without us."

"Maybe it was always like that," Alice had said. "Maybe you're just growing up." That's what had started the argument.

Smilin' Jack was still working out his course corrections with a chewed-up pencil. "So what are you gonna do now, Dave?" he asked, absently.

"Well, now that you mention it, I thought I'd take Alice to dinner and maybe a night on the town."

"Oh, I can't, David," Alice said. "I know it's a big night for you but I've really got to finish those case studies before I check in for reassignment tomorrow."

Smilin' Jack cleared his throat. "Yeah, well, what I meant was what are you gonna do in real life."

"Got a job."

"A job," Alice repeated, scornfully.

"A job in Bangkok." Sloane ignored her. "Not much. Not like New City or anything like that. A nice, easygoing sort of deal, know what I mean? Something I can get a grip on."

Alice gave a derisive snort.

"Yeah?" he told her. "Well, maybe that's what I'm after. Maybe that's what I think real life ought to be. Simple and straightforward. That's why I'm filling out these damn OC transfer forms, y'know. Because it won't be some kind of Chinese syndicate that has to fly this crate out of Bangkok tomorrow. It'll be some poor slob like us who's got a right to know what's going on."

There were a few licks of light turbulence and Smilin' Jack took the controls back from Alice and lifted the nose of the aircraft to climb over it. With her hands free Alice began to talk.

"Don't you think you're laying this 'brotherhood of the air' stuff on a little thick?"

Smilin' Jack rolled his cigar to the other side of his mouth and began puffing at it nervously.

26 . . .

"I mean it, David," Alice said. "If you're so almighty noble about the simple life how come you're taking up with the likes of Peter Voss?"

"Pete Voss?" said Smilin' Jack.

"She doesn't even know him," Sloane growled.

"I know *about* him," Alice said. "I've heard plenty about him."

"You mean *Captain* Pete Voss, that wheeler-dealer from I Corps?" Smilin' Jack shook his head respectfully. "By Jesus, I thought he was dead. I figured they'd got him sure as shit back there at the end. (Beg pardon, ma'am.)"

"Yeah, well, don't worry about Pete." He grinned. "He can get himself out of anything."

"Yeah, and at a profit." Smilin' Jack chuckled. He had a yuk-yuk kind of laugh that made his Adam's apple bob up and down. "Seems t'me the Commies missed a chance back in 'Nam. All that trouble we ran 'em through when all they had to do was make ol' Pete a good offer. He'd have sold 'em the whole kit 'n kaboodle and had us out a' there in a week. I c'n just see the sign on the door. 'Under new management.'"

"There, you see?" Alice said. "That's just what I heard about him, too. A real shady character, right, Jack? Hanging around with gangsters and . . . and war profiteers. How do we know this new business of his is on the up and up?"

"There's nothing 'shady' about Pete," Sloane insisted. "He just sort of knew how to get stuff on the sly, that's all. A little pilfering from army stores. Midnight requisitions. It's as American as apple pie. Everybody was into it. Right, Jack? A case of good scotch . . ."

"Radios, cameras," Smilin' Jack added. "A hundred gross pantyhose. Maybe a truck to carry it all in . . . Hey, remember that villa he had back at Cam Ranh Bay? Now that wasn't exactly officer's billeting, was it? Open house all the time. I remember a game of seven-card stud that went on for seven months. Girls, booze . . . why, there's nothin' Pete wouldn't do for his buddies."

"That was all just the war," Sloane said. "This is different. Now he's putting together a little company and wants to expand, maybe get into the export market. I know Bangkok pretty well so he wants me to help him out."

"Why, that's a fine idea, Dave," Smilin' Jack said. "Bangkok's a hell of a town."

"Thought I'd relax and enjoy myself for awhile."

"Damn straight. It'll be just like the good ol' days."

"Is that what they were?" Alice said. " 'The good old days?' Well, I don't remember them that way, see? And as far as this Voss character goes, it sounds to me like he's not much better than a common crook."

"M'be so, darlin'." Smilin' Jack looked over at her and smiled the smile that had made him famous. "But he surely does know how to treat his friends."

CHAPTER

3

There were two odd little men watching from the alleyway while Sloane got himself out of the cramped backseat of the three-wheeled tuk-tuk. They were skinny, square-headed, and out of place in the breezy, cosmopolitan atmosphere of Bangkok. Farmers, they looked like, squatting on the heels of their big farmers' feet and craning their necks like a couple of geese to gawk at him. The elder of the two wore the black peasant pajamas of the northeast and the younger a set of cheap ready-mades of the current metropolitan style.

Sloane figured them for Cambodians. Khmer refugees were showing up in the cities these days, those who could get away. These two probably escaped from one of the camps up along the frontier to look for work in the city.

He unwadded a few baht notes for the driver. "Soi Sunak?" he asked, just to make sure.

The driver folded the money into his shirt pocket and nodded toward the alley where the two little men were watching. "Soi Sunak," he confirmed as he slipped the gears and drove off at the head of a poisonous cloud of smoke. There was no marker, no sign. This alley was no different than a thousand others in this great maze of a city.

"Incredible." Sloane stretched his cramped legs and massaged his kidneys with his knuckles for a moment while he looked around. He wasn't familiar with this part of town and it took a moment to get his bearings. The golden late afternoon sunlight weighed heavily on the tall mango trees along Sathorn North Road. It was a wide boulevard lined with expensive homes and a number of the city's foreign embassies and divided down the middle by a muddy canal.

Bangkok had once had hundreds of such canals, *klongs*, they were called. But over the last twenty years or so most had been filled in for roads and malaria control. There had been a lot of changes over the last few years and not many of them to Sloane's liking. The city was growing and growing too fast. Gone were the days of leafy indolence. The old Silver Bazaar had been torn out for a new branch of the Bank of Tokyo and another nondescript hotel had sprung up where the silk dyers used to dry their cloth in long streamers along the banks of the Samkhan canal.

Bangkok was a vital city. Always sorting things out to make room for the new. Always ready to profit from the whims of fate as it had from half a century of war. For Bangkok, change had long ago become a part of staying the same.

The *soi* was little more than a gap between the walls of the Indonesian Counsulate's compound and the walls surrounding a rather sinister-looking group of tile-roofed buildings that had a brass plaque on the gate reading NATIONAL SECURITY CENTER, SECTOR 11. The *soi* was hardly three yards wide and was surfaced lightly with gravel. When the monsoon finally arrived it would turn it into a muddy bog.

The two little men reacted with alarm at Sloane's approach. They rose carefully from their heels and then, in a kind of controlled panic, they tried a step first this way and then that. Once in the open they were spotted by a band of street urchins who seized the opportunity for some mischief and began chasing after them, squealing and teasing the little men who fled, squawking and flapping, back into the shady green lots behind Embassy Row.

The *soi* led back into a different world. It followed an erratic course between the walls and rough fences of the jumbled lots, crossing one alley and then another before disappearing among the vines and trees. On either side the bungalows and shanties and little Buddhist shrines were packed together in such a way as to manage a kind of lush, packed privacy for everyone.

As Sloane approached the end of the security compound's wall he had the uncomfortable feeling that somebody was watching him. He turned expecting to see the two little men but the *soi* was empty behind him. And then:

"American?"

Sloane spun on his heel. Nobody.

"Oh, you must be American," said the rich baritone voice. "I can tell by the way you walk."

Sloane looked up and found a bull-necked police officer peering down at him from the top of the compound wall. He was amused by Sloane's confusion.

"I . . . who . . . ?"

"You seem lost, my friend," the officer said. "This is your first visit to Dog Alley?"

"Dog Alley?"

"Yes-yes. Soi Sunak," he said. "It means 'Dog Alley.' You must be looking for Peter Voss, isn't it." He leaned out precariously, a pair of binoculars pendulating from their strap around his thick neck. "Take that first left, just there." He pointed to the end of the wall. "It is a shortcut to Silom Road. Just before the footbridge you will see a new gate. First house on the right."

Sloane gave him a sloppy salute. "Thanks," he said, as he shifted the strap of his bag to his other shoulder and started off again.

"And tell him I said hello," the officer called after him. "A fine fellow, Peter Voss. I like him very much."

Everybody liked Pete. He wanted everybody to like him and he usually got what he wanted, that was part of his genius. Some say genius is more than just a measure of aptitude. They say it's an altogether different species of intellect. That's how it seemed with Voss. He had a kind of presence, a way with people just as he had a way with computers.

The bonds of friendship were like an alliance to him and if you ever did him a favor, as Sloane had, he was the kind who never forgot. And if he'd ever done one for you—well, he never forgot that either.

Perhaps it was some remnant of his past, this brash warmth, this engaging if sometimes abrasive style of his. Something from the Sisters of Mercy Institute in the Bronx, where he had been raised with his brother—the pliant charm an insecure child might learn in order to capture more than his share of love and attention.

There had always been this insecure child in Voss, in spite

of the bravado. It was this little boy part of him that women seemed to fall for, Sloane had long suspected. Each assuming she alone had found him out for what he really was. But she'd be wrong. Peter Voss was as complex as he was brilliant and his "little boy" bit was only a small part of what there was in him to contend with.

"It's amazing how gullible women are when they think they're in charge," he'd once confided.

It had occurred to Sloane once or twice that he didn't know him all that well either. Even after all these years it was sometimes as if Voss were acting out a part, as if he'd had to *learn* how to be one of the boys. Sloane didn't understand that vaguely strained forwardness of Voss's good nature. For him the easy exchange of human fellowship was as natural as getting up in the morning. Sloane could only attribute it to the remnants of Voss's childhood.

Voss had had a six-inch name back at "the Sisters." He'd changed it upon entering the army and never told anybody what it had been. He'd have changed everything, if he could, and buried his early years in some hole in the past where nobody would ever find it, but the mannerisms of his Bronx youth persisted. They were the style of the street, heavy-handed and quick and too much a part of him to shake off. He was fast on his feet, a con man who could spin an intricate deception with the skill of an Irish peddler.

His speech was hard and clipped like a street punk and he carried himself with the air of a gold camp gambler, an aggressive stance that suited that attitude of personable arrogance so popular with the army's officer corps at the time. He had quick eyes and big appetites.

The army had been the best thing that ever happened to Peter Voss. It spotted his talent, took him out of the Bronx, and made him an officer. It finished his schooling at MIT. It made exceptions for the eccentricities of his habits and his counterculture wardrobe, and when it went to war it gave him a chance for a place in the sun. The army was a system like any other, as impersonal as a tool in the hands of somebody like Peter Voss. As for the war, he seemed to think of it as just another fact of life. Like his computers, it was simply there to use.

They had known each other since 1969, when Air America renewed Sloane's contract and assigned him to flying supplies to some construction sites in the Laotian jungle. There were American private contractors there building microwave repeater towers that would link the data retrieval facilities at Nakhon Phanom Air Base in Thailand to the growing computer network in South Vietnam. An offbeat young Lieutenant Voss was one of the corporate army's brilliant new systems engineers, a member of an inspection team that was sent out from Da Nang now and then to keep an eye on things. He often flew out to the sites with Sloane and spent a lot of flying time trying to explain the essential absurdity of the situation.

"Look at all that out there," he'd say, settling into the number-two seat of the cramped cockpit with a can of Budweiser in his hand. "Fifty thousand square miles of jungle down there."

Below them the low hills of the Plateaux Montagnards rolled away like an endless green carpet. The only landmarks in sight were the glittering trickle of a river off to the right and the landing strip for an uncompleted repeater tower up ahead.

"Triple canopy of foliage, they say. Trees so thick there's villages down there that have never seen the light of day." Voss drank from his beer can and wiped his chin with his sleeve. "Want one?"

"Nope." Sloane was scanning the trees near the landing strip for signs of trouble.

"It just goes on and on like that, y'know? The proverbial 'green hell.' How can anybody fight a war in that mess?" Sloane didn't answer so he went on without him. "Well, the army's got an answer."

"Yeah?"

"Well, it thinks it does. See, the modern U.S. Army is run by its technocrats. The Green Machine, they call 'em. And the Green Machine can give you an answer for just about anything. This is all just a matter of logistics. This whole war. And that's what we're doin' out here, you and me. That's what all that electronics gear back there is for." He hooked a thumb over his shoulder to point back into the cargo bay. "The Green Machine's gonna revolutionize jungle fighting."

"Yeah?"

"That's right. It's gonna automate war."

"Sure." Sloane laughed. "Yeah, sure it is."

"It's true. Some programmers back in Virginia—smug little assholes who have never in their lives seen a sight like this." He nodded to indicate the soft green jungle below. "They're gonna sit down and design us a brand-new kind'a war."

As he explained it, the army was putting together what a think tank in Arlington, Virginia, had promoted as an electronic barrier that would stretch from the South Vietnamese coast to Terchephon, Laos. Not a Maginot Line, exactly. Rather what they wanted to call an "electronically prepared combat zone" set up to stop once and for all the flow of men and supplies along the vast reaches of the Ho Chi Minh trail.

The barrier had seismic counters and acoustic listeners and silent jet aircraft flying at treetop level sniffing the air for the ammonia in a porter's piss. There were microphones in plastic feces strewn from the air along the side of the trail, plastic palms that measured the doppler effect of marching feet. It had mini-mines that went off with a "bang" and activated a sensor that would register on an operations board 650 miles away.

A satellite hung in stationary orbit over Vietnam, old Lockheed Lodestars circled endlessly, gathering bits of broadcast data from the ground and sending them on. The microwave repeaters on their new red and white jungle towers were already relaying it all to Nakhon Phanom Air Base in Thailand and to Voss's Tactical Coordination Center, an extraordinarily advanced computer complex code-named Beach House 7 at Cam Rahn Bay.

The Tactical Coordination Center was there to sort out needs and measures; artillery could be called in from as far away as twenty miles from the suspected target. Missiles from fifty, and if it was worth it (as Ke Sahn would prove to be), B-52s could be called in all the way from Guam. All of this was lumped together under the unlikely code name Igloo White.

The alley opened under a stand of trees that drooped out over another, smaller *klong*. Along both banks tin-roofed shanties balanced out over the water on a forest of wooden pylons. In the water below them half a dozen women were washing piles of gaily colored laundry and joking with a passing boatman. The footbridge at the end of the gravel pathway teetered slightly as the boatman poled his way under it.

The two little men were back. Sloane saw them stick their heads up from behind a tuft of weeds and go scampering off again when they saw that he had spotted them.

The new gate was right where the police officer said it would be, a solid job made with heavy planks of raw wood still leaking blobs of amber sap. Behind it, what Sloane could see was a comfortably ramshackle compound based around a large wooden house that had never seen the threat of a coat of paint.

Sloane liked the place. It was basic and homey and quiet—but at the same time he wondered if there'd been some kind of mistake. It was a bit rustic . . . no, it was shabby. Hardly up to the luxury one associated with the fabled Peter Voss. For a moment Sloane wondered what he was getting into.

There was a high picket fence all around it, the same as the other houses on the *soi*, so that half the windows on the first floor looked out on its mossy boards. A broad-leafed ivy was climbing up the house's clapboard siding and reaching out for the passing power lines. The sunlight was filtered through a green world of towering eucalyptus trees.

"Cat-cat," came a cry from inside. Sloane had just drawn the hasp for a look inside the gate when through the crack shot a kinky-tailed alleycat with a limp fish in its mouth. "Cat-cat, you come back here," but Cat-cat was already long gone down the alley and under a fence.

"Cat-cat!" The gate burst open and a young girl rounded it in a fury, crashing headlong into Sloane who, unbalanced by the weight of his bag, stepped backward, stumbled over his heels, and went sprawling into the shallow culvert that ran along the foot of the fence.

"Oh . . . ! Oh, my goodness!" The girl cupped her open mouth in her hands, peering over her fingers to see what she had done. Graceful even in her embarrassment, she looked like one of Gauguin's island girls, slender but strong, wrapped in a loose red sarong that she had tucked provocatively at her high breasts in the country fashion. Her face was fine featured but with that special Siamese fullness to her lips and eyes.

"Oh, my goodness, I am so very sorry," she said as she stooped to help him to his feet. "That nasty cat agai'. This time he sto' one of my fishes."

Sloane got to his feet awkwardly and slapped at the dust on his pant leg. "That's okay," he assured her as she tried to help. "No, really. It's all right. Listen, is this where Peter Voss lives?"

The girl nodded, surprised. "Heavens. You must be Petah's

new partner." (She pronounced it "par-tin-ore.") "Oh, and I just now knock you dow'."

"Don't worry about it."

"*Sia jai!*"

"No, really . . ."

"Oh, Petah has told me all abou' you." She pressed her palms together in the prayerlike *wai* greeting. "*Khun* David Sloane, yes? And my name is Kiri Banserai. Maybe I think he has tol' you abou' me, too. Yes?"

"Oh sure," Sloane lied. "Lots of times."

The rutted parking space inside the gate was empty. Around back the corrugated roof of the house was extended to the out-buildings by means of a sway-backed breezeway that covered one full side of the patio. There was a charred hibachi against the back fence, a scattering of wicker furniture, and a frayed cotton hammock that hung between a pillar and a hook on the bathhouse door. At the farthest corner from the house, almost hidden in a patch of encroaching green, was a little shrine to the household spirits. Kiri's touch, no doubt.

"Kiri?" Voss appeared at the screen door, in a pair of army skivvies, unfolding the stack of computer readouts in his hands. "Kiri, where's my cigarettes?"

"Hi-ya, Pete." Sloane grinned.

"Dave!" Voss tossed the readouts aside and was through the door and down the cement-block stairs in a single bound. "Damn, man. You were gonna call me when you landed. I had a real five-star reception all lined up." They started by shaking hands and fell to poking and mauling each other instead like a pair of playful cubs. "You really look great, man. You really do. Do I look great?"

"You look great. You look like you always look."

"Great."

In fact, he was almost exactly the same. The same self-conscious bravado, the same performance he had always used to mask his feelings. He still had that disarmingly boyish face with its wide, smooth brow. His fine dark hair was still too long (he wore it tied back in a little tail to keep it out of the way) and he still wore his rock n' roll T-shirts. This one said JEFFERSON AIR-PLANE and bore a silhouette of Grace Slick with a halo.

If anything, he'd lost some weight. That's all. And there was something else about him that Sloane couldn't quite put his finger on. Something new and formidable in those clear brown eyes—the way they examined his own.

"Should'a called, Ace. I had the mayor lined up. I had dancin' girls. Everything."

"I know all about your five-star receptions, remember? The last time I had to get rabies shots."

Voss laughed. "They still talk about you at Madam Loo's."

"I'll bet they do."

"This is really great, man. And listen, you're gonna love this deal." He feigned a few quick jabs while Sloane dodged and parried. "You'll see. It'll be just like the old days."

Kiri had been watching their greeting ritual with a look of keen interest, as if there was something to be learned from their antics, and when Sloane caught her eye he grinned at her, embarrassed, and broke it off.

"Hey," he said, looking around. "Hey, this place is terrific."

"It's a dump."

"No, I mean it," Sloane insisted. "It's got character."

"It's got termites," Voss insisted. "That's what it's got. It's got warped windows and creaky floors and running water that doesn't run half the time."

"And your electricity goes off," Sloane offered.

"Every time it rains." Voss laughed.

"Just like my place over in Klong Toey. God, I've missed that place."

When he looked back he found that Voss had been watching him. "You haven't changed, have you?"

"Changed? No. Why should I?"

"I dunno," Voss said, helping himself to a Marlboro from the pack in Sloane's shirt pocket. "I was afraid this sort of thing wouldn't interest you. Not after being a big shot at New City Credit."

"Bit shot? Me?" Sloane started to laugh. "Hey, that whole board of directors thing was just a fluke, that's all. Just some big business razzle-dazzle. I didn't belong there."

"Not from where I saw it." Voss was serious. "You played a tight, hard game and you came out on your feet. You even had a write-up in the Business Week section of the *Bangkok Post.*"

"Read it," Sloane told him, taking a cigarette for himself. "Hype, that's all it was. Hype and jive. Fact is, I just blew it."

"The hell you did. In fact, I gave the Prince even odds you wouldn't take this job. That you'd stay in the big leagues."

" 'Big leagues.' " Sloane gave an ironic snort. He took a light off Voss's Zippo and avoided his friend's eyes.

The house was in shade now, only the olive-green treetops overhead still caught the evening sun. Voss let his smile fade as he surveyed the scene. "Not much like the old days, is it? Hey, remember that villa I commandeered? What a deal, huh?"

"And that flat you kept in Saigon?"

"Yeah, right around the corner from the Caravel Bar. You should'a seen the action I had goin'. I had to use the embassy computers to keep it all straight. All gone now, along with everything else."

"Yeah. Well, maybe it's just as well, Pete," Sloane said, surprised by this sharp note of regret. "Y'know, there were some who said you were into the blackmarket pretty deep."

"Nah. Nickel 'n' dime stuff, that's all," he assured him. "Anyhow, that's all pretty irrelevant by now. As it turned out, the NVA won the war ahead of schedule and cut me off at the knees." He looked away. "So as it turned out you were the one who ended up on the board of directors while I ended up starting from scratch in this . . . this fuckin' dump."

"Petah." Kiri scowled at him. "Really, Mr. Sloane. He can be so crude. And swear? Goodness, sometimes the air turns blue."

Voss grinned suddenly, as if remembering his better nature. He threw an arm around Kiri. "I see you've met my harlot, here." He gave her a squeeze.

"Your . . . oh, yes." Sloane gave her a wink. "Yes, I did. She made quite an impression."

"Cat-cat stole a fish," Kiri explained.

"Forget the fish, f'Christ's sake," Voss told her. "We're gonna celebrate tonight. We'll go to Yankee Daniel's. How's that sound? C'mon, let's get us a drink first. Somsak will put your stuff away. *Somsak?*" he shouted. "Where the hell is he this time?" He opened the screen door to the cookhouse. "Somsak?"

A pair of heavy green houseflies made their escape, spiraling lazily up into the pale evening sky when Voss stuck his head in for a look. Beside the door was a pile of old motorcycle parts. A dented gas tank, chains, sprockets, all stacked neatly against the foundation.

"The Kid's stuff," Voss explained. "He's always tinkering with something, you know how he is. There's another pile inside. Somsak's been pissin' and moanin' about it for a month. *Somsak!* What are you up to this time? Hey, was there a jeep in the drive when you came in?"

"I didn't see any jeep."

"Mistah Somsak took it," Kiri said.

Voss let the screen door slam shut. "He might have said something."

"He did. He said he be ri' back."

"Every time I need the damn thing Somsak's got something going. He jobs out with it, jeep and driver, trucking stuff around for the Chinese down in Sampeng Market."

"With your jeep?"

Voss shrugged. "Everybody's got a hustle in this town."

The house was roomy but sparsely furnished and the walls were just the flip side of the clapboard siding. It was typical middle-class housing, solidly built but unfinished so that the dampness of the season gave the bare wood a pungent, forest smell.

"Me and Kiri use that end of the house," Voss said. "And the Kid's got that room there. He gets upset sometimes if he's too far from the door."

Sloane's room was at the top of the stairs, open and airy with large screened windows on either side. There was a wardrobe and a matching dresser with a blue china pitcher and washbasin on it. At the far end was a brass bed under a tent of mosquito netting. A ceiling fan made torpid sweeps through the humid air.

There was somebody in the bed. Sloane could hear the rumble of low snoring coming from inside the mosquito netting but Voss just ignored it so he did, too.

"You can stay here as long as you want," Voss told him. "Or the company's got a rest house. An apartment over in Thonburi. You can use that."

"This'll do fine."

"Suit yourself. Either way Thai/Tech picks up the tab."

"That's very generous of Thai/Tech."

"It's the Prince's money." Voss shrugged. "And he loves you already. I told him what you did for the Kid and he wants you to give him lessons."

"Give him what?"

"Flying lessons," Voss said. "With the company plane. Keep'm happy and he'll keep us supplied with the basic operating funds."

"The company's got a plane?"

"The Prince is just great. With him as a partner and my computer system to run things we're ready to start a whole new game in this part of the world. I'm setting up a system based on the model I used for Beach House 7. Imagine the control that will give us as we diversify. We can increase the range of direct management by a factor of four—maybe five. All the production and marketing details under constant surveillance." Voss had a way of assuming the mantle of power by just talking about it. His eyes would glitter and his easy smile would harden at the edges as his attention fixed on the big deals swimming in his fertile mind. He made Sloane uneasy when he was like this.

"A computer system like that is going to eat up a lot of your capital," Sloane suggested. "Does the Prince have that kind of money?"

"Don't worry about capital," Voss said, with a wink. "It just so happens that I am about to take care of our capital problems once and for all. All it takes is a little piece of hardware and a lot of ingenuity."

" 'Take care of our capital problems,' did you say?" Sloane laughed. "That's a terrific idea, Pete. And just where the hell are you going to get a piece of hardware that can do that?"

Voss smiled. "Sea freight," he said.

The liquor cabinet was a low mahogany box beneath one of the windows and while Voss was rummaging through it looking for something worthwhile there were signs of life from the bed. A series of groans developed gradually into a spasm of ugly gargling coughs that rattled the crockery on the dresser.

"Ah-har-HARGLE-HARGLE-HARGLE!" A ghostly figure sat up gasping inside the netting. "Huh-huh . . . oh. Oh, my God."

"What do you want to drink?" Voss asked, apparently unable to find what he was after.

"Anything. Anything," the figure whimpered. A foot wearing

a ratty old desert boot was stuck out over the side of the bed to feel for the floor. There was some trouble with the netting before the owner could follow.

"Jake!" Sloane said. "Jake Berman. Well, I'll be . . . What are you doing here?"

Jake gaped around at the room. "My guess is I'm still here from last night." He scratched his crotch and looked back at the bed as if to see if he was still in it.

Jake had been a stringer for UPI and a pickup writer for any number of third-rate TV producers. Sloane had known him as the philosopher barfly of Voss's court of hangers-on. Always looking for an argument or for somebody to touch. Air America was an informal organization in those early days and its crews were given wide latitude in carrying out their assignments, so Sloane could easily be talked into giving a war correspondent like Jake a lift to the scene of a story now and then.

Despite this advantage and despite Jake's suicidal tendencies once he got there, he was singularly unsuccessful at his trade. Jake's objectivity had deserted him early on in the war and his horror had grown with each confrontation he had forced himself to endure. The war was lunatic, he discovered, and nobody would pay him to write that sort of thing.

Jake was wearing what was very likely the same sweat-stained bush jacket that he'd worn throughout the war. It was baggy and threadbare at the elbows and it had pockets big enough to carry his laundry in. He was putting on weight. A sagging sort of affair that had him slipping into middle age without a struggle. He was beetle-browed with sad little eyes and his complexion had all the sallow hues of someone in a state of perpetual hangover.

"Dave?" he said, offering his moist hand to be shaken.

"Been a long time, Jake. You're looking good. Putting on a little weight, I see."

Jake sighed. "The waist is a terrible thing to mind," he said.

Voss had half a dozen bottles out and was still searching determinedly through the rest.

"Somsak put all this stuff together," he said, taking a moment to indicate the rest of the room with a free hand. "God knows where he found that bed. He wanted to fix up the Kid's room, too, but the Kid doesn't like changes. Makes him nervous, y'know?"

"How is the Kid?" Sloane asked.

"He's doing all right," Voss said. "Kiri takes care of him. She's real good and he's totally devoted to her. And I've got a doctor over at Thomasat University that gets him the best medicine money can buy."

"He's worse," Jake said.

"No, he's not."

"He is," Jake insisted. "You've got to keep him doped up all the time so he doesn't get excited. And he seems set on making his world as small as possible, have you noticed that? Taking apart his motorcycle all the time and putting it back together? One of these days he's going to fixate on a carburator and the only thing Kiri's gonna be able to do is change his oil."

"That's enough, Jake," Voss warned from his bottles. "I don't want to hear you talkin' that way about the Kid."

"You've got to face it . . . Ah, skip it. I might as well be talking to the wall."

"Y'want to tell me about drugs? Listen. When you quit poppin' screwballs then maybe you can tell me about drugs. Okay? Until then if I need your advice I'll ask."

Voss wasn't angry, he was simply drawing the line, but Sloane felt obliged to change the subject anyhow. "Er . . . this Kiri seems like quite a girl. Maybe you ought to hold onto this one."

"She does the holding on for both of us," Voss said. "Aha. Here it is." And he pulled out a brown-labeled bottle that looked like it belonged on the back shelf of a college chemistry lab. "Polish vodka. A thousand years old. Much too good for those embassy paper shufflers so ignore the commissary stamps."

"Embassy? Commissary stamps?"

"Yeah. Things have been looking up around here since they computerized their inventory."

"I thought you were through with that kind of stuff," Sloane reminded him. "I thought it was 'irrelevant.' Listen, computer scams might be okay for a PX in 'Nam but this is real life."

"Hey, it's nothin', man." Voss explained. "It's a kind of a game, that's all. Like a puzzle. I use the Thai/Tech computers for a 'smart terminal' anyhow, right? So every once in a while I go for a stroll through the other systems in town, that's all. Their systems and remotes and networks all work through the phone lines, don't they? That sort'a makes them public property. So you could say they were askin' for it.

"And what's it cost them? Sometimes I hide a trapdoor in their program in case I need it someday. Or maybe I pick something up on the way through. It's nothin'. It's like a prize."

"Yeah? Well, do me a favor. If you're going to swipe things out of other people's computers you can leave me out of it."

"You don't swipe things from a computer," Voss told him, patiently. "You make the data that represents it go away. Without that data the item doesn't exist. The rush is on to computerize inventories but computers deal with bits and bytes, not 'things.' They have no sense of 'thing-ness,' no sense of ownership. See? That's where everybody makes their mistake. Computers don't do anything but count." He poured vodka into mismatched tumblers and passed them around.

"Nobody in here but us chips." Jake downed his drink with an audible gulp. Outside, a wet breeze was disturbing the trees and rattling the ivy against the screens. "Y'know, you're really something, Pete. Tell me, when you were doing all that computer stuff back in 'Nam didn't it ever occur to you that you were helping to foist a rather destructive value system on society? I mean, didn't it ever occur to you that body counts were just another kind of inventory?"

"Mmm." Voss was idly swirling the vodka in his glass, he had heard all this before.

"Nothing counts like the counting, right? So nobody counts much at all." Jake's face was flushed. He had a lot more to say but Voss cleared his throat and cut him off.

"As you might have guessed, Jake's still working on that great American 'why did we do it' war book of his."

"I'm up to page 7350," Jake said. "I was just getting around to Captain Rip-off, here."

"C'mon, Jake. Ease up."

"Nah, that's okay." Voss was back to checking out his stock of liquor and didn't look up. "Jake appointed himself my conscience a long time ago. He's harmless enough."

"The traditional symbiotic relationship between the press and the military," Jake said, unhappily. "Can't live with 'em, can't live without 'em. How about another drink?" When Voss had poured it out Jake took it to the bed, where he sat on the edge of the mattress with his feet dangling a few inches from the floor.

"Well, then," he toasted. "Here's to Captain Peter Voss and the fruits of his filching." He again finished his drink in a single gulp. "After 7350 goddam pages I'm no closer to the answer than I ever was, but I'll bet good ol' Pete could give us the answer quick enough, right, Dave?"

"Sure, Jake." Sloane had slumped into a canvas chair in the corner and was watching him over his glass. His legs were propped up awkwardly against his duffel bag. He hadn't been listening so much as watching Jake's raving. Some things never change. He had to work hard at keeping his amusement from showing.

"Yes, sir, push a button and you can get anything out of those things. He's probably got the answer to the whole thing wrapped up and stuck away back there at Beach House 7—right in there with all those ugly toys they gave you guys to play with. Like . . . like those smart bombs, right? The ones that go out looking for somebody to kill."

Jake waited for a moment as if summoning his strength and then, "BEEEEeeeow . . . " He pulled one out of the air and blew himself up. "POW! And 'Puff the Magic Dragon' with those electronic Gatling guns—B-R-O-O-M, B-R-R-R-O-O-O-M!—a whole football field wiped out. Badda-badda-badda . . ." He was jumping around in wild pantomime, shaking the whole room as he blasted away. "Bada-bada-bada, some little kid drinking his vodka. BOOM!" He threw a pillow into the air and dived for cover under another. "WHOMP, WHOMP, WHOMP! A whole village wiped out because it didn't jive with some asshole's computer program."

There was a pause while he reached out from under cover to find that his drink was miraculously unspilled.

"Jake?" Voss wasn't paying much attention, he was used to Jake's antics. He was sitting at the window watching the children below. "C'mon, Jake. Let's let Dave unpack and clean up. Anyhow, weren't you supposed to cover that news conference for the *Guardian?*"

"Oh, yeah." Jake sat up with a start. "Oh, shit, I can't fuck this one up. Loan me a hundred baht, will you, Pete?"

Voss pulled a couple of notes from his money clip and handed them to Jake, who stumbled past him down the stairs.

"Still popping screwballs, isn't he?" Sloane said when he was gone.

"Don't mind Jake," Voss told him. "He'll never finish that

book and he knows it. He thinks too much. He'd be better off if the war was still going on. It would give him a sense of scale, know what I mean?" He headed down the stairs. "It'd give him a job, too."

Cat-cat was doing a high-wire act along the top of the picket fence, its asymmetrical tail flicking carefully for balance while it eyed the cookhouse door. Voss was splashing away under the faucet in the bathhouse singing, "I can't get no . . ." trying to imitate Mick Jagger and a twanging guitar at the same time while Kiri sat up cross-legged in the hammock nearby, absorbed in the paperback she was reading.

Sloane was watching from his window above the scene as Cat-cat oozed to the ground and made a beeline for a rip in the cookhouse screen door. It had almost made it when a wet arm came out of the bathhouse and scooped it up.

"A-hah, y'little bastard!"

Cat-cat flattened its ears to its head and yeowled as if the end had come.

"Petah," Kiri warned, wagging her finger at him. "No you hurt Cat-cat."

"He's a pain in the ass," Voss teased. He took a sniff of the unhappy beast and wrinkled his nose. "And he stinks. What he needs is a bath."

"Oh, Petah, really . . ."

"A nice cold bath, what d'you say, Cat?" Cat-cat was looking for the exit. "Kiri will help, won't you, baby?" Kiri tried to grab the cat away but Voss kept it out of reach. "Sure she will. She'll look out for your interest." He ducked inside and turned the water back on.

Kiri looked quickly around. Sloane could see her trying to suppress a giggle as she drew at the folds of her sarong and let it slip from her breasts. She kept her back arched, pointing her breasts upward like a teenager showing off her new toys, and let the cloth fall in a silken circle at her feet. Her skin was glossy brown in the shadows and the sight of her below was enough to take Sloane's breath away. She took another quick look around as she touched her tongue to her lip, her eyes bright as a forest animal's as she disappeared into the dark doorway. A second later the cat was out of the bathhouse and over the fence like a streak.

Sloane was a little ashamed of himself for watching and went back to his unpacking to get his mind off Kiri's lovely bare body. For the first time in years he felt at home. The household seemed complete, somehow. Secure and self-contained. He emptied his bag on the bed and was whistling as he sorted his things into the dresser drawers when the quiet of the alley out front was broken by the roar of a poorly muffled engine.

The lot across the *soi* was vacant except for a lean-to somebody had built against the inside of the fence there. The bungalows on either side of it were much like Voss's but full of the large families that had peopled the alley with kids.

The noise got louder and there was a commotion at the end of the fence where the two little men went flapping past in a panic just inches ahead of a dusty green jeep with ARVN stenciled on the side of its hood.

The driver was a wiry, white-haired man in a bright sarong who swerved manfully around the corner without a thought for the two who fled before him. He was still at high speed as he cut the wheel hard and skidded toward the gate in a spray of gravel and dirt. Sloane could see his bony knees working away as he tried to brake or shift or anything but it was too late. He hit the gate with a bang that sent a shock wave rippling along the fence and a flock of green birds bickering off through the sun-streaked trees.

The driver saw Sloane at the window and nodded up at him soberly.

"Somsak!" Voss yelled from the bathhouse.

CHAPTER

4

Kiri was a bar girl. Most of Voss's girls had been whores of one kind or another, he seemed to like them that way. He'd told Sloane once that sex was a four-letter word and things would be a lot simpler for all concerned if it were treated that way. Straightforward and raunchy. And there was something about knowing the cash value of a screw that kept everybody in their place. He liked that, too.

But it was hard to say how he really felt. He often covered his complex nature with such barracks posturing, an image worn by a fast-talking kid from the Bronx who had learned how to live by his wits. After all, Sloane considered, it was plain to see that Kiri was something special, a prize beyond the reach of a crude man.

Voss had found her in the Mosquito Bar, one of those loud, brassy dives down in Klong Toey, where she'd spent the greater part of her adolescence warming the beds of Dutch sailors. Sloane knew the place well. It was hard for him to think of her that way. She was bright and sweet without any of those hard edges that girls of the profession seem to acquire with experience.

She spoke several languages. The dialect of her childhood village near Mai Sarang in the mountainous northwest territories along the Burmese border, the brisk Thai of urban Bangkok, and Dutch because most of the customers at the Mosquito Bar had been sailors from the nearby docks of the Holandia Line. So English was her fourth language and she was quite good with it, although like most Thais she was used to the light, bubbly cadence of her own language and so found it difficult to bother with the hard consonants that begin and end so many English words.

Her delivery was stilted and mannered like the paperback romances she liked to read, too precious for real life just as Kiri herself seemed to be. She was a moody girl beneath her cheery manner, not completely comfortable. A visitor determined to make a good impression.

And she adored Voss. It was as if he were the only man in the world. Her eyes followed him everywhere, watching him hopefully when he didn't suspect. She found ways to be near him, to touch him as she passed. She was bound to him, it was plain to see as the three of them made small talk over drinks in the twilight calm of the courtyard.

But Sloane knew his friend's track record. Voss meant well, he always did, but Sloane knew how little his friend could give to a relationship. It was a deal, that's all. That's why Pete loved whores. He needed to know the price.

But he liked Kiri. And he told her story with surprising sympathy, as if there was something he held in common with her. He told how she had been orphaned as a child by a cholera epidemic and was taken away by a woman who called herself "nanny." The old woman had brought her and some other surviving children to the far away city of Bangkok and the only profession that would have them.

There was a knock at the gate and after a moment Kiri came around to announce that "Major Chapikorn ha' come to call."

"Come in, Chappy," Voss said as the police officer from the wall of the security compound rounded the parked jeep. "I want you to meet my buddy Dave. David Sloane, Major Chapikorn. Internal Security."

Chappy was a barrel-chested man with dark skin and a wide smile. He wore a light, tailored khaki uniform and a Sam Brown belt with a .45 in its holster. He still had his binoculars.

"Dave's coming to work with us at Thai/Tech."

"Ah, but we have already met," Chappy said as he reached out and grabbed a fistful of Sloane's fingers. "I should have known it was you, David. May I call you David?"

"Sure."

"And you must call me 'Chappy' just as Petah and his friends do." He continued to hold onto Sloane's hand, pumping at it as he talked. "I heard all about you from Petah. What wonderful adventures you both have had. Tell me, did you really drive a tuk-tuk into the Barkley Hotel swimming pool?"

48 . . .

"My girlfriend was driving." Sloane wished Voss would quit repeating that story. "Cost me a bundle."

"Of course it did." Chappy laughed and pumped his hand all the harder. "Very much fun, I must say. Someday I must tell you of my adventures in San Antonio, eh?"

"Chappy took his Sec/Op training at Lackland," Voss explained. "That's how he got to calling this place 'Fort Apache.' "

"But in this case," Chappy said, "all of the savages are on the *in*side."

"Chappy's with the National Security Center. He's chief of the Sector 11 operation you passed out there by the road. They're there to spy on the Russian Embassy across the street."

"And the Laotians."

"And the Laotians down the street," Voss said. "Say, Chappy. We're all going down to Yankee Daniel's for some serious partying. Want to go along?"

Chappy dropped Sloane's hand. "But, Petah, my surveillance schedule . . ."

"C'mon, Chappy. Let somebody else count Commies for a while."

"All right, I'll come. But you should take this sort of thing more seriously, Petah. And those Khmer are back. They were following David when he arrived."

"Who?" Sloane asked. "You mean those two Cambodians?"

Voss gave him a nudge with his elbow and tried to look serious. "I suppose they're Reds, too, are they?"

"Of course they are," Chappy said. He could see they were making it into a joke and he scowled. "There is a third one sometimes."

"Curly, Larry, and sometimes Moe," Voss explained. "They've got a hovel stuck together behind that fence on the other side of the *soi.*"

"They are here spying on you, Petah. I am sure of it. And now they are spying on David, too."

"Yeah, yeah," Voss scoffed. "And tonight you'll probably catch them under your bed."

The heat-dazed city was coming alive again in the cool of the evening. The workaday traffic of trucks and exotic little carriers was gradually being replaced by crackling flows of motorcycles, growling tuk-tuks, and lightweight cars. Top-heavy buses were nosing about in the clamor picking up anybody who could find a place to hold on.

Somsak traded lanes with a motor scooter that had a girl sitting sidesaddle on the back and then bullied his way into a gang of three-wheeled carriers who were vying for a turning lane. Somsak entered into the spirit of the traffic as if he were entering into mortal combat: wary of any danger, alert to any opportunity, and ready to fight over every inch of progress. He scowled and muttered and sometimes made Kiri laugh with his black curses.

Voss sat beside him bracing himself with a foot against the dash while Sloane and Chappy lounged in back with Kiri squeezed between them. She was holding up a yellow bandanna, watching with a curiously detached smile as it fluttered in the slipstream.

Whenever a shrine or a wat or a temple came into view she would instantly compose herself, make a *wai* gesture, and nod behind it as if for a quickie prayer. She didn't miss a one, not as far as Sloane could see. She knew where each holy place was, or perhaps she could sense them—a gold-tiled stupa coming up on the right. A small shrine in the park, there, with garlands and X-ray plates of cured petitioners tacked to the tree beside it. Each got its little nod and a word or two and then was completely forgotten. She was like a little boy dodging cracks in the sidewalk for fear of some unnamed retribution.

The town was crass and unfamiliar to Sloane. So much had happened to it. Brand-new concrete buildings were going up sometimes before the old could even be properly torn down. The traffic was a steady roar in the harsh, wet heat and the air was full of diesel smoke. Sloane was watching the crowds, looking at the faces that made the mob more human. Now and then he would see a Westerner among them. He even thought for a moment that he recognized one of them but found he'd mistaken the ambling, tousle-haired youth with a girl on his arm for a friend who'd been killed in Vietnam. Dead a long time, now. Sloane often saw dead friends among strangers.

Chappy had to reach around Kiri and pat Sloane's arm to get his attention. "Are you enjoying?"

Sloane nodded, uncertainly. "City's changed some."

Chappy patted him again. "Is it not a wonderful place, this city of angels? To live here is to see the world as a child again.

Always something new, always something delicious waiting for you." He gave Kiri a pinch and settled back.

Silom Road bent to the left and entered a wide roundabout from the south. A white-helmeted policeman in polished combat boots stood in the middle of it all pointing and beckoning with gloved hands while being ignored by wave after wave of flying Hondas pouring out of Rama IV Road.

Somsak had hardly come to a stop when he saw his chance and gunned out into the maelstrom, splitting the unrelenting line at its weak point—a motorcycle loaded down with lumber. A cab had to veer out of his way, cutting off a second line of traffic and giving the jeep just enough room to carve a space for itself in the outside lane. Behind them the traffic from Silom Road had followed them out and taken command of the circle. The pack on Rama IV would have to wait now for a champion of its own.

Voss looked back, saw the look on Sloane's face, and grinned. "Relax," he said. "Somsak's the best there is."

Things changed when New Road was crossed and they neared the river. Gone were the boulevards and the trimmed trees along Lumpini Park. Everything seemed to narrow in and break up into back streets and uncharted lanes where local merchants conspired beneath their flickering neon lights late into the night. At last Somsak pulled up under one such sign that said ARAZONA BAR, Yan Ki Daniel, Prop and everybody piled out.

"Have it back by one o'clock," Voss ordered and Somsak nodded as he ground the gears and pulled away. *"And this time leave me some gas."*

Yankee Daniel's was stashed away under one of the old Chinese go-downs that line the back streets of Sampeng Market. A pair of round windows looked out from under the open porch, each with a neon Singha Beer sign hung a little off center so that the place looked cross-eyed.

"How did you end up with a Vietnamese Army jeep in Bangkok?" Sloane asked as they headed inside.

"Let's just say there was a goin' out of business sale." Voss winked as he pushed through the door. "Cash and carry."

There weren't many customers: a couple of Thai freaks smoking silently in the corner and a tired-looking merchant nursing a beer. The decor of the place was a muddle of good intentions, odds and ends gathered together as money and inspiration managed to coincide. In contrast the Formica-topped bar looked almost new; its toneless light reflecting up from work level had an eerie effect on the barman's face.

"How y'doin', Yankee?" Voss said to the barman while Sloane took stock of the girls that lined the bar. They smiled back at him and swiveled on their stools to show off their knees.

"Hi you, Petah," Yan Ki said, glancing nervously at Chappy's uniform. "Hi you, Kiri. Petah, why you not send this Kiri work fo' me, eh? She number one ba' girl."

"That's what I keep telling her, Yankee." Voss's eyes sparkled eagerly as they took in the scene. "A sex drive like hers she'd do better charging piece rates."

Yan Ki didn't understand but he laughed anyhow. He knew an off-color quip when he heard one. Kiri took Voss's arm and clung to it, looking at the faces around her to see if there was something she had missed.

Yan Ki pulled a bottle of Dewars from a private stock under the bar and began filling an ice bucket.

"Helped him set this place up," Voss said. "Went into the records of a couple of the local banks and did a little switcheroo on his credit rating, right, Yankee? A little 'creative accounting.' Listen, we'll be out back, okay?"

"Sho' thing, Petah."

"Dammit, Pete," Sloane muttered. "Can't you leave anything alone?"

"What?"

"Bank records, for God's sake."

"You worry too much." Voss laughed, hung an arm around his neck and headed him toward the back room.

Kiri had friends among the girls so she stayed behind to gossip while the others made their way to the back. The bar opened onto a larger room with an unused dance floor. The room was dim and smelled of spilled beer and stale tobacco smoke. Ceiling fans stirring up the muggy air only made things worse.

"Thai/Tech used to keep a guest flat in the adjacent wing, over there," Voss said as they picked their way through the tables. "Handy, but not much class. So we moved it into one of those new apartment blocks in Talatplu overlooking the river."

There were more people in the back and most of them seemed to know Voss. They'd nod or say "Hi, Pete" as he passed.

A set of French doors opened onto a wide wooden veranda out-side and the table just inside it was piled six deep with beer bottles and smoking paraphernalia. The half-dozen *farang* sitting around it had their eyes on something going on outside.

"Hey, Clyde," Voss said to the young black man in a green army shirt who seemed to be presiding.

"Yo, Pete."

"What's happenin'?"

"Jake's out there tryin' his act on another of the local honeys."

Voss groaned. The veranda was built out over the waters of one of the arterial *klongs* that angled in from the river nearby. A string of dim bulbs was looped from post to post over the railing and glimmered in the water below. There was a couple out there but the light was behind them so it was hard to make them out.

"You sure that's Jake?"

There was a short flurry of movements between the couple. Jake had made his move and the girl had replied with a particu-larly crude gesture of disdain.

"Oh, that's him, all right." Clyde held up a handful of money and showed his teeth with a mercenary grin. "Y'want in on it?"

"What are the odds?"

"Twenty to one," Clyde said. "Same as always."

Jake's bar girl looked up hopefully as they approached.

"I thought you were supposed to be covering that news conference," Voss said.

"Ahem, yes. Well, that's a long story. See, what they did was sort of . . . throw me out."

"They sort of what?"

"Look, maybe we can talk about all this later. As you can see I seem to have me a live one here."

They left him there and took a table near the railing. "So they threw him out," Voss said as a waiter showed up with the drinks. "Jesus H. Christ. Why can't he keep his mouth shut? All he's got to do is grab a few sexy quotes and make up the rest like all the rest of them do."

Chappy had chosen the chair that afforded the best view of the couple and was uncasing the binoculars that still hung from his neck. "Oh my, something's wrong," he said. "Yes, she is on her feet . . . She is angry, I can tell." The show was over already.

He sighed and rebuckled the case as the bar girl clip-clopped back inside like a little girl in high heels.

"Sweet girl," Jake explained as he pulled up a chair. "But afraid of emotional commitments, y'know?" The lights gave him a furrowed, tragic face. He had a sweater tied around his shoulders and his shirt was the same one he'd been wearing earlier. It smelled of his nerves.

"Well, Chappy," he said, as if starting afresh. "I see rank hath its binoculars."

"They are new," Chappy said, proudly. "Petah got them for me."

"More of that computer razzle-dazzle, eh? Another raid on the PX?"

"They're compatible systems." Voss shrugged. "Now, what happened at the news conference?"

Jake avoided his eyes. He rubbed his nose between a couple of pudgy fingers and said something that nobody was meant to hear.

"What?" Voss insisted. "What was that?"

"I said I can write my own fiction."

"And I suppose you told them so."

"Well, yeah," Jake admitted. "I guess I did, in so many words. Sure I did. Hey, Dave. Hey, how about buying me a drink?"

"How come y'always gotta fuck things up?" Voss asked him. "Huh? Why is that? Gonna write the great American war book, right? Well, how y'gonna do that when you can't even feed yourself?"

"I can feed myself all right," Jake muttered. "Anyhow, what else do you expect me to do when some fat colonel starts handing out all this shit about sending the refugees back into Cambodia to protect them from the border raids of the Khmer Rouge? That's the same as sending them back to their executioners, am I right?"

"And you said . . . ?"

"The Thais don't call them refugees, you know that? 'Cause the UN says if they're refugees you can't force them to go back."

"And you said . . . ?"

"I said 'bullshit,' that's what I said." Jake laughed. " 'You might as well take them out and kill them yourselves.' That's what

I told 'em. You should have seen their faces, heh, heh." He took a cigarette from the pack Voss had lying on the table and looked around for a light. "Mm, that's when they threw me out."

"No sense of humor," Sloane suggested.

"I try to call 'em like I see 'em."

"F'Christ's sake, Jake," Voss said. "You're supposed to be a reporter, not a referee."

They ordered up a feast of batter-fried grouper and prawn stewed in an earthen pot. There were puffed pork rinds, sticky rice, and a sour squid salad that everybody ate with their fingers and *nam pla,* the infamous Thai fermented fish sauce that made the Dewars taste like canal water. And when it all began arriving so did Clyde and his cronies from inside.

The conversation, by common design, did nothing to inhibit the eating and drinking and soon Sloane found it more pleasant to listen to the others while he regarded his place in the world through a mellow alcoholic glow. His attention drifted to the houses across the *klong,* with their porches and flimsy walkways. In the quiet there, a woman was sponging herself from a large, clay water pot under the light of a flickering oil lamp. Only Sloane saw her.

Something touched him on the neck. It was hardly more than a feathery rustling of his collar and it sent a shiver down his spine. He turned to find a huge young man gazing down at him with a half-open mouth and wide, uncertain eyes. He was very blond and very white and his muscular, veined arms hung awkwardly from his polo shirt. He'd withdrawn his hand timidly and was crumpling the seams of his washpants with it, hoping Sloane would speak first.

"Hi, Kid," Sloane said. "Gee, you look great."

Well, at least he looked better than he had that night on the tarmac apron of the airstrip at Cholon. It had been raining for three days straight and Sloane had almost given him up when a couple of local thugs showed up with him, sopping wet and thin as a corpse in the beam of the landing lights. They had all been lucky that night. Sloane's fledgling air service had only that one aircraft at the time and he had managed to get it in without a military cargo and out again before the tower caught on to his "electrical problems" ploy. That's how they got the Kid out of Vietnam.

Sloane got to his feet. He offered his hand and the Kid was grateful for it.

"Hi, Dave. Peter said you'd be in sometime today." The Kid had a strained, hoarse voice and had to choke out his words as if each was a struggle with silence. "I was gonna wait back at the house but I must'a forgot."

"That's okay. People forget sometimes."

"Yeah." The Kid seemed distracted for a moment.

"So . . . so how are you feeling?" Sloane asked. "Hey, sit down. Want something?"

"No, that's okay. I just wanna see Kiri." He started to turn and then remembered. "Oh, I'm feeling a lot better, Dave. Honest." He went back inside while everybody at the table found other places to look.

Sloane wiped an eye quickly with the heel of his hand and found he had to clear his throat to speak. "Listen, Pete," he said. "You can tell me it's none of my business but maybe Jake's right. Maybe it's time to take a chance on getting him someplace where they can help."

"You're right," Voss answered. "It *is* none of your business."

"Look, he's not really a deserter. I mean he's sick. They'll deal with that. Jake says . . ."

"The Kid's *my* brother, not Jake's, and I'll be the one who says what's the right thing to do and what's not." He looked around at the others and realized he'd been too abrupt. He played with his glass for a moment, biting his lip the way he always did when he was upset.

"Sorry, Dave," he said at last. "Hey, I guess if anybody's got a right to say what he thinks about the Kid it's you. Y'know? But I just can't let them get their hands on him. That's it. I've gotta handle this my way. Y'gotta take my word for it, I've got plans."

"We've all got plans," Jake said, and he drank down somebody else's drink.

The air was hot and still and the palm trees, dark with the aura of the city sky behind them, hung their shapeless fronds over the rooftops like piles of laundry. The long wait for the monsoon had left the water level low so the *klong* below them gave off a pervasive fetid stink that took steady drinking to keep at bay.

The talk had turned to war stories and other manly lies. There was lots of boisterous laughter and everybody seemed more concerned with getting their turn in than with what was being said. Alice was wrong, Sloane was thinking, happily. It was just like the old days.

Tied to the pylons down on the water were *hangyaos*, long, thin canal boats that drifted and nudged each other softly while their boatmen smoked and talked together. A bright light had appeared at the turn in the canal and was playing along the shanties there and silhouetting the docks along the bank. There was a lull in the conversation on the veranda and below the boatmen grew quiet. The light rounded the bend and its beam swept back and forth over the surface of the water revealing its leaden green translucence and catching the boatman in a brilliant silver pool. It seemed an unearthly thing, gliding above the water all by itself until it had closed on the drinkers and the gurgling of the motor could be heard behind it.

"Hey, look," somebody said as a white lapstrake launch slowed under the puny lights of the veranda. Besides the crew there were two men in the boat. One was a heavy Oriental in a linen suit and the other, standing in the bow, was a strange-looking *farang*, a Westerner with dark eyes wearing a trim gray suit.

"Hey, man, look who's here."

"General Washington."

"That's that guy . . . that guy used t'be scag man down by the Khanh Hoi docks."

"Janus," said Jake. "Janus Czyuresky."

"Can't be," Clyde said. "He's all dressed up. Must be Captain Ay-hab. Hey, Ay-hab? Still lookin' for that whale?"

"Who's this?" Sloane asked Jake.

"Crooks," Jake said, leaning back in his chair and rubbing his hands together expectantly. "That sleazy one up front is a real psychopath. One of those waterfront thugs the Reds ran out of Saigon with the rest of us. The fat one's a friend of Pete's."

"That's a friend of Pete's?"

"Sure." Jake eyed him for a brief moment. "Birds of a feather, right? What did you expect?"

The boat pulled up to a float that supported the hinged gangway leading up to the veranda and the one they called Janus got out to help the other in the wilting white suit over the gun-nels of the launch and onto the platform. They made the climb up to where the others sat, the heavier man sweating heavily and tugging at his collar as he paused to wheeze for a minute and let everyone see his toothy smile. He had a face like a bag of walnuts.

"Hello, Peter," he said. "Hello, boys."

"Well, if it ain't the Korean Navy," Clyde said.

Chappy leaned back on two legs of his chair and hooked his thumbs over his belt. "I thought you were finished with this fellow, Petah. What is he doing here?"

"My, my. Such a hostile reception," the Korean said to his escort. "How quickly they forget, eh, Janus?"

Janus made no reply. His coal black eyes had everybody covered.

"And where did you pick up this guy?" Voss asked him.

The Korean looked around as if to appraise the fellow for himself. "It is not an association I am proud of, I will admit. But I felt the occasion called for drastic countermeasures."

"Countermeasures," Jake said, surprising the assembly with his vehemence. "Y'know what an animal this guy is?"

"Everybody does, dummy," Voss said. "That's the point."

"Well, at least he got a new suit," somebody else said.

"Hope he burned the old one."

There was general laughter while Janus's face shriveled with malignity.

"Now, Janus," the Korean warned. "Remember what I told you. This is a business meeting. We are all going to remain friends, isn't that right, boys. Here, let me buy the drinks."

"I thought we agreed this deal was supposed to be private, Sung Dai," Voss told him. "Look, suppose you make the delivery, then we'll talk, okay? Just you and me."

"Well, actually . . . maybe we could just hear him out." Jake never refused a drink. "What d'ya say?"

"Ah, for once your Mr. Berman is quite right." The Korean gave the waiter some money and sent him off to the bar. "The least you can do is hear me out. You see, I am sorry to bring you some bad news about your friend Trang Van Thep."

"Bad news?"

"Yes. It seems I won't be able to deliver him after all."

"You what?" Voss stood abruptly. "You told me . . ." He

pushed his way through the others around the table and let the Korean lead him to the far end of the rail past the strings of party lights. "Wait. Hey, wait a minute, man. You gotta tell me what's going on . . ." When he'd caught up he took the Korean's arm and spun him roughly around to face him.

"Be careful, Peter," the man snapped, nodding toward Janus. "Be very careful. I know how much you dislike violence, but he does not."

Voss dropped the arm but Janus was unconvinced.

"Perhaps a little smile," the Korean suggested. "A testimony to our long association."

Voss never took his eyes off the glowering thug. He managed to spread his lips enough to show his teeth a little sheepishly while he said, "All right, let's have it. What's happened to Trang Van Thep?"

"I got him out, as we agreed. Sent him out with fishing boats and had them met offshore by a coaster with a lot of other refugees." He was smiling, too.

"A coaster? You put him aboard one of those *wrecks?*" The revelers at the table behind him grew quiet, trying to figure out what was going on. But a moment later the drinks started arriving and the general ambience rose accordingly. He tried again, this time with his anger under control. "I never agreed to stick him on some leaky old scow. You know as well as I do what's been happening out there on the gulf."

The Korean shrugged. "You said nothing about first class."

"He's valuable property, you fool."

"Not any more. He did not have the MAS Unit."

"He . . . he . . ." Voss stared dumbfounded at the Korean for a moment. ". . . didn't have it?"

"He never had it. He just wanted out of the country so he, what is the word? Concocted? Yes, he concocted a story he knew you would be interested in."

Voss swore bitterly and turned away to think, chewing at his lip while the Korean watched him warily. Voss always played the odds, he trusted no one. Surely he had allowed for a setback like this.

"Well, then, Sung Dai," Voss said at last. "Well, I guess that settles it, then. We lost, that's all. That's the way it goes sometimes . . ."

"We? *We* lost?"

"That's about it, isn't it? You and me both. It was my money too, y'know."

The Korean raised one eyebrow. "Oh?"

"I mean, try to be philosophical about it. Chalk it up to experience and maybe go out and tie on a good drunk. That's what I'm gonna do."

"That is not good enough, Peter. Not nearly good enough."

"Listen, man. Use your head," Voss told him. "Without that MAS Unit the system is locked up tighter than a drum. The deal's off, that's all. 'Cause there's nothing I can do."

"Oh, I am sure you can think of something," the Korean said, allowing an unpleasant smirk to spread across his puffy face. "You see, I believe in you."

"That's very flattering, I'm sure," Voss said. "But I'm telling you it's impossible. So ask Trang Van Thep. He knows what this means. He'll tell you the same thing, ask him."

"Ask him yourself," he replied. "I told you he did not bring the key."

Voss tilted his head as if he wasn't sure what he had just heard. "What have you done with him?" He leaned in until his face was only inches from the Korean's and said, "What have you done with him, you Korean cocksucker?"

Sung Dai's eyes bulged with instant rage. His face flushed and filled out like a balloon. "You . . . you . . . How dare you . . . ?" he sputtered.

"Where is he?"

"The last time I saw your Lieutenant Thep he was floating in the gulf with all the other garbage. I expect they will be up on the Ko Sua Reefs by morning."

"You *left* him there?" Voss grabbed the Korean's damp lapels. "You left him there? Idiot! He was our last link to . . ."

There was a scuffle behind him and a yelp from somebody at the table. Chairs crashed to the floor and somebody shouted, "Look out, Pete!" Voss looked back in time to see Janus come lunging through the tables at him. He had covered half the distance between them and was groping for something hidden beneath his new jacket. Only Sloane had made it to his feet in time but was slowed by the overturned furniture and too late to head him off.

"Let go of me," the Korean warned, and Voss did. The

Korean moved quickly to ward off his henchman, stepping be-tween Janus and his target with both hands out. "Wait, Janus. Now just wait a minute. Now what did I tell you about this one, eh? He mustn't be hurt, isn't that what I said?"

Janus hesitated.

"So, now. So you just go back to where you were and wait as I told you."

The thug did what he was told but he didn't like it. The Korean kept his eyes on him so when he spoke again it was difficult to realize he was actually talking to Voss.

"Our last link to what, Peter?" he asked.

"Huh?"

"You said something about our last link to something. What were you talking about?"

"Nothin'. The key's gone and that's that."

"No. You said 'our last link.' " He waited and then went on. "So it appears to me that even without the MAS Unit he was valuable, is that it? That means there *was* another way, eh? And perhaps yet another after that, yes? What a devious genius you have, Peter. I am sure you will find a solution to our dilemma." He plucked at the collar of his sodden shirt and turned to the tables to show off his teeth again. "Well, boys. How about an-other round, eh?"

He tossed a wad of bills on the waiter's tray. "I hate to interrupt such good times, so few are offered us in this life." His gusto faded momentarily when his eyes met those of Major Chapikorn. Perhaps he was overdoing it, he must learn more self-control. Then he saw Sloane.

"And who do we have here? A new member of the club, is it? And a cut above the rest of this riffraff by the looks of him. Wouldn't you say so, Janus?"

"Look here, Mr. . . . ." Sloane began.

"Mr. Park Sung Dai," said the Korean. "And you are?"

"Ellsworth Bunker," Jake said. "We bring him out once a year to explain himself."

"Shut up, you," the Korean snapped. Janus took a step closer to hover menacingly over Jake's littered end of the table. Jake was oddly relaxed. He was wearing that deceptive grin of the drunk who is looking for trouble.

"Take it easy," Sloane warned him.

"Nothing personal, right, Janus? It's just a job."

"Jake . . ."

Jake made a ring out of his thumb and forefinger and peeked up at Janus's face through it. "He's a freelance anus, that's what ol' Janus is. Asshole for hire. All that dirty shit that somebody like Park Sung Dai needs disposed of? Why, there's our boy, right there to take care of it."

Janus struck out at Jake's hand as if to snatch it away but Jake pulled back just in time. For a drunk he was surprisingly agile.

"Wa-hooo!" Clyde whooped. "Oh, he didn't like that at all."

"Janus! Control yourself," Sung Dai warned.

"He only pretends to be nasty," Jake persisted. "He's really just a pussycat. Loves children. Remember those little boys he got his hands on?"

"Knock it off, Jake," Sloane said. "You're picking fights again."

"I am not." Jake waved the notion aside. "I'm just trying to be entertaining. I'm just trying' to get him to say something for us. He speaks one of those Serbo-Slavic things with no vowels in it. You'll love it. It sounds like a tape recorder running backwards."

"Stop it, you fool," the Korean said.

"Like this: Myp nnnrpyt tytk snypt . . . like that. Right, Janus?"

Janus could hardly contain his fury. "Mypnnrpt tytk smrfft," he hissed.

"See?"

Clyde was howling. "Do it again, man. Do it again."

Janus's face twisted into something almost inhuman. He balled his fists and waded into his tormentors, pushing aside everything in his way. In a single motion he tore a quivering brown leather shaft from under his jacket and made a lunge for Jake.

"Look out!" Sloane grabbed at Janus's sleeve in time to deflect his whipping overhand. Jake leaped to his feet as the table went crashing over with everything on it.

"Whip it out," he was shouting. "That's right. Whip it out, you murdering motherfuck."

Some of the drinkers dove for safety while others joined in. "Grab him, grab him," Clyde yelled as he ducked a slash that was meant for him. It was a mad melee full of arms and legs and grappling bodies and that strange leather wand whizzing through the air with everybody grabbing for it. Bottles and glasses smashed to the floor, their fragments spilling over the side and splashing into the water below. Sloane shoved himself into the middle of the action, trying to get Jake out from under, sticking an elbow into Janus's face while he fended off the blows that were then directed at him.

Jake was no better than Janus. Shove him away and he'd just push back in, swinging one ineffectual punch after another. He was probably the one who kicked Sloane's feet out from under him and sent him sprawling against the rail.

"Stop it!" the Korean shouted as the fray threatened to engulf Peter Voss too, in spite of his struggles to get out of its way. "Stop it, all of you!"

Jake had hold of the arm with the weapon, trying to use it to throw Janus off balance, but Janus threw him off instead and landed a kick in Jake's groin that doubled him over and propelled him backward. Back he went through the tables and chairs with his little legs pinwheeling to keep up until he tripped and went crashing through the rail, yanking out the string of lights with his flaying arms as he somersaulted, slow motion, down into the canal.

Sloane got to the splintered rail in time to see Chappy go trompling down the gangway to the raft near the spot where Jake had surfaced, sputtering and splashing about in the slime.

"Get me out of here." Jake was blowing and spitting with disgust. "Get me out of this shit."

Janus had somehow gotten hold of Voss, who in turn had him by his wrist to ward off the flailing weapon. Voss tried to duck out from under just as Janus lashed out at him. He twisted away and took the blow with a loud thump between his shoulder blades. His eyes shot open and his mouth gaped with the cry he could give no voice to. Like an athlete with the wind knocked out of him he writhed backward, reaching for the wound as if a knife were stuck there.

"*Aiee,*" the Korean shrieked. "Not him, you idiot! Not *Peter!* Stop it, you animal, stop it or we will have nothing left at all!" He pushed his way through the scramble trying to intervene but he wasn't the one who broke up the fight. It was the Kid.

The Kid must have seen what Janus did to his brother because he emerged from the back room with murder in his eyes and Kiri at his heels.

"No, Kid," she was pleading. "Stop it, Kid. It is all righ'."

"Kid, don't . . ." Voss croaked from the wooden deck.

Janus knew that he'd made a mistake as soon as he saw the Kid's massive bulk heading his way. He tried to threaten him off with his weapon, poking and waving it at him as if it were a stiletto but the Kid was too light on his feet to offer a target. Softly he circled, dodging and ducking Janus's thrusts like a cat until—with his first lightning attack—he had him.

"No, Kid." Kiri was sobbing. "No kill him."

The Kid twisted Janus's arms behind him and grabbed his head by his hair. He swung him over his hip and ran him into the rail head first. There was a bang at the impact and then a creaking and groaning as the Kid began sawing at the rail with the side of Janus's head. Janus let out a shrill, warbling scream that went on and on as if his breath was endless.

"Stop it, Kid. Stop it," Kiri begged.

Blood was spurting from Janus's ear. His screams turned to grunts of animal horror between the wet, rubbery sounds of cartilage being ground away.

"Oh, Kid. You must stop." Kiri's face was streaked with tears and spattered blood. "They will come for you if you kill him. They will find out about this and they will come and take you away from me."

The Kid snapped out of it then. It was as if his mind had simply turned to another matter. He looked at the small, trembling girl for a long moment and then just let go of Janus, letting him drop at his feet like a piece of baggage. Janus's new suit and the side of his head were soaked with fresh blood. The Kid had rubbed off his ear. It was gone. Over the side and into the water. Jake saw it land.

"Eeech! Get me out of this shit!"

Docile now, almost innocent of the whole affair, the Kid let Kiri lead him back inside while Janus, still in a state of terror, struggled shakily to his feet, pulling a wad of Kleenex from his pocket and pressing it against the side of his head to stanch the dark stream of blood.

Chappy was already fishing Jake out of the drink as Sloane

came stumbling down the gangway to help. The sailors manning the launch showed no inclination to interfere. Up on the veranda their boss was panting heavily as he squatted beside Voss, who sat where he had fallen, working at a tender spot behind his neck with his hands while he got his breath back.

"You are not to try anything like that again," the Korean said. "No more taking chances like that, do you understand?"

"Taking chances, me? I was tryin' to get out of there."

"I mean it. I cannot afford to risk you like that."

"*You* can't afford . . ." He tried to straighten up but sat back with a groan.

"I did not come here for a fight. I came here to tell you that in spite of everything we remain partners. I believe in you, Peter. You used your wizardry to pillage my accounts and now you will use it to put it all back again. Who knows"—he plucked at the DOORS logo on Voss's T-shirt and shook his head—"maybe there will be enough left over for some decent clothing."

Then he left them, following his shaken and bleeding henchman down to the raft where Chappy was halfway into the water trying to fish Jake out. Sloane had him under the arms and was hauling at him when the inboard was started up behind them. He turned and found Janus's eyes fixed on his as the launch swung its stern around and gathered speed up the waterway.

The Korean's money paid for a lot of liquor and it wasn't long before the slapstick confrontation had been inflated into a deed of almost mythical dimensions. Especially for Jake, with his hair stringing down over his face and canal water still dripping from his shirt pockets.

"I hurt him, though. Didn't I?" He paused to light a soggy cigarette. "Did you see the look on his face when I got in that left hook?"

"Oh, you hurt him, Ace," Clyde said. "You surely did."

"Hurt him any worse he'd have killed you." Voss was grim.

"What was that thing he was waving around?" Sloane asked. "I thought at first he had a knife or a gun."

"God forbid." Jake snorted. "If that creep ever got hold of a gun he'd end up killing everything in sight. You know the kind. The war drew them like flies to pig shit. Should have seen what he did to a friend of mine in Da Nang. Remember that, Pete?"

"Huh?" Voss had been thinking about something else. "Oh, Janus. That's a blackjack he's got."

"A what?" Sloane almost laughed. "A blackjack?"

"A pimp's weapon," Jake said, getting angry all over again. "Silent, not much blood. The Nazi brownshirts used them back in the thirties in their early street fighting—leather-wrapped springs tipped with steel ball bearings. The whip action punches little holes in the skull. Little hemorrhages, like. I've seen what he's done. You might survive, but you'd never be playing with all your marbles again."

"What the hell were you doing, then? Trying to get yourself killed?"

"It was nothing."

"It was stupid." Voss was still massaging his sore neck. "Gettin' your rocks off over nothing. Next time you feel like acting out your death wish you can count me out."

"I . . . I . . ."

"I mean it. I'm sick of tryin' to keep you from getting hurt. Y'gotta quit getting drunk and pickin' fights all the time. I mean, look what you did to the Kid, f'Christ's sake."

Jake was dismayed by Voss's outburst but he recovered quickly. He winked broadly at Sloane. "Strike while the ire is hot, I always say."

The partying went on into the night with endless rounds of tiger beer and the rest of Yan Ki Daniel's Dewars. Some of the girls were showing up from the front. Bar girls have an unerring instinct for being where the money is.

Sloane finally took a break and wandered inside to see how the Kid was and found him slouched on his stool like a trained bear so that he could look into Kiri's face while she gossiped with her girlfriends. It was almost painful to see how the Kid worshiped her. And for her part Kiri held his pawlike hand in hers, patting it now and then with that curious tenderness that some women have for a man who's been ruined so utterly.

Jake bellied up to the bar beside Sloane and bummed a cigarette. "Tell me, Dave," he said as he hung it from the corner of his mouth. "Jus' what are you two up to anyhow, you n' Pete?" He was surprised by a hiccup and was spitting out bits of tobacco while Sloane lit one of his own.

"Up to? What d'you mean by that?" Sloane said. "I needed a job and he gave me one."

"Jus' like that?"

"Sure. Said he needs my 'sperience with these big international corporations but I'm not so sure."

"You figure he's jus' helpin' you out," Jake suggested.

"Somethin' like that."

"Good ol' Pete," Jake said, testing his grip on the bar. "Anything for a pal."

"Good ol' Pete," Sloane agreed.

". . . never asks what's in for him."

". . . never does."

" 'Cause there's *always* somethin' in it for him."

"Now, Jake . . ."

"Forget it," Jake said. "I didn't mean anything, okay?"

"Okay."

"It's just that he thinks he can have it both ways, y'know what I mean?"

"No."

"I mean he does business with creeps like that Korean . . ."

"He does?"

"Sure he does. Back in 'Nam. Park Sung Dai. You must have heard of him. He was one of the top black market operators in Southeast Asia. So Pete does business with somebody like that and then he pretends that he's better than they are."

"Yeah? Well, he's right."

Jake took a drink of beer and rubbed his wet chin pensively. "He was the same in the war. He knew that those electronic toys of his didn't have anything to do with real life. He told me once that the war was being taken over by programmers in Virginia who couldn't in their wildest dreams imagine what the war was really like. But he went along with it, yes, he did. He went along for the ride. Ask him about it sometime. All he ever says is 'garbage in, garbage out.' "

"We all made mistakes, Jake. Lots of us went along."

"He did more than go along, dammit. He fed off it. He thrived on the stupidity of the thing, it let him skim what he wanted off the top and go on telling himself he was above it all."

"C'mon, Jake. They're just machines, for God's sake. He just ran 'em."

"See there? Now we can all pretend it's not our fault. That's what his goddam computers have done to us. That's their real damage. They've helped us lose our sense of complicity."

The drinkers on the veranda were ready to move on. They came stumbling inside looking for a last drink or a girl to take home or just for some more action to round out the night. Jake paid no attention.

"Ben Franklin was right," he said to nobody in particular. "The national symbol should have been a turkey."

Somsak appeared in the doorway at exactly the appointed hour, frowning at the scene he found before him. The drinkers had come to that part of the evening when a heady sense of hedonism begins to overwhelm their better judgment. There was a feeling in the air that there was still some excitement worth looking for elsewhere in the city of angels. So the last swallows were taken from the last drinks, debts were paid off and fresh spending money borrowed. Some of the girls were divvied out while Kiri, tittering nervously with the others, kept her arm possessively around Voss's waist. Chappy was found in a heap singing to himself and Sloane had to help him find his way out into the cool night air.

For a moment everyone was spellbound by the moonlit quiet of the street, but the spell was broken when a cheer went up for Jake, who appeared from around the corner hanging from a tuk-tuk he'd fetched back from Charoen Road.

The jeep was waiting in front of the door and behind it was the Kid's motorcycle, a huge old Norton, relic of the Burma campaign, with its original olive drab showing through the sides of the tank where countless pairs of thighs had rubbed through countless paint jobs. Its only springs were connected up under the front yoke and its handlebars stuck out like a longhorn steer. It was held upright by a bomb-shaped sidecar with a dispatch case still bolted to the back.

The jeep was first off the line with those who'd managed to get aboard shouting up at the shuttered windows like drunken liberators. There were four in the backseat of the motor rickshaw and three more hanging onto the back so that the ungainly three-wheeler kept dipping up and down like a teeter-totter as it pulled away.

They'd stuffed Sloane into the Kid's sidecar and fitted somebody in on top of him. He was as loud as any of them. It was just like the old days, charging off after some senseless triumph somewhere, racing through the back streets of Thon Buri from one torrent of bright lights to the next, where sleepless bazaars peddled their special late-night wares. It was wild and woolly fun.

Sloane could see the Kid's face now and then as a light passed overhead. His eyes were clear and eager and his mouth was swept back into a steely grin. Nothing was wrong with him. He was full of life again, complete and whole. Oblivious to his part in reality, he was cheating time like the rest of them, caught up in some nihilist rapture all his own.

CHAPTER

5

First came the bright pink splot dancing in front of his eyes and then came the giggles. Sloane watched the splot for a minute or two and then he realized that he didn't actually have his eyes open. He tried a quick peek. One dry eye popped open unexpectedly and a dazzling beam of light seared the pupil and burned through to his sinuses like pepper dust. He swore with a strange deep voice and scrunched his eyes shut; he was going to sneeze and a sneeze was sure to kill him. The giggles continued as he made faces and rubbed his nose furiously. The pink splot went on dancing in front of him.

He'd been sleeping, that was it. And now he was awake and it was awful. He tried another peek and found a pack of bare-legged little boys hanging onto the side of the jeep while one of them twisted the rearview mirror around to reflect a blinding beam of sunlight into his eye. Oh, the heartless little bastards.

"HAAAARH!" he yelled and with a chorus of piercing laughter they scampered off to regroup at a safer distance. "HAAARH." He tried to sit up too suddenly and banged his head on the steering wheel. "Oow, oh shit. Oh, God."

His body had been draped across the bucket seats and his rib cage felt like he'd been run over. He tried a few deep breaths and found that his lungs were crinkled up in his chest like a pair of paper bags. Now there was a lump on his forehead from the steering wheel as well as a throb he could almost hear behind his right eye. He sat up carefully and shaded his eyes before he tried looking around.

It looked like the Thonburi side of the waterfront. The river was wide here, smooth and muddy green as it glittered in the morning sun. There was a briny, fish smell to the breeze and formations of white water birds were winging along close to the water. The sky was a perfect blue dome and a wind, a couple of thousand feet up, was pushing a few little clouds ahead of it, rolling and puffing toward the gulf.

Voss was just leaving a noodle stall near the pier, trailing smoke from the cookfire after him. He ambled over to the jeep and handed Sloane a glass of brown liquid that scalded his fingers.

"Coffee," Voss told him. "Got a couple of pastries, too. I'm not too sure what they are. How y'feelin'?"

Sloane was passing the glass from hand to hand trying to keep it from burning him any worse while he looked for a place to set it down. "Just a little headache," he admitted. Voss never got hangovers.

"The Prince will be along pretty quick."

"The Prince?"

"I called him a couple hours ago."

Sloane checked his watch. "It's six o'clock in the morning."

"C'mon. I'll show you around while we wait."

"I'm going to meet the Prince now? Like this?" Sloane said as he climbed out of the jeep. "Look at me, what'll he think?"

"He's very informal," Voss said. "Finish your coffee."

Sloane kept his eyes shaded with his hand as he followed him toward the river. "Never go to sleep," Voss was saying as they walked out onto the pier. "That's the whole secret. Party yourself out and then keep goin' until you're sober again."

The pier was huge. Acres of thick hardwood planks laid out in a herringbone pattern with knee-high davits down either side. An aging steam tender was tied alongside, rust streaked and low in the water. On the upriver side of the pier, under a forest of bobbing white masts, was a fleet of untidy fishing boats. They were all variations on a theme: twenty- or thirty-footers, diesel-powered with their deckhouses just aft of midships. They were tied off to the heavy hawsers that were stretched out from the pier by rows of red buoys.

The company offices were housed in a nondescript brick cube that rose from its own foundation in the center of the pier. It was two stories high and topped with oversized dormer vents and an elaborate grouping of antennae. On the end that faced the shore there was a large sign with the company logo that said THAI/TECH INDUSTRIES LTD., two lines of cartoon waves, and the motto "Riches from the Sea."

Voss led the way past a Sikh guard who was sleeping by the door and into the pleasant reception room, where he paused to let Sloane look around.

"Just like they got in the old country," Voss said as he unwrapped the pastries he'd been carrying. "Here y'go, have one. C'mon, eat something. You look like hell."

Sloane took a bite and made a face as his chewing reduced the greasy bun into a wad of fishy paste. He palmed the rest as Voss headed up the stairs two at a time.

The interior of the building was a study of Bauhaus practicality with small square windows and brown pipe railings running up the cement staircase. The overhead tube lights soaked everything in cold light. The computers were on the second floor, some humming softly as if they had been on watch all night.

Sloane gave a low whistle. "Some setup you've got here. Is this like the computer you had at Beach House 7?"

"It's a cheap imitation," Voss said. "But it's compatible." He sat down at one of the consoles and began punching up digits on the screen. "It's a matter of resources at this point. These old Sperry Rand tape units will have to do until we've got money enough to convert to drum storage. And we've got to keep it all compatible with the local networks like the one at Chulalongkorn University so those of our clients with remote terminals can tie in."

"What for?"

"Well, for one thing, with our own computers on line this whole system becomes a super-duper smart terminal. We can go through all those access codes and security systems out there like a dose of salts. It's gotten so we regularly use other people's systems for auxiliary storage and nobody's the wiser. That effectively doubles the capacity of what you see here."

"Doesn't exactly sound legal."

"I'm tellin' you, you worry too much," Voss said without looking up from the screen. "Come here and look at this." He pointed at some numbers that were climbing the left side of the screen in front of him. "There he is. ID code. Site code—I thought so. He's not one of ours. See there? Lots of people cross over the line once in a while. This one's using some of our statistics for his own research. Oh, we've got us a real eager beaver here, working early so we won't be around to catch him at it. Maybe he even programmed it to start by itself so he could stay home and catch up on his sleep."

"You mean he's using a computer to steal time on our computers?"

"Some people have no ethics." Voss smiled. "It's a kind of a game, that's all. Thai/Tech only uses an average of ten percent of our available time units. Then we contract out another eighty-seven percent to our clients for everything from sales and receivables to cash flow to production planning—all that accounting stuff. Then there's twenty percent payroll accounts, inventory, and cash flow projections with their own remote terminals on a time/share basis, and that's how we cover our initial investment."

"Wait a minute," Sloane said. "Ten percent and eighty-seven percent and twenty percent adds up to a hundred and seventeen percent."

"That's what I'm sayin'. So if we need somebody else's system for a while who's to know? We did the same thing in 'Nam when we were setting things up. We'd just go on-line and tap whatever system was handy. Saved us a lot of time."

"You mean that in effect you're renting time to your clients on somebody else's computer?"

"*Our* clients," Voss said. "And you don't hear them complaining, do you? Now give me a minute here while I have some fun with this guy." He began pecking at the keyboard while Sloane sat down with his thoughts and his greasy bun.

"Y'know," he said at last. "Alice had something to say about all this."

"Alice? Good God, are you still seeing Crazy Alice?"

"I'm seeing her tonight, as a matter of fact."

"Great. Maybe I'll finally get a chance to meet her."

"Yeah, sure," Sloane said. "Anyhow, this wheeling and dealing of yours makes her nervous. Now I'm not saying she's right, you understand. But this . . . this cavalier attitude you take with other people's records is pretty risky, isn't it? Just because you know so much about what computers can do . . ."

"Oh, I know something much more important than that," Voss said without looking up. "I know what they *can't* do." He waited for a moment while an event took place on the screen in front of him and then went on talking while he worked. "What they can't do is think. Computers organize, that's all. When you ask a computer for an answer it doesn't give you an answer, it gives you back a summary of its organized data. I don't know why that's so hard for people to understand what that means. What that *really* means."

"Okay, what does it mean?"

"It means it's the *data* that counts, not the answers. The rules you're so worried about don't apply with people like me. For us data has become a raw material like iron ore and coal and it belongs to those who know how to get at it.

"That's why Beach House 7 was plugged into much more than just Igloo White and its electronic weaponry. It was interfaced with the data base from the full range of the war effort. From the Statistical Evaluation Center in the basement of the American Embassy to the Marine supply depot in Da Nang. From the Resettlement and Pacification Program to the National Finance and Banking Administration.

"There's never been a weapon like it, a computer network wired into every facet of the host country's fiscal, agricultural, and logistical potential. A network whose sole purpose was the prosecution of war."

"So how come we lost?"

"Simple," Voss told him. "Garbage in, garbage out."

The characters on the screen began blipping out one by one until there was nothing left but the user's code blinking pathetically in the lower left-hand corner. Then it went out, too.

Voss grinned. "Boy, is that sucker gonna be surprised."

"That's the cannery." Voss pointed at the wooden building on the downriver side beyond the tender. It had a low, slanted roof, like the warehouses that cluttered the rest of the Thonburi riverfront, with a number of raw wooden additions and repairs that contrasted sharply with the darkly weathered siding. The heavy equipment was scattered around the pier like toys in a playground; light towers, an army forklift, and long stacks of tarpaulin-covered boxes. There was even an ancient chain-drive truck with solid wheels under a mysterious chute at the end of the cannery.

"We freeze some of it," Voss was saying. "We're modernizing the equipment but the priorities are a little mixed up at the moment. For instance, our computer model of optimum fishing patterns isn't working out."

He was leading him along the downriver side of the pier where a series of multitiered conveyer belts pointed out over the water between a light tower and a decrepit-looking crane.

"We make use of everything. Trash fish get sorted—that's the only canning we bother with anymore—and we sell it to the Japanese for cat food. God knows what they really do with it. The computer changes the composition every day according to availability, consistency, and price just like they do in the States with hot dogs. The rest—oh, you'll love this . . ."

He leaned against one of the davits and pointed over the side. "The rest, the bones and entrails and heads and all that garbage, we ship upriver. The Prince has muscled in on the *nam pla* brewing business up in Kambulak. That's that fermented fish sauce you seemed to like so much last night. See that? That's what it's made from."

Directly beneath the conveyer belt was a barge. A heavy vessel, not much more than a black steel hull with a cabin mounted in the stern and a wide cargo hatch near the bow that was nearly buried under a fly-covered mound of moist, pulpy garbage.

Voss went on without mercy. "Crush it, boil it down, and let it ferment for a while . . . Right now, of course, it smells a bit rank."

Sloane found that he still had the remains of his greasy pastry in his hand. He flung it into the water and watched in disgust as it dissolved into a rainbow slick.

There was a crewman bent over an electrical conduit box attached to a huge electric motor. A cable stretched from his hand to the dock while he probed with it through some of the protruding wires. Suddenly there was a blue spark and a loud metallic roar as the big motor turned over. The whole vessel convulsed and fell silent again. The crewman, who had been knocked to the deck, looked back at the two *farang* sheepishly.

"Good, he got it to work," Voss said, rubbing his hands together as if he'd done it himself. "Watch this, this is a great gadget." He shouted something to the crewman, who waved back, wrapped some wires together, and threw a switch. The bow reared up and settled again as the roar became a slushy grinding sound from deep in the bowels of the boat. The quaking visceral mound began to hollow as it emptied itself into the hold.

Sloane tried to turn away from the sight but couldn't. His attention was fastened on the repulsive maw and he could only stand there with his stomach churning as the pile collapsed into a pair of huge spinning blades below decks that reduced the offal to a gruel-like swill and drove it back into the stern.

"Oh, my Christ, Pete."

"Really something', isn't it?" Voss said. "Twin counterrotating worm gears. Draws it back and distributes it throughout the hold. Saves us all the man-hours it used to take to rake it out even. Some AID project up on the Mekong was using it for fertilizer . . . Hey, you all right?"

Sloane was reeling toward the dry land, taking in deep gulps of fresh air with each stride. Voss had to skip a few steps to catch up.

"And then we just reverse it for off-loading when we get it upriver."

"Must be quite a sight."

A second glass of coffee helped some. They'd gone back to the noodle stall where the local dockworkers were gathering and Sloane had the owner brew it strong and load it with condensed milk and coarse-grained sugar. Voss went on talking about the business while they found a bench under the tattered awning and Sloane tried his best to pay attention. He hovered over his slippery glass, breathing in the steam between sips.

There was time for another glass before the Prince showed up. The Prince had a bright red Fiat with dark-tinted windows and a whip antenna tied down to the rain gutter. He was dressed in what Voss called the Penny-Loafer Protestant style with a pair of aviator sunglasses that gave him a dashing look. When he spotted Voss he gave a cheery wave and leaned back into the Fiat to retrieve a well-stuffed clipboard.

He was a young man, trim and about Voss's size. The crease in his charcoal slacks was razor sharp and there was an array of gold pens along his breast pocket. He had a beige sweater rolled under his arm, though it was hard to believe he would need it on a day like this.

"Good morning, Peter," he said. "And this must be David Sloane. I cannot tell you how delighted I am to have you with us. Peter has told me all about you, you know."

"Prince Woraphan," Voss said to Sloane. "Our partner in crime."

The Prince took Sloane's hand and eyed him carefully. "Heavens, Peter. He looks terrible."

"I was just introduced to your fertilizer barge," Sloane explained.

"Oh, good." The Prince beamed with pride. "Isn't it splendid? It came into our hands because it was another of the refugee boats. It was packed to the rails, poor creatures. Many were dead down in the holds before the paperwork was complete and they could be shipped off to the camps.

"We get many boats that way. Fishing boats, mostly. They just keep coming. Government workers and soldiers from the 'reeducation camps.' The old, the sick, the useless . . . the Vietnamese have never liked their Chinese, of course, and the NVA hates Catholics as well. So the Communists rob them and the boat owners rob them and by the time they get here—if they get here —they have nothing left at all."

They started off down the pier toward the fishing fleet, Sloane sipping the dregs of his coffee while the Prince talked.

"But what is Thailand to do with them? Thousands—tens of thousands. Who knows? Those who survive are sent off to Songhia or, if they are Cambodians, off to the border camps. The boats are impounded, of course, so all we have to do is pay the duty on them and they belong to Thai/Tech."

" 'Riches from the sea,' " Sloane suggested.

"Now tell me, Peter," the Prince said. "What exactly did the Korean say?"

"He said that Trang Van Thep was adrift on one of those old China coasters and that he'd probably be on the Ko Sua Reefs by this morning."

"Mmm, that is bad." The Prince shook his head. "A very bad region. We will have to find him before the pirates do."

Sloane looked up from his glass. "We?"

"Yes, of course." The Prince brightened. "Oh, yes, indeed. This could well turn out to be a wonderful adventure, you know? I love adventures. Peter's good friend Lt. Trang Van Thep has attempted his escape from that benighted land and now is lost upon the sea. And something else, too, yes, Peter?"

"That's the bad news," Voss said. "He doesn't have the MAS Unit after all. That's why the Korean left him out there."

"No matter," the Prince said. "He must be rescued."

Voss was biting his lip again. "He said he'd collaborated with the new regime so he'll still have something useful to tell us about the network."

"Yes, well, all that is your department. The important thing is that he is your friend, so of course we must do what we can."

"All of us?"

"Of course, David," the Prince said. "Isn't it wonderful?" We are all going out for a little look-see."

"Sure." Voss slung an arm around him. "It'll give you a chance to look over the areas we fish. And you can check out the plane."

There was a pause in the conversation and after a few more steps Sloane began to lag behind. He was hiding his eyes by rubbing the bridge of his nose between his fingers.

"Oh, hey," he said. "I'd really like to, but there's something I've got to do today. It's Alice. See, Alice has to report to her site tomorrow . . ."

"Don't worry. I'll make sure she feels right at home."

"But you've done so much already. No, why don't you two go and look for this Trang Van What's-his-name without me? I really don't feel up to it anyhow."

"But . . ." The Prince looked around at him, helplessly. "But who will fly?"

"Who . . . who will . . ."

"Oh, yes, you must teach me, you know," the Prince told him. "I was getting pretty good when our last pilot quit very suddenly. It is very important that I learn to be a pilot. Come along, I will explain." He put a hand to the small of Sloane's back and ushered him along as he spoke. "You see, most of our fishermen were refugees and are afraid to risk going out on the gulf again even for a livelihood. Now Peter's computers have given us a fine statistical model for seasonal fishing patterns but our people will not follow it. They fish the river channels or the delta where they are safe and trust to luck.

"This will not do. Thai/Tech's original expansion was financed against the collateral of our fixed assets—the cannery, the fleet—so these operations must cover more than their capital expenditures or my uncle will not give me any more money."

"Sounds serious."

"It is," the Prince assured him. "Now what better way to instill courage in the hearts of our fishermen than to fly right out there with them, you know? Show the flag, so to speak."

"Uh-huh."

A *hangyao* is a slender craft, something between a skiff and a rowing scull and powered by a small automobile motor mounted on a kimble so that the long power shaft sticks straight out behind. The one the Prince hailed to take them out to the plane was driven by an elderly woman in a woven reed sun hat and blue worker's shirt.

". . . eighty liters of fuel," the Prince was saying. "I saw to it myself yesterday. All of it strained through a chamois skin. Seventeen hours only since the last overhaul."

"What kind of a plane is she?"

"She's . . . well, she's a Japanese plane."

"Really? What kind of a Japanese plane?"

"What kind?"

"Sure. Maybe I won't know anything about this kind of aircraft. Maybe I can't even fly the damn thing." The sun's glare made Sloane's headache worse. He shaded his face with his hand while he searched for their destination. "Single engine?"

"Yes. Single."

"What is it, float plane? Amphibian? Flying boat?"

"Floats."

"But what kind? What's her power? What's her range?"

"Plenty of power." The Prince patted Sloane's knee. "Plenty of range. You are being so practical. So American. For me it is enough to know what a lovely aircraft it is."

It was the ugliest aircraft that Sloane had ever seen. It stood tiptoe on a pair of ungainly pontoons that were covered with rivets and mysterious threaded plugs. The paint job looked recent, a dark silvery color which, if it was meant to look like metal, was betrayed by patches and templates that stretched the canvas skin like the ribs of a starvling.

"Oh, lord."

"A Mitsatsu 150," the Prince told him. "One of the light observation craft your navy code named the 'Zebra.'"

It was a biplane with blunt box kite wings, the top pair aft of the lower so that the windscreen fit almost flat behind the engine like a skylight. It had an oversized tail assembly and the fuselage was shaped like a coffin.

On the other side of the river the royal pendants were flying from the signal mast of the Naval Headquarters. A bell sounded clearly from the high-walled monastery behind while the *hangyao* circled the aircraft slowly, closer each time around until it passed under the wings and then the tail. Sloane signaled the old woman at the helm to cut the motor and reached for the tail skid as they passed under it. He hoisted himself up and gave the exposed ends of the control cables a few hard yanks before letting go and allowing the boat to drift on.

"The Japanese left it behind when they abandoned their reconnaissance base back in 1945. They left a whole warehouse full of parts, too, so it is all restored to number one condition. Molded plywood around the cabin, just like the Fairchild back in '34. A wonderful motor, you know? Water cooled. You can see the radiator where that section of cowling is missing."

"The doors are gone, too."

"We have seat belts," the Prince pointed out. "And may I say the breeze will do you good. It is a beautiful day to fly, the monsoon is late so the hot wet air will give us plenty of lift."

"It's the other way around."

There was a brass stirrup fastened behind the base of the lower wing and a grip Sloane had to stretch for as he hauled himself up to where he could back into the cabin.

"Be careful of the floor, just there," the Prince said. "Dry rot."

"This is ridiculous," Sloane said. "Pete, this is crazy. This thing ought to be checked out by experts. And anyhow, my head is splitting."

"No time, man. Trang Van Thep will be on the reefs by now. He won't have much of a chance if we don't get out there quick."

Sloane muttered something under his breath but he was

already hanging out of the other side tracing the spaghettilike wires and tinfoil-wrapped fuel line up forward in the engine compartment.

"There is aspirin," the Prince called up from the pontoon. "In the map pouch between the seats. Out last pilot wouldn't fly without them."

"I'm not surprised." Sloane followed the fuel line from the selector switch overhead until he found the booster pump under the panel. There was a bilge pump there, too, a brass cylinder with a wooden handle. He unhooked it and tossed it down to Voss to empty out the floats.

Sloane choked down a few aspirin dry and continued his inspection for another half hour before he was satisfied. At last he leaned out the door to check the control surfaces while he wobbled the stick. While the Prince cast off from the mooring buoy and Voss climbed into the cabin, Sloane went over the unfamiliar instrument panel and controls, checking them off one by one in his head. He switched the ignition switch back and forth until he was sure which was which.

"Switch off," he called down and began buckling himself in while the Prince positioned the blade from the end of the pontoon. Then he flicked the switch on again.

"Contact."

The Chao Phrya River turns from west to east above the city, first a widening of the banks where its current glides quietly over its alluvial bed, then an easy half-circle that separates Bangkok from Thonburi. There are times in the day when the schedules of commerce turn the waterway into a white-waked warren of activity and one of those times was fast approaching as they started off.

There was still an unobstructed right of way diagonally across the front of the ferry boat docks—or at least there was until a coolie in a flatboat came punting out from shore to recover his fish traps. He saw the plane come roaring along, as did a crowd of commuters on the shore. They were smiling and waving as the old Mitsatsu 150 went streaking by chased by a pair of rooster tails that misted into rainbows at the edges. It must have been quite a sight, especially from the coolie's point of view for he had paused to watch from a point directly in the airplane's path.

Sloane didn't see him at first. There's not much that can be seen when the windscreen is almost overhead. He couldn't even see horizon once he had powered the heavy floatplane into its plow attitude, and it didn't get much better when he opened the throttle and pulled back on the stick. The angle stabilized easily enough but when he let the stick ride forward nothing changed. The plane refused to leave the hump. It just went on pushing all the water ahead of it like a river barge, riding the backside of its own wake.

The prop wash was howling through the open cockpit, soaking them all with spray while Sloane felt around with the stick looking for the trim that would plane the aircraft up onto the "step" where the floats could hydro free of the water's suction. The nose lowered just a little and there was the flatboat, right in front of them with the coolie watching them in awe.

"Look out, meat-head!" Sloane shouted as he yanked back on the stick. Nothing happened. They had reached air speed, they were on "step," now what? He began working the ailerons against the rudder, flapping and hopping the plane from one float to the other, fighting the water's suction with long mushy leaps like the mating dance of some madcap seabird. The coolie watched in amazement, swaying on his skinny legs in unconscious imitation of the aircraft as it came barreling down on him.

Then there was a moment of hesitation. Sloane felt it at the base of his spine. A split airborne second between one float and the other, so he hauled back on the stick with both hands and held his breath. It didn't stall. It wanted to but when he nudged the stick forward the aircraft found some precious airspeed and ground its way into the sky.

Sloane let it climb. Nothing fancy for now, he just gave it its head and let it put some welcome distance between them and the ground while he gripped the stick with a white-knuckled hold and cursed himself for a fool. What a stupid stunt. Flying a piece of junk he knew nothing about while the Prince, sitting beside him, was having the time of his life. He would have told Sloane anything to get himself this joyride.

"Give me a couple more aspirin," Sloane shouted over the wind.

They leveled off at three thousand feet and Sloane tapped the throttle back and listened to the change in the engine's pitch.

Maybe it wasn't such a bad old beast after all. He relaxed his grip on the stick, giving it some play until it yawed gently to the left. Not bad at all—it's trimmed up pretty well, holds its altitude. He even allowed himself a little smile as he squirmed in his seat trying to work the stiffness out of his back.

"Isn't it wonderful?" the Prince yelled.

"Just proves the old adage," Sloane said. "Crank up enough power and you can fly a brick."

The Prince nodded happily. He hadn't heard him.

At three thousand feet they could see the Gulf of Siam and how the jade green river snaked toward it through a scorched checkerboard of rice paddies ahead of them. The Prince had a clipboard full of maps flapping around in his lap while he and Voss argued about the landmarks they were passing over. Sloane followed the river and waited for them to plot out the course while he tried to get the feel of the aircraft and decide what instruments he could trust.

The radio didn't work. It didn't even look like a radio, more like a toy safe with a couple of wires sticking out, but the compass looked about right. He pumped the stick a few times and worried about the flex of the wings. Rebuilt or just recovered? Why hadn't he asked?

There were towns and villages below, industrial suburbs along the river and farm villages bunched together amid their radiating fields. There were still canals, too, angling off from the river toward the jungled hills beyond Kanchanaburi.

The Prince shook Sloane's arm and pointed downward. The lower wing was well forward of the doorway so Sloane had to bank right until the wing tip was pointed down at the river. There were some boats down there. Not like the seagoing traffic that plies from the Chow Loong piers, but little clusters of waterbugs inching their random ways from one spot to another.

"You see?" the Prince shouted. "There they are down there, waiting for the fish to come to them. Let us give them a show. Let us dive down and tell them to do their jobs right."

"Forget it," Sloane shouted back. "I'm not diving in this crate."

"No time anyhow," Voss said from the back. "Look here, this is what we've got to do." He took the clipboard and held it up for Sloane to see the course he had drawn on the map with a wax pencil. "We've got to get to where this dark area is, here. The Ko Sua Reefs. We ought to be able to see them pretty well from the air, they'll be a couple of hours out once we're past Samut Pakran."

"Landfall off this point?" Sloane punched at the map with his forefinger. The Prince nodded.

"Do you trust this compass enough for dead reckoning? We'll be out over the water for a long time." This time the Prince shrugged.

Sloane made a slow turn to the south over the marshlands where the Chao Phrya disgorged its heavy billows of silt into the emerald calm of the gulf. The islands ahead looked larger from the air than they showed on the map because of the submerged reefs and coral shelves of the archipelago. Beyond them was nothing but a vast glittering expanse of water and an occasional solitary freighter.

Sloane kept his eyes on the horizon and the bobbing compass. He could detect a hundred impending calamities in every pocket of turbulence and every imaginary change in the drone of the engine. His mouth was dry and the aspirin had stuck on the way down. It burned in his chest like a live coal.

They flew on for another hour and a half, suspended in space and time while nothing in their world changed. Not the blinding sunlight, not the endless roar of driven air nor the shape of the great sea down below. Everything stayed just as it was until the coastline of the Isthmus of Kraw began to creep over the horizon.

"Down there," Voss called out from his place at the door on the Prince's side. He hoisted himself upright by the seat webbing and stuck his head between the two in front. "The reefs are down there."

Sloane eased the aircraft into a slow bank until he could see the wide patches of lighter green out the other side. "Looks like thirty miles or so of this stuff close in to shore." Voss showed them the map. "Man, we'll never find him in that."

The Ko Sua was a barrier reef, a huge stain of coke bottle green that lurked beneath the surface between the shore and the safe open sea. The windward side was strewn with wrecks, splintered and drowned beneath the surf where the edge of the reef merged with the darker waters of the deep. Others in the in-shore shallows seemed to be at rest at their moorings. Ages of tragedy in a crystalline showcase.

Sloane dropped to two thousand feet and began a rough search grid that would concentrate on the eastern perimeter where a boat with a coaster's draft would have a better chance of survival. Back and forth they flew, east to west and back again while their eyes burned in the hot blowing air and the blinding midday brilliance of the glittering sea.

"Nothin', man," Voss said after an hour of futile searching. "Everything's dead down there. Everything."

"Perhaps further down," the Prince suggested as Sloane climbed again for an overview.

"Like a needle in a haystack," Sloane said. "And besides . . ." He pointed at the fuel gauge, twisted the shuttlecock valve to draw on the reserve, and then tapped the gauge with his knuckle until the needle moved.

"We'll follow the coast up the peninsula," Voss shouted. "Cut back when we get to Prachuap. Who knows, maybe they made it."

"Not very likely." Sloane could see that even from this altitude. It was a treacherous place down there. Even north of the mass of the reef the endless coiling lines of surf swept over deadly coral crusts that surfaced more than a mile out from the jungle-fringed beaches.

In spite of his skepticism it was Sloane who saw the coaster first. He'd leaned out the door to check for the source of a streak of oil crawling back from the cowl when he spotted a dark shape through the circle of the spinning prop. He pointed it out to the Prince who pointed it out to Voss while Sloane took them down for a closer look.

"That's him," Voss yelled. "It's gotta be him, it's the only one around. God, it looks like they're sinking. The current must'a dragged them over that outcropping and into the channel tail first."

"There's still some people aboard her."

"What's that, a raft?"

The coaster was a wretched old hulk, almost alive in its final agonies. It had hung itself over a coral head and was wallowing in the surf line like a mortally wounded beast, grinding itself to pieces against the bottom. Sloane circled lower over the wreck while the other two crowded the door for a better look. The few survivors had tried to lash together some timbers for a raft but it was useless. The raft had hung up on the torn plates of the hull and caught in the rigging that had been swept over the side. Some men were hacking at it with machetes but each roll of the hull pulled it under. There were ten or fifteen people, women and children mostly, clinging to each other on the rolling afterdeck.

"Look down there," Sloane shouted to the others. "Out this side. There's dugouts down there! See them? Two, three, four, there must be a dozen of them. I'm going down for a closer look."

He headed in from over the southern stretch of beach and banked out toward the wreck at five hundred feet. There were more people down on the sand, some of them dragging dugouts and small boats out from the jungle line. They scattered before the approaching aircraft.

"Take it easy, Dave," Voss yelled. "I don't like the looks of this."

"Looks to me like help is on the way."

"Help, my ass," Voss said. "Take a look at that."

Sloane yawed the plane to the left so that he could see the vessel just behind the wing. The raft was awash with surf and struggling figures. A machete glinted in the sun and a figure fell back into the foam.

"Oh, my lord!"

"They're killing them! They're slaughtering them like pigs!"

"Pirates!" the Prince was shouting. "Good God. Women, children . . . we must do something."

"Forget it," Voss said.

"What do you mean, 'forget it'?" Sloane demanded. "We've got to do something."

"Use your head, man. What *can* we do?"

"Perhaps your friend is still down there," the Prince yelled. "Perhaps he is still alive."

"They're armed and we aren't."

"Yeah? Well, they're not going to get away with it," Sloane yelled. "It's going to cost them something."

"Hey, they've got guns. That's all there is to it." He'd never seen Sloane like this. "Hey, don't, Dave. What the hell do you think you're doin'?"

Sloane had yanked the plane over into a hard, banking climb. He held it there, up and up to the very brink of a stall and then he kicked at the rudder so that the plane fell back on itself and nosed over into a dive.

"Stop it! Stop it, man. You'll get us killed!"

Sloane took them right down to the deck, the guy wires screaming all the way before he hauled back on the stick. There were more boats in the water now, little brown figures scrambling into them and pulling for the wreck. Sloane was heading into their midst at a hundred and fifty miles an hour and so close to the water that the fliers were drenched in their own spray.

At first the pirates tried to scatter their boats ahead of them but then one of them with an outboard motor hit a curling wave wrong and was flipped over. Another lifted over the crest only to land on the cripple. The attack was falling into a chaos. Some crews jumped overboard in terror at the sight of the onrushing aircraft, others were swamped as they tried to turn for shore and the surf rolled over them. Sloane swept in low at full bore and then reared back into a climb.

"This is insane!" Voss was yelling. He was gripping the sides of the plane to keep himself braced while he bent forward, red-faced, trying to make himself heard. "You're gonna get us killed, do you hear me? You'll tear the wings off this . . . Oh, no!"

Sloane had them at the apex of the climb and he stalled them over almost onto their back. Again he kicked the rudder so that they fell off to the right, again the nose dropped into a screaming dive that leveled off at wave height. This time he flew in low over the beach, sending the pirates running for the trees and diving into hollows in the dunes. And this time somebody shot at him —a little puff of smoke from behind a palm.

"See that? See that?" Voss had Sloane by the collar and was shaking him and pointing out the door. "They know we've got no guns or we'd have used them. They know it's a bluff. If they hit us and we go down they'll get us, too, did y'consider that?"

Sloane paid no attention to him. He had been heading out to sea, picking up some altitude, and now he put the aircraft into a sharp right bank and aimed straight for the wreck.

They were too late anyway. The coaster had broken in half, its bow had sunk a hundred yards out and the rest was breaking up. The refugees had fought and lost, the aft section was heaped with bodies, their limbs slack and broken as the pirates picked through them. There were a few left even yet and the marauders were scrambling up the debris to get at them, too. What could they have that was worth such a horror? A few coins? Their women, the children?

Some of the pirates ducked at the sight of the diving aircraft, some others dived over the side. But there were others who were too intent on their prize to be intimidated. They cowered, yes, and hid while the plane passed over but then they were back at their terrible task.

The few remaining survivors had been hacking away at the ropes that entangled their raft but it was useless. There was no place to escape to anymore. More dugouts and outboards were closing in for the kill and the refugees had to fall back to protect their women and children.

A ragged fusillade of small arms fire opened up on the airplane from the trees and in no time there were guns going off everywhere. From the jungle, the dunes, even from the boats. Little white puffs that seemed to rally the rest the way blood rallies sharks.

There was a snap and sting on Sloane's cheek as a bullet ripped through the doorjamb and sent fragments flying. Then there was a hollow thud from a pontoon.

"That's it, hero," Voss shouted in his ear. "Get us the hell out'a here."

And that's what Sloane had to do. He was flying into a hail of bullets that was tearing up the fabric on his wings and punching holes in the cowling. A shot slammed through the firewall missing the Prince by inches, so on his fourth pass at the wreck Sloane pulled up short and climbed. As he passed over the broken boat and its doomed refugees he was forced to witness a tableau he would never forget. A huddle of women and children clung to each other in the stern while an old man—Sloane saw him quite clearly—armed only with a machette, had placed himself between what was left of his people and the pirates. There was no expression at all on his face as he watched Sloane fly away.

CHAPTER

6

They ought to make another language, Sloane was thinking. One with simpler kinds of words anybody could use to talk about the shape of their feelings. If he had the words maybe he could understand the feelings himself.

"He was just standing there, y'know?" was the best he could come up with. "I guess I've seen a lot of people die in this war but this was so . . . so insulting. So humiliating; to be killed, to let them be killed like that. Slaughtered like a bunch of pigs. It's like a lot of what I saw back in Laos. I remember I got to thinking that if their lives were so cheap then maybe mine was, too."

"You did what you could," Jake said, awkwardly. He kept his eyes covered with his arm. "That's got to count for something."

"It didn't." In spite of everything Sloane still tried to be a believer. He wanted life to have order and make sense and it was at times like this, when he was forced to witness these senseless horrors, that the awful doubt of the disillusioned began to darken his thoughts and eat at his sense of himself. "It made me part of it, again."

His face was streaked with heavy droplets of sweat and he had to squeeze his eyes shut now and then against the salty sting. He arched his back and scratched at a trickle racing down his spine to puddle beneath his naked buttocks.

"I read where ten thousand boat people entered Malaysian waters in just one month, this last spring," Jake said.

"I heard."

"Forty-three thousand in a camp there the size of two city blocks. And that's just one country, one camp . . . and the UN estimates that more than one-half of those who set out ever make it. They drown, they die of thirst, disease, pirates, they get used for target practice by Khmer gunboats . . ." He was wrapped in a towel and draped over the second tier of risers like a lounging walrus, protecting his eyes from the glare of the overhead lights by hiding his face in the crook of his arm. "This happens every day."

"Not to me, it doesn't."

The Wanchai Athletic Club had the best Turkish baths in Bangkok. Unlike the chrome and cheap glitter of its modern competitors it had a history that went back thirty years before Petchaburi Road saw its first invasion of GIs on R&R from Vietnam. It had a certain seedy dignity with its Old Kingdom artifacts and the dense potted ferns that thrived on the forced tropical heat. The white walls and floor had taken on a dull ochre patina with age and the brasswork and railings were burnished at waist level by years of passing clients. The cloying scent of jasmine tinted the hot air from the rubdowns the club's girls gave in the cubicles down the hall.

"Any sign of your friend?" Jake asked.

"Nope." Voss sat hunched over with his head in his hands, staring down at the floor. His hair was loose and hid his face in its wet folds. Kiri was kneeling behind him kneading the tight muscles of his neck and back with the concentration of a surgeon. Like the others she wore only a towel around her middle, letting her round breasts bobble unselfconsciously as she worked. The sight of her moist amber skin and the sloppy wet sounds she was making were driving Jake crazy.

"Um, let's see," he said, tearing his eyes away and adjusting his towel to hide the bulge between his legs. "Uh, Trang Van Thep. Yeah, I knew that guy, didn't I, Pete? He was around your place a lot. Real serious type."

"Yeah, that's him," Voss said. "He was what they called my 'Host National Counterpart' when they Vietnamized the war. He was supposed to be running things and I was supposed to be a civilian administrative adviser—sort'a bending the rules of the Paris Accords."

"So, in the end he got left behind, too," Jake said.

"Everybody did," Voss said. "Everybody and everything. Hell, I almost got left behind myself. I was up in Pleiku tryin' to do a little last-minute business when the shit hit the fan. Damn lucky to get out with my skin. I mean, who could have expected such a fuck-up?"

"Petah . . ." Kiri frowned at his bad language.

"The NVA had mounted a full-scale armored assault. They'd taken Ban Me Thuot, the Central Highlands, and overrun Quang Tri. Four ARVN divisions were running for their lives and what do we get from DOA at Tan Son Nhut? 'Now, boys,' they tell us. 'Let's not panic. Let's not scare the public with any of this loose talk about getting our asses kicked. This is all a diversion, see? So keep all this defeatist crap to yourselves.' "

"They'd been kidding themselves for fifteen years," Jake said. "I guess it figures they'd end up believing their own lies."

"So nobody would give the orders to retreat or shut down operations or nothin'. They just went on pretending . . ."

". . . until there was nothing left to do but run for their lives, too."

"You got it."

Jake rolled over and propped himself up on his elbow. "And what about all those fancy computers of yours? What about Beach House 7 and all those other fabulous toys?"

"Left 'em behind."

"That's it? Just left them behind?"

"That's it. It all belongs to them now, them and their Russian buddies. We didn't even turn 'em off."

"You didn't turn 'em off?" Jake gave a snort that shook loose a small shower of droplets from his pale face. "That's crazy."

"We never shut down," Voss explained. "Beach House 7 was there to survey and coordinate data from detection devices and weapons resources all over the war zone. A hundred megabytes of working memory data, all stored in a 'nonvolatile' system. Cut the power and everything's gone, just like that." He snapped his fingers. "If I'd been there I'd have shut it down, right? But I wasn't. And no ARVN technician's gonna take the responsibility for a disaster like that."

"So we just left it there," Jake said. "We just handed it over."

"That's about it." Voss stretched and worked the muscles of his lower back while Kiri dug her thumbs into his spine. "Don't forget, we left them the seventh largest air force in the world, too. And ten divisions of armor. Hell, they've got enough hand-me-downs to start another war. And those port facilities we built at

Cam Ranh Bay was like giving the Russians one of the finest harbors in Asia."

"Incredible." Jake reached back and yanked at the chrome-link chain near his head and held on while a hissing column of steam rose from the pot of hot coals and blossomed across the ceiling. ". . . couldn't even turn out the lights when we left."

"I guess."

"So, what about this Trang Van Thep?"

"Huh?" Voss looked up as if the question took him by surprise.

"This Trang Van Thep guy. What did you want with him, anyhow?"

"Nothin'." Voss swept his wet hair away from his eyes. "I told you, he was a friend of mine."

"C'mon, Pete," Jake insisted. "You can't tell me you guys went out barnstorming the gulf after some computer whiz-kid out of the goodness of your heart."

"Really, Jacob." Kiri sat up with arms akimbo. "Petah ha' much goodness of heart. You are always saying such bad things about him. You should be ashame'."

Jake was overwhelmed by the sight of Kiri's half-nude pose and gulped loudly before he dared reply. "I am," he said. "Oh, I am."

"Jake didn't mean anything," Sloane told her. "It's just his way of wondering if maybe there isn't more to this than meets the eye."

"Well, he should say so then," Kiri said.

"That's it," Jake said, braver now that he was addressing the issues. "I was thinking maybe he was after something a little more tangible than another dose of righteousness."

Voss stiffened. "I told you . . ."

"Actually, Pete"—Sloane was picking absentmindedly at the blisters on the palm of the hand he'd done most of the flying with but his tone of voice was insistent—"actually I was just wondering the same thing. I was thinking maybe this had something to do with that piece of hardware you mentioned last night. 'Sea freight,' you called it, remember? Going to keep the company out of hock?"

This tidbit brought about an interesting change in Jake. Some instinct must have stirred deep inside, for his body seemed

92 . . .

to revive itself from its torpor. He scratched. He cracked his knuckles and rolled himself upright. His little eyes grew bright as he regarded his companions from beneath his one bushy brow.

"Hardware, you say?"

"All right, yes. There was a piece of hardware he was going to bring out with him. That was the deal I made with Park Sung Dai to get him out but Thep blew it. Turned out he didn't have it after all."

"What was this piece of hardware, anyhow?" Sloane asked him. "How come he was so worked up about it?"

"It's called a MAS Unit." Voss looked up but Kiri pushed his head down again and continued massaging his neck, the muscles of her torso working rhythmically under her shiny skin. "See, all computers have entry codes and lockout programs of one sort or another. There are different levels of security in the data business but nothing like what we had at Beach House 7. To interface with Igloo White or the rest of the network required an entry code so complex that it had to use its own minicomputer to input. That minicomputer interrupted the line from the network so you had to go through it to get into the Beach House 7 computers. It was the Modular Access Security Unit. MAS Unit. See?"

Sloane blew a few drops of perspiration from his upper lip and nodded. "I guess so."

"Well, about two months ago Trang Van Thep gets word out to me that the Beach House complex is still on but it's locked up tighter than a drum. He says he'd managed to hide the MAS Unit at the last minute when the NVA came rolling into town and he figures if I can get him out of 'Nam he could maybe bring it out with him."

"Wait a minute," Jake said. "Let me see if I got this straight. Your guys left the Beach House computers on, right? And the NVA can't afford to turn 'em off because they'd lose all that data."

"More than just the data, they'd be without a high-level connection to the machine they'd just captured. They couldn't get into it. See? Couldn't load a program, couldn't get any data or readouts or even figure out how the damn thing worked. They'd need spec manuals, hardware manuals, block diagrams—everything."

"Couldn't they just take it apart and figure it out?"

"Nope. They'd have to trace every circuit, every chip, every buffer. Hell. They'd get more out of it if they just melted it down for junk."

"And they can't get in, either. Right? Because they don't have that MAS thing." Jake started to laugh. "I don't believe it. I mean, that's just amazing. What a nasty little present to leave behind. A prize they can't get at. Here's this fabulous computer system still buzzing away all by itself, right?" He giggled. "Still thinking all those top-secret thoughts, still dreaming all those official Pentagon dreams while all the Reds can do is stand around playing with themselves?"

"Computer's don't think," Voss said.

"I don't care what they do, it's too beautiful." Jake laughed. "My God, that's the best joke of the war!"

"So what's this key thing got to do with Thai/Tech?" Sloane asked.

"It's a long story," Voss said. "And it doesn't make much difference."

"I'm not going anyplace."

"All right, I'll tell you. It seems that Park Sung Dai had a lot of his illicit money stashed away in transferrable funds in the Bank L'Indochine in Saigon, where he could get it out quick if he had to. Unfortunately his timing was bad. The Republic of Vietnam closed up shop early and with it went the bank. It's very sad. Now our Korean friend doesn't even get visiting rights on about eleven and a half million bucks.

"So I got to thinkin' this was a good way to get Trang Van Thep out'a there, poor bastard. I owed him that much, at least. So I make this deal with the Korean. He's still got a lot of connections back in 'Nam, the black market's bigger than ever. I tell him if he gets Trang Van Thep out of there he can keep the MAS Unit. See?"

"Just like that?"

"Why not?" Voss said.

"What would he do with it?" Sloane asked.

"Peddle it," Voss said. "The Vietnamese would love to have the Beach House computers with all their data intact. Think how well it would complement the rest of the weapons system we left behind for them. They could reactivate parts of Igloo White. He could trade the MAS Unit for those transferrable funds of his, maybe. Or maybe for the eleven and a half million, since the accounts have been impounded by now."

"Why should the Vietnamese want to deal?"

Voss shrugged. "The war isn't over, don't forget. The Khmer are raiding into Vietnam, too. Most of the Igloo White Interdiction System is still in place along their mutual border so Hanoi would just love to get it working again."

"And the Russians?" Sloane said. "They'd have it then, too, y'know."

Until now Voss seemed absorbed in examining the details of his feet as he talked, flexing his toes and rubbing inside his ankles. But now he looked up almost defiantly.

"Look, this is all pretty irrelevant, don't you think?" he said. "Thep didn't get the damn thing and that Korean son of a bitch left him out there to die. Now y'got the whole story so maybe we can just drop it."

"Yeah, sure," Jake said. "Only you didn't say what you were going to get out of it. How was this altruistic endeavor supposed to improve the fledgling fortunes of Thai/Tech International?"

"Well, naturally, we'd expect a commission."

"Jesus H. Christ." Jake crossed his legs and tucked his towel under his crotch. "I knew there had to be something in it for you."

"Lay off, Jake."

"He had to be worth something in hard cash, didn't he? Otherwise he'd be just another of the boat people. Just another illegal alien."

"What was that?" Voss shook himself free of Kiri's hands.

"I didn't mean anything." Jake was a little abashed by Voss's reaction. "You know me."

"What was that about illegal aliens?"

"Huh?"

"The boat people. The refugees," Voss said. "That's all they are . . . legally, I mean."

"Yeah. The Thais won't give them refugee status."

"So they're subject to the same restrictions and penalties."

"I guess so," Jake said. "Like wetbacks. Why?"

"Nothin'." Voss jumped to his feet, spilling Kiri back on her haunches. "I just got a great idea, that's all. I should have thought of this a long time ago, it's so obvious."

"What's he up to this time?" Jake asked Sloane.

"I just figured out a way to fight back." And he headed for the door with Kiri chasing after him.

"You are all sweaty, Petah," she complained. "Not good you go out like tha'." She paused long enough to give Jake a scowl. "See when you upset him so? He will catch his death this way."

It was silent when they were gone except for the hiss of steam, and then Jake said, "I hate it when Kiri gets mad like that. She's the only girl I know who tolerates me."

"Well, you're pretty hard on her boyfriend sometimes."

"Maybe so," Jake said. "And maybe you're not hard enough."

"Meaning what?"

"Skip it." Jake stood up and rewrapped his towel. "Come on, let's get us a rubdown, too. You can charge it to Thai/Tech."

"I feel like a baked mackerel already," Sloane told him. "And besides, I'm supposed to be meeting Alice in a couple of hours."

"Yeah, I know."

"You know? How do you know?" Sloane gave him a suspicious look. "You guys aren't up to something, are you?"

"Nah." Jake took hold of his hand and hauled him to his feet. "Come on, strictly medicinal. They've got terrific girls here."

The massage cubicle looked like a Victorian operating room. It was tiled in the same white-turning-brown tiles and lit by a single cone-shaped bulb hanging from a cord that disappeared into the dark void above. There was a tub in the corner and two narrow tables that looked like a pair of torture racks. There was a lot of equipment around, things with nozzles and flexipiping and chrome fixtures near the tub and a set of infrared heat lamps that could broil a lamb chop at twenty paces.

The masseuses could have been twins, both square-faced Chinese girls of indeterminate age, both with big hands and deep chests. Jake's girl seemed to like him so of course he thought she was terrific.

"What did you mean by that comment about me not being hard enough on Pete?" Sloane asked. He was stretched out face down on the hard leather mat of one of the tables while his masseuse furrowed through the flesh along his backbone.

"Umph." Jake was reluctant to turn his head toward Sloane so he spoke directly into the mat in front of his face. His voice sounded like a cheap radio. "Has it ever occurred to you that our friend Pete is in trouble?"

"Trouble?" Sloane hadn't expected that. "Well, starting a new business would be hard on anybody."

"No. I mean something bigger than this Thai/Tech stuff. I mean, that Sung Dai character is big trouble."

"Maybe so," Sloane said. "And maybe that's a good reason not to ride him so hard. You can play this devil's advocate game of yours a bit too well sometimes. If he were in trouble I'd want to help him out. I'd like him to know he can count on me."

Jake was chuckling while Sloane spoke; his girl was playing pinch 'n' tickle with him, a game that finally had him doubled up like an armadillo. "Heh-heh-heh . . . y' . . . y'know, you're okay, Dave," he managed to say. "No, I mean it. Hee-hee . . . (Stop that, young lady.) You've got that plain-faced existentialist outlook that we writers love. Strong in character and weak in the head. See, the trouble is you want to believe more than you want to understand."

Sloane gave a telling groan but Jake ignored it. "For instance, how come the Korean could be smart enough to run one of the biggest black market operations in the world and still be stupid enough to leave eleven million sitting in a Saigon bank when he saw the end coming?"

"Maybe he needed ready capital," Sloane suggested.

"All right, but it was in transferrable funds. So why didn't he transfer it to, say, Singapore or . . ."

"Maybe he was out of touch someplace, too, like Pete was. Maybe he had clearing-house troubles, there were lots of people trying to get their money out of Saigon."

"All right, why did Pete get the Korean to go through all that trouble getting Thep on the boat, taking that risk when he could have made the deal with the Vietnamese right there in the country?"

"I don't know. Maybe he couldn't trust the Communists."

"But he could trust the Korean?" Jake rolled his head around to face him. "See what I mean? You'd rather believe in your old friend than understand him. Just like the war. Too much believing, not enough smarts."

"Yeah, well . . ." Sloane let it go at that. At least Jake had been right about the rubdown. The not very pretty girls seemed to have the right touch. Sloane's nerves were dissolving like butter, and when Jake patted and pawed and eventually made his excuses ("A-hem, I seem to have found me a live one, here") Sloane didn't even bother to acknowledge his exit. He listened while Jake went chuckling off after his girl to a room of their own somewhere down the long hall.

Gradually he forgot the point that Jake had been trying to make and he gave himself up to the hands that were working him over. The girl's touch grew lighter, the room grew quiet, and he felt himself slipping into a strange somnambulant state where he dreamed he was still awake. In this dream he was in a cubicle with a girl rubbing his back—not a pretty girl, but one who knew her stuff. She worked with scented oil that she melted into his pores with the heat lamps as she spread it lightly with her fingertips.

When he awoke he wasn't sure he'd been asleep. But when he listened he could still hear the girl. She was mixing something, it sounded like. The lights were off. It was dark and quiet except for the sound her mixing made, a soft kind of methodical slapping like the stropping of a razor. He tried to make out what it could be but he couldn't. Nor could he see what she was up to in the dark.

But why was it dark? He opened his eyes again and rolled over on his back. He was naked and alone in a cubicle in a vast empty room, alone except for that sound. He was suddenly tense and alert. What time was it anyway? Where was he really? It was like awakening in the grip of a nightmare. He felt for a towel and found none. He searched for a light and found the stainless steel stand that held up the heat lamps. Someone was breathing in the dark, sharp breaths through flared nostrils like someone aroused.

Where the hell was that switch?

He found the cord and felt along it until he found the plastic pod of the light switch and pushed the button.

"Aaaargh!"

The dark was ablaze with red-hot tungsten coils that scorched his eyes and drove him back into the leather mat with his fists in his eyes.

"Ow. Shit!"

The slapping sound stopped for a moment and then resumed. When he opened his eyes again he found himself exposed in a pool of red light. The blackness beyond the circle was filled with dancing fleets of neon coils that the lamp had burned into his retinas.

The slapping sound grew louder, more insistent, and then a voice in the dark said, "Put that away." And the slapping stopped.

"Who's there?" Sloane sat up cautiously, he had no idea what surrounded him beyond the circle. He searched the gloom as he dropped his legs over the side of the table. *"Who's there?"*

A match flared in the darkness and in its light he could see the end of a black cigar being toasted over its flame. Behind it was the puffy face of Park Sung Dai, the Korean. He took his light and blew the match out; the smoke was pink as it rolled through the circle of red light.

"Give me a towel," Sloane demanded. "Where's my towel?"

"No towel," said the Korean. "Not just yet. Janus prefers you as you are and I try to humor him where I can. You should, too, it's safer that way."

Janus appeared under the light as if just to let himself be seen. His head was wrapped in a bulky drooping bandage and one side of his face was scraped up but under the red light the rest of his face was altogether free of the lines and imperfections and any other tracings of humanity. It was a face empty of almost everything except the huge black pupils of his eyes. He was slapping his palm absently with his leather blackjack as he stared. It looked like something out of the Middle Ages, an instrument of the Inquisition. It was about ten inches long and tipped with a lump the size of a golf ball. The shaft flexed slightly with each stroke and then snapped straight again on impact. Sloane found himself staring at the thing in spite of himself.

"He likes you, Mr. Sloane," the Korean said. "That is a very dangerous thing."

Slap. Slap.

"I told you to put that away." Another puff of pink cigar smoke drifted into the light. "It is annoying."

Janus stepped back into the dark leaving Sloane alone, sweating and shading his eyes trying to see. "What is this?" he demanded. "Give me a towel."

"When we have had our meeting."

"Is that what this is? A meeting? I thought it was to show off your goon, here." He shifted on the table to get down but Janus appeared again.

"Stay where you are," the Korean said. "This will not take long."

"Damn right it won't," Sloane said. " 'Cause I'm leaving."

"Janus."

Janus moved in like a knife fighter with his weapon in his fingers. Sloane stayed where he was.

"Okay, okay," Sloane said. "So talk."

The Korean let Sloane sit there under the heat lamp and drip for awhile as he took a few drags on his cigar. The room reeked of its bitter stink.

"What are you two up to?" he finally asked.

"What's that, the sixty-four-dollar question? He gave me a job, that's what we're up to. I was broke and he gave me a job."

"I find that hard to believe," the Korean said.

Janus's lipless slit of a mouth spread into an imitation smile. He moved closer and lay his blackjack lightly across Sloane's thigh, winding it in his fingers so that it rolled up and down.

"Get him away from me," Sloane warned.

"Just tell me what I want to know," said the Korean.

Then Janus overplayed his hand. With his black eyes burning brightly he made a playful stroke at his captive's genitals and Sloane went for his throat. Blind to the danger he grabbed Janus by the neck with one hand while with the other he reached out to fend off the blow from the blackjack that, in fact, he had already missed.

"*Ho, Janus!*" the Korean shouted. "*Stop it!*"

Janus drew the blow short, snapping his elbow back so that the blackjack whistled past Sloane's skull a fraction of an inch from his ear.

"Stop it, both of you."

Sloane stood frozen where he was, incredulous at the speed and precision of the attack. It wasn't a draw, he'd have lost. He found he still held Janus by the throat, his breath hissing through his trachea that Sloane had squeezed beneath his thumb. And still that sick grin across his face.

"Let him go."

Sloane released him and shrank back to the table without taking his eyes off of Janus's face.

"Christ! What is this guy, anyhow?"

"Yes, I know the feeling," the Korean said. "It is an interesting sensation to have such a dangerous man at one's disposal, eh?" He seemed to reconsider the situation for a moment and then said, "Give him a towel."

Janus mumbled something that couldn't be understood but he did what he was told. The Korean's cigar glowed impatiently in the dark while his thug found a towel and Sloane wrapped himself in it.

"How about some lights, too?" he said.

"How about an answer?" the Korean suggested. "You were just going to tell me what you were doing with your friend Voss."

"Business."

"Business with Peter?"

"Why not?"

"And what kind of business would New City Credit have with the likes of Peter Voss?"

"New . . . ? Oh, I see. Listen, I have nothing to do with New City anymore, I left them a couple of weeks ago. Finished, see? Kaput. So now I don't represent any interests but my own around here. Does that answer all your questions? Now, I don't mean to be rude but I have plans for the evening."

"I see," said the Korean. More pink pulls, and then, "You left the board of directors of a major financial institution to come to work for Peter Voss."

"No. I mean that's not exactly how it was. There was a policy dispute and I lost. That's all. So I decided to toss in with Pete. Hey, where are you getting all of this?"

"I have extensive sources, Mr. Sloane." He leaned back on his stool, his feet sticking into the light. "And besides, I went through your billfold."

Sloane shaded his eyes trying to see into the gloom but he couldn't make anything out. His face stung from the burning lamps and the sweating made it worse.

"You can understand my concern," the Korean said. "A man of your history, a member of the board . . ."

"That was a fluke," Sloane said angrily. "I'm a flier, not a financier. I got stuck there by accident."

For the first time the Korean let his chair tip forward into the light so that he could be seen and his appearance was quite unlike the comfortable sonority of his voice. He looked frazzled and out of place. His suit jacket hung from the back of his chair, his wet white shirt stuck to him like wallpaper.

"I see," he said. "So we must continue to play this game. Very well, let us just stay where we are until you explain a few contradictions to me. I am a slow learner, you see. Not like our brilliant young associate."

"Explain what?"

"Tell me, why should a man of your caliber, a man who has achieved such inroads into the world of Asian finance, throw it all away? Why should a man who has a position of influence and trust take up with the likes of Peter Voss, eh? Do you think I am a fool? Do you think I cannot see that he is up to something?"

"I can't answer for your paranoia," Sloane told him. "Pete's a friend of mine. That's all there is to it."

"He was a friend of *mine,* too. In fact, he was my partner. Did he never tell you that?"

"I heard something about it," Sloane said.

"You 'heard something about it.' " The Korean examined Sloane's face for a moment. "Yes, perhaps it is true. Perhaps you have a great deal to learn about your friend. Perhaps you are only here to be used as I was used."

"I think I'd know it if I was."

"Would you?" The heat of the lamps was wilting the Korean. His slicked-back hair was coming loose and his pale face was darkening into a burn as he dabbed at it with a handkerchief. "You and I have had dealings before, Mr. Sloane. Are you surprised? Yes, it was that night four, no, it's been five years, now. The airstrip at Cholon, remember how it rained? And how we almost missed you because of the sentry dogs. Yes, it was I who looked after the one they called the 'Kid.' I was the one who paid off the police and kept him hidden away until you could fly him out."

"You?"

"Me. And I did it because Peter was my partner. It was my obligation, do you see?" He was sweating like a trooper, spraying the air with droplets as he spoke. "As for being Peter's 'friend,' I can tell you this. After going through all that trouble, yes, and all that danger, too. After jeopardizing my business just to rescue this . . . this half-witted murderer, then my partner—our friend

—showed his appreciation by turning his bloody computers on me. *On me!*"

By now he was almost choking with anger. He stood up shakily and reached around behind him for his jacket as if he could not take his eyes off of Sloane. Then he signaled Janus.

"We go," he said, and they headed for the door.

"Wait," Sloane called after them. "Hold on, what's this about the Kid? What's this murderer crap?"

"That's what he is," the Korean said without pausing.

"That's crazy. He had a breakdown. Battle fatigue. There was lots of that in Vietnam."

"Could it be so?" The Korean's face lit up and he laughed explosively. "You did not know? Did your friend not tell you? Your *good friend Peter?* The man I delivered to that airstrip was wanted by military authorities—I believe they call it 'fragging an officer.' A not-very-bright young lieutenant, as the story has it."

"That can't be."

"Believe what you wish." The Korean was still laughing as he and Janus headed off down the hallway. "Your friend has used you already, Mr. Sloane, and he didn't bother to tell you. He has made you an accessory to murder."

"You're crazy," Sloane shouted after him. *"You're* the one that's crazy!"

CHAPTER

7

Alice was staying at an old rest house that everybody called the Old Rest House, a relic of a bygone era nesting under a long corridor of trees that once led down to the riverbank. Now there was a glass office building in the way.

Sloane picked her up in the jeep and they drove north on Mittaphap Highway as twilight gathered over the outskirts of the city. The air had lost its close city character and a fresh breeze brought the wet, earthy smell of ripe humus. There was heat lightning off to the north that flickered along the horizon like distant artillery.

Alice relaxed easily on the seat beside him, taking in the sights. "They're sending me up to the refugee camps north of Aranyaprathet in a few days," she said as they turned onto the bridge over the black waters of Bang Su. Below them the Quonset-roofed barges slept like flotsam on a still pond. "I'm just supposed to look things over so I can put together a report for the Central Planning Committee meeting on the 23rd."

"Yeah?"

"They've been getting six hundred or so a week into those camps. They're so crowded that the army's even taken to forcing them back over the border."

"Yeah?"

She cocked her head at him. "And when I get back from Aranyaprathet maybe I'll shave my head and join an order of Mae Chi Nuns."

"Hm? Oh, I'm sorry. I was thinking of something else."

They followed a side street lined with rickety wooden houses to the crown of the hill, where a huge open-sided pole barn looked out over the canal. It was just the way Sloane had remembered it, a noisy confusion of pushcarts and makeshift counters known as the Nailert Market. The street vendors of the city gathered there two nights a week to hawk their wares through a thick smog of spicy cook smoke.

It was a smelly few acres of short-order chiefs and country floor squatters with piles of noodles and rows of glazed ducks ready for grills or woks or drums of hot deep fat. Each vendor had his place and each his special fare, strung up in glass boxes or smoldering over gas jets or charcoal-stoked fires.

"Having second thoughts about the job?" Alice asked as she bit carefully at a skewered ribbon of eel.

"Things will settle down."

"If you last that long," Alice said. "Look at you. Your face is flushed, your eyes look like road maps."

"Let's not talk about it. Okay? Let's talk about that stuff in the brown sauce, there. What do you think? Chicken? Fish?"

"Oh, all right. I'm just worried about you, that's all. I'm worried about what you're getting yourself into."

"Alice, we've been through this a hundred times."

"Sorry," she said. "I'm sorry. End of lecture. I just thought . . ."

"*Co' beer, here,*" somebody yelled from the crowd.

"What the hell?"

"*Ice* co' beer, here."

Sloane made his way back up the aisle for a look behind a pair of puffing clam steamers.

"Oh, no."

"Here y'are, buddy. Ice cold beer." It was Jake. The sidecar of the Kid's old Norton was a-slosh with ice and Jake was straddling it, fishing out cans of Coors beer for anybody who showed an interest. "How about one for the little lady?"

"You promised to leave us alone," Sloane said.

"I lied," Jake explained. "Anyhow, this wasn't my idea. It was the Prince's. He wants to meet Alice."

"Alice, this is Jake Berman."

"Hi, Jake," Alice said. "David's been telling me about you for years."

Now that Jake had a good look at her he seemed to be taken by a sudden fit of shyness. "Um, uh . . ." he said as he fumbled around in the ice. "Have a beer?" And he handed her another one.

"Who's the Prince?" Alice asked. "You didn't say anything about a Prince."

"That's him back there," Jake said, handing out some cans to the gathering crowd. "He's laying out a spread."

"David, hello," the Prince called from a square he'd laid claim to at the edge of the crowd. He was watching over a cook who in turn was watching over a charcoal brazier overflowing with hamburgers and franks.

"He's very big on picnics," Jake said. "Pete'll be along pretty soon. He had something to do and the Kid's motorcycle isn't working right." The Kid had been there all along, sitting in the sawdust behind his machine while he poked at a neoprene gas line with a straw. He got up when Alice's eyes fell on him, wiping his hands on his jeans.

"H'lo, Alice." He nodded and smiled at her.

"Hi, Kid," she said.

The Kid started to say something but it was noisy and there were so many people . . . so he just nodded again and sat down.

The Prince was at his best. He buttoned his blue blazer as they approached and bowed as he took Alice's hand. "I love American women," he explained after formalities were exchanged. "What I remember best about my schooling in Connecticut are the ladies and the picnics we all had in the summer. Now, see there? What would you like? And we have American ketchup and relish. Potato chips? Fritos? I have five kinds of dip. That one's shrimp."

"My goodness," Alice said. "Where did you get all this?"

"Peter got it all, of course," the Prince told her. "Peter can get anything."

"So I've heard," said Alice.

Sloane didn't like the look in her eye. "Listen, we don't really have much time," he said. "I don't want to eat and run but . . ."

"You must let Alice meet Peter, at least."

"Yes, it's time I met this Peter Voss, don't you think?"

Her eyes were bright and cheery, the worst sign. Sloane had a feeling she was up to no good. Voss arrived half an hour later in a motor-rickshaw that managed to plow its way a hundred feet or so into the crowd by beeping its horn until it could make no more headway. Then Voss alighted with Kiri on one arm and an open magnum of champagne in the other. Many in the crowd seemed to know him. They waved and called his name and a few held cups out for him to pour some champagne into.

Kiri was basking happily in the attention, waving back and trying some of the snacks people passed to her. The Kid was on his feet swaying slightly back and forth and beaming at her from behind his motorcycle. She waved at him, too.

Voss stuck the remaining champagne into the ice in the sidecar. "Hi," he said to Alice. "You must be the new kid on the block."

"That's me," Alice said. "Wanna fight?"

It was Peter Voss's show from the moment he arrived, just like the old days: his treat, his friends and his crowd. It was everything the way he liked it and he couldn't have made a worse impression on Alice.

"My goodness," she said, batting her eyes at him from the business end of her hot dog. "You seem to be some kind of hero to these people."

"It's nothin'." Voss waved it off. "The Prince and I do business around here, that's all. A few favors here and there, a little grease for the local machine. Stuff like that."

"*Noblesse oblige,*" Alice suggested.

"Nothing noble about it," Voss said. "Strictly business."

She'd gotten his range first shot. Alice was better at picking a fight than anybody Sloane knew. Win the battle and loose the war, that was Alice's way. Well, to hell with it. Whatever she was out to prove she could just count him out.

"Give me another beer," he said to Jake.

"And the champagne," Alice continued. "Wherever did you manage to find that? Was that some more 'business' or did you —let's see. What's the popular euphemism? Liberate. That's it. Did you liberate it? I've heard so much about your tricks."

"Oh, I get it," Voss said, looking her over more carefully. "You want to know if I ripped it off. I know your kind."

"I don't think you do, Mr. Voss. But yes, did you 'rip it off'?"

"I just take advantage of the system," he told her. "Wine, corporate records, bank accounts . . . it's all computerized. Ownership is assigned electronically now."

"Really?"

"Trouble is computers don't know anything about owning stuff. They're neutral. They'll do anything for anybody, all you've got to do is ask. All you've got to know is how to ask."

"And I suppose you know how to ask."

"I'm the best there is," Voss said. "There isn't much I can't get at, one way or the other."

"Really?" Alice said. "Like what?"

"Oh, like immigration records, for instance." Voss grinned suddenly and poked at Sloane to listen up. "There is a certain Korean gentleman, see. His name's Park Sung Dai. He's . . . well, let's just say he's the competition."

Sloane peered at Voss over his beer. He wasn't going to like this.

"This competitor has been giving us a lot of heat lately so I decided to take him down a peg or two. I relieved him of some of his assets by rearranging his file in the Bureau of Registry."

"What kind of rearrange?"

"I changed his immigration status," Voss said. "Now he's a refugee."

Alice turned to stone.

"I'd love to see his face . . ." Voss laughed as he shook a glob of Heinz ketchup onto Kiri's hamburger. "Now, as for the champagne—well, I have to confess that was sort of an afterthought. In fact, it was Kiri's idea, a little welcome gift. There's more in the rickshaw. Oh . . . this is Kiri."

Kiri was smiling expectantly but Alice hardly spared her a glance.

"You've got it all pretty well rationalized away, haven't you?" Alice said.

Voss had just taken a huge mouthful of his hamburger and was stuffing in the overflow with his finger when he stopped his chewing to size her up. He was catching on. "I do all right," he said.

"And what about this competitor of yours—this Korean? Does he do all right now, too?"

"He gets what he deserves."

"Oh, does he?" she said. "Tell me, while you're sitting around changing people's immigration statuses and reaching into their computers and taking what you want, doesn't it ever occur to anybody to shout 'Stop, thief'?"

"If you mean Park Sung Dai, he couldn't blow the whistle on a litter-bug, so why worry about it?"

"Because whatever you want to pretend about who theoretically owns what, it all comes down to the fact that you're pilfering amounts to a lot of very real money."

"It's *not* real money, that's the whole point," Voss argued. "It's more than real money, its data. Look, when money grows up to be big money it doesn't come in stacks of greenbacks and pound notes any more. And it doesn't get passed around in . . . in money bags or in suitcases. It becomes like a concept, see? It's an understanding among the rich that only has to be represented.

"Money has become data, an endless tally sheet being endlessly transferred from the computers of one banking center to the computers of another. Always changing, always adjusting for currency fluctuations and whatever local needs for fast moving capital. Always on the move between Hong Kong and Bern, between Singapore and Taipei to numbered accounts and Chinese Commercial Code accounts."

Sloane traded glances with the Prince. Voss was in his element, brilliant and cynical—almost wolfish. Sloane didn't like him this way.

"The world operates on a vast cycle of debt," he continued. "Go ahead, ask your boyfriend, here. He'll tell you all about it, that's what he used to do. That way the big shots like New City Credit can keep themselves plugged directly into the money market and keep us little guys shut out."

There was an unmistakable electricity between them, a connection that charged their argument with nervous energy and even began drawing a small crowd of curious bystanders. The raised voices and dangerous undertones had the Kid shaking his head and mumbling and flexing his big hands at his side.

"So you think that makes it all right to just take some," Alice said.

"To join in," Voss insisted. "For somebody like me it's like a huge artesian spring flowing under everything. All you've gotta do is dig a little and you can have all you want."

"And I'll bet you're a great one for digging," she said, squaring off in front of him. "You don't seem to care much about getting dirty."

Kiri knew an insult when she heard one. She had begun in

awe of this yellow-haired *farang*, a woman like herself but for whom life had been so vastly different that she might well have been dropped from the moon. Kiri had wanted to make a good impression but now it was evident that they shared little more than their gender. She was arrogant and rude and she made Kiri angry, and when Kiri got angry the Kid got upset. He was backing toward his motorcycle, making throaty noises like an animal sniffing a coming storm in the air.

"To whom you just think you are addressing," Kiri finally demanded. "My Petah nevah need listen to people like you. He is good to us all. He does what he mus', it is part of his profession."

"Damn right," Voss said. "Save your preaching for the real thieves and murderers, the ones who made the world what it turned out to be. I just go by their rules, that's all. I'm just a businessman."

"And this"—Alice pointed at Kiri with the remains of her hot dog—"I suppose this is your secretary."

"Secretary!" Kiri flared, making the most of her pert stature. "I am no secretary, if you please. I am Petah's harlot!"

Jake was in love. He could hardly contain himself with joy at seeing Voss meet his match, it was like witnessing a moment in history. He was straddling the sidecar and clapping his thick hands in delight when he lost his balance. The sidecar's metal sides, sweaty from their cold contents, gave no purchase between his squeezing thighs so he continued to rotate sidewards until he'd rolled out of sight. Then his pant leg got caught in the drive chain and trying to get it free kept him out of things for a moment longer so that when he finally emerged from the dirt and the sawdust he found the confrontation was all over. His disappointment was plain. He'd waited for years to see somebody cut this cocky wonder boy down a peg or two and he wanted more.

" 'Not afraid of getting dirty.' Did you see his face when she laid that one on him?" he asked Sloane later.

"I heard."

"She's terrific. Just . . . just terrific."

"Yeah. Sure." Sloane didn't think so at the time. "You'd like anybody who told Pete off."

Jake agreed eagerly. "It was love at first slight."

The Prince's picnic had fizzled out almost before it started. People were either upset or trying to keep other people from getting upset so that nobody thought about the Kid, who had taken refuge behind his Norton. He crouched there pretending to tinker with the engine while he tried to control his nervous shaking. He was mumbling incoherently to himself and watching through the spokes as Kiri continued her slow burn. She was the only stabilizing factor in his disordered mind and he had never seen her angry before. He couldn't keep track of the scene around him, not with the noise and the milling around. The crowd of curious people seemed threatening, the way they kept circling and snooping . . .

"You okay, Kid?" Jake pulled the plug under the sidecar and waited while it emptied into the sawdust like a pissing buffalo. He had already announced to the others that he'd be the one to ride back with the Kid. After all, there were still a few beers left inside. Jake was reknowned for such lapses in judgment.

The Kid didn't answer him. He hid his wild eyes beneath a pair of goggles and mounted his heavy machine like a bandit making his escape. The ear-splitting roar as he kicked over the engine hid his ragged shout.

By then Sloane had taken matters in hand and gotten Alice back to the jeep. They had just crossed the smelly *klong* and were still sharing an angry silence when there was a roar from behind and the Kid went by like they were standing still. Jake was in the sidecar holding on for dear life and the Prince's red Fiat was right behind him with everybody inside it yelling at the top of their lungs.

The Kid swerved into a roundabout, cutting it so sharply that the sidecar lifted into the air and Jake began waving his arms and screaming hysterically. The Fiat cut off the jeep as it swerved in after the motorcycle and bounced over a low curb. Both disappeared into a maze of dark streets off Sukhumvit Road.

"Something's wrong with the Kid," Alice said.

Sloane swore loudly. "Hold on," he told her and they took off in pursuit.

For several long minutes he was hard pressed to catch up and then he caught sight of the Norton just as it spun out of a side street and righted itself on the damp brick pavement. There was hardly a pause before it fired off down the next side street and the Fiat appeared coming the opposite way. The Prince's car had bashed its rear fender and the bumper was dragging. The trail of sparks was much easier to follow in the dark. Alice had her feet planted against the firewall and held on as Sloane skidded around a corner and screeched to a stop behind the Fiat, which was just sitting there amid the trash baskets in a dark commercial *soi.*

Sloane hauled himself up behind the wheel. "What happened?" he called to the others. "What's going on?"

"He just . . . he went crazy for some reason," the Prince called back. "When he got his motorcycle running he just went crazy and began tearing up the bazaar with it, driving through the booths trying to find a way out through the crowd. He seemed to think everyone was after him. Oh, it was a terrible mess, I can tell you. He's someplace in there, we think, and if he is he is trapped. It is a dead end."

Sloane switched off the jeep's engine and in the quiet they all listened.

"I had no idea . . ." Alice whispered.

"Shhh," Sloane said. "I think I hear him."

It was Jake's whimpering Sloane heard, then came the low rumble of the Norton's big engine.

Dum-ba dum-ba dum-ba dum-ba dum-ba.

"I hear him, too," Alice said.

Ba-ruuum, ba-ruuuum.

In the Fiat they were all pointing up the *soi.*

Bruuu-WAAAAA!

The berserk Norton roared out from an intersecting alley, skidded directly into their path, and came roaring down on them head on. At the last second it swung right, hit a concrete step, and reared up over a freight platform, pulling an awning and a rack of cane down behind it. Jake's head could just be seen above the cowl of the sidecar; he was shrieking pitiably as they landed again and rocketed off into the night.

Voss sat behind the wheel of the Fiat, staring off in the direction of the motorcycle's disappearance. He was too stunned to pick up the chase so Sloane swung around him and set off in the jeep. He had almost caught up when the Kid turned onto a side street and scattered a formation of orange-robed monks who were filing out of a stupa after vespers. Sloane had to pull up sharply to avoid them and before the monks could gather their wits and get out of his way the Kid had turned off over the hump of the railroad tracks and was gone down Petchaburi Road.

They finally found the motorcycle back in Dog Alley, sizzling and snapping as it cooled in the shadows of the moonlit *soi*. Sloane swung down from the jeep and approached it as if it were a wounded animal gone off by itself to die. Alice followed.

"Jake?" he whispered.

A silvery hand felt its way out from the sidecar and snatched at Sloane's pant leg.

"G-G-Get me out of here," Jake pleaded from inside.

He had himself crammed so deeply into the toe of the sidecar that he was stuck there. All that was free was an arm that, in the gloom, seemed to belong to the machine itself. Alice tried to help. It was her idea to push his head down between his knees while Sloane pulled him back by the belt. It took a few tries but it worked. Jake was leaning back and breathing deeply when Voss pulled up.

"Where is he?" He was out of the car and panting hard as if he'd been running all the way. "What's going on?"

"He was gonna kill me," Jake whimpered. "He was gonna kill everybody."

"Where'd he go? Where is he?" Voss demanded, jerking Jake around to face him and squeezing his cheeks so that his mouth pursed like a fish.

"Hey, take it easy," Sloane said. "It's not his fault."

"He was gonna kill me."

"Yeah, sure, Jake," Sloane said. "Listen, where is he now? Did he go inside?"

"In-inside," Jake stammered. "I thought he was gonna kill me for sure but then he went in there after somebody else." His one free arm waved at the house. "In there."

"Somebody else? Who?"

"In there, that's who," Jake said. "There's somebody inside the house."

"Who?" Voss demanded. "A burglar, a prowler?"

"Somebody, anybody," Jake shouted. "If there's anybody in that house he's in big trouble."

"There wouldn't be anybody in there but . . ." Voss looked up at Sloane. "Somsak."

"He wouldn't hurt Somsak," Sloane said.

"He's crazy, I tell you," Jake said. "He wouldn't know Somsak from Jack the Ripper."

"Oh shit." Voss caught a glimpse of Kiri racing for the gate. "Kiri, no." He caught her in three strides, grabbing around the middle so that she swirled around into his arms. "There's nothing you can do. You'll only get hurt." He handed her over to Alice and then he and Sloane opened the gate and crept inside the dark compound.

"Kid?" Voss said tentatively. He cleared his throat and tried again in a normal voice. "Kid, where are you?"

There were no lights in the house.

"Take it easy, Kid," Sloane said quietly. "Everything's all right."

Somebody made a noise just above their heads. There was a thumping and banging at the barred window of the front downstairs room.

"He's got somebody in there."

"Kid!" Sloane yelled.

"Kid, no! There's nobody here but Somsak and us."

They rounded the corner quickly and ran along the wall to the back door, where Voss threw back the screen and tried the lights. Nothing. It was black and silent inside the house. The thought of a crazed giant lurking in the dark brought them both to a halt.

"What's the matter with the lights?"

"I don't know," Sloane said. "Give me your lighter."

They had to feel around for each other and then Voss pressed his Zippo into Sloane's hand. He flipped it open but before he could light it something swung out of the darkness, knocked it from his hand, and sent it skittering across the varnished floor.

"Oh, lord!" Sloane hit the floor and began crawling after the lighter, feeling along in front of him until he found it in the corner at the base of the stairs.

"Take it easy, Kid," he soothed as he felt his way back along the wall. "Take it easy, now. You know me. It's Dave. And your brother's here, too. There's nobody here but us and old Somsak and you don't want to hurt him."

He flicked the lighter. There was no flame but the spark lit up the Kid's ghastly figure right in front of him. The shock of the sight propelled Sloane back against the wall. For a second he just clung there with his heartbeat pounding in his ears. The Kid had been facing into the room, his eyes bright with some awful zeal. He had his brother locked in his arms, with one slablike hand covering his mouth.

"Kid, for God's sake!"

He tried the lighter again and this time the Kid was gone. He was in the room, a lurking violence searching out its victim. Voss had been dropped to the floor.

"Kid!" he was pleading. "Kid, stop it. It's only Somsak."

Suddenly there was an almost womanly scream and a potato-sack sound as a body was slammed against the back wall and sent careening through the furniture. There was a pause and then a flurry of muffled blows.

"Stop it, Kid. Stop it!" Voss was yelling.

Sloane gave the lighter one last try and the spark of the flint strobed the gruesome scene in the room, freezing the Kid with a rubbery rag doll figure over his head. The flash made the image last longer than the moment itself, for it had hardly registered when the body had already been hurled across the room. It crashed into the iron bars there with such force that it ripped the frame loose and the whole window plug pulled away from the studs and went crashing to the ground outside.

The night seemed to hold its breath, and then someplace in the room the Kid began sobbing.

Sloane made his way through the wreckage to the hole where the window had been. His heart still banging away, he climbed through the hole and dropped to the ground. The body there looked like part of the debris, all steel gray in the moonlight. He was feeling the limp wrist for a pulse when the screen door of the cookhouse slammed and a figure with a flashlight came stumbling toward him, grumbling loudly at the disturbance.

Sloane watched with momentary confusion and then let himself sit back in the dirt. He took a deep breath of the clean night air and rubbed at his eyes with his fingers. They had awakened Somsak.

He was in a very white T-shirt and a pair of striped shorts as big as a tent. He handed the flashlight to Sloane to hold and bent over the victim, who seemed to be still alive. Oddly, in the victim's clinched hand Somsak found a paper and a brass electrical fuse. He must have taken it out of the box beside the backdoor to assure himself the cover of darkness, Sloane thought. Good idea, if it hadn't been for the Kid.

Somsak turned the victim's face to the light and Sloane recognized it from the first day at the mouth of Dog Alley. Somsak shook his head slowly.

"*Khmer,*" he said.

CHAPTER

8

When the neighbors began gathering, one of them was sent for Major Chapikorn back at the National Security Center compound and the jeep was pulled around so that the victim could be examined under its lights. He was breathing unsteadily, there was a rattling noise from deep in his chest, and the blood bubbling from his nose was purple under the headlights. His arm was broken, the bone protruding through the flesh above the elbow, and his leg was bent back impossibly from his hip.

Above them in the dark house the Kid was raving incoherently like a child lost in a nightmare and desperate to awaken himself.

"I have been expecting something like this, you know," Chappy said when he got there. "Peter likes to make it a joke but I told him all along these fellows were spies."

"And just who are you?" Alice demanded, pushing through the neighbors gathering at the gate.

"Ah, I am Major Chapikorn." Chappy touched his cap and gave her a little bow. "Call me Chappy."

"That's dumb, Chappy," Alice said. "He's no spy. He's just another refugee. He's like a thousand others I've seen."

"A pint-sized burglar," Sloane said. "They're probably half-starved over in that shack of theirs and when this guy saw we were out he decided it was his chance to swipe something. That's all."

"Mmm," Chappy replied. He gave the victim a quick search and when he was done he got the two men who'd accompanied him from the barracks to carry the broken little man out to Sathorn North Road. "I will find transport as quickly there as anywhere, not to worry. I will take care of everything."

Before he left he took Sloane aside. "A moment, David, please," he said, squeezing his arm affectionately. "You must take care of your friend, will you do that? He has been pretending very hard that his brother will someday be better, so what has happened here tonight will surely be a hard lesson. There is really so much about life that he does not understand, you know? He is needing someone who understands what life is all about, someone like you for that."

"Me? I . . . I . . ." Sloane tried to think of something to say but could only look away, embarrassed. Chappy understood. Americans are like the Siamese sometimes.

When Chappy had left, Sloane got the fuse from Somsak and took it around back to the box. He pressed it back between its two prongs and patted around the wall until he found the light switch. The only lamp in the room was lying across the overturned cot, its hot bulb scorching the tissue globe while it cast nightmare shadows up the walls. Sloane found Voss with his brother on the floor.

The Kid was hyperventilating, gasping for air and trembling uncontrollably. Voss was holding him from behind, rocking him in his arms. His eyes were hidden in shadow. He was mumbling huskily, his face close to his brother's ear, his words like the cooing a mother uses to comfort a child.

". . . I'm here, Kid. I'm always here," he was saying." They'll never get at us again, that's all in the past. Nobody's gonna get at us. Honest."

There was a noise outside, rubble being cleared, and then the gate slammed and the Kid stirred but Voss held him fast. "Kiri!" he yelled. "Where's that goddam Thorazine?" He looked up, nose running, his face streaked with his tears, and saw Sloane standing above him. "All my fault," he told him, wiping his nose on the back of his hand. "You were right, man. I should'a seen it, too."

"I didn't mean it that way, Pete."

"I know what you meant," he said, angrily. "And you were right. I just can't analyze this kind of thing. I'm just no good with feelings. My own brother . . . I could never just look at that lost look of his and see it for what it was. I wanted to think he was getting better so I did, that's all."

The Kid's breathing was still irregular and he gasped and

clutched at his brother's arm. "Shhh, it's okay, man. It's okay. Shh. Shhh."

The Kid wasn't listening. His eyes were darting about the room like a trapped animal. He looked like he was still dangerous.

"I'm scared, Dave," Voss said. Sloane didn't know what to say so he just stood there and let him talk. "The Kid used to take care of me back at the 'Sisters,' did I ever tell you that? Mom dead, the old man in jail half the time, we had nobody but each other. I was always in trouble and he was always there. The heavy. The big guy. So now that it's my turn, look what happens."

"You're scared?"

"Sure I'm scared. I'm scared I'm gonna lose him and it's gonna be my own damn fault." He'd said more than he intended. "*Kiri?*" he called out into the hallway.

"Pete, can I do something?" Sloane knelt awkwardly beside him. The moment was gone. He felt like an intruder.

"Nah." Voss waved him off. "Family business. *Kiri!* Where the hell is that shot!"

Kiri was in charge of the Kid's medicine. She appeared with a black strongbox from which she drew a glass vial. She filled a syringe and tapped it expertly into his arm.

"Hold on, Kid," Voss was whispering as the milky liquid emptied into the muscle. "You can't give out on me now, not when we're almost there."

In all the years Sloane had known him, Voss had never let this side of himself be seen before. To see the Kid's tragedy reflected in the anguish of his brother was to see Peter Voss in a new light. With his bravado stripped from him he seemed more real than he had before. In his grief he was more human. Sloane swallowed hard. He stood up and turned to leave them there alone and found Alice standing silently behind him. She had been watching them, too, and she wore a look Sloane could not fathom.

The neighborhood kids were lining the fence outside and the women were all clucking about foreigners. The men were trying to pry a few of the details from Somsak but he shooed everybody away. Bad enough he should miss his sleep, he wasn't about to become part of a spectacle.

A doctor from the other side of the canal arrived, a shuffling old man in a white short-sleeved shirt who had the sad, folded face of one who had seen it all. He seemed to know the household well. He gave the Kid another shot and waited out the result, sitting quietly beside Kiri until he was sure the patient was safely unconscious and then he shuffled away again without saying anything.

When things had finally settled down, Sloane found Voss sitting by himself in the far corner of the courtyard leaning against the marble column that held up the household shrine. The faint light made his face look grimy and worn. His eyes were dark circles. It was a steamy, tropical night but he was shivering as he took long swigs from a black bottle.

"Here," he said, offering some to Sloane. "You'd better have some, too."

There was still some activity at the front of the house but it all seemed far away. Sloane found that he had a couple of mangled cigarettes left. He gave one to Voss and stuck the second in his mouth. Then he took the bottle and squinted at its label in the dark.

"What is it?" he asked.

"I don't know."

Sloane squatted down beside him and took a couple of swallows. "Some kind of whiskey," he said, and then they just sat there in silence for a few minutes.

"Is he safe in there?"

"Yeah, I guess so." Voss held out his hand for the bottle. "He'll be all right, at least for the time being."

"Then what?"

"He's just got to hang on a while longer, that's all."

"Then what, Pete?"

Voss took a hard drink and pretended he hadn't heard. "Somsak never did like those Cambodians," he said. "He lost some family up near Bhan Toey to one of the Khmer Rouge border raids last year. What a mess, huh?"

"Listen, Pete, we've got to talk," Sloane said, waving off his turn with the whiskey.

"I'll bet this war's never gonna end," Voss said. "It's been going on for two thousand years, did you know that? It's tribal, it's racial . . ."

"Pete, I know why you can't take the Kid home for help."

"Yeah?"

"I had a run-in with that Korean, Sung Dai."

"I told you to stay away from that guy."

"He told me the Kid fragged an officer."

Voss didn't look at Sloane. He had another drink and sat watching the lighted window and Kiri at work inside. "He didn't 'frag' him," he finally said. "He wrung his neck like a chicken."

"Why?"

"Something about botched orders," Voss began, then he looked down at his feet. "No, that's not right. He did it because he was crazy. He did it because he'd spent three tours in 'Nam and two of them as a LURP off in the boonies and almost everybody he'd ever gone out with was dead."

Alice found them there and without a word she made some room for herself at the foot of the ivy-covered fence. Voss passed her the bottle.

"They were always trying to split us up when we were kids. The courts, the orphanage, the foster homes. But we'd refuse to go or we'd run away or whatever we had to do. He did my fighting and I did his thinkin', y'know? We were like a team. It took the draft board to break us up.

"I did okay in the army." He swirled the whiskey in the bottle, rubbed his hand over the top, and took a drink. "Yeah, I did great. I took what I needed and let the rest go by, but the Kid. Christ, they just kept sending him back. It was like they'd singled him out, or something. Like they'd said, 'let's see how far we can push this guy, let's see how far he'll go before he breaks.' So back in '70, when he went with the 101st into the Ashau Valley and had to be medivaced back to the States they told him, 'No good.' Stateside is 'bad time.' Ten months, five days you gotta spend 'good time.' That means y'gotta spend it *in* 'Nam or none of it counts. Ten months and five days—or they just sent you back.

"So four months later it happened again, shrapnel, concussion, and they sent him off to Hawaii. Another month in the hospital and they sent him back to start his tour all over again."

"Why, for God's sake?" Sloane said. "All they had to do was look at him. All they had to do was see what he'd been through."

Voss shook his head. "It's all computerized," he said. "Ain't that a kick?"

A cricket began its song behind them in the weeds and Kiri came to the window to look out at the moon-washed courtyard.

Then she closed the shutters and behind them she dimmed the lights. Voss watched her for a minute and then said, almost to himself, "I could have saved him, I know that now. I could have traced the system back to the deployment manifest and pulled him out myself. But it was all like a new toy to me back then so I didn't think of it until it was too late."

Sloane butted out his cigarette. "So where does the Korean come in?"

"Park Sung Dai was one of the big racketeers in Saigon at the time. He heard someplace about this little wire transfer trick I used to keep the good times going. Booze, cigarettes, stuff like that, and he got real interested. He even made me a few offers but I wasn't interested. So when the Kid got into trouble he heard about it first. He paid off some cops and hid him out until I could get hold of you to fly him out of the country. The deal was that I had to cut him in on my little schemes.

"Well, they didn't stay little for long. Sung Dai took my nickel-and-dime tricks and turned them into a big-time black market operation. What could I do? I had to go along. And anyhow, what did I owe to the system?"

"I see what you mean," Alice agreed. The sky was bright with stars but her face was hidden in the shade of the tree above her.

Without looking, Voss took the bottle from her and took a couple loud gulps of the whiskey. It was Sloane's turn but he waved it off.

"Now the Korean's mad," Sloane said. "Why?"

"I screwed up on my timing, just like everybody else," he said. "I'd put a lot of the money we made from the operation into transferrable accounts in the Bank L'Indochine branch in Saigon."

"*You* put them there. And he didn't know about it?"

"Hey, the Korean's a crook. He'd have run off with the whole thing, all the money the minute things got hot. Where would I have been then, right? It was costing a fortune to take care of the Kid. It was like insurance. It was simple, the bank's computers were interfaced with the National Defense Network, same as the military and everybody else. So all I needed was the terminal at Beach House 7 to go in and release the accounts when the time came.

"Trouble is the time came a lot sooner than anybody expected. I was a long way from a terminal so I couldn't release anything. The Korean lost a lot of money and so did I.

"Now he's got the idea that I owe him something, like it was my fault we lost the war. That deal for the MAS Unit was supposed to square us, but instead it only got Trang Van Thep killed.

"Oh, he's a real son of a bitch, that Korean. And he's got this idea I'm some kind of magician or something. He thinks there's something more I can do, but I can't. I mean, what more can I do, right?"

They passed the bottle around again, Sloane drinking deeply from it and rubbing his mouth with the roll of his sleeve.

"You should have told me this, Pete."

"What for? This is my problem, not yours. And anyhow, you'd have done the same thing, right? You'd have gone in there and faked the engine trouble until you got the Kid on the plane. You'd have waited because that's the kind of guy you are."

Sloane got to his feet and brushed himself off. "I had a right to know, that's all," and he left them there in the dark.

It was quiet for a time after he had gone. The screen door banged shut as he went back into the house and low voices from inside. Voss was shivering again. When he looked at Alice he found her sitting upright, her face out of the shadow of the tree. She had been watching him carefully, staring into his eyes as if he had something more to say.

"Well?" he said, defiantly. "Looking for bones to pick?"

Alice turned away. "I guess I'd better see if there's anything more I can do." But as she was getting to her feet Voss suddenly reached out and touched her hand.

"Don't . . ." he said. "I mean, I'm sorry. Don't go, okay? I guess I don't want to be alone right now."

"So," Alice said quietly, taking her seat on the rock beside him again. "So you're not such a tough guy, after all."

Swells from the wake of a passing ferryboat rushed the seaplane in muddy green ranks, splashing over its pontoons and rocking it just enough for a 9 mm socket to make a break for the waterline. Sloane grabbed it and tossed it into the metal toolbox with the others. The lines to the oil drum buoys stretched with the strain and then dipped into the water as the aircraft settled back into the river's easy drift.

Sloane had a platform of rough boards laid crosswise between the pontoons and was sitting in the shade of the wings tinkering with the oil cooler assembly, taking it apart, cleaning each part in a paint can full of kerosene, and laying it out with the others so he could visualize their assembly sequence.

He was dressed like a castaway in a pair of raveled cutoffs and Indian thongs. He'd spent the last three days familiarizing himself with Thai/Tech's marketing data in the mornings and working on the aircraft in the afternoons, checking every detail that he could get at. He was dirty, sunburned, and happy as a pig.

It was quiet on the river this time of the day; the midday heat slowed things down. It would be like this until the rains came.

Sloane liked being alone out here, it gave him a chance to think. He was totally absorbed in his task and didn't hear the *hangyao* draw up alongside and lag back against the easy current. Alice was standing in the bow.

"Hi-ya, sailor," she called out. "New in town?"

Sloane shaded his eyes and squinted into the glare. "Hi, lady," he yelled back. "What are you up to?"

She wore a carelessly buttoned light cotton blouse that fit her snugly around her breasts and made her look like a carved wooden figurehead. Her skirt was brown and practical and her sunny blond hair wafted gently as her skiff lifted over each wave.

Sloane hadn't seen much of her since the night of the Kid's breakdown. There'd been plenty of work for each of them to get started on and Alice had the additional difficulties of trying to cut her way through a wall of red tape. In-country travel was restricted for foreigners because of recent Cambodian incursions.

"Can I come aboard?" she asked. "I brought a lunch."

"Perfect timing," Sloane said and began scrubbing up with the kerosene as the *hangyao* bumped alongside.

"What is this thing, anyhow?" Alice asked. She had to stoop slightly to fit under the fuselage.

"It's a Mitsatsu 150," Sloane said. "It's Japanese." He soaped himself in the river water while she looked around.

"No wonder they lost the war."

"Hey, this is a great old machine," Sloane told her. "See that radiator up there? Water cooled."

"Imagine that." She didn't care how the water cooler radiated. "Anyway, I went shopping down in Sampeng Market and found a couple of stalls that had all these natural macrobiotic munchies . . ." She lofted a checkered tablecloth and let it settle in the after end of the platform away from the work area, then she started laying out white paper canisters and neat packages wrapped in rice paper. "Here, open this. I got a jar of curd and chives and raw bean sprouts you can dip in this stuff here."

Sloane picked up a plain little bottle and sniffed the cork. "Oh, God," he muttered. *"Nam pla* sauce."

"No complaining," Alice said. "This is all very healthy food, and you need it. You never . . ." She paused to stick a finger into a canister she'd just opened and tasted it to see what it was and then laid it out with the rest. "You never pay enough attention to your diet."

Sloane tied off a couple bottles of Singha beer and hung them over the side to cool in the water while Alice spooned things out onto clean paper squares.

"I got brown rice and, here. You'll love this," she said. "Pickled kelp."

Sloane made a face. "Bring anything to eat?"

"Very funny."

The city on the far side of the river was shimmering in the heat and the large white yacht near the bank there let out more cable, shifting for a better anchorage in the soft silt of the river bottom.

They took their time over the food, talking about Alice's job. It had her all wound up just as it always did; she seemed to save all her pent-up anger and frustrations for these moments when she had Sloane all to herself. He'd been part of the backwoods war and understood her feelings about the Montagnards and Meo and Hmong tribals whose fate had been sealed by the American pullout.

"It must be a madhouse in Cambodia," she said. "The Khmer Rouge is slaughtering its own people by the thousands. It makes no sense, they kill their weak, their doctors, their landed peasants, everybody. They kill the educated, they kill each other. We're getting half a million refugees in the next six months and somebody's got to protect them."

Sloane looked out over the glimmering water, his thoughts running through the scene again, those poor doomed outcasts on the bow of the sinking coaster as the airplane passed over them on its way to safety.

"The Khmer Rouge have even taken to raiding over the border into Vietnam and Thailand, even attacking the camps themselves for rice and slave labor."

Sloane marveled at the way Alice could talk about such awful things while going about the task of eating like a horse. Even now she paused only briefly to stick a particularly gooey sweet in her mouth and lick her fingers before going on.

"Mumm, there's going to be another war over all this," she said. "Wait and see."

"It'll be the same war," Sloane said. "Pete says this is all one war that's been going on for two thousand years."

"He said that?" Alice looked up from her eating for a moment. "Funny guy, your Peter Voss."

"Funny?" Sloane tried the kelp and found it wasn't bad. "That's not what you called him the other night."

"No, I didn't."

"Thief, I think that was what you said."

"I know, and I spoiled the fun, too."

"Criminal."

"I didn't call him a criminal, David. I was only trying to make a point."

"Well, you certainly did that all right."

"My point was that his way of life is much different than yours. You're wasting your time playing 'Terry and the Pirates' all over again. You've come a long way from your Air America days, why do you have to pretend you're still some kind of a hotshot kid?"

"Y'know what I like about flying?" Sloane said. "I like it that the problem and the solution are both self-contained. You've got a physical problem and a physical result, keeping eight and a half tons of airplane in the air long enough to get from one place to another. Everything is right there, you're directly in touch with all the critical elements of your life for as long as the flight lasts, and I like that kind of control. What I need to do is to change the scale of things so I can reach out and take control of my life again."

"And you think this job with Thai/Tech will let you do that?"

Sloane hesitated. "I hope so." He opened the second bottle of beer with a pair of pliers, took a drink, and handed it to Alice.

"And this grease monkey stuff? Is this what vice presidents are supposed to do at Thai/Tech?"

"Yeah." Sloane was touchy about Alice's ideas about what he ought to be doing when there was so much she didn't understand about him. The truth was, though, that there wasn't all that much for him to do back at the offices. If it wasn't for this old plane he'd be bored to distraction.

"Yeah. Right there in the job profile it says, 'Vice presidents will have damn little in the way of office work but will be expected to go out periodically and get dirty.' " He wiggled his fingers menacingly in front of her face but she only laughed.

"I know what you mean," she told him. "I like it dirty sometimes, too." Sloane dropped a chopstick into the bean curd.

A light breeze stirred the humid air and lifted a brown pelican from his perch on the nearest buoy. Sloane was leaning against the strut watching the fishing boats at the company dock bobbing at their moorings while Alice lay with her head on his lap. Her eyes were closed but she was awake. At last she stirred and said, "I've found something for you."

"Pepto Bismol? Maalox?"

"Stop it, you. I'm serious. I told our district supervisor about you and he said he had a position he'd like to talk to you about."

"Alice . . ."

"A responsible job," she insisted. She sat up so that she could face him. "The People Project needs somebody at the regional level who can deal with distribution and fiscal allocations. Oh, David. It's just perfect for you."

"Alice, do we have to go through all this again?"

"No," Alice said. "No, you don't have to say anything yet. Just think about it, okay? That's all I'm asking you to do."

"Mmm."

"Just think about it?"

Sloane looked at her uneasily. "Yeah, okay," he finally said. "I'll think about it."

Alice grinned. "You do that, Flyboy." She ran her fingers into his kinky hair and grabbed a handful. "And while you're at it you can think about this." She kissed him lightly at first, their lips just touching. And then as they nibbled at each other she began closing in hungrily. Then to Sloane's surprise she broke away, her blue eyes a little unfocused.

"It's awfully hot for this sort of thing, don't you think?" She wore that mischievous look, like a child who'd just thought up something new and unwholesome to do. "Let's go for a swim." She was already unbuttoning.

"Out here? Right in the open?" Sloane asked.

"The boats are in the way."

"What about the other shore?"

"Too far away," Alice said. Her blouse was already undone and she was pushing her loose cotton skirt down her legs. "Anyhow we'll be in the water, so what's there to see?"

When she was nude she turned to see how he liked her, holding her breasts in her hands and rubbing them absently so that her nipples jiggled between her fingers. Her face and arms glowed with a warm brown tan that ended with a v below her neck and made her seem all the more naked with her milky white skin and pink private creases. She waited for a moment, letting his eyes move over her and knowing the quivering he was feeling in the pit of his stomach and the power she had over him. Should she swim? Or perhaps submit to some readier delight?

Then an upriver ferryboat tootled as it pulled into the channel and the moment was gone. She turned quickly and dove cleanly into the water.

"Oh, lord." Sloane gave another look around and then hooked his thumbs over his shorts and shoved them down without unbuttoning. He felt more naked than she could possibly feel. "What am I getting into this time?" He took a quick look around and dove in after her.

He went thrashing upstream, exhilarated by the cool flow of the river, until he passed Alice and saw her long legs tredding water as the current drew her back into the shade of the wing.

Sloane felt clean and free. Lolling over onto his back, he watched the seabirds circling high above him. All the world seemed liquid and clear, everything far more real against that perfect sky.

"You're not the swimmer you used to be," Alice said as he drifted into her arms.

"My rudder gets in the way," he said.

"And maybe you've been working too hard." She spoke very softly, he was very close. "Maybe what you need is a few days off, a few days in the country . . ."

"You're up to something."

"Why don't you come up to the Aranyaprathet camps with me?"

"I know what you're up to." He was clinging to the pontoon with one hand and running the other over her slippery breast. She watched him stroke her, her nipples a light blush like her cheeks, and let her legs float up around him.

"Um, you could see about the job," she said.

"I know."

"You could . . ."

"I know, I know."

The far bank of the river was indeed too far away for anyone to see what Alice and Sloane were up to unless that anyone had a heavy set of binoculars steadied against the rail of the Korean's yacht. That's what Janus had to use or he'd have missed all the details. He was excited and breathing hard and the eyepieces kept fogging up. It was almost too much.

He stepped back, drew a square of folded Kleenex from his pocket, and mopped his forehead where his perspiration was beginning to loosen his dirty bandage. Then he refocused on the couple, watching from behind as their cautious lovemaking grew in intensity until they were thrashing about in the water like a pair of rutting carp. Janus was grunting and running his tongue over his lipless mouth.

The image was excellent, he could see every detail. He could see . . . *Damn!* The looming black bow of the upriver ferryboat came slicing through the image like a closing curtain cutting off Janus's view at the most tantalizing moment.

Janus lowered the binoculars and cursed the ferryboat and all aboard her with a string of vile-sounding utterances while the passengers who lined the rails of the tall double-decker drifted past unconcerned, facing into the breeze trying to get some coolness from it. There were a few who were looking his way, though. A couple near the back seemed familiar, even at this distance. Janus frowned and tried the glasses again, running their view along the crowded rail until he came to a girl he remembered from that night at Yankee Daniel's. Yes, it was Peter Voss's whore. It was Kiri, dressed for a summer's outing in a bright print frock and a slip of lavender cloth around her neck. She was smiling and waving his way. No, no, she wasn't just waving in his direction, she was waving directly at him as if there were only a few yards separating them. And—yes, he thought so. Beside her was Peter Voss. He was smiling, too, that smug, insolent smile of his. He must have known Janus was watching, he was waving at him with childish enthusiasm and pointing at something upstream.

At first the signal was lost on Janus. It was a trick. Some kind of elaborate ruse to interrupt his fun? No, they were pointing at something, even the whore had taken it up, pointing and waving as if it was all some wonderful joke.

Janus turned to see what they were pointing at just as the Korean came hustling out onto the deck.

"Give me those," the Korean said, grabbing the glasses away before the henchman could unhook the strap from around his neck. "Give them to me."

The Korean growled to himself in his native tongue as he focused in on Voss's impudent face. Then he followed the gesture that he and the girl were making, scanning the water for a minute until the view was suddenly full of longboats and uniformed sailors. The Korean took the glasses from his eyes but they were still there, a flotilla of Coast Guardsmen sporting sidearms, M16 rifles, and boarding hooks. In the bow of the lead boat stood the unmistakable figure of Major Chapikorn, chest out, one hand at his waist. He filled the lenses of the Korean's binoculars as he stared back at him through a pair of his own.

The flotilla surrounded the yacht and in an air of general confusion and a great deal of shouting the boat hooks were brought into use and a number of grappling hooks were heaved over onto the deck. Their lines were tested by some of the Coast Guardsmen while others motored out a few yards and covered with rifles those who were boarding. Their excitement was high but not so many were agile enough to make it first try. Hooks slipped and dumped some of the men into the water and several more found the polished hull too smooth for their feet to grip and were left hanging above their longboats.

The Korean was scarlet with rage. "What is the meaning of this!" he was shouting. He turned to Janus. "Do something, you fool!"

Janus ran down to the main deck where the Korean's own sailors were pressing against the deckhouse and hiding where they could. There he scurried about yanking at the hooks and lines and managed to send a few more of the boarders into the drink. When the others began raising their heads above deck level he went at them with his blackjack, but at an order from Chappy one of the riflemen from the outer ring of boarders aimed his M16 in Janus's general direction and ran a stitch of bullets along the bulkhead just over his head.

The gunfire shattered the drowzy afternoon on the river, interrupting the naps of dock workers nearby and sending Janus and the crew scrambling for cover.

". . . hereby detain and impound said vessel under Immigration Statute A-14, and C-21. Said confiscation . . ." The young officer who read the order of seizure on the bridge of the yacht had a bad complexion and a high-pitched monotone. He must have known that he cut less than a dashing figure for he overcompensated by holding forth like a sample-sized martinet. Chappy, on the other hand, kept modestly back in the ranks playing the role of the observer who had just come along for the ride. But the Korean wasn't fooled. Major Chapikorn's eyes betrayed his merriment.

The Korean stiffened his resolve to meet the occasion. There was nothing he could do for the moment, it was an indignity to be suffered in silence, so he strode manfully to the rail and looked out over the river while his ship was officially seized. It was humiliating, being taken for an illegal alien, it would be expensive to erase that stain but until he did he would be little better off than a common refugee. He would take care of it all somehow. He had to. And when he did he would make Voss pay for it.

The ferry was gone now, a half-mile upriver, and his eyes fell upon the Thai/Tech docks and the old seaplane tied up at its buoys. He put the glasses to his eyes and watched as Sloane and a young *farang* woman whom the Korean did not know hailed a passing *hangyao* and went buzzing away in it toward the company docks. In the binoculars they seemed to be gliding along a wall of green water. A pair of marsh terns flew up from the reeds ahead of them. Everything seemed so close.

CHAPTER

9

The first elements of the convoy formed up near the RSF headquarters on Wireless Road. There were two rattling stake
trucks hired for the trip and a white Land Rover with the blue
helping hand insignia of the People Project decaled to the side.
The rest they picked up at an army cantonment out in the Din
Daena Sector: two army trucks full of burlap rice bags, boxed
packets of protein supplements, and cartons of basic medical
supplies and a GMC with a crude red cross painted over its tarp
and its end flaps roped up tight.

They shared the Land Rover with its nervous driver, who had
a habit of adjusting the dainty spectacles on his nose as if his many
close calls with traffic were merely a matter of viewpoint, and
Alice's boss, the SEA section chief. He was a browless, middle-
aged man with a colorless beard that sprouted from his pock-
marked face like an erosion project. Once they were on the road
he apprised Sloane of the various relief projects that were trying
to get relief operations under way.

There was Oxfam, of course, and the World Council of
Churches. The UN was only now beginning to admit to the atroci-
ties of one of its members and even if they managed to muddle
through their internal politics, it was unlikely the Thai authorities
would let the UNHRC intervene in any measurable way. It would
only spotlight the Thai shortcomings. The International Committee of the Red Cross had begun to show an interest but they
were more inclined to work within the governmental framework.
He went on and on. His offhand attitude and the way he had of
reciting endless lists of facts and data made him sound like he was
reading it all from the notes of a particularly tedious lecture that
he was in a hurry to finish.

"So of course we find ourselves with the worst of the lot, the Nong Kai camps. The Thais don't recognize these people as refugees, you know. None of them. That would make them responsible for their care under the UN charter, so they call them illegal aliens and treat them as a temporary affliction."

"So I hear."

"Well, places like Nong Kai are the result. The Thais don't want to have to worry about the place so they just don't recognize it. Some of the clients there call themselves Free Khmer and go back and forth over the no-man's-land as if it were their private domain. Some are resistance fighters, to be sure. They escort refugees, guard some of the camps, and gather intelligence for the Thai Army so they're tolerated by the border police. But some of them are just smugglers . . ."

"Only a few of them," Alice insisted.

"Gold, gems—even teak. Freebooters who make trouble for us with the Thai Supreme Command."

He was keeping an eye on traffic and signaling instructions to the driver as he spoke, a habit that annoyed the driver. "Nong Kai is a renegade camp. Dispensable, if you ask me. Officially it isn't there at all."

"There's fifteen hundred people there," Alice protested.

"Well, there shouldn't be. Half of them are Communists with a price on their heads running from other Communists and the rest won't let themselves be properly processed."

"They'd have them behind barbed wire in a week. Or worse, they'd force them back across the border again."

"Nevertheless, Miss Brodsky." Jorgenson gave her an icy glance. "Those are the rules."

It took the better part of an hour before they had escaped the city and were rolling out into the sun-bleached countryside to the northeast, where the riverine world of rice paddies and wallowing water buffalo seemed to go on forever. Once in the open on the flat lowlands highway they made good time, picking up almost half the distance to the border before noon. The small towns and sleepy villages and fly-blown bazaars along the highway hardly stirred at their passing.

They pulled up around noon at the town of Sa Kaeo, which had grown up around the fork where Highway 9 went on without them over the Bang Pakong River and into the jungle toward the border. Nobody went that way much anymore, there had been too many incidents, and it took a major commitment of troops by the Thai Army to keep the area sealed off from the Khmer Rouge.

The foreigners lingered over a light lunch beneath the striped awning of a roadside cafe while the drivers took their siesta and then the convoy started north along Highway 10, the trade route of the provincial planters of Prachin Buri, a solid highway now. Not the crowned macadam Sloane remembered from the early days of the war. There were some low hills off beyond the flat farmlands toward the border, and the countryside seemed more derelict as they converged with the river to the east.

Jorgenson continued with his appraisal of the People Project's plight. He spoke almost casually of the slaughter and dislocation to be found along the frontiers of Cambodia and Laos, maintaining a carefully detached attitude and letting the statistics speak for themselves. A necessary psychological defense for somebody with a job like that, no doubt, but one that lent a vaguely bitchy air to his mannerisms.

"This delivery represents the updated allocations for the refugee centers in the frontier district. We are expecting an increase to two hundred clients per day maximum and have already allowed for the increase in our contingency plans."

"I heard you're getting twice that number and it's getting worse all the time," Sloane said as the column started off. "I hope your contingency plans are flexible enough for that kind of short-term adjustment."

Dr. Jorgenson had an arm stretched along the back of the Land Rover's front seat. He turned so that he could look over it casually into the back.

"We try to make plans," he said. "Not guesses. If the situation were as unstable as all that I do think we'd have heard."

"Maybe."

Twice the column was stopped at checkpoints while soldiers examined everyone's papers and searched the trucks. They were held up at the second, a barrier made up of dirt-filled oil drums lined up across the road, so Alice got out and sorted through the bags. The troops stood around in their battle gear until she produced a packet of travel papers and the manifest of the cargo in the trucks. The harassed-looking officer explained that a Khmer raiding party had crossed the border during the night and the army was sweeping the district for stragglers.

Half a mile later they passed through a village where some of the houses had been burned and the cinder-block face of the district offices riddled with light weapons' fire. Worried villagers clogged the roadway, slowing the trucks to a crawl. Horns blared and tempers grew short.

Once past the village the Land Rover's driver kept a sharp eye on the rest of the convoy to make sure everybody kept ranks.

Aranyaprathet lay close by the border in a landscape of lightly wooded farmland. It was a growing town, packed in tightly upon itself and scarred by the addition of makeshift buildings that catered to the sudden burgeoning of the foreign element and illicit trafficking in smuggled heirlooms and relics brought in by the refugees.

The convoy was broken up here, and for an hour the supplies were redistributed among the trucks for delivery to the individual sites scattered along the ill-defined border. The Land Rover and one army truck struck off again to the northeast until they found themselves traveling along the rugged, dusty roads beside the lazy waters of the Cheom Bai River. It was late evening by the time they had made their way into the forests of the Dangrek Mountains to the town of Nong Kai.

The chief industry of Nong Kai was the yearly pilgrimage of the faithful to the astonishing landmark that towered over the town: the huge temple of Wat Duang Jan that dominated the southern valley with its bell-shaped stupa and its towering spire that glimmered as if it were sheathed in polished silver. Beyond it were the hills of the Khorat Plateau turning red in the afternoon sun.

"The Temple of the Moon," Alice told him. "Isn't it marvelous?"

Sloane agreed. "I've seen it from the air," he said. "Just where are these camps from here?"

"The one we're going to is two or three kilometers past the temple," Alice said. "Down in the valley."

"Not a very good site for a refugee camp," Sloane said. "The river marks the border along here. They must be sitting ducks. The Khmer Rouge could raid the camps from across the river whenever they felt like it. There's no cover, it's all floodplain."

"We don't have much choice."

"Have you some expertise in the local geography, Mr. Sloane?" Dr. Jorgenson asked from the front.

"In a way, I guess. I used to fly over this area all the time."

"Ah, yes, I had forgotten you were a pilot." He craned his neck for a better look at the temple. It had been built like a crown on the top of an even larger granite promontory that rose so abruptly from the low, modeled contours of the valley that it looked like it had been dropped there from the sky.

"Fourteenth century, I should think," Dr. Jorgenson said. "It must be two hundred feet high."

"Two hundred and sixty," Sloane corrected. "Three hundred more when you add that rock it's sitting on. It's a primary landmark on the OSC navigational charts. It lines up on the secondary approach to a Nakhon Phanom Air Base."

Dr. Jorgenson looked back at him with a new interest. "Oh? Did you fly into Nakhon Phanom?"

"Sure," Sloane said. "All the time."

"And for whom did you pilot, Mr. Sloane?"

"Air America."

Dr. Jorgenson's waxy blue eyes narrowed as if Sloane had committed a not-unexpected social gaff.

"Something wrong?" Sloane had seen that look before.

"You were a 'spook'?"

Something turned in Sloane's stomach. "I was a flier for an airline that was under charter to the CIA, if that's what you mean. I flew supplies in support of a cause many people believed in. That doesn't make me a spook."

"You probably supplied the weapons these people waged their senseless war with."

"Useless, not senseless," Sloane told him. "And as for my role in it, I guess I lack this gift of prophecy everyone seems to have these days. All I could do was what seemed right at the time."

"I suppose they teach you that, don't they? How to rationalize these wantonly destructive policies your country's secret services seem to enjoy."

Sloane leaned forward, barely able to contain his temper. "I wasn't privy to their policies and I didn't know much about their recreation either. I've noticed, though, that a lot of people seem to get their kicks out of blaming everything on the CIA. It didn't invent the Khmer Rouge, right? And it didn't invent the boat people."

"Of course not. These are not unique entities in this . . . this bloody morass, they are the direct result of American interventionist—"

"Indochina was a 'bloody morass' long before we got hold of it."

"David, please," Alice inserted.

"Hey, what am I doing here?" Sloane demanded. "What is this? Did you two invite me along so we could have this little chat?"

"David, stop it!"

"Didn't she tell you what I did in the war?"

Dr. Jorgenson eyed Sloane with eager dislike. "She didn't tell me you were a spook."

"There's got to be some kind of record in all this." Alice was seething. "Let's see, fewest civil words ever spoken at an interview. Nearest thing to a fistfight in a car owned by a charitable organization . . ." Sloane hated the prig anyhow so it was impossible to tell Alice he was sorry and Alice refused to let him off the hook. She wouldn't even let him help her get her bags out of the back of the Land Rover.

Alice's camp was hardly a camp at all. Just a patch of land at a border crossing point where the refugees had settled in. It was about an acre of raw red dirt cleared of scrub and elephant grass by the same slash and burn technique the local farmers used for cropland. There was no barbed wire or any other sign of Thai supervision yet, but there were slit trenches along each side and sandbagged shelters near the center. The river was a hundred yards away, almost hidden by a thicket of gum trees.

"Interview? Was that what this was all about?"

"You know very well what this was," she said. "You said you were interested."

"Interested, that's all. Only interested. Mostly I came up here to be with you." Sloane followed her past an arrangement of open-sided canvas tents full of listless groups of men and silent, hollow-faced women and their naked children. The administration was quartered in a pair of sturdy thatch fishermen's huts built on stilts a few feet off the ground. The bags had to be negotiated up a ladderlike set of stairs.

"Nobody said anything about an interview," Sloane said. "In fact, I didn't even know that asshole Jorgenson was coming along."

"You know what I think? I think you did it on purpose." Alice refused to even look at him, bouncing her bag along beside her in the dust. "You never wanted this job, you want to go back to your nowhere friends and their nowhere ways and pretend you're twenty-five again." She turned on him at the doorway. "And who are you to call Dr. Jorgenson an . . . an asshole?"

"And just who was he to treat me like I was some kind of a war criminal?"

"He did not."

" 'Spook,' he called me," Sloane told her, holding the screen door open while she bumped her bag up over the step. "I put a lot of sweat and tears into that job because I thought I was doing the right thing and he treats me like I was some kind of a lackey or something."

"Did it ever occur to you that Dr. Jorgenson is doing what he thinks is right, too? He's put a lot of 'sweat and tears' into all this, too. Maybe he deserves a little understanding when he gets like that."

"And I don't, is that it?" he demanded. "Maybe he did pay his dues, so what? What right's he got laying all that sanctimonious crap on me? He's not a hell of a lot better for his part in the system than I was for mine. We were both somebody's lackey, we both were used.

"Look around you," he said, taking her arm roughly and pointing her toward the scene outside. "Just look at this place."

The refugees were clustering in miserable little groups for the evening meal, brooding over their bowls, while a group of confused newcomers looked on from a safe distance waiting to see what they could expect from the mercy of strangers.

Most of those hunkering around the fires were plainly sick and malnourished from their ordeal. Cut off from everything that had given their lives stability and order. Their existence had become the purposeless routine of the camp and their hopes the squalor of despair.

"What do you think this place is for? Do you think it's for

them? It isn't, you know. It's for the ones who made this mess and can't be bothered to clean it up. It's for the arrogant Americans and the barbarians in Hanoi. It's for the Koreans and the Australians who want to stem the yellow tide and the Taiwanese dope peddlers and all the others . . .

"This is a holding pen, lady. An internment camp. A place where the ones who got us all into this fiasco can stick these people away and forget them. Your Dr. Jorgenson can call me a spook if he wants, because all those little rules and all his petty narrow-minded attitudes—hell, he's no better than a warden."

"How dare you?" Alice sputtered. "This is *my* life, too, you know. This is what I do, this is what I am, just like that . . . that asshole Jorgenson. Honest to God, David. Sometimes you make me so mad. You keep twisting things around just so they'll fit your stubborn . . . pigheaded . . ." She threw down her bag and gave it a kick. "Anybody else would just say yes or say no but you've got to make everything fit what you always intended to do in the first place. You could be honest with yourself just once in your life. Even Peter can do that."

"Pete?"

"Yes. At least he knows where he stands and he doesn't try to fool himself. He may be afraid but he's willing to start over, not hide in the past like you're trying to do. Yes, and he knows when he's been wrong and he can admit it, too."

"Pete? How do you know what Pete can do?"

"We talked, is that so surprising? We had a long talk that night with his brother and I learned a lot."

"Oh, he told you so, did he?" Sloane said. "And did he tell you how he got me to get the Kid out of the country? Well, he might have been honest about it, but he was a little late, wasn't he? I was supposed to get the Kid out of Vietnam, there was nothing about a killing or about aiding and abetting."

"But it was his brother."

"That's not the point."

"Besides, you'd have done it anyhow. You couldn't resist an adventure like that."

"Maybe so, but I had a right to know what I was getting into, that's all. Like with you, riding up here with that hypocritical bastard."

"You're angry with him," Alice said in surprise.

"Of course I'm angry with him."

"No. I mean you're angry with Pete."

"Pete? No. Not angry." He found a spare cot behind a bamboo partition that had been strung from a back rafter and dumped his bag on it. "I just don't like it, that's all. Maybe there's more he hasn't told me, how do I know?"

"So that's why you came up here," Alice said. "You're having second thoughts after all, aren't you, Fly-boy?"

"I don't know why I'm up here, if you must know," he said heatedly. "But even if it did have something to do with second thoughts . . ." He checked himself.

"Even if it did you wouldn't tell me, is that what you were going to say?" she demanded. "Has it come to that?"

"Why do I always have to account for everything with you? Why does everything have to be in black and white?" Sloane was throwing his clothes out on the bed, pretending to sort them. "You want answers? Go ask Pete. He's got an answer for everything."

"I might do that," Alice snapped. "I just might do that."

Sloane threw down a rolled T-shirt, grabbed a blue nylon windbreaker, and banged out the door to cool down. The night was clear but the stars were clouded by the smoky haze of the cookfire logs. He paused near the ladder of the open veranda, where the open-sided hospital tent was clearly visible. Bamboo mats covered the dirt floor where some two dozen people lay. Some were injured, limbs blown away by the mined borderlands and battlefield wounds bleeding through their bandages, others were emaciated and sick.

From where he stood his gaze fell on the open eyes of a wasted woman of indeterminate age lying on a vinyl pad in the corner nearest the porch. She was naked below the waist, covered with festering sores. There were tubes of intravenous fluids leading from a clear plastic bag on a tripod to the needle taped to a vein in her foot. She was little more than a skeleton. Her skin was like parchment stretched over her small bones.

A woman sat beside her rubbing salve into her sores and a little girl in a drab cotton wrap sat on the ground at her feet. She was thin but still a pretty child. Her face was wan and empty of the quick charm that Sloane always enjoyed in Cambodian children.

A dying madonna. Sloane knew that look. Those wide, passive eyes, that open-mouthed expectation. She'd been too long getting here. She'd given too much of her own to her daughter. Her malnutrition had crossed over the point of no return.

As he watched she turned to look at him and it seemed to him the same look as that of the old man on the boat, the one who could do nothing but watch as they flew away and left him. Sloane's anger drained from him. He met her gaze for a long minute and then climbed down the ladder to ground level. He entered the tent and for the sake of modesty he tapped on the tent pole near where the woman lay so that the girl could cover her with the checkered cloth she had folded beside her.

Nobody seemed to mind or question his place there. He knelt beside the dying woman, touched her hand tentatively, and was surprised when her fingers gripped his hand and held him there. Her crusted lips were moving but he couldn't make out what she was saying.

The child at her feet watched him in silence. Embarrassed, he tried to get her to smile but she wouldn't He stayed by the woman's side for a long time thinking the thoughts of a man who'd had a part in all of this. Then a doctor came by on rounds. He was Thai, an overworked volunteer who showed up when he had time to spare. A dangerous charity in these parts. He preferred to speak in English.

"Why is she holding on to me like this?" Sloane asked him. "Why that look on her face?"

"There are no *farang* left in Kampuchea," the doctor said. "Seeing you here like this she knows she is at last away from that place. She knows she is safe."

"I see."

Sloane stayed with her until she slept and then made his way through the other longhouse shelters. The place stank in spite of (or maybe because of) the breeze flowing in through the open sides. People had hung sheets of colored plastic for privacy but each cubicle seemed to be packed with people.

Most of the men had gathered around a smoky fire at one end of the shelter away from the women, smoking and talking in a variety of dialects—a couple that Sloane could roughly understand.

Most were peasants but some were city people, educated and

suspicious. All wore their drab peasant pajamas and red woven kramar, the checkered scarf that was good for everything from head wraps to slings for babies. There were Chinese ethnics, among the first to be driven out by the brutal horror of *Angkar*. A few others had found their way here, too. Tribes from the highlands to the far north, Meo, and even Hmong in their floppy blue leggings and their uncut hair.

Much later, sitting with some of the elders and eating fried *pla taw* caught fresh from the river, Sloane passed out the last of his cigarettes and tried to understand the stories of death and havoc the war had brought these people.

Thai/Tech seemed far away, life was more real here among these people. Now and then, he would think about his argument with Alice and feel ashamed.

A week and a half had passed since Sloane had returned from Aranyaprathet and it was getting harder for Somsak to get the jeep to himself. Kiri, for instance. He'd had to promise to pick her and the Kid up later that night at the *Vasakha Puja* celebrations. She didn't like the Kid driving at night anymore. And Sloane would have liked a ride back from Yankee Daniel's. Somsak was lucky to get it at all and it wasn't fair. After all, he had a business to run.

It was late evening in the dingy inner districts of the Sampeng Market. Fat, wet clouds obscured the season's early moon and there weren't many lights among the warehouses and pocket factories that lined the back streets.

Somsak was in a foul mood. He was trucking a consignment of pigs for an up-country wholesaler he didn't like and he was delayed by some last-minute haggling over the price. In the end he was forced to carry twice the load that he should have. The wholesaler seemed to feel that there was always room for one more. After all, the pigs didn't mind. Each was crammed into its own woven wicker cage, stacked high in the back and roped down with the rest.

Damned farmers. They were all alike. Always trying to get something for nothing. Somsak's mood didn't improve when he found his regular route out of this labyrinth of back streets blocked by an empty flatbed truck. It took ten minutes at least and the help of several shopkeepers to back down the street and find another way out. The new route was blocked too. Another truck, this one stalled with a young sailor at the wheel. The only alternative was a narrow lane he'd never seen before.

The bumpy stone surface of the alternate *soi* had the pigs squeeling like demons as they bounced along in the back. Instead of delivering him out into the evening traffic on New Road, the detour lead him deeper into the closing core of slums where there was little room to maneuver and on crossing alleyway wide enough to follow. The crumbling walls seemed to lean in overhead, almost blocking the fading light from the sky.

The district looked abandoned this late in the day. A couple of half-naked kids were playing in the rubble. A lone skinny dog got in a few barks as the jeep passed but then there was no sign of life but the stink of sun-baked urine and some forgotten movie posters pasted up in bunches.

Somsak's anger was giving way to anxiety. He had a lot of money tied up in his cargo and he had less than an hour to get them out of there and across town before the butchers shut down their warehouse. The *soi* kept closing in, he felt trapped.

Then more sailors. A gang of them ambling along ahead of him. There were five or six of them dressed in white with nothing in particular on their mind, it seemed, and no place they needed to be. They seemed friendly enough, maybe they knew a quicker way out of here.

Somsak pulled up and beeped the horn but as the sailors turned he found that there was something about them he didn't like. It might have been their nervousness or the furtive way they had of looking back over their shoulders. They were up to something, that was sure. Then it came to Somsak what they were up to. The pigs. They were after his pigs. His eyes grew cold as he weighed his chances, he was a ruthless man when he had to be. There was no room to turn around and only inches between the fenders and the high distempered walls.

He eased the shift into first gear and waited while the sailors approached. Sure enough, another nervous look around, a traded signal between them, and suddenly they were rushing him.

The first two were already clambering over the fenders when Somsak revved the engine and popped the clutch. The jeep, tail-heavy with its noisy cargo, reared as it lunged forward and threw the first sailor against the windscreen and over the side where the skidding flank of the jeep smashed him against the wall. His cry, if he'd managed one, couldn't be heard above the squealing pigs.

The second sailor lost his balance when his jump landed him on the rearing hood and he was flipped over into the crates, where, grabbing at anything he could get hold of, he tore loose the rope that held the stack in place and sent the whole load tumbling to the bricks—pigs and straw and upended cages went flying everywhere. The sailors had botched it.

The remaining half-dozen, seeing the old man bearing down on them, turned on their heels and ran for it up the *soi,* yelling and pulling over some empty barrels behind them to slow him down. Then they were running from the noise of the jeep crashing through the steel barrels as much as from the jeep itself.

With his tires still screeching on the slippery brick and the blue smoke of burning rubber blowing out behind, Somsak kept his foot to the floor until he'd caught up with and run down one of his attackers, ker-lump, under the right front tire. Surprised by the sound and shocked by the violence of the brief action, Somsak hit the brakes and the other three jumped a loading dock and made their escape.

Some people will steal anything. Somsak was grim but pleased with himself. So, the old man still had some fight left in him after all. Then he made his mistake, he went back to see to his load. The *soi* was littered with stunned hogs and two of the sailors. He threw a couple of the empty basket cages back up onto the back and shouldered a full one into place, then he carefully retied the stack. He eyed an escapee grunting and snuffling away up the gutter but decided to cut his losses. Half his load was gone. This was going to cost him plenty.

Fifty feet farther up the *soi* the walls opened onto a round loading plaza for an abandoned manufacturing complex and there Somsak found that his attackers had reorganized.

Janus was waiting there, too, watching from the top of a concrete stoop but Somsak wasn't afraid of him either. He swung right and entered the plaza with the idea of using the open space for a high-speed turnaround so he could head back down the alley without stopping, but three of the sailors were waiting behind the first corner and jumped him before he could get up the speed to outrun them.

They swarmed over the jeep, wrestling with him clumsily, kicking and punching, trying to pry him from the seat. One of them grabbed him around the face but let go with a howl when Somsak bit off a piece of his thumb. The old man held the wheel with both hands, it was the only thing he had to hold onto. He gripped it with all the strength that he could muster while his attackers fought to tear him free. The sinews of his wrists strained at his skin like packing cords, the knuckles of his fists were white from his grip.

The sailors pulled and tore and beat him around the face, they'd have him out of his seat in another moment if he didn't do something. So he swerved unexpectedly and drove the jeep flat into a wall.

The crash honeycombed the windshield and cut up the face of one of the attackers, who was thrown into it. Another smacked his head against the steel dashboard, rebounded limply back into the seat, and stayed there. But there was still one left and he had Somsak under the armpit, yanking and hauling at him while Somsak held onto the wheel for dear life. He was beginning to slip, his foot had to stretch for the gas pedal and the clutch. He shook and elbowed and fought but he lost. The engine stalled.

It was Janus who put an end to the fiasco. He jumped down from his perch and motioned the sailor to let go and give him room. Janus's eyes glittered wetly as he drew out his blackjack and tickled the old man with it. Somsak stared back at him fearlessly while Janus tapped the old man's fingers one at a time and smiled. Then he went to work pounding at the knobby old hands, smashing at them until there was no way they would hang onto anything again.

Somsak was supposed to have joined them but he was very late and Kiri was worried. It was not like him to forget a promise, especially on the night of the *Visakha Puja* with the glittering festivities at all of the temples in town. It was the birthday of the Buddha, and the day of his enlightenment and death. It was the festival of lights, with thousands of tiny candles burning in long lines around the wats and the holiday crowds with their smells and noise.

She was glad the Kid had come along. She often took him to one or another of the city's hundreds of holy places. The atmosphere was so very different there, a peaceful and godly place with tinkling wind chimes and orange-robed monks in little hushed groups. It calmed him as none of his medicines could.

He was rarely as happy as he seemed on this night. His eyes were bright with wonder as he held her hand and pointed out the colorful sights and curious faces in the crowd, the fireworks and bright lights.

He was laughing at Kiri's little jokes and telling her stories about Christmas and his childhood with Peter. He knew she liked to hear about him. They walked about in the bright bazaar eating snacks that took his fancy from the stands and pushcarts set up outside the great western gate.

"What's that, a charm?" he asked, holding up a crude little amulet from the shining array laid out on the ground before a smiling peddler. "Maybe we could give it to Peter. He could hang it over his computer, maybe. Just for luck."

"Just for luck," she repeated to herself, hugging his arm as they moved on. It was good to see him enjoying himself away from Dog Alley, away from his mysterious, gloomy preoccupation with the past, but she had reasons of her own for being here, too.

Life is a mysterious affair for the Siamese, rich and deep in so many ways and yet with few certainties to rely upon when they are needed. There are not many who can grasp the subtleties of Buddhism enough to enjoy the rewards and sustenance that religion gives to daily life, so over the years the void has filled with spirits and demons and forces that a person can appeal to with veneration and sacrifice.

Kiri had spent much of the afternoon on the temple grounds with the Kid—several hours at least in one of the graceful peaked *bots* of a monastery, praying with a small crowd in front of the rows of Buddha images lined up along one end of an alcove. Kiri was disturbed by a growing spectrum of doubts. Something about her life seemed to be slipping from her grasp and today was the day to pray for the magic that would bring it back.

The Kid never left her side, repeating what prayers to his own God that he could remember and trying impossibly to look inconspicuous as he knelt beside her in the midst of the crowd of much smaller supplicants.

As evening settled in they joined the throng of worshipers

outside the wat's pillared reliquary listening to the drone of the *Pali* chanting. This was Kiri's festival, the one most auspicious to her karma, an astrologer had once assured her. The correct day, then, for her to follow through on a task she had set for herself weeks ago. It was time to replace the broken-down little spirit house in the courtyard.

It was not a simple task. It required great care and the proper alignment of omens and the stars to attract the favor of the household spirits that dwelt there. There would have to be a small *puja,* a secular ceremony of welcome to ensure the harmony of the change and the right medium to perform it.

She had heard of just such a medium, an old Yeo woman from the Black Thai regions of the far north who sold potions and herbal medicines from a makeshift tent outside the wall. Kiri was to see her there before the procession of the relic began and so, with the Kid in tow, she pushed through the growing crowds and made her way out to where the fortune tellers and sellers of charms and talismans sat.

The smells of hot cooking oil and hissing kerosene lamps blended strangely with the heavy incense smoke drifting on the air from inside. There were tents laid out like offices with framed charts and instruments of chance. There were a number of mediums there counseling clients from all walks of life. They generally wore street clothes or even business suits. Some had their diplomas and endorsements on exhibit beside their astrological charts and diagrams.

The Yeo woman had none of these things. Her tent was gloomy, dank, and filled with discolored glass jars containing mysterious objects and sheaves of dried plants and skins curing from strings overhead. She wore her tribal costume: a heavy black turban, brocade skirt, and a dark red sash around her tiny waist. There were wispy white hairs growing from her chin and her voice crackled like a witch's.

The medium took Kiri's smooth hand and held it between her own and searched her eyes as if she could see something there in the dim lamplight. The Kid sat in a corner a little away from them, gaping around at the grotesque specimens on display. She spoke in a dialect of the north, one that Kiri remembered from her childhood.

"So, you have come at last, little one," she said, as if she had known her all along. "Oh, but you have waited so long. Already it may be too late."

"It is about . . ."

"A man. Yes, I can see this." Her Thai was modified by the harsh singsong of her northern dialect. "He is *farang*, like the giant, here."

"His brother, yes. But not like him."

"But he is. They are bound together, these two *farang*, just as they bind you." The Kid fidgeted under the old woman's quizzical gaze. "You share their fate, my pretty, and their terrible fortune."

"Terrible . . ."

"There is only misery from these two."

"That is silly," Kiri told her. "The Kid is my friend."

"And his brother your lover, is it?"

"No more of this," Kiri said firmly. "I am here to engage a medium to install a new spirit house. Nothing more."

"It is no wonder the spirits have fled, for in the end you must flee, too."

"What are you saying?" Kiri was taken aback by this unsolicited warning. "I will do nothing of the kind."

"Oh, you must," the old woman told her, caressing her hand more tenderly now. She waited for a long moment as if she wasn't sure whether to go on. At last she did. "For in the end you will find only betrayal and death."

"Stop it!" Kiri cried. "There are other mediums I can deal with, I do not need a witch like you!" She jumped to her feet and the Kid, taken by surprise, rose with her.

"What's the matter, Kiri? What'd she say?" Kiri didn't answer, all she could think of was to be away from this hag. In her hurry she pushed past him toward the back flap of the tent, knocking over a jar of filthy liquid that shattered on the hard dirt floor.

"Kiri, wait!" But before the Kid could stop her she was gone. He turned to the Yeo woman. "What did you say to her, old woman? What did you tell her?"

The medium said nothing for a moment. Her hostility for the big young foreigner was plain. But abruptly she smiled, baring a broken row of yellow teeth, and in English she said, "Fifty baht, mistah."

It was some time before Kiri came to herself again. Breathless and exhausted, sickened by the dense sweet smell of incense
and the milling crowd inside the fortresslike temple grounds, she
paused to try to collect her jumbled thoughts and spotted, near
the heavy, inlaid double doors of the westernmost entrance, a
woman with pale blond hair who had entered with the worshipers
and made her way past the tall *chedri* towers near the courtyard.
It was that woman. David's woman. This woman had been ungra-
cious to her, she had upset Peter and stirred feelings in Kiri's
heart that she had never had to deal with before . . . but no. This
was not the time to think ill of a guest. Kiri tempered her feelings.
Perhaps the bitterness of their first meeting had been caused by
the heat of the moment. There must be some goodness to her,
after all she was David's girl and Kiri liked David.

She was calmer now. Away from that old woman she'd been
able to breathe again and see how foolish it all had been. She had
better go back and find the Kid, but first—there was that woman.
Perhaps Kiri had been hasty, perhaps she should set aside their
differences. Surely ending their animosity would help bring order
to things once again—so she followed after her, trying to catch
up in the crowd. After all it was an auspicious night to make
amends and to do so would earn merit.

Her heart quickened, she felt better already. This was indeed
her special festival. The crowd of worshipers thickened near the
central wat and Kiri had trouble making headway. She bumped
into a man with a candle and had to stop to apologize. For a
moment she was night-blinded by the flickering flame but then
she saw the woman just as she rounded the corner of another
pavillion.

"Miss? Oh, Miss Alice?" But the rhythmic chant around her
drowned her out. There was an excited murmur as a formation
of monks in saffron robes appeared parading a favorite relic to be
venerated and the crowd began closing in on itself. It was too
packed to get through so Kiri gathered her dress and trotted
around the crowd's perimeter until she could see the foreign
woman again. "Miss . . . ?"

Alice was waving to someone, she was not here alone after
all. Kiri stopped dead. The throng parted like water and flowed
around her. The reflected torchlight from the golden tiles of the

nearest shrine cast the figure in silhouette but she could make out quite clearly the long tied-back hair and the familiar angular posture. Her heart froze in her breast. It was Peter.

For years the Municipal Planning Commission had been talking about filling in the *klong* that runs down the center of Sathorn North Road and paving it over. There was hardly any water traffic these days because with all the talk about filling it in nobody bothered to dredge out the accumulating silt and water weeds— and because of all the silt and water weeds there was a lot of talk about filling it in.

The hour was late and the road running along either side looked empty. Its streetlights were shaded by the leaves of the tall trees and had little light to spare for the pavement below. The chirping of the crickets fell in and out of unison like the breathing of lovers in their sleep. It seemed to be a quiet street but there was a lot going on.

First, a solitary figure showed itself beneath the streetlight far up the street, then was lost in the dark again.

Then there was a small commotion in the undergrowth across from the mouth of Dog Alley, where a very skinny boy, the younger of the Cambodians, poked his head out of cover for a better look at the figure coming their way from up the road and then ducked out of sight again.

There was someone else there, too, an older man with a cruel look about him that set him apart from the other two. He knelt in the dry crackling reeds and watched for the figure to reappear. When it didn't he signaled the boy, who left his cover dragging a heavy Chi/Com radio pack with an extended antenna that kept catching in the weeds.

While they worked to free it the ghostly figure appeared again, staggering through another circle of light and then was gone again, this time without the others noticing. When at last they started across the road they were stopped, this time by the sound of singing from down on the waterway. They were looking around for the source of the merriment when the figure appeared once more under the next streetlight. It was the old man who drove the jeep. Quickly they turned the bulky radio around by the strap of its canvas pack and dragged it back under cover.

Somsak's face was ashen, his eyes fixed, and his mouth agape

as if he was astonished by his own suffering. He was holding his
mangled hands to his chest like a pair of precious red mittens,
testing every movement he made as if to measure its cost in pain.
The singing from up the road grew more raucous as he turned
into Dog Alley and disappeared.

Kiri never said anything about her discovery to the Kid. She
found him waiting by the western gate and they got a ride back
to Dog Alley in a tuk-tuk. She'd given him his medicine and then
gone outside to sit by herself in the moonlit courtyard to wait for
her lover's return. She was still there hours later, shivering in the
chilly night air, when she heard a noise at the latch. Thinking it
was Peter, she ran to the gate, opened it, and recoiled from the
sight that greeted her there.

"*Khun* Somsak!" Kiri cried as he sank to his knees and folded
into the dust.

"Oh, my goodness. Oh my . . . *Kid!* Come quickly, it is Mistah
Somsak!"

The singing was coming from one of the skiffs being punted
through the weeds down on Klong Sathorn.

> "You're goin' home in a body bag
> doo-da, doo-da"

"Jake . . ."

> "You're goin' home in a body bag . . ."

"C'mon, Jake. Knock it off."

> "Oh, doo-da day."

"Sit down, Jake. You're gonna sink us," Sloane said from the
front of the first boat. "I thought you were gonna lay off those
screwballs. They always mess you up like this."

"Remorse's more fun than regret," Jake replied. " 'N besides, whose idea was it to cheer things up around here? Too bad
Pete couldn't join us."

"I told you, I don't need to be cheered up."

"Nonsense. Everybody needs cheering up. Here, just try one of these little babies."

"Sit down, Jake."

The skiffs were pulling up in front of Dog Alley, and the Cambodians, caught between the waterway and the open road, broke from cover and darted across the road into the dark mouth of the *soi*. The younger, too small for the job, had to skuttle along sideways and drag the heavy radio along after him.

There was a lot of banging around when the boat was shoved in to shore and then a lot of pidgin bargaining with the boatman while the other boat went poling past them on its way to the river.

"See ya,' numb-nuts." It was Clyde and some others from Yankee Daniel's, laughing and waving as Sloane struggled to get Jake out of the boat and onto the shore without them both ending up in the canal.

"Yeah, sure."

Sloane had to keep a hold on Jake as they stumbled out of the boat to stop him from falling backwards into the water. The boatman was glad to be rid of them and poled off rapidly as soon as they were safely on shore.

"Now, remember, Jake. No more of those screwballs. I don't want any of that stuff you do when you're doing dope."

But by the time he got him up onto the road Jake had found something in his pocket and furtively stuffed it into his mouth. It made him laugh.

"Hch, heh, heh."

"C'mon, old buddy." Sloane took him by the arm and aimed him into the alley. "Up here where I can keep an eye on you."

"You can't put me on point," Jake protested. "I'm noncombatant."

Once into the darkness Jake grew quiet and they became aware of the scraping noise made by the two ahead of them dragging their field radio over the loose gravel.

"There's s-somebody else in here," Jake whispered. The screwballs had him sweating and shivering at the same time.

They stopped and so did the noise. The Cambodians had come to the end of Voss's fence, where the dim house lights of the neighbors lent a little more light to the lane that crossed before them. The elder of the two tried a step and the younger bumped into him. The elder shushed him, turned, and with his very next step walked smack into the Kid.

The Kid was carrying poor Somsak in his arms, heading for the road to get him to help. God knows what the Cambodians thought. The elder made a strangling noise and dived for the hole in the base of the fence across the *soi* while the younger pivoted around on the strap to his radio pack and tried to flee with it back to the road. But there was Jake Berman.

"Ambush!" Jake yelled and flattened himself against the fence.

"What the hell is goin' on?"

"What's that? What's he got?" Jake blubbered in his opiated panic while the Cambodian spun around again and went scrambling after his colleague through the same hole and out of sight. It took a few yanks at the strap before the antenna bent and the radio disappeared through the fence after him.

"It's a radio." Sloane laughed. "I'll be damned, he's got himself a field radio. Maybe he really is a spy."

"Not that," Jake pleaded. "Not *that*. My God, what's that the Kid's got?"

CHAPTER
10

It almost rained that night. A wave of saturated air had come and gone and left the bare wooden house smelling like an old dog. The blades of the ceiling fan spun slowly through the heavy air, chilling the sheen of perspiration that covered Sloane's back. He'd been lying there all night like that, not trying to sleep but drifting off now and then only to dream strange dreams full of blood and filth and that familiar primordial dread that follows men home from war.

It must have been the hospital, they always got to him. Or maybe the ride in the taxi they'd found to get Somsak to the Chulalongkorn Medical Center. Or the seawater smell of fresh blood. At the medical center they'd cut away Kiri's makeshift bandages, snipping away long ribbons of gauze caked with brown dried blood, snipping skin away from the splintered bones so white and wet . . .

"NAA-aah!" Sloane jerked himself upright in the bed and blinked around. His heart was beating like a trip-hammer. Slowly he lay back again and forced himself to take a couple of deep breaths. God, he thought, rubbing his eyes between his fingers, what's happening to things around here? What's happening to me?

There were strange sounds out in the courtyard and he lay in the gloom trying to collect them and sort them out. Voices. Baritone chanting, low monotonous rhythms that hung on the air as if the night itself had been given voice.

He swept back the mosquito netting and climbed wearily out of bed to burrow through the pile of dirty clothes on the chair for his shirt. There was a crumpled pack of cigarettes in the pocket.

He shook one out and lit up as he went to the window to watch for the dawn.

The early light was just beginning to sift through the dark leaves and the courtyard was carpeted with coiling vapors of ground fog. Jake was snoring just below the window, folded almost in half in the white string hammock where they'd left him a few hours earlier. Cat-cat was there, too, settled on its haunches on top of the fence watching Kiri and the Kid and a Chinese medium from the neighborhood, who were busy installing a new household shrine in the far corner of the courtyard.

The ceremony seemed makeshift and spur of the moment. The medium wore his crimson robe slung loosely around him and the dopey look of somebody who'd just been roused from his sleep. His hairline was a smudge on his shaven head. The new plaster spirit house was a poor choice, garish with gold and red enamels and too large for the slender pedestal on which it now rested. They must have burned the old one during the night while Sloane lay sweating in his restless sleep. The ashes were piled beside a hole in the shallow strip of garden.

The medium rang a little bell and yawned while the Kid swept the ashes into the hole with his hands and filled it with dirt.

There was a low table set out like an altar before the shrine and on it the medium's utensils: a tambourine, some bottles of colored powder, the bell, and a cheap brass sword. Fat green flies buzzed in lazy circles over bowls of sacrificial rice and oil. Heavy bundles of joss sticks smoldered all around, their cloying smoke mingling with the ground fog and the prayers. It was motionless and serene, like a scene from the bottom of a tropical fish tank.

Sloane sat on the sill watching it all while the depressing rush of the day's first cigarette pumped through him. A little spirit house, a handful of rice, and a few sticks of incense and even a lowly bar girl could hope to influence her fate. It was one of those times when he recognized what it cost him to be an outsider.

He stretched and scratched at the loose curls of hair at the nape of his neck and then got up to put on a pair of dirty jeans. The cigarette was still in his mouth so he made ridiculous faces trying to keep the smoke out of his eyes while he tucked himself in. Then he went downstairs to brew up some coffee.

Kiri looked up from her prayers when she heard the screen

door close and came to the cookhouse, where she found him scooping coffee into the pot.

"David. Please, not to drink coffee this morning," she said. She was wrapped tightly in a sarong that bound her small breasts to her torso. She seemed delicate and vulnerable.

"Hm?" Sloane looked up from the match he'd just struck to light the stove. "No coffee?"

"Tea," Kiri said. She was serious. "Special tea, it is part of the ritual."

"Yeah, what's all that about? A new spirit house?"

"I had to wake Mistah Chang," she said. "I tol' him it was an emergency."

"You mean because of Somsak?"

"Yes. And mo'."

"More?" He sniffed and rubbed his nose with his furry forearm. "Yeah, maybe so. There's a lot going on around here." He pumped up some gas into the stove, put the match to it, and ducked when it went off with a muffled "whump."

"Please, David." She touched the hand that held the pot and he set it down.

"Look, Kiri. I'm not up for that stuff this morning."

"No coffee," she insisted. "The tea is blessed and all who come must drink of it. Everyone. It is the act of hospitality called fo' in the ritual."

"Oh, all right." Tea in the morning, he grumbled to himself. No way to start the day.

"Tea," Kiri said. "And a portion rice with ghee."

"I'm really not very hungry."

"Neither were the others, also," she replied. "But they are willing to show their respectables."

"Others?" Sloane asked. "What others?" He followed her out through the screen door and into the breezeway, ducking under the cotton cords that held the hammock in which Jake lay trapped. Around the corner of the cookhouse he found the two he had least expected to find there, the Korean and Janus. Both were sitting uncomfortably in the planter's chairs with a cup of tea in one hand and a brass platter of lumpy rice in the other so that they had no way to partake of either.

Janus was apprehensive in the presence of the Kid, his large black eyes hardly strayed from him as he hunkered at the feet of the chanting medium, blissfully absorbed in every move of the ritual.

"I don't believe this," Sloane said. "What are these two doing here?"

"They have been here for a long time," Kiri said as she knelt beside the Kid.

"More than an hour," the Korean told him. "I did not want to miss Peter's return."

As if on cue there were footsteps on the gravel out in the alley and Voss swung the gate open. He stopped where he was when he saw what awaited him inside. "What the hell?"

"Petah?" Kiri jumped up and went running across the cement squares with that curious elliptical motion girls have to use when they're hampered by tight clothing. "Petah." She took his arm and held on as if he might change his mind and disappear again back into the foggy *soi*. "Petah? Where have you been? I have been so worried—I mean, poor Mistah Somsak . . ."

"I know. Chappy told me," Voss said without taking his eyes off the Korean. "I've just come from the hospital. What the hell is goin' on here, anyhow?"

"Shhh," Kiri said. "Do not interrup'. You see? A new spirit house?"

"Yeah? And what's he doin' here?" Voss shook Kiri off and crossed the courtyard, leaving a wake in the fading vapors as he made for the Korean.

"Now, Petah, be good," Kiri said, catching up. "Hospitality is required . . ."

Voss never took his eyes off the Korean. "Hospitality? Are you nuts? He's the one who beat up on Somsak. He's the one who mashed his hands and left him for dead, him and his faggot thug."

"Petah, please." Kiri wouldn't be brushed aside again. "This *puja* must be done with best correctness."

"Tell her." Voss was like a terrier on a leash, emboldened by the leash that held him back. "Tell her what you did to an old man who never did nothin' to you. Right? And then we'll see about all that 'correctness' crap."

"Him?" Sloane was suddenly wide awake. "He did that to Somsak?"

"Somsak was conscious when I got to the hospital," Voss told him without taking his eyes off the Korean. "He said it was him. Janus. 'The Snake,' he calls him. He said the Snake beat him up and took his pigs."

"Please," Kiri said, trying to quiet them. "Please. This shouting . . . you will spoil everything." The Kid saw that Kiri was upset. His face soured and he stood up slowly just in case. The medium ignored the commotion. He was on his knees, immersed in his own reality, in the ritual, the chanting, and the little bell.

"Is that true?" Sloane demanded. "Janus did it?"

"Of course he did it. Who else?"

"And what if he did?" said the Korean.

"What if he did!" Voss demanded. "So what're y'bringin' him around here for? Showin' him off, is that it? Or maybe y'want the Kid to have another crack at him?"

"Janus will start nothing if you do not. He may be crazy but he is not stupid."

"Yeah?" Sloane said. "Well, why don't you just get out'a here? Both of you. Then it won't matter what he is."

The Korean was about to respond when there was a loud snorting and sneezing from the hammock. Jake had awakened. He had opened his red-rimmed eyes and found himself facing his knees, a perspective that seemed to confuse him.

"Umph," he grunted, tipping dangerously in his net as he felt for the ground with a free hand. "Harumph." He had a foot wound up in the cotton netting and was in danger of capsizing as he tried to free himself.

"It is beyond my understanding"—the Korean looked around from his tall straw chair to see what Jake was up to—"why you have always found my presence offensive and yet find yourself quite at home with this . . . this degenerate . . ."

Jake paused in his struggles. "Only a degenerate knows life for what it truly is," he replied, mustering what dignity he could. "Cause and effect."

"You see?" the Korean said to Sloane. "And yet you persist in assuming that it is *I* who do not belong. That *I* am the one not good enough."

Jake held his hammock steady while he tried to focus on the Korean. "What are you doing here, anyhow?"

The Korean stopped and took a deep breath as if to regain his calm. "Penance, perhaps." He smiled his strained, humorless smile, his doughy face creasing heavily under the burden.

He held up his teacup to show his good intentions. "Not an admission of any particular guilt, mind you, but an explanation —and a warning. You see, what happened to your houseboy was not my doing. It was the upshot of a dangerous little game your friend Peter has been playing with his computers. And, of course, of Mr. Janus getting . . . well, getting out of hand—so to speak."

"Game!"

"Petah," Kiri warned. She was determined to salvage what she could of the ceremony.

"Janus was only to take away the jeep," the Korean explained, as coolly as possible. "You stole my yacht so I took the jeep. Not a very good exchange, perhaps, but I had to prove that you are not invulnerable. I had to show that I could get at you, and the gesture seems to have made its point."

"What?" Sloane pinched the cigarette from his dry lip. "Stole your what?"

"Please . . ." Kiri begged.

"What's he talking about, Pete?" Sloane asked. "Have you got something of his?"

"Hell, no."

"C'mon, Pete," Jake coaxed from the hammock. "C'mon, what is it?"

"I haven't got it. Immigration's got it."

"Got what, dammit!"

"His boat."

"His boat?"

"His goddam boat, that's what."

"That's right, my boat!" the Korean said, springing to his feet and spilling his tea. "My yacht! Surely you know of it? The big white trawler anchored across from the Thai/Tech docks. It will cost me a fortune in bribes to get it back again. I shall have to pay off Customs and then the Immigration authorities.

"Oh yes, Immigration is the worst. But do not worry, I shall have it back. I shall have everything back." He thrust the hand behind his back as if to keep it out of trouble. He was red in the face but making visible attempts to calm himself. Losing his temper in front of these round-eyes would do him no good at all. Let them see he was reasonable.

He sat down again and managed a sip of what was left in his

cup. "Mm, this tea is rather good, actually. Perhaps I should have this fellow over to bless some of mine."

" 'Immigration authorities'?" Sloane turned to Voss. "Immigration . . . that's that computer trick you were bragging about to Alice. That one with the Bureau of Registry. Jesus, you mean that's what this is all about?"

"Yes! Yes, of course, it was!" The Korean got up again. There was no hiding his anger now. "You got into the Bureau of Registry's machines, didn't you? Yes, I knew it was you as soon as I saw that damned Major What's-his-name . . ."

"Major Chapikorn?"

". . . out there giving orders. And do you know how they got away with it? Do you know what they called me? An 'illegal alien.' They said I was no better than one of the boat people." He was almost pop-eyed. *"Me,"* he said. "They treated me like *trash!* Threatened to send me to a refugee camp! Well, I couldn't just let Peter get away with it. I had to make my point somehow, isn't it?"

"Make your point?" Sloane said. *"Make your point!* You crippled an old man to make a point? His hands were crushed! One of them may have to come off. Don't give me any crap about 'making your point' and 'poor exchanges.' "

"He wouldn't let go," the Korean said. "So much in life depends on knowing when to let go. Isn't that right, Peter?"

"I wouldn't know."

"Well, thcn, let me tell you," he hissed. "The time is now. Do you understand me? I do not wish to go around having old men hurt. I do not wish to take jeeps or fight with your friends, it is all so . . . so demeaning. But the time has come, Peter. Time to let go. *Give me back my money.*"

A breath of air stirred the ground fog along thc alleyway, revealing the split in the fence across the way and for a moment the face behind it. A plank was slipped aside and the younger of the Cambodians peeked out. He was little more than a boy, a cool, unpretty young boy with the cheerless look of a child forced too soon into the mold of manhood. He wore loose shorts and a ratty yellow undershirt.

He'd been awakened in the early hours of the morning by the sounds of the *puja* and the aromatic smoke of the incense drifting on the fog. Strange goings-on, indeed. And now there was shouting—something was afoot and it was up to him to find out what.

Keeping an eye on the *farang*'s front gate, he turned himself sideways and wiggled out into the *soi*. The field radio crackled behind him but the rest of the alley was still asleep.

In the open he was vulnerable, so he looked about quickly and made a dash for it, bounding lightly up the path and around the corner. Giant fruit bats, hanging like fleshy sacks from the lower branches of a eucalyptus, stirred at the boy's passing but it was still an hour until daybreak and little else seemed awake.

He followed along the fence toward the noise of the angry exchange going on inside to where a rotting stump gave him the footing he needed to climb to the top of the fence. There he would have the cover of the banyan's drooping branches. But when he hoisted himself up he found himself facing Cat-cat who, until that moment, had been balancing comfortably on the top rail.

Cats don't like surprises. It spat and boxed the intruder smartly before abandoning its position for the nearby tree trunk. The boy almost lost his grip. He banged a knee but got an arm over the top, and was rubbing the scratch on his nose when he heard a sound behind him in the alley.

Then everything happened at once. The stump beneath him groaned and before he could look around somebody had him by his skinny legs and was shaking him loose from his post.

He tried to hold on but all he got was splinters under his nails and some nasty scratches down his chest. He fought and kicked and almost had a leg free when his hand slipped and back he went, tumbling through the prickly leaves into the arms of Major Chapikorn.

Kiri gave up trying to quiet them. The *puja* was ruined altogether, so she sat down miserably beside the medium, who went on about his business as if all the world were in perfect harmony.

"I *can't* get the money back, you fool." Voss was almost shouting. "It isn't even there anymore. Get it through your head, we lost the war. And even if I could get your money back I wouldn't do it. Not after this. What d'you think your threats can do to me? Huh? I ain't scared of you."

"No?" Sung Dai squinted at him. "And maybe you are just

too vain to see how vulnerable you really are. That could have been *you* driving the jeep."

"You wouldn't dare. You can't afford to have me hurt," Voss reminded him.

"But there was your houseboy, yes? And how about these others, eh? How about your friend Mr. Berman? Or Mr. Sloane, here. Maybe even Miss Kiri. You see? Your alliances are your weakness, Peter. Not your strength. They make you vulnerable to someone as determined as I."

"Yeah? And just what's that supposed to mean?"

"Hey, what the hell is all this?" Sloane demanded. "Alliances? Bargaining position? What's with you two, anyhow? Trying to pass this thing off like it was just a business deal? What kind of bargaining position is it that lets an animal like this come along and cripple a man? What's he got on you that you let him talk like he's a regular human being?"

"It was not my doing, you see?" The Korean turned to Sloane. "I acted in good faith but now I must apply persuasion by whatever means I may. And as for the question of what I 'have on him,' I would say that it was the other way around. Wouldn't you say that, Peter? All those tricks with all those computers . . ."

"He told me all about them."

"*All* about them? All those devious larcenies he has gotten himself involved in?"

"Yeah." Sloan tried to look like it didn't matter. Remembering his cup of tea, he swirled the dark sediment around the bottom and took a sip. "He told me."

"Just like he told you the part about how his brother was a killer?"

"Hey, leave the Kid out'a this," Voss told him. "This business has nothing to do with him."

". . . and of course he told you about the funds he stole from my company," the Korean cut him off, sharply.

"Stole . . ."

"That's right. *Stole.* Eleven and a half million right out of my accounts, intercepted somehow as they were being transferred from the Saigon branch of the Bank L'Indochine to the home office in Hong Kong. It took the best technical consultants in Tokyo more than six months to figure it out but I knew right away who was responsible."

"Yeah? Well, that's not the way I heard it." Sloane glanced at Jake, who had a cigarette lit by now and seemed to be tuning himself in to what was going on. "The way I heard it, you left your money in those transferrable funds yourself and now you've got the idea he can somehow get it back for you."

"Is that what he told you? Oh, no, Mr. Sloane. I am not a fool. I would hardly have risked leaving that sort of money in Saigon with the communists practically at the gates of the city, would I? Of course not. I would send it someplace safe. Someplace secret like a commercial code account in Hong Kong. Yes?"

"I suppose so," Sloane admitted.

"Of course I would. It would be safe from everyone there. Everyone, that is, except Peter Voss and his damned computers."

"I believe 'm," said Jake from his hammock. He'd gotten both feet safely to the ground by then, one on either side to keep him from capsizing, but the rest of him remained stuck the way it was. "I really do. Gentlemen, I believe we have wronged a great man and his lizard. I think it's time we righted this wrong and let him go out and smash up somebody else."

"I am not in the mood for this, Mr. Berman," the Korean warned.

"Anything to what he says, Pete?" Sloane was beginning to see how much more there was to the association of these two men than he could ever know. That in sharing their illicit past they were both still bound to it . . . and now, dammit, so was he. For just a moment Sloane saw his friend as a stranger. "Well, is there?"

"And what if there is," Voss said, turning away and waving off the whole assertion. "What can he do about it? What can anybody do about it now? Even if the money was still there y' couldn't get at it. Trang Van Thep is dead, the MAS Unit was the only way back into the Beach House complex and now it's gone, so that's that. What's this asshole gonna do to change the facts, man? What's he gonna do besides beat up on old men and swipe cars?"

"Oh, there is much more I can do, Peter. Much more, indeed." The Korean's eyes were blazing. "There is a way to get my money back and there is a way to make you do it." By now he had worked himself into such a state that even Janus was beginning to fidget uncomfortably. "I still have my deal with

General Giap's people in Hanoi and you will play your part or your houseboy's hands will be the least of the damage. Do you understand?"

"What's this . . . ?" Sloane tried to interrupt but the Korean paid no attention.

"I am through with these games," he continued. "I am through with your cleverness and devices. I am a crude man, you have said so yourself, and so I have crude ways."

"You can't threaten me."

"Think not?"

"What's this about a deal with Hanoi?" Sloane demanded. "What have you two been up to?"

"There are many deals to be made," the Korean replied. "And not just with Hanoi. Many with the most extraordinary people you can imagine. I know, you see, because I have made deals of one kind or another with almost everybody.

"You could say that is what this has been about, deals about money, deals about power, deals about people—it is all the same no matter what your friend might like to pretend. Each feeding off the other. Peter thinks it's only money. He thinks he can separate one from another, but he can't and that's his weak point —and that is where I can hurt him." He was sweating heavily, swabbing his face with his big white cloth.

"What can I do, Peter?" he asked, puffing himself up like the big bad wolf. "Well, first, I can take away your toys."

"The jeep?" Voss gave a short laugh.

"First your toys and then all of this!" the Korean shouted, waving his free hand to indicate the whole of the compound. And, as if he could think of nothing else to illustrate his fury, he gave the table beside the chanting medium a kick. The leg buckled under and the table collapsed, sending the ceremonial accoutrements, sword, teapot, bowls of rice, all tumbling to the ground.

"Aw, now hold on."

The medium looked up from his prayer.

"I can isolate him." The Korean was pleased with this unexpectedly dramatic spectacle so he went on to scatter the nearest bundles of smoldering joss sticks with his foot. "I can take away everything he uses to carry out his bloody tricks."

"Stop it!" Kiri cried. "Stop it, you."

"Hey!" said the Kid.

The Korean paused, looking around for something else to do. "And . . ." He threw down his teacup, snatched the brass bell from the hand of the cowering medium, and threw it awkwardly at the little peaked spirit house. He missed and it hit the wooden fence behind with a disappointing thud. "And every*body*, too. Understand?"

"I understan' okay." It was the final straw for poor Kiri. "I understand you a crazy-man."

Janus scowled and took a step in her direction but the Kid was there, kicking the table out of his way and backing him up against the fence. The gentle ceremony had dissolved into a farce. There was pushing and shoving and threats from both sides and Jake was grunting and cursing and flopping around in his hammock like a carp caught in a net.

The medium had to scurry out from underfoot and as soon as he was free he gathered up his robe and fled to the gate. He didn't escape, though. The gate banged open and there was Chappy.

"What is happening here?"

Chappy was all-confident, the instant master of the scene, like a hall monitor catching some of his lower school boys at their pranks. He stood like a rock, chest out, feet apart. His uniform was sharply creased and his free hand rested on the flap of his holster while the other held the Cambodian boy around the neck.

"Hi, Chappy. What'cha got?"

"Hi, Kid."

The Kid liked Chappy so the distraction made him lose track of what had just been happening. In fact, everybody broke off the confrontation in the face of Chappy's authority.

"What is happening here, eh?"

"Uh." Voss stuck his hands into his back pockets and let his shoulders slump nonchalantly. "Nothin' much, Chappy. What's happening with you?"

But the Korean was still simmering. He was used to buying and selling petty officials like this one. "I know you," he said.

"I know you, too," Chappy replied. "Yes, indeed, I know a great deal about you."

"What'cha got, Chappy?" the Kid repeated.

"Ah, yes." Chappy brightened. "My little prize. I caught him in the act this time. Oh, he was spying, all right. He was peeking over your fence and I caught him at it." The boy began squirming and Chappy gave him a good shaking to make him stop.

"This time I'm going to interrogate him, Peter. Did you know they have a radio back there? A Chi/Com field radio. Eh? What do you think of that? Maybe he will tell me what it is for, eh, young fellow? Maybe I can find out why he and his friends are so interested in you."

"He's not interested in . . ."

"Radio?" The Korean's demeanor had suddenly changed. All at once he was calm and inquisitive. He approached the frightened boy, appraising him as if he were livestock. "A field radio, did you say?" He took him by his hair and turned his face upward roughly for a better look. "He has a radio, eh?"

"Oh, no," Voss said. "Not you, too."

"C'mon, Sung Dai." Sloane took him by the arm. "Leave him alone . . ." But the Korean jerked loose.

"I do not like this, Peter," he said.

"Who cares what you like?"

"He's just a little boy," Jake said.

"Yes, yes." The boy made an ugly face and the Korean gave his hair a yank. "Dangerous little boys, most dangerous of the Khmer Rouge cadres. Pol Pot calls them his 'untainted eyes.' "

"Is everybody nuts around here?"

". . . Angkar's assassins."

"You're crazy," Sloane said. "This whole thing's crazy."

"Is it crazy of me to protect my investment?"

"What is he talking about, Peter?" Chappy asked. His catch puzzled him now that the Korean was interested in it, too.

"How the hell should I know?" Voss said.

"I think you do," the Korean told him. "Is it so surprising that the Angkar hierarchy would be interested in you and your magic weapons system with all the border skirmishes they are having with Vietnam? They are at war even now, you know. Raiding into the 'Parrot's Beak' in Vietnam just as they are raiding over the border here in Thailand. Use your head. If Hanoi and their Russians want you so much, wouldn't Angkar and their Khmer Rouge hear of it?"

"Yeah? And just who would they hear about it from?"

"Your weapons system is placed along their border with

Vietnam. I suggested a deal. I need options, Peter, and you are a very valuable commodity. Not to them, of course. It seems they just want you dead."

Kiri gasped and the argument faltered. Then Sloane said, "This is a madhouse. A goddam madhouse."

The Korean let the boy's head drop. "You know, Peter, for all your genius, in the world of dirty money you are still a child. I tell you, it is all part of the same package. All of it: money, politics, war. That is why you need me. That is why you have always needed me. You were never any good at judging that scale of risk."

"Bullshit."

"But it is true," the Korean said. "You see how it all mushrooms? You see how stealing is a much more dangerous business than you suspected? You don't have to believe me. Just let your lackey, here, interrogate this young fellow . . ."

"Lackey?" Chappy cocked an eyebrow. "I am an officer in Internal Security and *I* will say who is interrogated and who is not."

"We know what you are," the Korean told Chappy. "You are another of Peter's errand boys. Well, go ahead then. Take him away. Though what we can expect to learn through a petty buffoon like you . . ."

"What? Buffoon, did you say? And just who are you calling a petty buffoon, Mr. Park Sung Dai?"

"Forget it, Chappy," Voss said. "C'mon, let the boy go."

"You, that's who. Yes, I remember you," the Korean said. "You were on the boarding party. You took my boat away."

"Impounded," Chappy corrected. He was glaring at the Korean and as he sized him up he let the boy slip from under his arm. He held him easily by the scruff of the neck and let him struggle for a moment and then, quite on purpose, he let him go.

The Korean gasped. "You . . . !"

"All very legal, seizing your boat. Even if one is but an 'errand boy.' "

"See there, you silly ass," the Korean said. "Your man is getting away."

"He is, isn't he." Chappy didn't even watch as the boy scrambled over the nearest fence and disappeared. "Now, then, let me see your papers."

"You . . . you just let him go? Just like that? Must you do everything Peter tells you to do?"

"Petah is my friend." Chappy shrugged. "Your papers?"

Jake was chuckling loudly nearby, his weight in the hammock making the rafters squeak. The Korean shot him a look that could kill and began fishing for some ID to show.

"Nothing else?" Chappy asked, examining the scribbles and stamps in the Korean's British passport.

"All right, Peter," said the Korean. "Enough is enough. Call him off."

"Perhaps I am only a lackey and a buffoon," Chappy said as he flipped through the pages a second time. "But I know this passport is out of order. Where is your reentry stamp? Your visa extention?"

"Peter, call him off."

"What do you think I am, Petah's errand boy?" Chappy folded the passport into his breast pocket, unclipped the flap on his holster, and dropped his hand to the butt of his pistol. "Come with me," he said, indicating the gate with a flip of his thumb.

"What?"

"Your papers are not in order," Chappy said without a hint of irony in his voice. He nodded toward Janus. "And neither are his. We will go back to the Security Compound, I think. And there maybe you will learn how much trouble a 'buffoon' can make for you."

Jake's laughter rattled the tin roofing over the breezeway and followed Chappy and his prisoners down the *soi*.

CHAPTER
11

"Wait a minute, Pete."

Traffic was already thickening out on Sathorn North. A battered taxi was pulled up under the tree in front of the Indonesian Counsulate. The driver was still asleep, his sandaled feet sticking out of the open window, his arms folded peacefully in front of him.

Sloane had to skip a few paces to catch up. "Hold on. We've got to talk."

"Can't," Voss said, sidestepping a young girl on her way to the canal with a bare-bottomed baby on her hip. "Gotta get to the office. Gotta figure something out."

"We can talk on the way," Sloane told him and gave the snoozing taxi driver a shake.

"Look, some other time," Voss said. "Okay?"

Sloane grasped the rear door by the window frame so that his arm blocked Voss's way. "Now."

"Hey, you guys . . ." Jake had had a hard time catching up and when he had he slumped heavily against a fender, panting for a moment before going on. "Okay . . ." He was swabbing his sweaty face with his sleeve, his jacket was already soaked through. "Okay, let's have it, Pete. What have you got your hooks into this time?"

"Look, you two," Voss said. "This is between me and Park Sung Dai. Personal, y'know what I mean?"

"Personal?"

"Right. And anyhow there isn't enough time to explain. I've got to figure out my next move." He made another try for the backseat of the taxi but Sloane stood his ground.

"You've taken casualties," he reminded him. "A Vietnamese refugee and an old man who had no part in this scheme of yours. I don't call that 'personal.' "

Voss hesitated. He turned and sighted along the line of passing cars as if looking for another cab. There were none and when he turned back again he seemed to have deflated slightly.

"Yeah," he said. "Yeah, I guess you're right." He found himself a place on the fender beside Jake, and crossed his arms over the Santana logo on his T-shirt.

"Okay. So go ahead. What do you want to know?"

"First I want to know if it's true," Sloane said. "Is it?"

"Is what true?"

"What the Korean said. Is it true you stole his money?"

"Hey. No problem, man," Voss said, plucking his sticky T-shirt free of his clammy skin. "No problem at all. Chappy can keep him tied up for days. Maybe weeks. That's all it takes, y'know; friends in high places. He can harass him, jail him, even expel him from the country. Park Sung Dai knows it, too. Did you see the look he gave us when Chappy marched him off?"

"I saw."

"Me, too," said Jake. "And I didn't like it."

"And whatever Chappy needs in the way of legalities I can arrange through the Internal Security data banks."

"I didn't ask if you could get away with it." Sloane told him, bluntly. "I asked if you did it."

"I can beat him on this," Voss said. "Honest."

"That's not the point," Jake told him.

"It's the only point that counts right now," Voss said angrily. "Now, y'want a ride? Fine. Otherwise get out of my way so I can get to work. There's probably a dozen ways out of this mess if you'll get off my case and let me figure them out."

Sloane traded glances with Jake as he let Voss past him into the cab. *"Bye Fong Thon,"* Voss told the driver and he gave him directions to the Thai/Tech office while the other two climbed in from either side.

The driver nodded sleepily, ground the gears, and pulled out into the path of an overloaded truck. Horns blared and brakes screeched and he grinned around at his passengers as if he enjoyed his first near miss of the day.

"C'mon, Pete," Jake said, settling uncomfortably into his

portion of the small seat. "Let's have the rest of it. And don't hand me any more of that 'personal' garbage."

"Yeah, Pete," Sloane added. "Maybe I missed something, back there, but it sounded to me like Sung Dai was threatening the lot of us"

"It won't come to that." He took a cigarette from the crushed pack in Sloane's shirt pocket and stuck it in his mouth.

". . . Chappy for sure. He's his clearest threat. Then there's Jake and me and God knows who else. That makes it our mess, too. All of it. Kiri, for God's sake. She's in this, too. Even the Kid . . ."

"Nobody's gonna hurt the Kid," Voss cut him off. "Not while I've got the tools to fight back. What d'ya think this is all about, anyhow? I gotta protect my brother, don't I? Y'know what it'll cost to get him the kind of help he needs and still keep him hidden? Switzerland, that's what it takes. And there's an institute in Buenos Aires with specialists. It'll cost a fortune but I'll do it, see. I'll take care of him the way he used to take care of me."

"That doesn't cut it, Pete."

"Look, I didn't make this mess, y'know. I didn't start the war. Y'want to bitch, go bitch at the military. Go bitch at the system. After what they did to the Kid I had a right."

"Oh, you had a right," Jake said. "Oh, well, then . . ."

"You're trying to make it sound like it's my fault. I mean, it wasn't me who left Trang Van Thep out there on the gulf. It wasn't me who beat up on old Somsak. All I did was fight back. And I'm gonna keep on fighting back, see? 'Cause I've still got an ace or two up my sleeve."

"Yeah?" Jake was not impressed.

"Yeah. Park Sung Dai'll never get the Kid or you guys or anything else, see? I'm tellin' you, I can beat him at this."

"Beat him?" Jake said. "Beat him, f'Christ's sake! You make it sound like some kind of a game."

"Look, Jake. Why don't you go back to your screwballs and your Mekong Whiskey and that endless book of yours and keep your nose out of things you can't understand, okay?"

"Hey, I don't have to take . . . !"

"Can it, you two." Sloane half-turned in his seat. "Let's skip this 'who beats who' stuff and get a few things straight for a change." He was going to get an answer this time or else. "I want to know what you're going to do about Sung Dai. I want to know why you don't just give him his money back."

"I told you, I don't have it. D'ya think I'd be living like this if I had his eleven and a half million? Hell, no, man. Use your head!" Voss took a deep breath as if to start again.

"Look. That money was our operating capital. In the black market you're only as good as the money you can move around quickly. Got it?

"Okay, but what's to keep Park Sung Dai from just running off with it? They're tranferrable funds, right? So what's to keep him from transferring them? . . . to Zurich, say. Or Hong Kong.

"So I had to take it out of his hands. After all, it was my money, too."

"What do you mean, take it out of his hands?" Sloane asked him.

"I used the access I had through the National Defense Network to insert a monitoring program into the Bank L'Indochine's computers. Any change in the stable state of the accounts would deflect them into different accounts where he couldn't get at them."

"What 'different accounts'? Where's the money now?"

"Yeah. Where's the money?" Jake demanded. His stomach was growling loudly enough to be heard above the road noise, his face was a cool shade of pale. Screwballs and booze always left him that way. "You took it and now you've got to give it back. That's the bottom line, isn't it?"

"No, it's not." Voss was plainly exasperated. "That's what I'm trying to tell you. Okay, so I deflected some of our funds. But that was just data, got it? Not real money at all. There's no cash buried in the backyard someplace, no safe full of jewels or . . . or bearer bonds ready to cash in. There was just a lot of data mixed in with all the rest. Credits and debits stuck away with all the rest in the Bank L'Indochine computers.

"There's nothing left of that now. I was too late to get to a terminal to transfer it out of the country in time. So what am I supposed to do about it?"

There was silence in the cab while the driver negotiated his charges skillfully into the flow of traffic down Rajdamnari. Then Jake said, "Bullshit."

"Oh, Christ." Voss threw up his hands. "Here we go again."

"Bullshit. I don't believe a word of it. What about you, Dave?"

"Hell, I don't know." Sloane was shaking his head, his eyes on the traffic ahead. "I guess I've got to believe him. After all, I don't understand this computer stuff."

"Nobody does," Jake said. "That's where they've got us. We're intimidated by the technocrats. We abdicate our moral judgments to them because we haven't the skills to fight back."

Voss sighed. "Jake, do we really need a lecture?"

"Not a lecture, just a few points to ponder." He was leaning forward, addressing Sloane as if Voss wasn't there. "I mean, why believe him this time? What's his track record? He had his fingers in everything dirty in that war, I don't care what his excuse is."

"That's not the point."

"No? What kind of excuses are we always getting from him, huh? What's the line he's always giving us?"

"You're not above takin' my handouts," Voss said bitterly.

"All we ever get is this bullshit about 'poor little boy genius, brutalized by a wicked war and forced against his will into the black market . . .'"

"Shut up, Jake. I'm warnin' you."

". . . where he made a fucking fortune and lived like a king while his machines went on with the slaughter. 'What could I do about it?' he says. 'I only did it for my poor brother.'"

"Listen, Jake . . ."

"I don't like it either," Sloane told Voss. "There's a lot you don't bother to tell us, like the way you never told me about how the Kid had killed somebody. I had a right to know what I was getting into, instead I end up feeling like I was tricked.

"And you should have told us about who really lost those transferable accounts. So what's next? What'll we find out next that you didn't bother to tell us? You can't explain this away because of your brother, and you can't chalk it up as some . . . some accident of war. You were just working on another one of your bigger-than-life computer scams with Park Sung Dai's money, that's what it all boils down to. And now we're all in a lot of trouble."

"I'm tellin' you, I can beat him at this."

"Tell that to Somsak," Jake said.

"Or Trang Van Thep."

"Hey, how'd I get to be the heavy in all this, huh? And who says it was even his money? Who do you think made that son of a bitch that eleven and a half million in the first place? *Me,* that's who."

"And which of you is responsible for the ones who get hurt along the way?" Jake demanded. "You can't have one without the other."

"Hey, I'm going to make it up to old Somsak. I mean it."

"Going to give him back his hands?"

"I'll set him up for life. I'll give him a government pension. I will. I can do it, the Civil Service payroll is completely computerized."

"Will you stop!" Jake shouted. "Pull over here, driver." And while the taxi worked its way out of the inside lane of traffic he rummaged through his pockets until he found a five baht note that he tossed into Voss's lap.

"What's this?"

"I'll pay you the rest later. I'll pay you everything later, just spare me all that wheeler-dealer double-talk. I'm tired of it. You're like a spoiled brat who thinks winning is just a matter of changing the rules."

"What d'ya mean 'change the rules'?" Voss protested as Jake struggled out of the car and picked his way into traffic. "There aren't any rules, dummy. There never were."

"I'll get out here, too," Sloane said as he shouldered open the door.

"Y'know what he wants? Do you have any idea what the Korean's gonna try to make me do?"

The driver saw a break in the line and pulled out into traffic again so Voss had to shout out the window at Sloane's retreating back. "He couldn't sell them the key—hey, listen to me, wise ass! —he couldn't sell them Trang Van Thep's MAS Unit so he sold them *me.*"

But by now Sloane was too far away to hear, hotfooting it across two lanes of traffic between a squad of light Hondas and a swaying blue motorbus bearing down on him with its crushing load of commuters on their way to work.

Jake kept a couple of rooms on the fourth floor of the Coronet Hotel, a decrepit antique that was slowly collapsing into the

Klong Sarasin Marsh. Getting there after leaving Voss in the taxi had taken an hour's walk and an undignified ride with an acquaintance in the back of a delivery scooter loaded with crates of iced prawn. He'd never learn. These grand gestures always worked out this way.

For appearance's sake he left the scooter on the broad parkway of Wireless Road and was walking the last block toward the marsh when he spotted Alice on the corner he was about to cross to.

She looked wonderful. Like a bouquet of flowers, fresh and full of life. Her dress was simple and yet it showed the fine, slim contours of her body. Jake stood bedazzled for a moment, she was every American girl he had ever lusted hopelessly after. She was sweet and real and yet as impossible as the dreams of his boyhood. She was hope itself, standing there on the corner just waiting for him to say hello.

Jake panicked. He looked around for a way out. What could he say? How could he let himself be seen in this condition?

"Jake?"

Too late. She'd seen him. He tried to brush the wrinkles out of his bush jacket.

"Jake, hello."

Jake grinned weakly and waved back. He tried to keep an air of inner calm as he crossed the road to greet her. Oh, God. He probably smelled like fish.

"Why, hello there." Should he shake her hand or something?

"I was just on my way to work," Alice said, taking his hand to give it a squeeze. "For heaven's sake, what brings you into this neck of the woods?"

Jake flushed. "I . . . I live . . ." And he pointed in the general direction of the Coronet.

"Oh?" Alice knew what things were like in that part of town. "What a coincidence, the People Project's offices are just over there. How about inviting me over to your place sometime?"

"Well," Jake began, avoiding her eyes.

"Oh, it's okay," she coaxed. "It can't be so bad, and I do need somebody to talk to."

"Well, sure. If you need somebody to talk to."

"Wonderful. Give me half an hour to file some reports and I'll be there."

"Half an hour?" There was so much to do. He'd never have the place straightened up in time. "Great. Just ask around for the Coronet Hotel. Everybody knows the place." And not daring to trust his luck any further he backed away and took his leave with a jaunty wave. Forgotten were the events of the past night and the angry words with Pete.

God, she's neat.

Jake made tea out of something that left an oil slick. He had it waiting (lukewarm by the time Alice got there) so there'd be no reason for her to see the condition of his kitchen.

He'd cleared the only chair in the room for her but she seemed content to roam around examining his books, repeating a familiar title when she found one, and pulling a volume out now and then from the rows and stacks and piles of books that swamped the room. She was also interested in the view from his shaky veranda.

"What's all that?" she asked.

Below was a network of spindly walkways and tin-roofed shacks balancing out over the bogs and stagnant pools of the marsh. There were lines strung with gaily colored laundry stretching in all directions and scores of chattering young women tending them. Vendors plied their wares along the walkways and children were playing and scuffling together everywhere. The hubbub that reached the high porch was like the jingling of bells.

"Who lives down there?" Alice asked.

"Mostly they're bar girls from the clubs over on New Petchaburi," Jake told her. "I only stay here for the view."

"Well, it's a very nice place," Alice assured him. "It's cozy."

There was a table with an old Smith Corona on it and boxes everywhere filled with typed sheets of paper. A rattan basket beside the table overflowed with crumpled paper and torn-up discards.

"I don't get many guests," Jake said.

"Of course not. It's sort of a study, isn't it?"

"You could say that, I guess."

"This is a place to work, not to entertain."

"Right," he agreed. She understood exactly. "That's right."

"Anyhow," Alice continued. "From what I hear Peter's place is where everybody congregates. I wonder why that is?"

"Lack of parental supervision," Jake suggested. "Breakdown of America's moral fiber . . ."

"No, I mean it, Jake. Why is he the center of things wherever he goes? Why do people find him so . . . so fascinating?"

"You're worried about your boyfriend, aren't you? You're afraid he's fallen under the wrong sort of influence. But Dave's not like that. Whatever's going on in his head he can work out for himself. Maybe the rest of us are a bunch of losers but not him. He's his own man."

Alice didn't seem to be listening. She spent a moment pressing idly on a typewriter key. In the quiet Jake was acutely aware of the noise of the flies buzzing around in the kitchen behind him.

"Do you remember that night at the Nailert Market?" she asked. "Remember how Peter came out of that crowd like he was a movie star or something? My first thought was that he was bigger than me, isn't that funny? That he was bigger than any of us and he was going to spoil our fun. Like the rest of us were a bunch of little kids or something. I don't know why, but it made me hate him."

"I know," Jake said. "You were terrific."

"I knew you'd understand." Alice smiled and Jake's knees almost buckled. "And even though I keep thinking maybe it wasn't fair . . . I mean, with his poor brother and all."

"It wasn't," Jake said. "He should have told Dave the whole story from the start or left him out of it. Left us all out of it, but that's not the way he operates. Pete uses people, that's all. He wrings them out whenever he needs something and then files them away until next time. I can't figure out why they put up with it."

"I don't know." Alice took a sip of her tea and immediately cleared a spot on the table to set it down. "There really is something fascinating about him. There's that intensity to him and yet that vulnerable little boy, all at the same time. He seems to be looking for help. Looking for somebody to guide that restless genius of his, don't you agree?"

"Agree? Well, I mean, sure I do."

"I knew you would."

"Lack of guidance is one of Pete's big problems—that and his bottomless well of rationalizations."

"Yes, he's really quite rational," said Alice, thinking she had agreed. "He studied with the Jesuits, you know."

Jake stifled a giggle just in time. "I rest my case."

"Oh, what's this?" She had been shuffling absently through some papers on the table and come across a tattered, yellowing title page that read: *The March Hare, The American Experience in Vietnam,* by J. Aaron Berman.

"Why, it's the book," Alice said. "It's the famous book I've heard so much about." And she began sorting through the pages for a part to read.

"*No!*" Jake reached out suddenly and snatched the few leaves of paper from her hands—and just as suddenly he regretted it. "I . . . I'm sorry," he stammered. "It's just that it's not finished yet."

"I know that, silly. I'd just be reading it for fun."

"I've never let anybody read it before." He was confused and embarrassed. Why hadn't he hidden it or something? "Well, actually nobody else ever wanted to read it before. It's embarrassing the way it is, I don't want anybody to see it until I've gotten it to make sense."

"I'm sorry, Jake." Alice touched his arm so that he'd look at her again. "I had no idea it would mean so much to you."

"No," Jake said. "Oh, no. I'm the one who should apologize. How could you know? Anyhow, it's not that it means so much, it's that it doesn't mean anything much at all."

"It doesn't mean anything to you?" Alice was puzzled.

"To me. Right. That's it," Jake said. "That's it exactly."

"What is?"

"It doesn't mean anything to me, not the way it is anyhow. I can't get at the . . . the real guts of it. I just flirt around the edges like every other dime-store historian. Everybody talks about strategies and American resolve, about politics and logistics, but that's not what the war was all about. I just know there was something fundamentally wrong with our view of the world that cost us all those lives and all that guilt. I know all that, but I just . . . I just can't seem to get a handle on what it is.

"See all this?" He started rifling through the manuscript as if he were looking for the answer in the text. "It just doesn't mean anything. Thousands of pages, years of work, and it might as well be paper towels. Go ahead, maybe you should read it. You'll see what I mean."

"Oh, now, Jake. I'm sure you're wrong about it. Why, David and Peter both have very high opinions of your work."

"Pete? Nah. Peter thinks I'm a drunk and a bum and for once

he's not far wrong. He keeps me around like those medieval courtesans who used to keep monkeys and dwarfs around to make themselves feel that much more superior."

"Oh?" Alice said. "And why do you stay around if you feel that way?"

"Because I need him." Jake's eyes met Alice's. Seeing such perfect blueness and such guileless interest in what he had to say led him to offer up ideas he'd never dared voice before.

"It's that genius of his," he told her. "I don't know what it means, but I know it's got him plugged into a world that moves faster than mine. Like he's tuned to some kind of essential wavelength that I've been missing."

"I know," said Alice. "He makes me feel that way, too."

"It's as if he's found a loophole in the laws of perception, a ruthless vantage point that gives him a clearer view of the world than the one the rest of us have. It's people like him, the technocrats, who have the real authority. They've sold us more than their machines, they've sold us their way of thinking. We've become suckers for the 'quick fix.' War? Hell, how can we lose when we've got all these . . . these fabulous toys?"

"Huh?"

"Sure." Jake's eyes glittered. This was terrific, just having her around to listen. With every word came another idea. "Because he was plugged right into it all. That's his genius. He's a product of his time just like the war was."

"You make it sound like he started the war," Alice said.

"He did."

"Oh, now, Jake . . ."

"Yes," Jake insisted, surprised by the thought even as he gave it utterance. "Yes, he did. Him and his kind. The Vosses of this world are the most dangerous of its creatures, you know. They're like packagers, not technicians. They can wrap up the most fabulously complex problems in pretty packages so they look all neat and tidy no matter how much junk is inside.

"They make war into the business of selling packages. A corporate army for the technological society, see? It's all getting mixed up. Public relations, newspeak, buzzwords. Let's run it up the flagpole and *make* 'em salute."

Jake's eyes were fierce and eager. He loved this new line of thought almost as much as he loved Alice.

"Y'know, that's not bad. Not bad at all. I could use that idea like a running theme throughout the book. Jesus! I could even base the whole thing on Pete."

"Jake . . . ?"

"Sure. By showing Pete's corruption within the system I'll have shown the corruption of the system itself. See what I mean? 'Garbage in, garbage out': 'kill ratios' and 'collateral damage'— y'know what 'collateral damage' is? That's when you bomb your friends."

"But what . . . ?"

"And how about 'circular error probabilities'? That's even better. That's when you bomb your friends on purpose. And then there's 'denying the enemy his population resources,' that's a great one! That's when you kill *everybody!*"

"But what's this got to do with Peter?" Alice was bewildered by his inspiration. "Really, Jake. Why single him out?"

"Because he *knew,* that's why," Jake said. "He understood the whole misbegotten blunder and he went along for what he could get out of it. He knew that all that doubletalk and all those gadgets we had to play with weren't winning the war, they were sucking us in deeper. Technology wasn't the answer after all, it was part of the trap."

The children of Dog Alley were bored with the Cambodians so they didn't bother with them much anymore. That left the elder of the two free to tinker with the field radio and the boy undisturbed at his post.

When the moon rose its light was cold and diffused in the hot, damp air so it was hard to make out any but the most familiar shapes outside the fence. There was nothing to see of the foreigner's compound from where he crouched but he didn't want to risk getting any closer. The major from Internal Security was in there again, he'd come earlier with the one called Peter, and the big one had opened the gate for them. There was no sign of the jeep nor of the injured servant.

The boy reported all this from his place at a split between the fence slats while the elder nodded glumly and fiddled with the dial of the missing field radio he couldn't get to work. There was no discussion about what the observations could mean in part because the organization of their cell did not permit opinions in the face of authority and in part because only by silence could the elder maintain the illusion that he understood anything at all about what was going on.

There had been no one else about for a long time and the boy was growing drowsy at his post when he heard the sound of light footsteps cautiously picking their way along the gravel. A shadow flickered past the split from which he watched. In the moment it took him to slide the plank back for a peek whatever had been out there was gone.

The evening meal was solemn. The table was set up in the courtyard, as usual, with kerosene flambeaux burning with low, sooty orange flames along the cookhouse wall. Kiri had cooked a batch of rice and spicy eel-like fish that tasted like shark because of the oil it was fried in. It was not very good. Chappy said it was, though, and he and the Kid ate heartily while the other two, Voss and Sloane, just went through the motions, toying with the food until it looked well used if not eaten.

There was an odd sort of disharmony to the night outside the compound just as there was inside among the friends. It all made Chappy very uncomfortable. He had the feeling that the two friends had had a falling-out but it was not his place to ask them about it. And Kiri; her fine features were tight and apprehensive. She was defensive with Peter, something Chappy had never seen in their easygoing relationship.

It was a good night for the Kid, though. He had an appetite like a horse, always a good sign.

Voss brought out a bottle of brandy and shared a few glasses with Chappy. Sloane wasn't drinking. He seemed to prefer the company of his thoughts to that of the others at the table and looked as if he might soon find an excuse to leave them, but he stayed.

Then, after a long period of silence with the soggy air muffling the sounds of the frogs and crickets out in the trees, he changed his mind about the brandy and poured himself one.

"We've got to talk, Pete," he said at last.

Chappy assumed this was a hint and, hoping that discussion would restore the amicability of the household, he excused himself diplomatically and took his brandy for a walk around the courtyard to look at the garden and Kiri's new spirit house.

"I've been thinking about the war a lot lately," Sloane began.

"I haven't done that for a while but now this one particular incident keeps popping up in my mind. Something that happened late in my second hitch, just before I closed out my contract with Air America." He was turning his glass absently in the fingers of his big hands. "An evening like this one. Hot, grubby—up near Dulong Pass. Did I ever tell you about that?"

Voss shook his head and sipped his drink silently.

"I had to pick up about fifty or so bodies. An ambush, I guess. Montagnards and a couple of American advisers all torn up and bloated from a couple of days in the heat. And I remember watching them bag them up and load them aboard and thinking that I had a hand in them dying like that. That by just being there I was helping things like that to happen.

"And I remember the stink, that strange sweet smell—that's how they look for the bodies a lot of times, did you know that? In deep undergrowth where they'd have trouble finding them they just wait a few days and then just go around sniffing them out.

"Anyhow, I guess that's what it finally took to get me out of the war, that stink. I must have smoked a hundred cigarettes that night and nothing helped. It stuck to the slats in the cargo bay, to the fabric of my clothes, to the inside of my nose . . . it seemed to permeate everything. It seemed to me to be what it had all come down to. What my life had become. No more 'honor and duty.' No more rationalizing, that's really what my work was all about. That smell. Know what I mean?"

Voss nodded.

"Good. Because, Pete, I've got to tell you; I'm beginning to smell that smell again."

"I understand," Voss assured him. "I really do, but this all rests on the Korean's back. He did it. We've got nothing to be guilty about."

"It doesn't work that way. You can pretend you're just playing some kind of computer games or just switching some money around but that's not what it's all about. I got to thinking that Park Sung Dai was right. It's all part of the same thing—power, money, and suffering. You can't traffic in one without the others."

"You sound like Crazy Alice."

"Yeah, maybe so. Maybe in our different ways we've come to similar conclusions for a change."

Voss shifted in his chair uncomfortably. "So you've come to a conclusion, have you?"

"It was there all the time. It was there on the face of that poor bastard we left to the pirates. It was in the eyes of a little girl in Alice's refugee camp, and it was right there in front of me in the emergency room of the Chulalonghorn Medical Center when the doctor was cutting the dressings from Somsak's battered hands."

Voss had set down his drink and was watching his friend apprehensively. "What are you saying, that you're quitting?"

"That's about it, old buddy. Sorry."

"Right when I need you the most you're going to just walk out on me?"

"No, of course not." Sloane leaned forward on his elbows, his lower face hidden behind the *v* of his hands. He was watching his perplexed friend sadly. "No, I'll stay until you set things straight with the Korean."

"Yeah? And just how am I supposed to 'set things straight'? D'ya think we can work out an installment plan? D'ya think he'll garnish my wages for the next thousand years? Hell, no. I'll tell you the deal he's got in mind. He's gonna make me go back."

"What?"

"I'm serious, man. He expects me to go back to Vietnam."

"But . . . but he can't do that."

"He's already made the deal, that's what I'm trying to tell you! He's made a deal with Hanoi and their COMECON Russian allies to have me reopen Beach House 7. They think I can just flip the right switch or something and *presto!* Then Hanoi will have the weapons activated along the Cambodian border and the Russians will have the technology to build a fancy computer complex just like it.

"That's crazy."

"That's the deal. And when I'm done we're all to rely on their good graces to hand over the Korean's money."

"And you?"

"What d'you think? Think they'll g'me a pension and a gold watch? Hell, no. They'll never let me out of there. Who else can run the damn thing?"

Sloane sat there for a moment in stunned silence, then he gave a low whistle. "God, Pete. What a mess."

*　*　*

On the other side of the courtyard Chappy was rotating slowly on his heels surveying the hazy night sky through a small clearing overhead. He had just taken a sip of his brandy and was about to return to the table when there was a suspicious sound from the other side of the fence; gravel scuffled underfoot and then a fence plank creaked slightly as if someone had tried to rest his weight against the fence and thought the better of it.

He stood still, listening, but he heard nothing more. He shrugged. Everybody was on edge that night, that's probably all it amounted to. Peter was right. Chappy was too suspicious sometimes—no. There it was again. Farther down the fence this time, near where the others were sitting.

Chappy feigned a casual air, sipping at his brandy as he traced the fence line back toward the breezeway and listened for some other giveaway. Yes, something behind the fence, just there; a shadow behind the crack between the planks. The young spy was back. Chappy followed beside him for a few steps, the sounds stopped when he stopped.

What to do? To say anything about a prowler was to risk more of Peter's jibes and perhaps upset the Kid. Perhaps it would be enough to just have a little look-see for himself. He sighed to himself. The burden of command, the call of duty. Major C. V. Chapikorn, Station Chief of National Security, Sector 11, always vigilant.

He returned to the table to set his brandy down and picked up the thick Malaysian cheroot he'd let go out earlier in the evening in deference to Kiri, who had been sitting downwind.

"If you will excuse me for a moment," he said to the others and without explaining any further he left them, sticking the cold cigar in his mouth as he strolled toward the gate. He peered over the top before opening it and then headed off down the alley, the gravel crunching softly underfoot.

He paused when he came to the spot in the fence where he'd seen the shadow pass. Nothing there now. So with even greater care he crept past it along the fence toward the corner.

He had just passed the place in the fence nearest the diners inside when he heard something rustling through the weeds up ahead. Chappy smiled to himself, all of his senses were alert and keen for the hunt. He had been prepared for moments like this by years of exacting training. Carefully he unhooked the flap of his holster and rested his palm on the grip of his revolver as he moved stealthily toward the spot from which the sound seemed to be coming.

He stopped long enough to note how the spot lined up with the table on the other side of the fence and then he crossed the moonlit *soi* in a half-crouch.

Once in the shadows he waited for his eyes to adjust again to the shadows of the scratchy sumac and the knee-high grasses. He wheeled in the darkness at the sound of something and smiled at his foolishness when an alley cat darted out of cover and ran off down a shallow culvert with its kinky tail flicking behind it like a flag.

The moonlight was dull because of the haze but enough to have him confused in the pitch black of the undergrowth. His eyes hadn't fully recovered when he heard footsteps, someone running lightly down the alley. Just a few steps, that was all, but it was enough for Chappy to tell that whoever it was was headed toward the *klong*.

He wiped his mouth with his hand, this hot pursuit business was nerve-racking. He set off after the runner, moving swiftly and surely back and forth across the *soi* and keeping to the shadows as best he could until he came to the footbridge that arched over the tributary canal.

The Cambodian boy was there, hiding in the muddy water beneath the footbridge and listening to the major's hoarse breathing while he waited for his next move. He would have to wait for many long minutes in cold water up to his chin for Chappy had elected to hold up there under a banyan tree just a few feet away. From there amid its airborne runners and vines he could look out on a hundred feet of peaceful scenery on either side.

The waterway was lined with drab little shanties on slender pilings. The footbridge was a jerry-built configuration of bamboo stilts and worn hardwood slats, the kind of footbridge that was better left simple since it would only have to be rebuilt after a few rainy seasons anyway. There were a couple of boats tied up to the uprights, squat little barges, for the peddlers that plied these smaller *klongs* often did so with their families under the tent in the stern.

Chappy held his breath and listened to the sounds around him but he heard only the crickets and katydids. A bat came crashing out of the branches above him but he paid no attention. He narrowed his eyes and watched, waiting for his quarry to make a mistake. He waited for half an hour but nothing stirred on either bank.

At last he stepped out from his cover. Perhaps he had been wrong, perhaps the ambient sounds of this wooded place had fooled him, maybe he'd wasted his chance chasing a ghost. Chappy squirmed at the thought of his foolishness and buckled the flap of his holster.

It was odd, though. He had to have come this way, any other and he'd have had to cross fences and private properties and that would surely have raised a row. Maybe a look from the other side would explain it, so Chappy walked down to the foot of the bridge. He tested his weight on a step, it was not a very steady span. Carefully he climbed the steep incline, pausing at its highest point to examine the shadows along the bank he had just left. The water reflected the bright night sky like a mirror.

Nothing.

He had started back, still watching the shore, when he felt the footbridge quiver beneath his feet. He turned suddenly and there was Janus with a heavy automatic pistol in his hand.

Beneath the bridge the Cambodian listened for some sign of what was going on but for a long moment neither man did anything. Total silence, only the night noises all around and the lapping of water at the pilings around the boy's hiding place. Chappy just stood there, stunned by this egregious turn of events. How could this have happened? This was a predicament one might expect of a recruit, not of a major in National Security.

What a fool he had been. Janus hadn't been running from him, he'd been drawing him here.

Janus smiled, he knew what Chappy must be thinking, and then he fired. Chappy was spun around against the rail where he could only watch as Janus casually approached for an easier shot. Ashamed to die so cheaply, Chappy summoned the strength to try for his gun so Janus fired again. This time the force of the heavy slug struck him full in the chest. He was punched back heavily against the bamboo rail, which split away under his

weight. Arms outstretched, his eyes full of surprise, Chappy toppled over the side and crashed through the canvas tent of the boat
below.

There must have been a woman inside the tent. She
screamed when the heavy body landed on her, rocking the boat
and pleading for help as she struggled to free herself of the dead
weight. There was a baby down there, too, maybe more than one
for the night was full of screaming as Janus, shivering with antici-
pation, stood at the broken rail and smiled.

Chappy lay with the tent crushed under him, a puddle of
blood spreading over his chest. Beneath him was the terrified
woman crying for help and the screaming baby. Janus lifted the
gun again and began firing down into the melee, round after
round until he was out of bullets and the crying had stopped.

The night held its breath. It would stay quiet for a few more
moments while the noise of the massacre registered on the sleeping neighbors all around.

The Korean was there, too; he'd been there all along. He
climbed out onto the bridge from the place where Janus had been
lying in wait. He was breathing hard and pressing his linen handkerchief to his mouth. Warily he crossed the bridge, his eyes wide
with dread as if some dark compulsion were drawing him toward
the broken rail for a look over the side at the carnage.

For a moment he just stood there, his handkerchief clamped
to his mouth. Chappy was full of holes, the canvas was full of
holes, and a small hand stuck out from under it. There was a
barely audible hissing sound and the slender barge began to
settle into the black water. The Korean had seen enough, he
turned away in disgust. Without a word he held out his hand.
Janus put the gun into it and followed him back into the shadows
beyond the shoreline.

The boy waited in the water until he was sure they were gone,
then he climbed out of the water as fast as he could and disappeared back into the trees before the first of the neighbors dared
come out to see what had happened.

Jake hadn't had to do any running since the closing days of
the war, when an unexpected firefight caught him in the open
with a camera crew. He hadn't been fit for it then and he wasn't
fit for it now. He was gasping and drenched with sweat by the time

he rounded the corner of the *soi* and came upon the scene at the footbridge.

Voss was standing off by himself. He'd had no time to get a shirt on and his skin was colorless from shock. He watched expressionless while Sloane waded around in the water below, up to his waist in the canal, with a couple of grim policemen trying to free a woman's body from the sunken barge. Her eyes were open, that was the worst part. Her head hung back loosely as the men in the water hauled at her so that she seemed to be staring up at Voss. He couldn't take his eyes off her.

It was early morning and the first rays of the sun were just beginning to penetrate the trees. Chappy's corpse lay on the hard dirt bank beside that of a baby. Neither had been covered yet.

"Oh, God," Jake moaned as he knelt beside the bodies. "Oh, my God, Pete. Look at him. And a baby, for Christ's sake!"

Voss stood like a man carved out of wood. His jaw was clenched and his mouth pinched like a child's sucking a bitter pill. His veined hands hung limply at his side and his feet were planted in the mud as if he'd grown there. His eyes were damp and showed the nausea and horror he was struggling with. He seemed unable to help, only to watch as Sloane tugged at the arm of the dead woman so that one of the policemen could rip away the canvas in which she was tangled.

A uniformed officer behind Voss was reading back the brief statement he had just given from a form fastened on a clipboard. When he was finished Voss nodded and added his signature to the bottom. The policeman thanked him brusquely and went back to directing his men at their grim task.

Voss cleared his throat. "He says whoever did it blew the bottom full of holes," he said to Sloane. "That's why it sank."

Sloane looked up from his efforts. "What do you mean, 'whoever' did it?"

"Yeah." Jake was fighting back tears. He took off his jacket and used it to cover the child's little body. "Yeah, we know goddam well who did it, don't we? The question is what are you going to do about it, Pete?"

The body of the woman had come loose from the weight of the sunken canvas and Sloane came slogging out of the muddy water leaving the rest to the police, who slid her up onto the muddy embankment while the neighbors closed in. They were clucking and whispering among themselves and answering questions put to them by the policeman taking the notes. Sloane paused to watch as blankets were finally thrown over the bodies and a neighbor gave Jake back his jacket.

"Say something," Jake demanded when Sloane stood dripping beside him. Both were looking at Voss. "What are you gonna do, man? Somehow you've got to give that son of a bitch what he wants."

"He's right, Pete," Sloane said. "There must be something you can do."

Voss squinted at the opposite bank. "Christ." He seemed to be talking to himself. "I never thought . . . How could he do something like this? Even Park Sung Dai. What kind of an animal . . . ?" He was shaking his head, his eyes fixed on the bundled-up bodies as if he were in a daze. "Who'd have thought he could ever do something like this?"

Finally he looked away, but he still avoided the eyes of his two friends. "I guess I've gotta tell you guys now," he began. "Actually there is a chance to stop all of this."

"Yeah?" Jake regarded him suspiciously. "You just now thought of it?"

"No. I'll admit it. It's an ace I've had up my sleeve all along. I guess now's the time to play it."

"You're going to go back to Vietnam?" Sloane asked. "Back to Beach House 7?"

"I don't have to. I can do it from here."

"Do what?"

Voss took a small pad from his back pocket and began figuring on it while he explained. "Beach House 7's communications linkup with the outside world was through its own microwave transceiver, but there was another way, too. The National Defense Network had a transceiver of its own in Saigon. I used it all the time when I needed a spare line.

"So, if one is shut off to us without Trang Van Thep's key module maybe I can get the Korean to use his connections in the Hanoi government to give us an alternative. Maybe he can get them to switch on the old National Defense Network again. Then we can get back into Beach House 7 through the back door."

He stopped to watch Chappy's body being carted away and

didn't pick up the threads of his plan again until they were headed back to the house.

"Will they know how to do that?" Sloane asked.

"They shut it down quick enough," he told him. "Them and their Russian technicians. The very day they took Saigon they had the captured computers freeze the Central Bank's overseas assets and shut the National Defense Network down. If they can do that they can just turn it all back on again, that's all."

"That's it?"

"That's it. If they turn the network back on I can broadcast the sequence of commands from the Thai/Tech computers to the National Defense Network's microwave transceiver in Saigon. If I can do that I can use the Thai/Tech computers to pick the lock to Beach House 7 from inside the network. There's a lot of details to work out but it can be done."

Jake whistled. "That's some ace you had up your sleeve."

"Will it get the Korean off our backs?"

"Yeah, sure," Voss assured him. "Why wouldn't it?"

"And you could have done all this before?" Sloane demanded.

"It's the last trick I've got to play," he replied, ruefully. "I was waiting for a bigger pot."

CHAPTER

12

A breeze from downriver disturbed the coals of the noodle stall's fire and blew the smoke into Sloane's eyes as he sat with Jake on the bench facing the Thai/Tech dock. The barge that carried the fish renderings was being scrubbed down by its crew after its weekly upcountry run. Beyond it, out near the channel, he could see the plane shift on its cable into the wind.

The afternoon was darkening and there was speculation among the workers under the stall's awning about the likelihood of the season's first rain.

Jake was picking specks out of his coffee and muttering to himself when the Prince pulled into his parking space on the dock. Voss was with him. He was first out of the Fiat and headed straight for the office without so much as a nod to the others, who had been waiting for word since early that morning.

The Prince seemed to take it all in stride; as he joined them, he was rubbing his hands together as if he had just finished up a job well done. He nodded to Sloane, who was immersed in his thoughts.

"Are you all right, David?" he asked as he peeled an expensive pair of driving gloves from his hands. He signaled for a glass of coffee and from a wide wicker hamper he picked out a pastry like the one that Sloane had deep-sixed on his first morning. "Hello, Jacob."

"Well?" Sloane asked him when he'd settled on the bench beside him.

"Mmf . . ." The Prince shook his head as he bit into the fishy puff. "Mm . . . all is well," he said. "It is a deal. Peter says it was Park Sung Dai who had the difficult part, convincing Hanoi and its Russian technicians to agree. Even with the prospect of gaining entry into the Beach House 7 complex the idea of opening the old National Defense Network to an outsider was hard for them to swallow."

"I can imagine."

"But word came about an hour ago that they had agreed to Peter's proposal."

"And nobody else gets hurt?" Sloane asked.

"That is the agreement."

"Is it possible? Can he do it?"

"Peter can do anything," the Prince said. "But how he can do it—well, I leave all of that technical business up to him. It makes no sense to ask about things when I wouldn't understand the answers. Yes?"

"My point, exactly," Jake growled. "People like us can't understand the details so we concede to the technocrats. Why's the world so screwed up? Because people like Pete can win by default."

"That's pretty good, Jacob," the Prince allowed.

"I'm using it in the book. I'm starting off on a whole new tack. The war as a technological phenomenon. I got the idea from Alice." He sucked off the top half of his coffee and peered hopefully over his glass at Sloane. "She probably told you about it."

"You saw Alice?" Sloane was surprised. "When?"

"Couple days ago. Tuesday, I guess. She didn't tell you?"

"I didn't see her." Sloane frowned. "Probably just in for the day. She had some big conference coming up."

"She'd be great at a conference," Jake said. "She'd steal the show. She understood the whole technology concept right off, like she could read my mind."

Sloane decided it was time to change the subject. "You know, there's something about this scheme that's bothering me."

"What scheme?"

"Pete's Beach House 7 idea, turning it on from the network."

"What about it?"

"Like how come he used to need a MAS Unit to get into the Beach House 7 computers. Remember that? And now he doesn't?"

Jake had been stirring his tea with a finger, trying to mix in an overdose of sugar. "Doesn't what?"

"He's getting in to open up the Beach House 7 computer system for Hanoi but he still doesn't have the key. I mean, the way I understood it, that MAS Unit was like a real . . . a real thing." He made a shape like a box with his hands. "Like Beach House 7 was a house with a front and a back door to the outside world and only that one key could let you in."

"Or out," Jake added. "Y'know, I think you're onto something there. So why doesn't he need the key to get in this time?"

"I am sure there is a technological explanation," said the Prince.

"I'm sure there is, too," Jake told him. "He's up to something."

The next week and a half were hard on everybody. Without Alice around, Sloane began to see for himself how estranged he'd become from his past. Now and then he would look out over the river and the city that crowded its banks, and think about himself as a younger man and how taken with this place he had been.

She'd been a dreamy, spindrift sort of town back then. A bit tawdry, maybe, like a camp follower with the war going on all around. But more than anything she'd been a state of mind and Sloane was beginning to see that he could no more return to the Bangkok of the past than he could to the youth he'd so willingly squandered there.

"Okay, Prince," he yelled from the cockpit. "Prop it over easy and stay clear of that manifold. She'll probably backfire."

The Prince was out on the starboard pontoon trying to get enough of his weight on the propeller to pull it over. His face was smeared with oil and his overalls had been tailored too tight, they were blotted through with sweat.

"Grab hold further out," Sloane told him. "You'll get better leverage."

"It will not turn over."

"Sure it will. The compression's a little tighter since the overhaul, that's all."

"Is it really necessary that we do all this ourselves?" The Prince paused long enough to pull out a monogrammed handkerchief and dab at his face.

"Anybody can teach you how to fly," Sloane told him. "But how many can teach you to appreciate it? Right?"

"I suppose so."

Sloane had continued with his paperwork in the mornings, outlining the cost projections for some of the Prince's pet projects; simple tasks that left him with plenty of time in the afternoons to continue his work on the airplane. With the help of a local aviation maintenance company he finished the overhaul in a week, bench-tested and bolted the strange engine back in place. He and the Prince got in a couple of test flights and had spent the time in between puttering with the details. Today it was the magneto.

Voss hadn't shown much of himself since his project with the Korean and the Hanoi government had been started. In fact, he'd grown increasingly mysterious, showing up at Dog Alley just long enough to pick up his razor or some papers and then he'd be off again.

"Everything's coming along great," he'd say when they ran across each other. "Don't worry about a thing."

Poor Kiri didn't know what to think. She was afraid she was losing him and sometimes in the night Sloane could hear her sobbing softly. He had tried to explain Peter's troubles to her, he tried to explain the pressures and worries that were taking up all of his time but somehow she always ended up making him feel as if he was the one who didn't understand.

The Prince gave another pull and the engine kicked over with a flutter of blades and a loud bang that blew a cloud of high-test smoke into his face.

"Can that guy really fly this thing?" Jake was in the backseat, slumped out of sight except for his feet, which stuck out of the empty door frames.

"He's a menace," Sloane said and signaled the Prince to give it another try. "I'd be surprised if he could ride a bicycle."

"How come you don't tell him?"

Sloane shrugged. "Because he's the only fun I've been having around here, that's why."

Things had been especially hard on Jake, obsession and exhausting work habits on his book were getting the best of him. When he could work no more he became erratic and unpredictable, like a switchboard that was shorting out. For days now he'd been showing up at odd hours, stoned or drunk or whatever one gets on screwballs, pestering Sloane with his ideas.

"Give it another try," Sloane yelled down to the Prince as he pumped the throttle a few times.

Jake practiced a few words to himself before trying to say anything further. When he was in this condition he often over-compensated by pretending that his speech (and therefore his thinking) was actually more precise than ever. He only fooled himself, however. Just as often the complexity of communicating became too much to bother with at all and he would fade into an impenetrable snooze.

He had been laid out in a stupor in the backseat since early afternoon when the sun was white-hot overhead and now, for some reason, he was ready to simply pick it up where he'd left off.

"Say, how come you guys call her 'Crazy Alice'?"

At the moment Sloane was more interested in the Prince's struggles with the propeller. "Who calls her that?"

"You guys. You and Pete."

Sloane frowned. "Must be her reputation."

"Well, she's not so crazy. She caught on to Pete right away." He hoisted himself up onto one arm. "And she was the one who got me thinking about a new direction for the book and that got me to thinking about what you said about how you'd need the key to get into Beach House 7, and a couple ideas started to fall in place."

"Like what?"

"Like how Pete claims he first tried to just sell the key module to Hanoi to get Park Sung Dai off his back. Remember? And then how you and I got to wondering about why he had to bring it all the way back here to Bangkok. Well, I finally figured out why."

"Yeah?" Sloane smelled gas fumes and waved off the Prince. "Yeah? Why?"

"Simple," Jake said. "Maybe he wasn't going to sell it. Maybe he was going to use it."

"Use it?"

"Just maybe, you understand." He pulled in his knees and sat up as straight as he could. "I'll bet he could have hooked the key up to his Thai/Tech computers right here and transmitted its code to Beach House 7. It's an electronic process, right? I mean, that's not so much different from what he's trying to do now."

"That's a pretty big maybe, Jake."

"It makes sense, though. Right?"

"Look, this microwave transmission stuff is a lot more complicated than that. And anyhow, what would he want to do all that for?"

"Huh?"

"What for?" Sloane had forgotten where he was in the wiring and had to start over again. "You've got it all worked out, so tell me what for."

"I don't know what for. How the hell should I know what for? He's up to something, that's all. Maybe he's made his own deal with the Reds. Maybe . . ."

"No more maybes, Jake," Sloane said without looking back. "You think you've got something on him, let's hear it. Don't give me maybes."

"Well, whatever it is you can bet it's got something to do with that Korean's money." He leaned forward. "I've been keeping an eye on the yacht and I've got to tell you, it gives me the creeps. You've got little Oriental guys in cloth caps and business suits running around, and a bunch of Russians from the embassy with briefcases and pocket calculators coming and going at all hours. I mean, it's scary. This has got to be a very big deal to these guys, for Christ's sake. Think about it, he's gotten them to turn on the whole damn network for him."

Sloane leaned out the doorsill. "Be sure that cowling flap is open," he called down to the Prince. "Let's air out the fumes for a minute." Then he turned for a better look at Jake.

"What are you saying, that he's trying to con the whole Vietnamese government? The Russians? Come on, Jake. Be serious."

"Why not? He's done it before. He'd use them, he'd use us —he'd use anybody. Don't you see? He's got it all arranged. And y'know what else? Y'know what I don't see around the Korean's yacht?"

"What?"

"I don't see Pete. If they're all working so hard together how come he's never there?"

"Well, so what?" Sloane said with a look over his shoulder. "See, you just miss a lot and you can't admit it. I can tell you that Pete's over there all the time."

Jake pursed his lips and shook his head widely.

"He is, I tell you. He's there all the time working out their programming. He told me so."

"Nope," Jake said. "I told you there was more to all this than meets the eye. There's no sign of him at the boat. Hell, he could be working on a different plan altogether."

"Hey, maybe he's just got other things to do while you're watching."

"Yeah, sure. Maybe so. Maybe he's got himself a live one someplace and wants to get his rocks off without Kiri finding out."

Sloane dropped his handful of wires and turned around so he could get a good look at Jake. "Now don't start getting paranoid on me, Jake," he said. "I'm pretty upset with Pete right now, too. But making everything into some fiendish plot . . ."

"Everything plays a part in his world. What about this Thai/ Tech thing, for instance? A collection of failing businesses, a pile of junk for a factory, right? A nutty prince and a plane that would be condemned by the Mongolian Air Force. There's only one thing the company's got that's worth anything and that's that Buck Rogers computer of his. What the hell's he got that thing for? Everything is here for a reason. Everything and everybody."

"Yeah? Well, I'm here because he's a friend of mine."

Jake looked frustrated. "That's what I mean." His hair was matted in flat strings against his forehead and his single black brow flared out on either side like the fenders of a vintage sedan. "That's what I'm talking about, his friends, too," he said. "What d'ya think I've been talking about? Why not? Yes, even you. You watch, you're here for a reason."

"Listen," Sloane said. "I've seen you like this before. You get your teeth into an idea and you can't let go. You put your two and two together and when they come up five it damn near kills you. You go off on a jag, like that time in Hue, remember? And it's people like Pete and me who have to put you back together again." After a minute of Jake's examining his fingernails, Sloane smiled. He tousled Jake's hair and said, "Come on, let's call it a day. You can clean up back at the office."

Jake pulled away bitterly. "I've got work to do," he said. "Look, you just think about it, okay? You just wait, when the time comes he'll use you like a pop-up Kleenex."

The setting sun cast a soft glow over the city on the other side of the river as their *hangyao* sliced through the darkening calm. On the docks above them a pickup crew had just left the noodle stall to see to their duties aboard the barge and left behind the strange *farang* who had spent the greater part of the afternoon watching the activity on the old airplane out on the river. He had terrible foreigner's eyes and a large purple scab where his ear ought to have been. They were glad to be rid of him.

By the time Sloane had found a taxi for Jake and gotten him into it with a hundred baht for the fare and something to eat, the Prince had showered and changed and was sitting at his desk drying his straight wet hair with a towel while he went through some field reports in manila folders.

"Where is Jacob?" he asked cheerily. "Off to Yankee Daniel's for happy hour?"

"He's got some new idea he's working on for his book."

"Ah, yes." The Prince shook his head sympathetically. "There is always a new idea. Another chance. We call a fellow like that *'kam tam tua khong.'* "

Sloane searched his limited Thai vocabulary. " 'One of the doomed?" he guessed.

" 'Doomed of himself,' actually. There are many like him among Bangkok's *farang.* Poor doomed creatures who come here to make their last stand." He opened a desk drawer and found a towel there for Sloane.

"Like me?" Sloane wiped his brow roughly and was surprised to find he'd left a dirty smudge on the cloth. "Think I'm one of your 'poor doomed creatures,' too?"

"Difficult to say," the Prince said, uncomfortably. He was not used to being so candid. "You are not like the others. Even Peter, you are not at all like Peter. I often wonder what you are doing here."

"I'm beginning to wonder myself," Sloane said. "You know, when you think about some of Jake's ideas, well . . ."

"Come, David. You may speak freely. I know many things about Peter. More, I think, than you might expect."

"Well, Jake's gotten into this technology angle pretty deeply, you know how he goes off the deep end sometimes. Anyhow, he started getting suspicious about some of Pete's story."

"Go on."

"What he's getting at is that Pete's still up to no good. He's not trying to open the Beach House 7 computers at all. Not for the Korean, not for Hanoi and, more important, not for us."

"And do you believe him?"

"I have to admit, a lot of what he says makes sense."

"But you do not wish to believe him," said the Prince. "You do not wish to believe that your old friend is still being devious."

"That's about it," Sloane said. "If he wasn't playing it straight at this point, after all that's happened. I mean, with people around him being murdered and crippled. Jake wants me to believe he's still at it."

"Oh, Peter never meant for it to come to this."

". . . Come to this?" Sloane sat himself on the corner of the desk. "It's not a matter of degree, it's a matter of basic ethics."

"But surely you knew what his ethics were like before you joined us?"

Sloane blinked a couple of times and then straightened. He slung the towel around his neck and gripped it by both ends.

"Yes," he had to admit. "I guess I did."

A door closed down the hall behind him and he looked around in time to see Voss almost pass the Prince's door.

"Ah, there you are." Voss joined them. He seemed weary and ill at ease. He was going through the motions of cordiality, as if the format would carry him through. The pat on the back. The squeeze of the arm. That "how y'doin' " grin that politicians affect when they're after something. "God, am I glad to see you." He tossed some papers on the desk and clapped a hand over Sloane's shoulder to turn him toward the door. "Listen, we gotta talk. You mind?"

"No, no." The Prince waved them off. "We were only discussing philosophy."

"My office?" Voss said to Sloane.

"Yeah. Sure." Sloane let himself be led down the linoleum-tiled hallway to Voss's glass cubicle.

"See, we've got a sort of a kink in the plan. Sit down, sit down." He slid a chair under Sloane while for himself he elected to remain on his feet, pacing around the little glass room. "It's my fault, really. I should have known this problem was there all along but there are so many details . . . Anyhow, this is one you can help us out on."

"Me?"

"It's crucial to the whole plan. It really is."

"Sure. I mean, if it's crucial . . ."

"Great. I knew we could count on you." Voss pushed a dirty coffee cup and a pile of loose paper out of the way and rested his weight on the edge of his desk. "I mean, if you can't count on your friends . . ."

"Yeah, sure. What do you need, Pete?"

"Here's the thing. The only way back into Beach House 7 is through the old National Defense Network, right? Well, see, that means that the only way back into the network is through the commercial microwave communication system. There just isn't any time to set up a transceiver of our own."

"A commercial tranceiver?"

"Like the Post Office uses. Development agencies and financial institutions. Like your New City uses for their overseas transactions."

"Yeah, I know." Sloane didn't like the sounds of this. "Now don't tell me you guys at Beach House 7 had to use a commercial transceiver."

"Once in a while," Voss answered. "I mean, *I* used it once in a while."

"You did?"

"Sure. I've been trying to tell you, it's all on the same network. The National Defense Network."

"Oh lord." Would it never end?

"So now, without the MAS key unit that's the only way back in. See? Now comes the problem I was talkin' about."

"Which is?"

"We've gotta use an authorized entry into the worldwide commercial network through an established customer, see? And that's where you come in."

"You don't need me. You need test keys and . . . and Telex operators. You can't just go marching into the international monetary system like it was some kind of rinky-dink local outfit."

"We don't need 'em. We only need to get in, that's all. No Telex operators—and we'd never get a test key code anyhow, that's one the banks never let go of."

"New City changes their's every week."

"Right. But they wouldn't have changed yours."

"My what?"

"Your tag."

Sloane let himself sink into his slippery red leather chair and eyed his friend for a moment before he said, "What are you up to, Pete?"

"Up to?" Voss slid off the edge of the desk and began pacing around the room again. "Up to, f'Christ's sake. I'm tryin' to save our asses, that's what I'm up to. Look, you were a big shot at New City, right? So you must have had access to their computers. A personal code. A tag. A number. Five, maybe six digits."

"So?"

"So, that's all I need. A modem and a long-distance phone call and your personal access code will let me through New City's computers and into the commercial microwave service and that will let me into the National Defense Network back in Saigon."

Sloane rose to his feet. "Dammit it, Pete!"

"Hey, what's the matter, man?" Voss was surprised. "I mean, it's hardly even illegal. New City's Telex access, that's all I need to finish this thing once and for all."

"And what will you need next? Who else are you going to drag into this mess? Who's next on the list? How many more Somsaks and Chappys and those people in the boat. . . . Damn it, Pete. What the hell have you gotten us into?"

"Listen, Ace." Voss tried to calm him. He was very quiet, very deliberate. "We started the war together, you and me and the Kid. Jake, too, remember? Does it sound like I'm just using you or does it sound like we're all in this together? Didn't we take care of each other? Think about it, if y' haven't got your friends then what d'ya got left? Huh?"

"Yeah, I guess so."

Voss had grasped Sloane by the arms as he spoke and now seemed to be holding him in place, waiting for the answer he wanted to hear. "C'mon, Dave. If you can't ask a friend at a time like this . . ."

"All right," Sloane said, looking away. "Okay, I'll give it to you. It's back at the house someplace in my papers, I never could remember the damn thing. You want me to go get it now?"

"The sooner the better," Voss said. He looked much relieved. "Don't worry about a thing, Dave. Everything's gonna be okay now. Everything's gonna be fine."

It was already late when Sloane came out of the Old Rest House and found Jake teetering up the terrace toward the lobby door.

"Jake?"

Jake stopped, and tried to focus on him. The night around him was damp and the wind came in sharp, uncertain gusts.

"What are you doing here?" Sloane asked him. "Are you all right?"

"I thought I might have a little visit with your Alice." He staggered slightly and reached for the wall to steady himself, only to find it was too far away. "Hope you don't mind. I have a few new ideas I want to try out on her."

Sloane turned him up the *soi* toward the street. "Me, too," he said. "Only it turns out she isn't there."

"But I called the People Project office and they said she was coming into town tonight."

"So did I," Sloane said, affecting an air of indifference he didn't feel. "Must be she's staying someplace else."

"Ah," Jake replied. "That's a pity, because I'm sure she would understand the quandary I find myself in. You see, I have the answer almost all worked out and nobody seems to want to hear about it."

"About the book?"

"Nope." Jake searched for Sloan's eyes in the gloom. "About our friend Peter Voss."

"Right."

"There, y'see? Nobody wants to listen."

"I'll listen, Jake. I really will. But let's wait till you're sober." Jake stopped suddenly. "Oh, now . . ."

"What have you been doing to yourself this time?"

"Well. I did manage a few of these little beauties, here." He reached deep into one of the many pockets on his bush jacket and rummaged around until he produced a 35mm film can. "The conclusions I have come to are sobering, indeed. So I popped a few before setting off. Want some?"

"What are they?" He took the can and sniffed at the contents.

"Opiated hash."

"Opiated . . ." He gave it back. "So that's what screwballs are."

"Nah. Screwballs are the shmucks who take 'em." Jake gave an ironic snort. "People like me with a fire burning in 'em and no way to put it out."

"And that stuff helps?"

"Sometimes. Tonight, for instance, it got me t' thinking about loyalty and trust and all those things you seem to regard so highly in Pete and it got me to thinking that maybe your girl would listen even if you wouldn't. And maybe she could get through to you."

Sloane continued his walk to the main road with Jake hustling alongside.

"What I was thinkin' was," Jake took a sticky little ball from the film can and stuck it under his tongue. "That the problem is that if you can't envisage the scale this all works at then you can't understand what he's done. You've got to be able to get this image in your mind of what the war was doing to us."

"Jake, for the last time. Pete isn't any more responsible for that stuff than the rest of us."

"Isn't he? Don't forget, his genius wasn't for making it operate, but for understanding its effect on the basic function of things." Jake was trying his best to be precise. " 'Garbage in, garbage out,' he always says. Damn. He could sum up the whole fucking war while I sat for years, beating my brains out on a typewriter."

"That's stretching it a bit, don't you think?" They were out onto Suriwong Road and Sloane waved at some taxis that slowed for a look but then passed them by.

"And you can't seem to stretch it enough," Jake was offended by Sloane's patronizing tone.

Sloane tried for the next motor rickshaw and when it had passed them by too he said, "Yeah. Okay, I'm listening."

"Are you?"

"Yeah, I've had to do some thinking of my own. See, I sort of loaned Pete my tag code from New City."

"Your what?"

"My tag, the code that gave me access to New City's computers."

"You did what? You gave him your code . . . my God, that's

it! *That's gotta be it!*" Jake shouted. His face lit up and he opened his arms as if to receive a long forward pass. "That's it, don't you see? I told you to wait. I told you he'd use you, too, didn't I? Now you can see what he's doing, can't you? Heh-heh . . . oh, this is wonderful. That's what you're here for. Heh-heh-heh."

"What's the matter with you?"

"That's what he hired you for, can't you see that?" A taxi turned onto the street from the next block. "Stop this guy. Stop him," Jake yelled, flapping his arms and staggering out into the glare of its headlights. The taxi tried to swerve around him, braking hard at the last second. "Hey, you. Stop!"

"Those screwballs are going to kill you," Sloane said as the taxi pulled up at the door of the office.

Jake had himself worked up into a weird sort of craze, half anger and half jubilation. He was determined to confront Voss and have it out with him face to face. Sloane was just as determined to keep up with him until he was cooled down enough to tell him what the hell was going on.

"Wake up, you moth-eaten Sikh," Jake shouted at the Indian guard. "Where's your boss?"

"Jake. It's eleven o'clock."

"The lights are on."

But it was the Prince, not Voss, who was working late. Jake went past his door at a high rate of speed, without giving him a second glance until he drew up short at Voss's cubicle at the end of the hall. There was nobody there. His terminal was on, numbers and letters dancing up and down its screen in random patterns.

"Where is he?" he demanded of the Prince. "Where is that son of a bitch?"

The Prince gave them a quizzical look but Sloane could only shrug. "He's got this idea . . ."

"More than an idea," Jake cut him off. "I know what he's up to and it's . . . it's just wonderful. That's what it is. I mean, there he is with his goddam computer going. He's running a program, isn't he? And he isn't even here."

"Well," the Prince began. "Peter can . . ."

"Yeah, I know. Peter can do anything. In fact, who knows what he might be up to right this minute, eh?"

204 . . .

The Prince was calm. He'd seen Jake like this before. "All right, Jacob. Let us just see what he is up to, shall we?"

He reached over the arm of his chair, turned on his terminal, and waited for a second until "ready" appeared on the screen. "I am still a novice at this but Peter has taught me much of the basics." He punched in his code.

When the directory came on the screen he selected "operations in use" and a list began scrolling up the screen like credits in a movie.

"There's one of his codes," the Prince said, and typed it into his console. "We can watch over his shoulder, as it were. Hmmm." He rested his elbow on the arm of his chair, stroking his chin with one hand while he scrolled the list over with the other.

"Know what it is?" Sloane asked.

"Hmmm."

"Well?"

"Um, not all of these other things," the Prince said. Then he tapped at a five-segment sequence of digits on the screen. "But this one is a commercial code account, an account in New City Credit in Singapore."

"What? New City?"

"In fact . . ." He returned to the directory and then called up another category. When he had read the list that presented itself he turned to his guests with a worried look.

"In fact, it is *our* commercial code account."

There were still some signs of sleepy latenight life down on the klongs and ditches of the Wongwien Yai district of Thonburi. The roads that ran along the causeway were almost deserted this time of the night, but it was still slow going for the Prince's red Fiat because Jake was determined to help.

"Jacob. Please." The Prince was prying Jake's fingers from the steering wheel. "Perhaps you would be happier in the back."

"That way, that way!" Jake was hollering. "Shortcut, short-cut!"

"No. Please, that's the river."

"Leave him alone, Jake." Sloane was wrestling with him from the back seat. "He'll get us there."

"Slow and steady wins the race," the Prince said as he slowed for a right-hand turn.

"Can't drive any better'n he can fly," Jake grumbled.

They were on their way to Dog Alley because Jake was sure Voss would be back at the house and by now the other two knew they had a stake in finding out what was going on. Even the Prince was upset.

"He's a chameleon, that's what he is," Jake had been keeping a commentary going the whole time but each interference by him of the Prince's steering was so jarring that it was nearly impossible for the other two to keep track of his reasoning. "He could change his colors from army green to anything he needed to be. Prankster, tactician, black marketeer—it was all in the way he could manipulate data. All part of the same game.

"Trouble is, it's the Peter Vosses of the world who make the rules, not us. When the NVA cut him off from his computer terminals that should have been an end to it. But no. He just made up some new rules and here we all are, back in the action again. Back to finish the game."

"What rules?" The Prince demanded. "What game?"

"Left here!" Jake lunged for the wheel but Sloane had him from behind and held him so the Prince could look both ways before entering Rama IV Road.

CHAPTER

13

"**C**ome out with your hands up, Peter Voss. We know you're in there."
Jake waited by the gate while lights went on all over the neighborhood. Voss wasn't in there, only the Kid, who peered out of the window, shading his eyes from the headlights trying to see who it was.

"Jake?"

"Where's Pete, Kid?"

"I dunno. Hey, y'goin' out someplace? Can I go too?"

"Yeah, Kid. Sure."

"Let's leave him out of this," Sloane said.

"Yes. In fact, maybe we should wait, too," the Prince suggested. "And then when Jacob is feeling better . . ."

"I've never felt better," Jake insisted. "And it can't wait. Who knows what he'll get his hands on next? Guys like him can get into everything because y'can't get anybody to believe what they're up to."

The back screen door slammed and the Kid came shambling out into the car lights. "What's the matter, Jake?" he asked, squinting through the glare at the others. "Hey, you guys mad at Pete or something?"

"Are we, guys?" Jake asked the others. "Are we mad at Pete? We ought to be, y'know, 'cause this is all a setup."

"What's that supposed to mean?"

"This." Jake waved at the courtyard around him. "All this. The house. The Prince. The business. All this stuff is a setup."

Sloane was getting mad. "Are you going to give us a straight answer or not?"

"Of course. After all, you're part of it," Jake said gleefully. "Yes, you. Reliable, trusting . . . good to the last drop David

. . . 207

Sloane; just part of the same setup. 'Be a sport, ol' buddy,' is that what he said? Or was it, 'Uh, by the way, Dave. If you're not using your tag code how about lending it to me? I wanna take my girl to the movies.' "

"He said it was critical to the whole operation." Sloane was ready to grab Jake and shake the story loose. "What was I supposed to do? Tell him to forget it? Pretend those years we've known each other don't mean anything? Go ahead, tell me. What was I supposed to do?"

"You were supposed to do just what you did, dummy. That's what you're here for. He can do without the key but he can't do without you."

Oddly enough, Sloane was beginning to see the pattern of Jake's brainstorm.

"Do without the key . . . ? Oh, lord!" he said, in amazement. "I don't believe it! He doesn't need the key to get into Beach House 7 because he's not trying to get into Beach House 7 at all. He's trying to get back into the network!"

"That's it! That's it!" Jake doubled over with laughter. Tears were streaming down his face and he was gasping for air. "That's . . . that's always been it. Y'see how fabulous it all is? He gets the Prince to put all this together: this house, this company, this everything—all so that he can have the computer he needs. And then he hires you, not for your experience, not for your grasp of the cutthroat world of Asian business. No, sir. What he needs you for is your access to the New City computers and its access to the commercial microwave data communication system. That's all.

"See? Isn't it fabulous? Heh-heh . . ." He rubbed his wet face with the back of his hand and gave a loud sniff. "He's . . . he's not going to try to open the Beach House complex, he's going back for the eleven and a half million, ha-ha-hah."

"But he can't be," Sloane interrupted. "It's not even there anymore. The new regime confiscated the funds left in the banks. The piestre isn't even the currency there anymore. And even if it was, he'd have to have a test key to move any money around. The telex operators check every transaction and the test key codes are changed every week."

"What setup?" The Prince was pleading. "What are you talking about?"

"No. That can't be it. He must be up to something else."

From his lower line of vision Jake was the first to spy the familiar pair of legs rushing up the alley into the headlight beams.

"Petah?"

"Kiri," said the Kid. "They're mad at Peter."

"Oh, please, is something wrong fo' Petah?"

"Plenty." Jake's laughter was replaced by wheezing, his brow fell. "There's plenty wrong and you've got to help us find him."

"C'mon. Let's leave her out of this."

"Not on your life," he said, pushing away from Sloane. "Nobody's left out in this game. Everybody's a player, don't you see that by now?"

"Something has happen' to Petah?"

The Kid was looking around as if for his missing brother. "Peter? Where's Peter, Kiri?"

"It's okay, Kid." Sloane put a hand lightly on the Kid's arm. Even in the icy glare of the Fiat's headlamps he could see the first signs of distress in his eyes and knew that something was stirring in the Kid's sedated brain.

"Nah. Nothing's happened to Pete," Jake said. "We just want to know where he is, that's all. And I'll bet his little girl here can tell us, can't you?"

"No." She was haughty in her denial. Professing her ignorance with a rough shake of her head. "No. I do not know."

"Where does he go when he wants to be alone, hmm? Where does he always go, let's say, when he's got to be alone to think?" He took her wrist harshly.

"Hey, don't do that," the Kid said.

"Yeah, Jake. That's enough."

"Y'wanna find out what the hell is goin' on, don't you? Or maybe you just wanna sit around with your thumb in your ass?" Jake turned back to Kiri. "We're not blind, y'know. We can see his interest in you is, shall we say—not exactly what it once was. Why do y'suppose that is, eh? Too wrapped up in his work?"

"M-maybe so." Kiri's lip was quivering but she did her best to defy her tormentor. "Yes, he works too much, I think."

". . . or maybe he's got himself a live one, someplace."

"Jake!"

"Hey, it's nothing new for him. He's always had something going on the side, remember?"

"I cannot imagine to what you refer," Kiri insisted. By now

she had her small fist pressed to her mouth and was avoiding his eyes.

"Lay off, Jake."

"C'mon, you can tell us. Where's he go for a quick screw where he thinks nobody's gonna find out? Huh? Where's he go when he's got something going on the side?"

"Jacob, really!" said the Prince.

"Yeah, leave her out of it."

"But she's already in it," Jake said. "Even if she won't admit it, she's in it. Let her take her lumps like everybody else."

"Where's Pete, Kiri?" the Kid asked. His anxiety was growing. His eyes were tense and he was balling his fists at his side as he spoke.

"Come on, Kiri. Where's he keep his little love nest? Didn't he used to take you there?"

"All right!" Kiri said at last. "All right, but he nevah take me there. Nevah. I am his special girl, not just another tart." She was angry, her eyes blazing through her tears. She tried to swing at Jake, but he ducked and caught her hand just in time. For a moment she was just another bar girl turning crudely on a petty tormentor.

"This is not the proper way, Jacob. I am surprised at you. Some things it is more proper not to know too much. Everybody gets hurt just so you can find out bad things."

The Prince was much impressed by Kiri's brave defiance and reached out to her to reassure her but Jake misunderstood his intentions. Assuming he was about to interfere, Jake pulled her away by the wrist he still held so the Prince ended up grasping at her awkwardly as if she were the object of a tug-of-war.

"Don't do that," the Kid warned, pushing Sloane aside to get at the other two.

"No, Kid," Sloane said. "It's okay."

But the Kid wasn't convinced and in the confusion Jake grabbed Kiri away by the arm and had thrown her into the front seat of the Prince's Fiat before anyone could stop him.

"I'll drive," he said.

Voss took another puff from the cigarette protruding like a fuse from the lather on his face and went on scratching at his throat with a silver safety razor. The blade was dull and he didn't shave all that often so it was something of an ordeal.

He wiped a streak across the fogged-over mirror in front of him and paused at the sight of the face peering back at him.

"Oh, God." He looked haggard. His eyes were bloodshot, their sockets dark from overwork. His wet hair hung like seaweed around his ears. "God, I look awful," he said aloud. "I'm getting old. I'm getting stupid. I'm too strung out for this scene. Maybe with a couple hours sleep . . ."

He took another puff. The smoke erupted through the shaving cream leaving a yellow stain behind where his lips were hidden. He removed the cigarette and laid it beside the butts of the half-dozen others he'd started and forgotten since he'd begun his bath.

He felt grubby already. He felt silly and guilty and desperate all at once. It came in waves—and he was in the middle of just such a wave now. How the hell had he gotten himself into this one? At last he wrapped a towel around his middle and went to the door for another look from the high porch. On the way he scooped up his filthy T-shirt, wadded it, and tossed it into the kitchen wastebasket.

The Thai/Tech guest house was less opulent than the typical modern flat or private bungalow today's Asian corporations often keep for their executives and official visitors. It was a modest, stuck-together sort of place stacked with a number of others just like it in a faceless complex rising above the forest near the edge of town.

Once again he found himself watching the roadway running past from the Thonburi bottomland even though he knew he still had an hour to kill. The Thai/Tech docks could be seen a half mile away, still lighted for the swing shift. There were no stars and the marketplace at the foot of the rise was quiet. Every gust of muggy wind seemed to blow a little life out of the city.

He stuck another cigarette in his mouth and discovered he was still wearing his shaving cream. He swore and returned to the bathroom, where he found that the electric geyser had quit and he had to finish the shave with cold water. When he finished he went to check the road outside again and began to feel like a fool. It was all wrong. It was an unfamiliar element in his life, something he couldn't control and he hated it. Anyhow, she probably wasn't even coming.

He checked his watch and went back inside to finish dressing (a clean cotton shirt with stays in the collar) and then did what he could to tidy up the place. When he was finished he took a last look around with a critical eye.

Another dump. There was a dowdy old easy chair and a matching sofa that sagged in the middle and yellowing chintz curtains on the windows. No class. He shook his head. No class at all. The marbleized cement floor was pretty well covered with woven reed carpets and there were a few colorful batik wall hangings from Java. Funny. He'd never been embarrassed by this place before.

He made himself a stiff drink and sat down with it to speculate nervously on what the evening held in store. As it turned out he had time for several more (and needed them) before he heard steps on the outdoor stairway leading up to the landing. Should he wait for her knock? Maybe so, but he didn't He met her outside on the landing.

"I didn't think you were coming," he said.

"Neither did I," said Alice.

"But here you are."

"Yes." She looked around. "Yes, here I am. It's very nice here." She went to the rail. "And just look at the view!"

"Yeah. The view's nice." Was she coming inside? "Y'want a drink or something?"

"Oh, no, thanks. I just stopped by . . . I mean, I came here to tell you something, I guess. Something I've got to tell you, that's all."

"Tell me something?"

"Really. And then I'm going," she said. "I really can't stay."

Voss tried out his little boy smile. He put his hands over his ears. "S'pose I can't hear what you have to say? S'pose I can't hear anything until morning? Y'like this view? You ought'a see it in the morning over eggs and Bloody Marys."

"Peter . . ."

"Nope. Can't hear a thing. Stress, probably. I've had a lot on my mind lately."

"I know. And I've been thinking about that, too," Alice said. "I don't know how to explain this. I mean, it's wonderful to see you make this change in your life. To put your past behind you and all . . ."

Voss was scratching his head roughly as if he thought it was wonderful, too. "You don't know the half of it," he told her. "Just remember, it's gotta be anonymous. Nobody can ever know."

"Just you and me."

"Just you and me. Now c'mon inside and let me get you a drink."

"And it means just *every*thing to my organization—imagine, eleven and a half million dollars. That's enough for a dozen field hospital units of our own."

"It'll just show up, you know. A little at a time. If it works it'll just show up in the People Project account," Voss pointed out. "It's gotta go through Singapore."

"Oh, but it'll work. I know it will. Oxfam, IRC—they'll have to deal with us, now. It's the largest private donation I've ever heard of. It's the kind of money that gives a program clout."

"Easy come, easy go," Voss said. She looked wonderful. Bright, bubbly, and warm like a schoolgirl off to the prom. He felt like a lecher. "C'mon. A drink to go with it."

"All right. Maybe just one." She went inside with him and looked around the flat, examining the batiks while he found some glasses and poured.

"It's the company guest house." His eyes followed her every move. "The custom around here is to keep a place for company guests and for official functions."

"And for executives and their not so official functions." Alice laughed, nervously. "We're onto you guys."

He scooped some crushed ice from a Thermos bucket into a couple of glasses, poured a reckless dose of J&B over it, and handed her one while she looked around. When she had taken a few sips he reached out and brushed back the lock of her hair that always fell over her eye.

"Please don't," she said, quietly.

"No?"

"No, really. It isn't right. David . . ."

"I thought you'd broken off with David."

"Oh, we never really break off. We have these little tiffs and then we always . . . this is so different. You're so different than I'd imagined."

"Is that why you've come? Because I'm different?"

"I've come to explain."

"Explain." He sipped his drink, glumly. "You keep explaining things like everything's supposed to make sense. I'll bet that's why they call you 'Crazy Alice.' "

Alice nodded. "Maybe so."

"But what about the things that can't be explained. Things that just happen, like how I feel about you. How you feel about me." He put his hand behind her neck but she averted her eyes.

He looked away, too. "I guess you're right. I guess I was hoping for too much." He returned to the bamboo bar and poured another drink. "We've talked a lot, you and me. You made me see things in a different way and I guess I'm grateful. I figured I could prove to you how much I've changed by giving the People Project what it needs to carry on its work."

"It wasn't the money," Alice assured him. "Oh, that's important all right, but it's where it came from. That you cared enough to give up the rewards of your . . . your . . ."

"Criminal past?"

"I was looking for a better way to put it."

"Well, that's what it was even if it was for the Kid. But it was also the only way I could prove to you that I was through with all that. I thought that by disposing of those accounts, by transferring them into something . . . something really worthwhile that I'd be rid of the past once and for all. That I could be . . . I don't know."

"What, Peter?" Alice said, following him to the bar. "What could you be?"

"More worthy, I guess. Be the kind of man you would find, well, more worthy."

"But you are," she said. "You really are."

"We could do a lot for each other, you and me." He turned and, taking her by the top button on her blouse, drew her closer. "I'm a weak man, Alice. I need your help."

"Don't," she said, closing her eyes. "Oh, this is all so confusing. What about David? He's such a little boy in some ways." His arm slid around her waist. "If he ever found out . . ."

"Does he have to find out?" He took a step toward the bedroom door and found that she had turned with him. "Does he?"

"I . . . I guess not."

Sloane was riding behind the Kid and the Prince was in the sidecar. It was a hard ride with the hot, wet wind blowing at them and the earsplitting rap of the exhaust pipe as the Kid downshifted into the turns. They had lost the Fiat in the dark back streets off Klong Yat.

"Maybe he's lost," the Prince yelled to the other two. "Maybe he has passed out somewhere from his drugs."

"Too much to hope for," Sloane said. "No, he's been working up to this one for years."

"Maybe we shouldn't be chasing after him like this." Every bump and bang of the sidecar could be heard in the Prince's voice. "He might do something dangerous."

"He *is* doing something dangerous."

"Then why are we chasing him?"

"Because he could be right."

"There!" The Prince pointed down the avenue as the red Fiat raced through the intersection under the lights.

The Kid was after him before Sloane had even seen what was going on, swerving hard over a small bridge and down a walkway to cut him off. Small groups of pedestrians had to crowd up against the walls and leap out of the way. The Kid dodged them deftly and was behind Jake at the next crossing.

"Jake, stop!"

But Jake went weaving through the few cars waiting for a traffic light at Sampeng Lane and took a sharp right-hand turn toward Memorial Bridge. They were all heading for Thonburi.

There was a tall window near the bed and the light from the market below gave the hushed room an eerie footlight glow. Alice looked into Voss's eyes the way a trapped mouse looks into the eyes of a viper. He kissed her lightly, hardly brushing her lips, and then harder and hungrily as if he could somehow consume her.

"I knew you wouldn't go," he said, tugging her blouse from her loose slacks so he could press his hand against her naked back. "After what you've done for me. After what I've done for you.

Her arms were around him now. "You didn't do it for me . . ." She spoke in whispers between his kisses. ". . . you did it . . . because it was the right thing. Because it was . . ."

"I did it, that's what's important," he said. "The program is running right now. Transferring the money, shutting it all down. It's all behind me now. It's been a long time since I've done anything I've been proud of and I owe it all to you." He was unbuttoning things as he spoke.

"Mmmm . . . yes." She sighed. "Oh, yes. You're such a good boy." As her breasts slipped from her blouse she tipped herself back in his arms to offer them up to his searching lips.

"Don't," she said in a voice that wasn't meant to be heard. "Don't, please."

"Alice," he whispered. He was maneuvering her into alignment with the bed as he felt her defenses take the turn he had hoped for.

She put her hand against his chest as if to push herself away from him but somehow she managed to open his shirt and rub her nipples into the light spray of hair she found there. ". . . such a good boy."

He ran his lips along the base of her neck and up her throat. She was lost to him, holding her breath as he licked her ear and lolled the lobe wetly over his tongue. Carefully he took her weight and lifted her toward the bed, his mouth devouring her hotly— when some part of him as yet uninvolved in the seduction became aware of a small, indefinable kind of movement someplace behind her.

It was hardly the moment for a pause in the action so he angled himself to the left and opened one eye to get a look over her shoulder without losing his place. There was a shadow framed by the window against the distant lights of the Bangkok side of the river. It wore a familiar evil mask that leered in at them from the porch outside. That aquiline nose pressed white against the glass, that cadaverous skull. That scab.

"Jesus Christ!"

"What!" Alice cried. "What is it?"

Janus smiled at Alice's sudden panic. He ran his tongue along the slit of his mouth as she turned and her nakedness was exposed. Slowly he raised a finger and tapped on the glass.

Voss stood frozen, holding Alice to him while she fought him for a look to see what was the matter. Then he threw her to the bed and rolled off with her onto the floor. "That son of a bitch, sending that . . . that psychopath . . ."

"Who?" Alice pleaded in the dark. "What psychopath?"

"Shhh." The windowpane rattled behind the bed but he couldn't see what Janus was up to. So he wedged Alice roughly

216 . . .

between the bed and nightstand, where she'd be out of sight, and got to his knees for a look. Janus was still there, squinting at the bed from the window trying to find where they'd gotten to. His features were weirdly lit by the lights of the street below.

"You stay here," he told Alice.

"Don't leave me!"

"Shhh. Don't move, that's all. Don't say anything and don't move until I come back for you."

He crept across the floor keeping an eye on Janus, who'd picked Alice's form out of the dark and was content for the moment to just watch her there, sprawled and disheveled on the floor.

Voss stopped at the door wondering what to do. How had he found them? What was he up to? It was all Voss could do to risk the light from the living room by opening the bedroom door but that's what had to be done. Still on his hands and knees he exited the room and started for the kitchen alcove. Maybe there was a knife or something he could use to scare him away . . .

"Get up, Peter." There was another visitor. The Korean. He was in the living room sunk deep in the velveteen easy chair where he could see Voss's undignified exit. He was stiff and tired looking and his polished fingernails kept up an impatient tattoo on the chair's carved mahogany arms. "Get up, I said."

Voss got to his feet. "Janus . . ." he said lamely, pointing toward the door.

"He won't hurt her. Not yet."

"What d'ya mean, 'not yet'?"

"It didn't work, Peter," the Korean said. Voss approached him cautiously. This wasn't the confrontation he had planned on.

"What are you doing here? How did you find me?"

"The bloody thing didn't work." The Korean sounded ill. The floor lamp beside him made his skin look like oatmeal. "The latest word from Beach House 7 has it that the complex remains as it was. It has not been unlocked, the technicians there cannot log on. Nothing's changed. Your 'long distance' scheme hasn't worked."

"What's that animal of yours up to out there on the porch?"

"Beach House 7, Peter."

"What's he after?"

"Why isn't it working?"

"Call him in here," Voss demanded. "I want him where I can see him."

"Why isn't it working, Peter? I have half a dozen Russians onboard my yacht. What am I supposed to tell them?"

"Tell 'em it takes time," Voss told him, changing his tack. "Tell 'em they haven't given it enough time for the program to run yet. Now call Janus . . ."

There was a commotion down on the road outside: the screech of brakes as the Fiat pulled up, the garbled shouts above the racket of the motorcycle, and then what sounded like a mob trampling up the stairs to the landing.

"I don't believe you," the Korean rose to his feet. "And neither do the Russians. They are angry with Hanoi and Hanoi is angry with me . . ." His eyes were squeezed almost shut. "They'll kill us, Peter. You've got some very quick thinking to do."

Jake was first through the door, dragging Kiri after him. He had somehow raced up five flights with the struggling girl in tow and now he was near collapse.

"W-well . . ." he began, but then he could only stand there gasping for breath and weaving on his feet like a sailor in high seas. He began again. "Well, well. What have we here?" The only thing that held him in place was his grip on Kiri's wrist. He looked around. It was not the scene of carnal debauchery he had prepared himself for but after a few seconds of gaping he managed to muster to the occasion.

Kiri was ashamed to be there. For all her protesting, she too had expected the worst and now that there was nothing in evidence she began to wonder if she had just let herself be intimidated by Jake's suspicions and compulsive bad manners.

"What is this?" the Korean demanded.

"So." Jake panted, spitting out the sweat that dribbled over his lips. "So, what are we up to this time? Waiting for accolades from the Reds, maybe? Waiting for Hanoi to cut you in on their winnings?"

"What's goin' on?" Voss stammered. "What the hell are you doin' here?"

"We've just stopped by to see how your little scheme has turned out."

"What *is* this?"

"Stay out of this, Jake," Voss warned. "You don't know what you're getting into."

" 'Cause . . . 'cause . . ." Jake didn't really know what to do next. He was just standing there reeling drunkenly in the middle of the floor when Sloane and the others came bursting in behind him. And then, like a Victrola needle jarred back into its track, he picked it up again from where he'd left off. ". . . 'cause if that's what you're waitin' for—a slap on the back and all that money back—you'll be here till hell freezes over."

"What is the meaning of this?"

"It means if you're still after that eleven and a half million you can f'rget it."

"Get him out of here, Dave," Voss warned. "He's gonna ruin everything."

"No-no, let him speak," the Korean said. "There is something to be learned even from the lowest of creatures."

Jake swung around to face him. "You can laugh if you want. But in fact the joke's on you."

"Is it?"

"You tell me, Mr. Big-Shot. You tell me, does it work?"

The Korean lost his smirk. "Does what work, you drunken fool?"

"Beach House 7, asshole. Does it work or not? Is it on-line? Did your Reds get into their new computer? Huh? They didn't, did they?"

"What do you know of this?"

"I know your boy here isn't going to get into that computer complex for you or the Communists or for anybody else. He *can't.*"

"He . . ." The Korean looked stunned. "He can't?"

" 'Course not. His last chance went down with Trang Van Thep. Without the MAS Unit the Beach House complex is completely separate from the National Defense Network. That's the way Peter described it to us a few weeks ago. It can't be turned on from the network, it's 'off line.' "

"But . . . but all that work! All the plans . . . they've opened the network."

"Opened the goddam network, have they?" It was Jake's moment of triumph. "That makes them about a dumb as you, doesn't it? 'Cause . . . 'cause that's what he was after in the first place, a way back into the network. And you . . . you sucker. You gave it to him. You went right on bullying everybody around until you finally forced him to do just what he wanted you to do all along."

"Back into the network?"

"Sure. All he ever wanted from that MAS Unit was its access *out* of Beach House 7. Get it? Out of Beach House 7 and *into* the National Defense Network. He had it all set up but then—poof! No MAS Unit. So you come along and think you're a regular Henry Kissinger 'cause you talk all those big-shots into opening up the network."

"Goddammit, Jake!" Voss yelled.

"Look at him." Jake laughed, still using Kiri as an anchor as he tilted one way and then another, addressing the others in the room. "He's a marvel, this guy. I mean, think about what he's managed to do. It's his biggest computer scam yet, f'Christ's sake. He's managed to hoodwink the government of the Socialist Republic of Vietnam."

"The network?" The puzzled gangster stood gaping at his weaving antagonist. "The Socialist Republic . . ."

"The *banks,* dummy. The national banking system where your eleven and a half million is stuck in cold storage. It's wired into the same National Defense Network as all the other computer systems. He's gone back in after your money."

"Jake . . ." Voss moaned.

The Korean was dumbfounded. "Into the network?" he stammered. "Into the bank? But the deal . . . the Vietnamese expect to have the weapons system back in operation by spring. And the Russians!"

"Well, they can forget it," Jake was panting, his eyes not entirely focused. "And you can forget your bank account, too." For a moment he savored his victory, and then Voss said, "Well, Jake, you really fucked it up this time."

Jake's brow began working up and down as if he were trying to focus. "Oh, yeah?"

"Jake," Sloane said, reluctantly. "There's no money left in any bank account in Vietnam."

"O-oh, yeah?"

"That's right," Voss said. "Yeah, that's right. We lost the war, remember? The Piestra is a defunct currency, it wouldn't buy spit. The accounts are confiscated, the banks are under new management."

Jake stood there stunned. Could it be true? Could this all have been a mistake? He looked around for reassurance from the others in the room. He got none.

"Well, this is terrific. Just terrific," Voss said, making a bid for the upper hand. "Here I finally had this son of a bitch by the balls and you come bustin' in here and blow it all on another of your drunken tirades.

"And the rest of you, my old buddies. You go along with it, right? You'd rather believe his harebrained accusations than trust me. And what d'you know about it, huh? Any of you. What d'you know about the complexities of systems architecture? About the network and the software and the hardwired fail-safes and emulation and all that stuff, huh?

"I mean, what d'ya think, just because you didn't understand y'figure I was settin' you guys up? Okay, I'll tell you what this was all about. I was gonna go back into the network to shut it down." The Korean gasped. "I was gonna use the National Defense Network to dismantle itself, to end my usefulness once and for all. I was gonna close up shop and slam the door behind me. But then you guys let some drunk talk you into coming around here and fucking things up. I could have . . ."

Then the Prince did something nobody dreamed he could do. He lost his temper. *"Enough!"* He shouted. "Enough of this wounded honor nonsense, Peter. I won't have another word."

"Prince?"

"Correct, Peter. And Prince means prince of the realm, so? And as such I will not be treated like an idiot. I no longer choose to disregard your artifice and broken promises of the past. Not this time. This time you have gone too far.

"My uncle agreed to finance our enterprise only if the computer could pay for itself. That was the bargain. Nothing was said about opening our company accounts to your scheme. Nothing about risking these good people like so many poker chips. We went along with you until now, but frankly it is time to draw the line.

"You see," he told the others. "The eleven and a half million may not be in Vietnam. . . ."

"Don't!"

"But the code to transfer it is."

"Jesus, Prince. Whose side are you on?"

"Something called a 'test key."

"A what?" Sloane interupted. "A test key?"

"You know of it?"

"Of course. Financial institutions use them to authorize their money transfers."

"So, you see?" the Prince insisted. "Peter is up to no good. He must be. If it were otherwise why would our Thai/Tech Commercial Code appear in his program? Eh? What have our accounts in New City Credit to do with a computer network in Vietnam?"

"Accounts in New City?" Sloane's jaw dropped. "Thai/Tech's got accounts in New City Credit? That's where I used to . . . and a test key code stuck in a computer back in Vietnam."

"Wait a minute, I can explain."

"Nope." He shook his head. "Nope, it still doesn't make sense. They change those key codes every few days. He'd have to have a current one to use the exchange. And anyhow, where's the money?"

"Yes! The money!" the Korean repeated. "Where's the money?"

"What does it matter," the Prince said. "Peter will just have to give it back, you see? He will give the money back and then we can all get on with our business." He clasped his hands behind him and beamed around at the others as if he'd altered the course of human folly.

"I'm afraid it will not be that easy," The Korean's voice was barely under control. "Oh, no. Peter has had me playing a very dangerous game with the communists and someone will have to pay for it."

" 'Course they will," Jake swayed forward dangerously and took a step to catch up. "Right, Pete? Sombody's gonna pay for it, but what do you care? You just stick to your guns, ol' buddy. You deserve it, don't you?"

Jake's little eyes burned like coals. He was edging toward Voss, spewing droplets of sweat with every word. "You're no better than this asshole, are you? And Janus, did he kill Chappy or did you? Did he mutilate old Somsak or was it you? Huh?"

"Shut up, Jake," Voss warned, as he backed away. "I don't

have to answer to no junkie fuck-up like you. I don't need you laying your ego trip on me. Y'hear?"

"Fuck-up, eh?" Jake made a lunge at Voss only to find himself hanging over the span between them with only his own grip on Kiri's wrist holding him up.

"Stop it, Jacob."

"Hey," the Kid warned.

"Jake . . ." Sloane stepped between them. "Stop it, Jake. We got the point."

But Jake turned on him. "Did you? Did you really?" he snarled. "And just what point is that?"

As if in answer there was a sound from the bedroom and Jake heard it. His flushed face lit up like Christmas. There was evidence of duplicity at hand, after all. A sadistic smile curled one side of his face. "I'll bet we all knew the point all along, that's what I think. We knew but we were more comfortable with lies. Like our little Kiri, here."

"No." She'd heard the noise, too.

"She'd rather believe his little lies than face the truth, wouldn't you, baby?"

"No, Jacob. Please."

"Hey, let go," the Kid said.

" 'Cause the truth hurts, doesn't it? Well, it's time we learned to deal with the truth. Time we checked up on old Peter's little lies. What d'ya say?" And with that he went lurching off toward the bedroom door dragging Kiri along behind him.

"Jake, no!" Voss cried.

Sloane got hold of Jake's arm but it was too late. Jake reared back in front of the bedroom door drove his heel into it. The wood splintered around the latch and the door flew open. The light from behind them stretched into the dark room.

The sight that greeted them was almost too much for poor Jake to comprehend. His mouth dropped and he fell back against the wall. At last he let go of Kiri and she fell in a heap.

"Alice!"

Alice was still on the floor where Voss had left her. She had herself leaned against the side of the bed with her knees together and her blouse still undone. She kept her eyes on the floor as if she couldn't bear to look up.

"Oh, David . . ." she said, miserably.

CHAPTER

14

A prim young nurse dozed at her desk outside of the emergency room while an orderly swabbed down the corridor with methodical patience, sliding his plastic bucket over the wet tiles after him. It was very late in the old wing of Chulilonghorn Medical Center, a crumbling Victorian edifice with lofty ceilings where fans with big wooden blades mixed the stinging smells of disinfectant and floor varnish into what little breathable air was available on a hot summer's night. Most of the rest of the hospital was sleeping and in the gardens outside the tall open windows, even the whirring of the locusts had fallen off.

"Good. Good," the Prince kept saying, annoying the young intern who pinched the split in Voss's swollen upper lip together, slid a curved needle through the puckered flesh, and tied off another stitch. "Nicely done, Doctor."

"Enjoying yourself?"

"Shhh!" the intern said.

When the orderly had worked his way into the emergency room the Prince pointed out that much of the mess being mopped from the small white tiles on the floor was from Voss's bleeding.

"Must you?" Voss's face went a shade paler. He flinched as another stitch was tugged tight and tied off.

"He's doing very well, Peter." The Prince was observing the doctor's first aid with intense curiosity, making mental notes on the procedure and giving his partner's thigh an occasional squeeze of encouragement. "Very well, indeed."

"I'm glad," Voss said, thickly. The split had required six stitches so far and his left eye was swollen and blackening. It kept watering, the tears adding to the sticky smear where the flesh was numb around the sutures. "And how do I look?"

The Prince considered for a minute. "There are those who would say that you never looked better."

"Mmmm." Voss tried to touch his wound but the intern brushed the hand away and said something to the Prince.

"He suggests that if you do not like the pain you should not get into fights." The Prince grimaced as the needle pierced the skin again.

"Tell'm I got cold cocked by my best friend," Voss said when the thread had been drawn tight again. "See what he has to say about that."

When the last suture had been tied off the intern took a moment to inspect his handiwork roughly, tilting his patient's head back and forth under the blinding light to see if he'd missed anything. He hadn't. There hadn't been time for much more damage, all it had amounted to was a fast combination: a quick left-right and it was over. Voss guessed the lump on the back of his head was where he'd hit the floor but he couldn't be sure.

"What happened when the lights went out?" he asked.

"Mmm. Let me see. Kiri took it the hardest, I think. She blamed it all on Miss Alice, you see. Such verbal abuse . . . never have I seen her that way. She actually tried to attack her as if we were all back in the Mosquito Bar and Miss Alice was just another whore like herself. I had to physically restrain her."

Voss groaned and hid his face in his hand. "What else?"

"Well, after David got control of himself again he put Kiri in the care of the Kid and sent them home in the motorcycle. Then he took Miss Alice."

"What'd he do to Alice?"

"Do to her," the Prince said, archly. "What do you mean 'do to her'? What do you expect? After all, David is a man of honor. A gentleman, in his way. I had almost forgotten you had such countrymen."

"What'd he do?"

"He said he was sending her back to Aranyaprathet, where she'd be safe. There was, after all, the consequences of your scheming to deal with. Park Sung Dai will be more dangerous than ever. He was furious, Peter. He was almost insane with frustration—well, who wouldn't be? His man . . ."

"Janus."

". . . Janus. Yes. He was out on the porch the whole time."

"I know."

"Well, they went off together without him doing anything, I guess because the Kid was still there."

"Mmm."

The Prince paused, tapping at his cheek with a finger as if he'd left something out.

"Jake," Voss prompted.

"Jacob . . . oh yes, Jacob acted very oddly. He was terribly shocked at finding Miss Alice in such a . . . such a situation, though with a past such as his I can't think why. He left in a daze. Yes, and he was sick out on the veranda. Vomiting down on the cars coming up the hill."

"What happened to him?"

The Prince shrugged. "I wish I knew," he said. "He went off somewhere during all the confusion, that's all. The rest of us were too concerned with the women and with that Janus fellow showing up the way he did, so we didn't go looking for him." The intern stained the wound with some Mercurochrome and gathered up his instruments. A respectful nod for the Prince and he was off without further comment.

The Prince cleared his throat. "You know, Peter, it is not the habit of my people to make judgments about the behavior of others, particularly of foreigners whose values we do not fully understand. Still, I must say that your behavior in this affair has been disappointing. Tell me, did you lie to Miss Alice as you have lied to the rest of us?"

"Maybe half a lie," he admitted. "I told her I was dismantling the operation. Giving it up. Starting with a clean slate."

"Ahah. And she believed you?"

"Of course." He got shakily to his feet and checked out his image reflected in the glass of a cabinet full of surgical instruments. "As soon as I had the test key program out I used it to transfer the Korean's money to the People Project accounts."

"You *didn't!*"

"Why not?" He turned around to face the Prince. "Look, y'gotta understand. I've got feelings in all this, too, y'know. Honest. She's not like all the rest. We're a lot alike, her and me."

"All of it?"

"All of what?"

"The money."

"I'm trying to tell you what this girl means to me."

"But eleven and a half . . ."

"Petty cash, my friend." Voss made his way across the ammoniated floor, steadying himself against any furniture that came his way until he'd gotten to where his bloodied new shirt was hung. "I can't get you to understand how big this all is, can I? We are now piped into the international monetary exchange. You don't seem to realize what that means."

"I do so."

"Well, then, what was that crap about the company's commercial code? What the hell are you worried about?"

"Well, after all that Jacob and David were saying . . ."

"Y'got cold feet, I know." He unraveled a strip of gauze from its spool and wadded it up to dab his runny eye with. "You thought I'd rob from the company. Accounts with less than a hundred and ten thousand in 'em, think I'd stoop to that?"

The Prince scuffed his oxfords over the floor absently as if he were counting the tiles at his feet with his toes. "How much is in them now?"

"It's almost beyond counting," he said sadly. "Too bad we can't keep it."

A nurse appeared and began berating Voss for being on his feet but by then he had his shirt buttoned and enough confidence in his legs to head for the door.

The Prince was held up explaining things to the nurse and then to a burly matron she had summoned so he had to hustle to catch up with Voss on the steps leading down to the street.

"Where do you think you are going, Peter?" he called after him. "It's three o'clock in the morning."

"I've got work to do."

"Park Sung Dai is out there waiting for you. He is not done with you yet."

"I'm not done with him, either," Voss said.

The Chowloon Club was a sinister hole in the wall near the Klong Toey docks. It was dirty and smelly, with only a couple of dim bulbs to light the whole place. It was hard to make out faces, hard to make out what the figures clustered in dark corners were up to, and nearly impossible to see what the wall-eyed bartender was serving out for drinks.

It was a dangerous hangout, its patrons were the denizens of the Siamese underworld, its atmosphere as thick with conspiracy as with layers of smoke from tobacco and hashish. The talk was low, a murmur made of a dozen tongues except for the one that rose above the rest.

"*Sic semper* fidelity." It was Jake. "Y'know what I mean?" The bartender nodded. Jake was balanced on a bar stool looking no better than the rabble around him. His face was beefy red and he had a week's growth on his face.

"The way I figure it, if I can just make it through the night, this will all have happened yesterday."

The bartender paid no attention. He was licking his thumb and rubbing the sore-looking line of welts along the inside of his arm.

"G'me another one of those," Jake said, waving his chubby finger at the collection of dusty bottles and while the bartender poured him another Jake popped the last of his screwballs.

It took a while but at last the opiated cannabis concoction began to catch up with the residual drugs that he'd been stewing his brain with for the last few days and he felt himself slipping back into that numb, spinning twilight world again.

He found no solace there. The image of Alice kept intruding. Alice naked. Alice letting Voss fondle her, humbling herself beneath him, her private-most parts welcoming his . . . his . . .

With his sodden brain reeling under the onslaught of these explicit horrors, he found himself fighting for distraction in the reality of the barroom around him. He finished his drink and looked around at the fuzzy lights and the nightmare faces. There was a girl sitting beside him, her face swimming out of the turmoil. He tried to focus on her, screwing up his face as if he were squinting at fine print. At last he managed to recognize her as the plump bar girl with a puckered red mouth who'd been watching him since he'd come in.

"Hello, there," he said. She replied with a limp smile. He couldn't be sure of her qualities or indeed if she even had any besides her chilly silence. Patiently, she attended him, regarding him with cold, tired eyes while he regaled her with an hour of incoherent nonsense.

"Don'cha see the joke?" he concluded. "Jus' like the March Hare." He paused to stifle a belch. "Y' think he's crazy, runnin' around like that, heh-heh. But it's mating season, see? He's jus' lookin' f' somethin' to fuck."

She didn't care and Jake liked that. Life didn't mean shit to this one, she was vapid and distant, and the shimmering vision of her passionless screw began growing in his mind. She was bored and stupid and her face never pulled out of its fatal pout even while Jake blurted what words he could to buy a few moments of time between her open thighs. He was treading water in the black pool of his despair, he was starving for the cold touch of this heartless whore. He would pay anything, promise anything.

He paid off the bartender with a wad of uncounted bills. "I think I got me a live one," he confided and he followed the girl out into the night.

The buildings near the docks on this side of the river smelled of corruption and decay and number ten oil drifting down from the ships up the line. The slum behind was a jumble of raw wooden shacks under a pall of industrial fumes and heavy gases bubbling up from the muck of the ditches. The walkways were like tunnels between leaning wooden walls leading off in uncertain directions along the railway tracks.

There were ruins there from the beginnings of the city. There were iron-grilled go-downs and neglected piers and more shanty house saloons, all packed in together in a faceless, Dickensian nightmare.

Jake got mixed up. The walls were everywhere and the way the whore was leading him made no sense at all.

She was just ahead of him; sometimes he lost sight of her and a little nudge of panic would creep in. He was like a rat in a maze, they'd been creeping along these empty alleyways for what seemed like hours and he was vaguely aware that he was lost. That, in fact, he couldn't even find his way to the street. He should say something to the whore, but what?

That was simple enough. He'd just explain things. After all, he wasn't choosy. A quickie was all he was after. Hell—anywhere along here would do. He paused, breathing hard at this unexpected workout, but before he could speak the whore turned to him and for the first time she smiled. Wherever it was she'd been taking him, they must have arrived. She beckoned him with just the lightest turn of the head and Jake giggled.

"Heh-heh-heh, you little devil." He pulled a long handkerchief out of his back pocket and wiped at his upper lip as he trotted after her up a trash-strewn alley to where a cyclone fence cut off the way. There was dark all around, for the light of the city nearby was hidden behind the scrub that grew out of the brackish waters of the nearby estuary.

For a moment there was nothing to see but the dim patch of sky overhead, nothing of what was near at hand. Panic was creeping in from the edges of his opiated world, but the whore was there. He could hear her breathing and the compulsion that had driven him this far blotted out his apprehension and drove him after her into the dark.

He had drugged too many of his senses so it was only when his eyes had adjusted to the dark that he began to understand the danger. There in the shadows was a familiar object. Big and angular like an animal hunkering down, ready to spring.

"Why . . ." Jake said as his short legs continued propelling him forward in spite of his misgivings. "Why, it's the jeep."

He braced himself against the square fender, looking around for the whore. "Where are you, baby? What are you doing with Pete's . . . ?" Then he saw who was sitting at the wheel.

It was Janus.

Alice sat with Sloane until morning in front of the RSF offices on Wireless Road. There was a shrine to the starving Buddha, a handsome bronze that someone had wrapped in yellow crepe paper to clothe the naked figure and thus to earn merit against some future accounting. The stubs of burnt joss sticks and candles lay at its feet. The shrine was set on a simple rock pedestal under a heavy tree.

They sat in silence, Alice on the low rock, her back straight, her expression wistful as if her thoughts were far away, Sloane against the smooth, veined trunk of the tree with his leg propped up so he could rest his chin upon his knee. He was drawing patterns absently in the thin layer of dirt in the hollow of the rock near his foot.

They had said almost nothing until dawn broke and life was

taken up again in the shops along the boulevard. Then she tried some small talk to open him up but each attempt was left to dangle. It was worse than shouting or tears. It was nothing.

She could see how hurt he was but he sat like a stone, refusing to allow her even the comfort of his anger. It was as if she'd done much more than lose him, it was as if she'd lost all their past together, too. All those happier days with him were poisoned now and could never be tasted again.

"Say something, David."

"I think you've said it all this time," he replied and he got to his feet. "Here's the truck. They must be forming up early today."

She took his hand and held onto it so that he couldn't pull it away. "Don't do this, Fly-boy," she said, afraid to look up at his face. "We mean so much more to each other than to let this . . . this stupid thing ruin everything."

Tears came to Sloane's eyes but he stepped to one side so that she would have to either turn with him or let him go. She let him go.

"Here comes the Land Rover," he said. "And I see that Jorgenson guy has come along, too. Now you'll have company on the trip."

He left her there. He waved down a tuk-tuk, reached out, and swung himself into the backseat before it had time to come to a full stop.

Tall thunderheads had been tumbling down from the northeast since first light and now the air was thick and wet and the bright morning sky had been blotted out. Sloane could smell the rain long before he felt its cool sting against his skin: the smell of ozone, the tang of forest wetness that filled the air just moments before the heavy droplets began to fall.

The monsoon had begun.

Traffic was quickly thrown into chaos. Deep puddles swallowed up motorcycles and buses stalled in the middle of intersections. Schoolchildren in their uniforms crowded together under communal umbrellas. The crowds were in a merry mood, laughing and shouting, running for shelter with newspapers over their heads or just letting themselves get drenched. It was a joyful time in spite of the mess.

Sloane's tuk-tuk almost bogged down in the wake of a painted-up Mercedes truck but managed to reach the high ground past the Dusitani Hotel. The spray blowing into the back was soaking him but he didn't care. The tuk-tuk was sputtering down Sathron Road, the driver twisting his accelerator handle to keep the damp motor going, when the brake lights went on behind the truck up ahead.

Sloane was blinded by the torrent so that all he could see through the windshield was a refracted scattering of bright red lights. Something was blocking the way.

"What is it?" he asked the driver. "What's the matter this time?"

He stuck his head out into the rain and saw that a long red Toyota fire truck had managed to wedge itself into the entrance to Dog Alley like a spaniel with its head stuck in a burrow. Wheels were spinning, frantic firemen were shouting and pushing but the truck was stuck solid between the walls of the Security Compound and the consulate next door. A willing crowd was gathering in the pelting rain but nobody knew what to do.

Sloane paid off the fare with the handiest bill he could find and ran past two of the firemen, who were shouting at each other. The heavy pumper was blanketed with men in all states of attire trying to free their equipment and hoses from the compartments along the side of the boxy truck, many of which were wedged shut against the walls.

"Oh no." Sloane jumped up onto the bed of the truck, scrambled over the roof of the cab, and paused up there for a look. Over the fences and trees a column of heavy black smoke climbed skyward. "Oh, lord, it's the house!"

He jumped to the ground and wrenched a CO-2 extinguisher from its clamp behind the cab and chased after the few firemen who'd thought to do the same. Down the gravel path he ran, that hopeless, sinking feeling growing in the pit of his stomach, his clothing and hair plastered against his skin by the rain.

It looked like the house as he ran down the alley that led to the footbridge but then from the turnoff it seemed to be something else. It was something inside the compound, all right. And if anything it was getting worse. The column of smoke had grown thicker and had already climbed high enough to flatten against the low, dirty rain clouds. It was as dark as evening and the air was filled with an urgent din as the citizens of Dog Alley bumped and shoved and yelled in the downpour for children unaccounted for and neighbors with news. Even the Cambodians had stuck their heads out to see what was going on as Sloane rounded that corner of the fence.

He vaulted the gate and found that the stolen jeep had been returned. It sat in the center of the courtyard well away from the house, ablaze from end to end. The heat struck him as soon as he landed, it was a roiling inferno of burning gasoline and stinking black rubber smoke. It was the stench of battle and it triggered instincts that Sloane had forgotten, pumping adrenaline through his limbs and channeling his senses. This is it. Fly or fry.

The wind shifted, blowing the hot smoke into his face. Choking him. Trying to drive him back from the fire even as he ran toward it.

Voss was already there, he and the Kid. They were like shadows in front of the blaze, locked together as if in some childish wrestling match. The Kid was tossing his brother around like a rag doll but Voss held on.

"Get back," he was shouting above the roar. "Get back!" He was hauling at the Kid by whatever he could get ahold of, trying to keep him from the flames but the Kid went on trying to throw him off. His skin was already red and blistered and still he drove himself toward the fire, shielding his face with his arm as he beat uselessly at the flames with a blanket.

Sloane tried the puny fire extinguisher but it was as useless as the Kid's blanket. He threw it aside and went to grab the Kid, too, but then he saw what the Kid was after.

"Oh, no," Sloane said. "Oh, my god." Nausea gripped his stomach and he crept a few inches closer to the inferno to see for himself. There was somebody inside.

Something gave in the wreckage and the jeep tipped suddenly and then collapsed in on itself in an explosion of sparks. A conflagration spilled from a ruptured gas line, lighting the courtyard against the darkness of the storm so that the corpse could be seen quite clearly, black within the brilliant fire. Its hands had a death grip on the wheel, its head was tilted back against the iron skeleton of the seat, eye sockets empty, its charred, shrunken flesh drawn back from the mouth as if in some last hideous laugh.

Sloane turned his back on the blazing heat and backed toward the flames, blinking hard as the heat stole moisture from his eyes, ducking his face into his armpit as something went off with a bang and blew out a cloud of flame.

Another step, even the Kid could get no closer, and Sloane dropped and threw himself at the Kid at knee level. The Kid was off balance with both arms out ahead of him so the tackle bowled him flat just as the gas tank erupted in a ball of fire at the other end of the wreck, hoisting the rear of the jeep into the air so that the corpse toppled forward and dissolved into a heap of sizzling gore.

Sloane kept the Kid down until the fury had lifted, then they both crawled away from the heat to where Voss lay gasping for breath. Sloane fell against the fence, retching.

The first of the firemen had finally made it over the wall by the time anyone had the breath to speak.

"What . . . who . . . ?" Sloane panted.

Voss lay on his stomach, his convulsions subsiding, his face buried in his hands.

"Jake," he said when he could.

CHAPTER
15

"What day is this?"

"Friday," the Prince said. "June the twentieth."

"June twentieth." Voss put his hands behind his head and stretched painfully in his rolled leather desk chair without taking his eyes from the screen of the terminal before him. "It's springtime back in the Bronx. Baseball in the lot behind the school . . ."

"You're tired, Peter. Take a rest." The Prince had been sitting quietly nearby, neat and colorless under the computer room's fluorescent lights. He had closed the Thai/Tech office the day of Jake's death, sending home the few secretaries and clerks it took to run things while Voss settled in for a marathon session at his console.

"I used to know a couple of guys like Jake back in the Bronx. Nobody liked 'em much when they were kids because they were smart and wiseass and hard to get along with. And the more nobody liked 'em the more wiseass and hard to get along with they got. Trouble is they were usually right. Just like Jake.

"I was just thinkin', it was a guy like that, a boozer like Jake, who got me started on computers back at Trinity. One of the Jesuits. Got me a couple of scholarships, too. I loved him a lot.

"He told me once that the world's gonna turn itself inside out for these things. That nothing's gonna be left the same. 'The search for truth is over,' he used to say. 'We've settled for magic.' Man, if he could only see me now. Right? A little razzle-dazzle, a little sleight of hand and here I am."

"Yes, indeed. Here you are."

Voss checked the cigarette pack on the desk beside him and,

finding it empty, began poking through the ashtray for a butt long enough to light. "I shouldn't be surprised, I guess," he said. "Garbage in, garbage out."

"I don't like this, Peter," the Prince said. "I don't like any of it. It was enough to ask for money and power from those machines of yours, but justice, too?" He shook his head. "No, it is asking too much. We have been fools, my friend. There is nothing to this electronic world of yours but the greed of those who try to exploit it."

Voss chewed pensively at his injured lip, testing the pain behind the ugly black stitches as he inspected the stub of a cigarette that he had just rescued from the brimming glass ashtray. His black eye was still swollen and there was a bloodless, abandoned look to the rest of his face. His long hair hung slack and oily over his ears and his Frank Zappa T-shirt was beginning to smell.

"Yeah, maybe so," he said, as much to himself as to the Prince. "This is the way to end it, though. You've got to admit. A real masterpiece. Computers were practically invented to break codes, y'know."

"No. I didn't know that."

"Sure. An early IBM prototype called 'Colossus,' designed for Ultra, the British cryptological research that broke the German Enigma codes in the Second World War."

"Mm."

"As soon as I was sure I'd rescued my own little Ultra from the data banks of the National Defense Network I knew I had a chance to knock off the Korean once and for all."

"It sounds very complicated to me."

"Simplest thing in the world. I'm going to use it to give the Korean eleven and a half million dollars."

"Give him his money back?"

"Not *his* money. I already gave that to Alice. Nope. Somebody else's money. Somebody who won't like it a bit."

"I don't understand."

"That's okay. He will. When he sees for himself right here, right on this CRT screen here, he'll know that it's out of my hands. That it's come to an end for both of us."

He stuck the crooked cigarette stub gingerly between his injured lips, lit it, and managed a few nervous puffs before turning back to the screen where a sequence of diagrams had just finished and the word "ready" was blinking on the screen.

"Ready to run," he said.

"What do we do now?"

"We wait. He ought'a be showing up pretty soon." He rubbed his good eye with the heel of his hand. The Prince was right, he was tired. As tired as he'd ever been. He'd set to work the morning of Jake's death and kept himself going all day and all night on coffee and cigarettes. There was a foul, dry taste in his mouth and a hammering headache someplace deep in his skull. He was bleary-eyed and nursing an aching back but he'd stuck it out at his terminal hour after hour, punching out the end of a dream.

"That's him," he said at the sounds of intruders on the staircase. "Did you bring something like I told you?"

The Prince pulled a light, pearl-handled pistol from his jacket pocket and showed it to Voss, who didn't hide his misgivings.

"Oh, swell," he said. "Looks more like a cigarette lighter."

"It was all I could find."

"Okay, okay. Know how to use it?"

The Prince shook his head. "I don't like this. You're only making things worse."

"I don't like it either. You know how I feel about guns."

The double doors hissed open and a pair of the Korean's sailors entered. Cowed like country bumpkins by the futuristic environment of the computer room they were fondling their slung Bren guns for comfort. The doors swung closed behind them while Park Sung Dai, visible through the glass panels, paused on the landing outside to compose himself, hiking his white linen trousers and brushing at the wrinkles in his lap before making his entrance.

He was still out of breath from his angry climb up the staircase but he did his best not to let it show. His tie hung wilted from his collar and his wet shirt stuck to his midriff like wallpaper. He had removed his jacket and folded it over his arm, an uncharacteristic informality.

"Where's your thug?" Voss asked him, swiveling around and propping himself with his elbow against the arm of his chair. "Back in his cage?"

"On an errand," the Korean replied, inspecting the room nervously. "Picking up something to encourage your . . ."

"I don't need 'encouragement.' "

"Insurance, then."

"I told you I had the solution, didn't I?"

"Ho?" The Korean tilted his head suspiciously. Then he let an unpleasant smirk play along his lips. "So at last you have decided to see things my way. I wonder why."

"I didn't say I saw anything your way. I said I had the solution. The trouble is you've had the wrong idea about what this is all about. You act like this data business is just so much plumbing. Like I can just twist a valve here and unscrew a faucet there and the money will just flow to wherever you want it."

"Do not lecture me, Peter." The Korean scowled.

"I don't want any misunderstandings, that's all."

"You promised on the phone you had the solution. Is it so or not?"

"Absolutely," Voss assured him. "And there it is." He pointed at his keyboard. "See that button? That red one, there? That's a reset button. That's the button that changes the status of the computer and tells it to run the program. Shall I push it? There's a program all ready to run—well, more than one, actually. This one breaks a security code so I can transfer a lot of money into your account . . . are you following this?"

"A lot of money?"

"Eleven and a half million credited to your accounts in Hong Kong."

"So!"

"I'm sure your Russian technicians, back on the yacht, are monitoring all of this. They'll probably tell you how it works later. I just wanted you here to watch the fireworks firsthand. I want to be sure you understand."

"What are you up to?"

"Up to? I'm not up to anything, man. I'm finishing it. I'm calling a halt to this feud of ours the only way I know. You'll see. Go ahead, push the button yourself. That red one there."

"Me?"

"Sure. Why not? I told you, it's the solution to this whole mess."

"Oh, no."

"You don't want the money?"

The Korean eyed Voss suspiciously. "This will give me my money? Really?"

"Sure. And a whole lot more. Go ahead. You'll see."

The Korean's puffy eyes were jumpy with avarice and indecision. "All of it?"

"Every cent. I know when I'm licked."

"And our deal with Hanoi?"

"It'll take care of that, too, believe me."

"This . . . this red one?"

The tension was unbearable for the Prince. He squirmed and shifted his little pistol from one hand to the other in his lap as he watched the perspiring Korean extend a trembling finger toward the button.

"God, how I hate you."

"Push it!"

He stabbed at the button and jerked his hand away as if it had been red hot, looking around for the sirens or the explosions or whatever was supposed to happen. When nothing did he glanced around at his men sheepishly.

"Now, that wasn't so hard, was it?" Voss said as the screen before him became a riot of projected data filling and refilling the screen until it settled down into strips of twelve-digit numbers running from top to bottom. Now and then a number would blink out and the whole line would shift for another number to be added to the bottom.

The Korean waited, holding his breath for a sign but for a very long minute Voss seemed to have lost interest in him.

Finally, without looking up, Voss began talking. So calmly and so rationally he might have been explaining the rules of golf.

"When I got back yesterday," he began. "When I got back and found what you'd done to Jake I had this . . . this *thing* inside me. This scared, sick, awful thing that's been eating at my guts like some kind of animal. 'Kill him,' it keeps telling me. 'He doesn't deserve to live. He's a murderer. He's a leech. Kill him.' But I couldn't, see? You know me. I'm no good at rough stuff. And, anyhow, it came to me that I'm no better than you. A crook and even a killer, nothing more. I killed Jake, too. I might as well have lit the match. Complicity, Jake would have called it. I can't change all that now; about all I can do is call a halt to it."

"On my terms."

"On nobody's terms."

"But you just said . . ."

"I said you were going to get the money, but you won't want it."

"This is another of your tricks."

"Call it what you want, I'm shutting this whole mess down. I can still call the shots around here, see? Because I've still got all the smarts. In fact, I've got more than that now. A hell of a lot more. I've got a program that'll get me access to the world's monetary transfer system."

"Program? Access? What are you talking about?"

"Money. That's what I'm talking about. I'm talking about all that money I made for you and how little of it I ever saw."

"We had a deal."

"Promises, that's all I had. Eleven and a half million sitting in the Bank L'Indochine and the end of the war in sight—I knew when things started getting rough you'd cut and run and I'd never see a cent.

"So I decided to keep an eye on my investment by using the Beach House 7 computers to monitor the account. That's how it all started. Just a status check every thirty seconds through the National Defense Network. As long as the account remained in a stable state everything was cool, but when you tried to transfer it I was gonna grab it. Now that's reasonable, right? I mean, what could be more fair?

"But that's when things began getting complicated." Voss swung his feet up onto the desk and paused long enough to give his lip another chew. "See, you can't just 'grab' data, you've got to put it somewhere, you've got to move it around. And if you're gonna move money around you're gonna need a 'test key,' a unique corporate code one banking institution sends another to verify the authorization of the transfer of funds.

"Now, a test key doesn't stay the same. That would make it vulnerable to theft or to the cypher-breaking capabilities of another computer, so it's altered every week or so on a regular schedule.

"So I designed a cypher-breaking program and hid it in computers of the National Defense Network's operations center to monitor the activity of some other accounts the Bank L'Indochine handled. I called it 'Ultra.' Oh, I was real proud of it. I must have spent weeks at it—but it didn't work. It just didn't have enough data to penetrate the code. I was almost ready to give it up when one day a telex operator made a mistake on a funds transfer message. An insignificant mistake, it would seem, but that's all it took.

"The transmitted mistake, the reply and the correction set up a series of anamolies by which my program was able to break both the 'test key' code and the 'template' by which it was altered. It was like forging the signature of one bank to change its orders to another.

"After that it was easy for me to arrange things so that the minute you tried to transfer your account you activated a program that deflected the data to where you'd never find it; to hide it in some accounts I set up under the name of a legitimate institution where the transfer of eleven and a half million bucks would look like an everyday transaction. An institution where it would be safe until I could set up a corporate account of my own to transfer it to.

"That meant New City Credit, of course, where my old buddy Dave had just been appointed to the board of directors. Y'never know when you're going to need a friend in high places with an access code of his own."

The Korean took a backward step in the face of Voss's growing eagerness to vaunt his wizardry.

"Everything worked the way it was supposed to except for the war. With things closing in so fast everybody started pullin' out at the same time. Shell Oil, Chase Manhattan, Mitsubishi, Colonel this guy, and Senator that guy . . . everybody. Then you tried to pull out and the program intercepted it. But before I could get to a computer terminal to retrieve the money, the National Defense Network was shut down. Locked up tight with my little Ultra code trapped inside."

The Korean's eyes had grown round as the outline of the conspiracy took shape. "So . . ." he said when he was finally allowed to speak. "So that foul-mouthed . . . that insulting fool was right."

"Jake?"

"You were not honoring your commitment to open Beach House 7. This has all been a trick to get back into the network."

"Right. But not for the money. The money wasn't even there, it was hidden away someplace in the New City's accounts back in Singapore where nobody'd even know they had it. No, the money wasn't in the network but my little 'Ultra' program was. The program that could never be duplicated without the same telex operator making the same mistake. That's what I had to get or I'd never access those New City accounts again."

"So . . ." He was breathing heavily. "So you have the money now?"

"Nope. Gave it to Alice."

"Argh!"

"To her favorite charity, actually. To the People Project. What the hell, I didn't need the money much anyhow. The program was worth a lot more that that. Think about it. Access to almost any bank account on the system. Chase Manhattan, Kowloon and Shanghai . . . even the Singapore branch of the Moscow Narodny Bank is on that system. In fact . . ." Voss looked up at the Korean, his eyes as hard as steel. "In fact, *that's* where I got the money to transfer into your account."

"My . . ."

"Moscow Narodny is the British bank that handles the economic transactions between the Socialist Republic of Vietnam and the outside world."

"This will not work, Peter. They'll find out."

"That's right. You got the money you wanted, but you got it right out of the accounts of the Socialist Republic of Vietnam. Boy, are they gonna be mad."

"Aargh!"

"That's the end of our 'partnership,' Sung Dai. And maybe the end of us, too. And they'll certainly restructure the encoding system when word of this switch gets around so that's the end of my 'Ultra' program as well.

"So that's the solution, y'like it? You're all paid off. There's no more money, no more business, no more program, no more threats. We're through, Sung Dai. The only thing left for you is to get the money out of your accounts and run for it. Run as far and as fast as you can and try to find a place where the Communists won't find you, because even if the Russian technicians back on your boat haven't figured it out yet, there's still a lot of paperwork to a deal like this. A paper trail that follows after the transfer to confirm the transaction for the records. Sooner or later they'll find out what happened and when they do they'll know that this deal you made about accessing Beach House 7 was a trick. They're gonna be after you like a nest of hornets."

"T-the Communists?" the Korean sputtered. "But surely they will not be angry with *me.*" The Korean was mopping his face in spite of the chill. "After all, it was you who engineered all of this."

"It was your deal, not mine. Remember?" Voss dropped his feet to the floor and stood up. He rested his hands on the desktop and leaned forward on his knuckles, glaring at the Korean with fierce bloodshot eyes. "You were the one who carried the plan to them. You were the one who delivered the messages and instructions back and forth."

For a moment the Korean looked like there was something stuck in his throat. He made odd, involuntary noises through his nose and was moving his hands about in the air as if he were juggling something. Then his corpulent face seemed to expand, his puffy eyes squeezed together, and his fury burst.

"*Aaaargh!*" he screamed. "*Aaaargh!*" He spun around and snatched the Bren gun from the nearest sailor, kicking at him to free the strap and tripping backward over himself when it came free.

"Holy shit!" Voss flung himself to the floor.

"Stop this machine. Stop this money transfer! *Stop-it-stop-it-stop-it-stop* . . ." The Korean cocked the little submachine gun, braced its wire stock in the crook of his arm, and directed a deafening burst of automatic gunfire into the terminal beside Voss. Everybody else in the room had hit the deck, even the sailors. Shards of glass from the CRT went flying and an erratic string of welts burst through the back of Voss's console, spewing color-coded pieces all over the room. One of the sailors was crawling for the door.

"You can't stop it!" Voss was yelling. "You can't stop it from here. We can only monitor the system!" He was cowering behind his desk, hiding his face from the flying fragments. At the first pause he looked around for the Prince and found the chair he had been sitting in empty and spinning like a top. "Shoot back! Shoot back, f'Christ's sake." But the Prince was nowhere in sight.

"*I'll stop it myself!*" The Korean could hardly be understood.

His shouting was thick with hatred and phlegm. He let go with another volley that shattered the plastic face of a storage unit. Behind him another monitor, another column of digits.

"What're you trying to do?" Voss was shouting. "Y' can't stop it from here!"

"You lie!" And with that the Korean blasted out the other monitor, too, and then sprayed the storage units on the other side of the room, screaming and yelling Korean obscenities while a broken cable leaked sparks out all over the room. One end of a light unit dropped from the ceiling and glass was falling like a hailstorm.

"I'll stop it, I'll stop it, I'll stop . . ."

The clip was done but the Korean wasn't. He pounced upon the second sailor and tore his gun from him. Then he went looking for Voss.

"Wait, wait," Voss was yelling in a panic. "Wait, I'm tellin' you, y'can't stop it from here!"

The Korean paused long enough to cock his weapon and then fired again, a quick burst that made a sound like a power tool as its little bullets chewed up the room. Voss was scrambling from the cover of one desk to the next on his hands and knees, looking for the Prince. "Gimme the gun, Prince! Gimme the . . . where'd you go?"

The Korean jumped over the desk where Voss had been sitting, checked under it, and then followed the shouting to the other side of the room.

"Gimme the gun! I'll shoot him myself." Voss spotted the Prince's legs as they disappeared behind a filing cabinet. *Gimme the gun!*

The Korean had clambered up onto the next desk in line, hopping to the next one and the next like a monkey. ". . . *Stop-it-stop-it-stop-it!*" He caught up with Voss and shot up the linoleum just inches from his hand. The noise rang in Voss's ears as splinters flew, stinging his fingers and peppering his face.

"I *can't* stop it, I'm tellin' you." He tried for the desk again but the his pursuer leaped to the floor, sidestepping along beside him until the futility of escape was apparent. The Korean skittered around him and squatted there, bouncing on his haunches. He was strangely exuberant in his rage, breathing hard but undefeated. His calculating mind was still working.

Voss lay on his face, helpless and exhausted, trying to come up with a lie that he could use to reason with. "Wait . . . wait, listen." Voss was gasping. "Listen . . . say y'do stop the program somehow. Okay? I mean if you wreck the program how y'gonna get your money, huh?"

"Get it? Get it?" The Korean shook his head as if to clear it. "Why, from your Miss Alice, of course. Yes, that was the 'insurance' I sent Janus after. You gave it to her and she can just give it back."

"What? But she can't," Voss said into the linoleum. "She can't, you idiot. I told you it was out of our hands."

"*Liar!*" The Korean probed at his victim with the snout of the gun but he checked his temper. "I have found your weakness, Peter. You can fight me no longer. I may not be clever but I can still win this game my way."

"I gave it to the People Project," Voss pleaded. "To her relief fund. To the agency that she works for. From a blind endowment fund based in . . ."

"Aranyaprathet? Eh? You see? I know where she is. I looked her up. Nong Kai, in the Dangrek Mountains north of Nong Chan. A very dangerous place, that part of the border. No border police, isolated. All those border incidents. Anything can happen there these days. I'm sure Janus can persuade her—or persuade you."

"But I'm tellin' you, nobody can stop it," Voss shouted after him as he backed toward the door with his sailors. "Look. I'll show you. It's right there on the screen!"

"And you will explain it to the Russians, too," the Korean said, still waving his weapon around the room. "You will come to my boat and explain it to the Russians before I am through. Show all this to them and they will see that it was not my fault."

The doors hissed shut and he was gone. For a long time there was no sound but the occasional electrical sputter from somewhere in the ruptured circuits. And then from behind the filing cabinet the Prince said,

"Perhaps he understands all too well."

CHAPTER
16

The children along Dog Alley were already tired of the rain. They were huddled against the afternoon deluge under scraps of polyethylene sheeting they'd swiped from a construction site over on Silom Road, watching impassively as the elder of the two Cambodians (whose hiding place behind the fence could be little better than a bog by now) climbed the corner fence post to secure his radio antenna with a rag. He slipped near the top and banged his shin but the children weren't amused. They were drenched and bored.

Sloane watched the scene without seeing. He had gone to close the shutters against the rain that was dripping back under the eaves and ended up staring idly out through the tunnel of trees, lost in his morose thoughts. He stood there a long time, holding the same pair of socks in his hand that he'd been holding when he started his packing half an hour ago, and didn't come out of it until he saw Kiri trudging through the mud to the gate.

"Kiri," he called down to her. "Hey, where have you been? The Kid's been out looking for you since this morning."

She gave him a nod and a vague little wave. She hadn't really heard. She was clasping her arms in front of her, stooped against the steady drizzle with her straight hair streaking down over her face.

Sloane tossed the socks down next to his duffle bag, emptied the last of the drawers onto the bed, and left the rest of the job until later so he could go down to see how she was.

He found her out back under the breezeway. She was cleaning the curdled milk from the saucers she had left for the cats the day before and laying out clean ones with fresh milk from the icebox. Cat-cat was at her feet along with a half-dozen others, yeowling their Siamese yeowl and rubbing themselves against her ankles, their fur pasted to their scrawny flanks by the rain.

"The Kid's out looking for you," Sloane told her again. "You okay?"

"You should not have le' him out by himself," Kiri said without looking around.

"There was no stopping him."

For a moment she just stood there, watching the cats, and then her face began to wrinkle up and he could see she was going to cry. At first she tried to hide it, turning away when he reached out for her, but then she let herself fall into his arms, burying her face against his chest and sobbing softly as he rocked her with clumsy tenderness. He wasn't very good at this sort of thing but he was as gentle as he knew how to be, hushing and patting her softly as she wept.

"Oh, David," she sniffled. She turned her face and wiped her nose with the back of her hand. "What I will do now? Who will take care of me?"

Sloane gave her a hug. "I don't know," he said gently. "None of us knows, I guess."

"Oh, yes. I am sorry. I forgot, she is your woman."

"Was."

"Was your woman. How awful she must be to do this thing to an excellen' person like yourself."

"No, she's not awful."

"Please, but I believe you mistake her," Kiri said. For a moment she pulled back to look into his eyes with a strange fierce certainty that caught Sloane off-guard. She could be sad, that he would understand. Or angry. But this was the face of someone resigned to the treachery of life. An actress in a Greek tragedy committed to the fate she knew awaited her character.

"I know something of these *farang* women. I learn as much from this Miss Alice as I have learned from my books and your American cinema. They all talk of it, this power they have over men. They not want to love their men but to possess them, I think." Tears welled up in her eyes again. "What will I do without Petah? He was my whole world and now a woman like that . . ."

She left his arms and turned her back to watch the cats crowd their noses into the milk.

"Girls like me," she said. "We hide from the truth. We preten' it will go on and on and these men from the war will never leave us. But I think we are only for play until they are found by a woman of their own kind. Strange women with their big bosoms and eyes colored like the eyes of ghosts. They cast spells, these *farang* women."

"Oh now, Kiri . . ."

"They do. I have read much literature and there is much talk of how men fall under their spell. It is like the Goddess Kiratai, I think. Casting her magical net to capture the fishermen of Marn. This woman of yours from Nong Kai, she has cast such a spell over Petah. Isn't it so?"

Sloane took Kiri's hand and gave it a squeeze. "C'mon, Kiri, don't talk like that." There must be something more he could say but nothing would come. What could he tell her that would make any more sense than what she wanted to believe? Her fable was sad perhaps, but the truth of the matter was no better.

It was an hour and a half in rain-stricken traffic before Voss and the Prince reached Dog Alley. Voss was angry and desperate with each new delay, for by now there was only one way to reach Alice before Janus and only one man who could do it.

"David?"

The Prince opened the gate and slopped into the courtyard first, tracking heavy clumps of mud across the concrete squares as Sloane showed himself. He was about to greet the Prince when he saw that Voss was with him.

"Petah!" Kiri cried.

For a moment Sloane was surprised by his condition. "Your face!" he said. Voss's eye was puffed almost shut and the stitches were vivid against his pale skin.

"That was your doing, remember?" the Prince reminded him.

"Yeah?" Sloane braced his shoulders. "Yeah? Well, in that case he doesn't look so bad."

"Petah?" Kiri hovered there, ready at the smallest signal to run to him and take her chances. "Petah? What has happened?" Then she lost her resolve. He needed her, all muddy and bedraggled like that, but when she ran to him she got only a perfunctory hug.

"We'll talk about this later, okay?" he told her. "Right now we've got a big problem."

"Petah?"

"Not now."

"Ahem," the Prince interrupted. "There is a terribly urgent matter we must discuss with you, David."

"The only urgent matter that I care about is getting a cab to the airport. That's what that fat lip of his is all about, in case you haven't figured it out. I quit."

"Now stop it, David." The command was brusque and royal, so unlike the Prince that Sloane was taken aback. "The point of our meeting is not to be your jealousy or even the duplicity of certain other members of the company, do you understand? We have a serious problem that must be seen to at once."

"Yeah? Another of his problems?"

"Stop it, I said."

Sloane did. "Okay. All right."

"It's Alice," Voss said.

"Yes. Poor Miss Alice. Now we will never catch him on the ground."

"What about her? Catch who on the ground?"

"Park Sung Dai has sent his man . . ."

"Janus."

". . . Janus after Miss Alice. Aranyaprathet, wasn't it?"

"Oh, my God." Now they had his attention. "The camp? No, it's north of there. Nong Kai. What's this all about?"

"We will explain on the way."

"The plane," Voss said.

"Exactly. We must take the airplane."

"It's late," Sloane warned, looking around at the clear violet sky above the clearing. "A water landing after dark . . . ?"

"Petah, no!"

"Stay here, Kiri," Voss told her as they headed toward the alleyway.

"Petah, you stay here, too." She ran ahead and tried to block him at the gate. She tried to hold him but he unclasped her hands carefully and took her face in his hands.

"Not now, Kiri. I've got to go."

But Kiri would not be passed off so easily. She was shaking her head hysterically, tears washing down her face as she clung to him. "Let her bewitch someone else. Let her go and we can have it all as it was before." Voss looked around at the others, bewildered by her ardor as he pried her fingers from their grip on his wet shirt. "Stay with me, Petah. I have nothing but you."

"Not now, dammit." He tore the shirt getting free of her hold. "We'll take care of all this later. Honest, Kiri. Later." He held her hands to keep them away, squeezing them with pretended affection as he backed out of the gate after the others. When he was free he had to hurry, sloshing off comically after the other two, hustling after them as best he could for they were already at the corner of the *soi.*

"Petah . . ." Kiri cried after him. "Stay with me."

"Kiri, please! What d'ya want me t'do, huh?"

"Don't go."

"They're liable to kill her, don't you get it?" he called back, waving his arms beseechingly and slipping in the muck beside the fence. "I gotta go. It's all my fault."

"I do not care," Kiri screamed. "I do not care if they kill you both, do you hear?" She stood at the gate watching them disappear around the corner, then she turned and followed their path from inside the fence. "Do you hear me? You are no better than that *farang* sorceress. You have taken what you want from me and now you throw me back like a fish. But it is too late. I cannot live now. And you . . ." She chased after them, tracing their progress from inside the fence, keeping up until she came to the end and then hoisted herself up on a rail to see over the corner. ". . . Maybe you cannot live either," she shouted. "Do you hear me? Maybe I have some magic of my own." The three of them continued trudging up the alley toward the road. Voss kept his eyes on his feet as he slogged through the mud. The Prince was ashamed to look around. Only Sloane turned in time to see the look on her face, but he had to leave her there, too.

The children watched from under their plastic and the elder Cambodian was peeking up over his fence to see what the yelling was all about. His yellow eyes caught Kiri's for a moment. What could these foreign devils have done to her? Then one of the urchins squatting nearby shouted something that made the others laugh and the Cambodian lowered himself back into his hovel. Kiri wiped her eyes on the back of her arm.

The answer had come to her at almost that very instant. That miserable little man, that boy waiting all this time behind the fence. Could it be true what Major Chapikorn had said? If it was, then her terrible course had been revealed to her with the clarity of a bell. She let herself down from the rail again and turned toward the house. It was as if she were plotting for somebody else, for even then she knew it was an act she would regret for the rest of her life.

She returned to the house and found an old Pan Am travel bag that Voss had given her and packed a few of her belongings in it. She went out to the bathhouse and took some dimestore cosmetics, her hairbrush, and her small bottle of scent. She opened it and smelled the fragrance from the plastic stopper while she sat there on her knees, thinking about her idea, letting her thoughts go racing down those few bleak channels of reason that are left to hurt and jealous lovers when their world seems to be coming to an end.

At last she got to her feet and looped the strap of the travel bag over her shoulder. It was evening by now. The rain clouds had lifted and the sky over the trees was touched with the crimson of the setting sun. The rich smell of wet foliage filled the alley as she carefully closed the gate behind her for the last time. Without looking back she crossed the alley, jumping the muddy ruts until she came to the plank in the fence that the Cambodian used for his door. The antenna was waving in the light breeze and the sound of static could be heard even through the thick wood.

Kiri sat for a moment, wringing her hands lightly as if she were reconsidering. It was so hard and yet it was the easiest thing, too. All it would take was a word. Just the name of a town in the Dangrek Mountains far away. She stuck a knuckle between her teeth and held her breath against a moment of indecision. Then she gave a quiet knock.

The promising fresh breeze of the afternoon rain had been smothered by the damp heat of the season. The river was flat and motionless, stirring only with the wake of the evening ferries and the deep-bellied barges.

The Korean was frightened. The Soviet engineers were on

to him already, he was sure of it. Even now they were meeting in his wardroom where their equipment had been set up and he could hear their raised voices from the privacy of his bridge. There they were, Peter Voss and company. Three figures at work on the old biplane near the Thai/Tech pier not two hundred yards away.

The figure down on the pontoons must be Prince Woraphan. He had pulled over the big wooden propeller four or five times now, and each time there was a loud backfire, a cloud of brown smoke that hung in the motionless air and nothing else. There was much yelling back and forth with the pilot climbing down to lend a hand.

The Korean hadn't thought of the airplane. Was it possible? Could they reach the girl before Janus could? What would he do if Janus failed? How could he make Peter come here and confess that it was he who had tricked them? Surely there was something he could do to force Peter's cooperation once and for all. Something that he valued above all else. Something—the Korean squinted at the big figure that had just come running up the pier —something close at hand.

"Peter!"

"Look, it is the Kid," the Prince said. "Up there on the pier."

Voss climbed down from the cockpit so he could see around the wing. "Yeah. What's he so excited about?"

"Water in the fuel line." Sloane swore and emptied the sediment bowl into the river.

"Hey, Peter!"

"He seems pretty upset, Pete."

Voss cupped his mouth and yelled back, "What's the matter?"

"She's gone!"

"Who?"

"Kiri. Her bag, her stuff from the bathroom . . ." His voice broke. The three on the pontoon stood there helplessly while he tried to control himself. "She's gone away, Pete, and it's your fault."

"Aw now, Kid . . ."

"It's true. She's leaving us 'cause of what you did."

"Oh, Jesus," Voss said. Then he called back, "Hey, don't worry about it, Kid. Hey, wait . . ."

The Kid was looking around as if trying to decide what to do.

"You'd better do something, Pete."

"No telling what he's capable of when he gets like this," the Prince agreed. "Go along. We'll see to Alice."

"I don't know." Voss hesitated but he never took his eyes off the Kid. "Jesus, what am I gonna do?"

"You're going to go take care of your brother." Sloane had already signaled a *hangyao* tied up near the dock. "We'll be better off with just the two of us anyhow. Come on, Prince. Let's try it again."

This time the engine sputtered and caught. When the *hangyao* had pulled away with Voss, the Prince braced himself against the prop wash and let go the line to the anchor buoy and the ungainly biplane began to make headway against the current.

The Korean continued to watch for a moment and then turned his binoculars on the huge figure up on the pier again. He followed the progress of the *hangyao* until it was out of sight behind the tall pilings of the pier and then lowered the binoculars to rub his sticky eyes with his fingers.

The surface of the river was like pudding. The aging biplane was especially cumbersome in the wet monsoon air. It burrowed along the waterway in a long half-circle from the Thonburi piers to the river bend at Klong San until there was lift enough to hump it up onto its step. Then it lifted gracelessly into the air and banked toward the east as soon as it had cleared the river traffic. The horizon was a bright red ribbon of setting sun and the low angle of the light enhanced the contours of the flatlands city.

"How the hell are we supposed to find the place?" Sloane shouted, trying to read the wrinkled map on the Prince's clipboard. "We won't get there until dark and by then our only landmark will be the stupa."

"The Temple of the Moon? But it is so big," the Prince said.

"Not in the dark and not from two thousand feet. Then we've got to set her down. How many flares y'got? Where did you get them anyhow, did you ever try one out?"

The Prince shrugged. "They were good enough for the Japanese," he shouted back.

"Oh, lord." Sloane wiped his face in his free hand. He was trying to remember the bend in Cheom Bai River, the clear straight run to the north and his ride along it from Nong Kai in the Land Rover. Was it really long enough to land an aircraft as heavy as this one?

"Hey, got any more of those aspirins?"

The hedgerows and jungles softened in the twilight as they passed under the aircraft's wings and the rounded mountains of the Dangrek Range hove up out of the eastern gloom.

Sloane was scared. It was hard to tell about the Prince. It was growing dark. The sky had cleared and there was light from the stars overhead. Below there were only the clustered lights of a few towns. Ranchet, Burubai, and some others too small for names. And then—nothing. They might as well have been flying over an empty sea, for the broad, faceless jungle now covered what villages might be down there and it was a couple of hours yet until moon rise.

Sloane trained a flashlight on the compass to check his northeasterly course while he mumbled a few words to the divine.

A light cloud covering began to thicken below, hiding the ground with reflected starlight. Sloane gave up some altitude and as they slipped out from under there appeared a thin string of lights wavering slightly in the darkness below.

"Boat lights," he called out to the Prince. "Must be the river."

"Torch fishing," said the Prince, leaning close and shouting over the noise of the prop wash. "Risky business with the Khmer Rouge so close at hand."

"See anything of the stupa?" Sloane asked. "It's got to be down there someplace and without it we'll never know where the hell the camp is."

He flew up the river for ten minutes and then back around again, this time lower.

"Further north," the Prince shouted.

"Yeah?"

A half hour passed before Sloane turned downriver again. He spent a few minutes trying to get his bearings, checking the empty jungle out both sides while the Prince leaned out for a look below them and ahead, keeping a tight hold on the empty doorjamb and shielding his eyes from the prop wash. The torches down on the river looked like fireflies on an August night.

"No sign of it," the Prince shouted. "At least, not from up here. We really must go lower."

Sloane was swearing aloud. "All right, then," he finally said with a quick look at his copilot. "But I'm not gonna like it." And he started down for a closer look.

He throttled back and let another thousand feet settle out from under him until they could make out the black shapes of the taller trees rushing by. Neither spoke. Following the river torches and the weird glow they left on the ground haze, Sloane began to feel his way along the gap left by the river, swooping around sharp bends and taking the unexpected rise in the bluffs along the eastern side in leaping climbs and sudden half-circle banks. The river swerved and twisted and so did the ancient aircraft, dodging unexpected shadows that came at them out of the dark and jumping shapeless hazards jutting out from the water below.

The Prince was leaning dangerously out of the door, his eyes peeled for the unexpected out ahead. All at once he gave a cry and, without pulling himself back in, began grabbing at Sloane, shaking him frantically and waving at something out ahead of them.

All Sloane needed was a brief glimpse of the massive black shape coming at them to stomp on the rudder pedal and suck the stick into his stomach. The aircraft replied sluggishly. Hoisting its nose up and tipping a wing at the sky, it fell off to the right as the dome of the great stupa swept by and the echo of their engine clattered loudly back at them from the surface of the lordly dome. And then, just as suddenly, it was gone.

They hadn't time to think. Sloane had a fight on his hands to right the falling aircraft. They were so far over they had almost fallen into the trees before he had the plane level again. He banked around toward the river before they lost their way again.

"My goodness," the Prince said.

Sloane swallowed hard. "Well, at least we know where we are," he said. "Now let's get a few of those flares ready, and remember to wait until I bank it your way."

He followed the course of the river for another five minutes, keeping low to the trees while he matched the shape of the terrain with the inch he'd memorized from the map. There was little similarity between the two and the flight became a hair-raising bobsled run as they careened along through the trees. There were no torch fishermen here, no sign of life until the first pinpricks of light from the camp itself, the watch fires of the refugees against the hostile borderlands on the other side of the river.

The walls of trees grew wider as the aircraft drew near the camp. In what light there was from the rising half moon they could see into the marshes that lined the banks. The fires were the only signs of life on either shore.

CHAPTER

17

"See anything?"

The gale blowing through the open cockpit was worse at this slower speed, gusting with the turbulence of the shifting ground winds and deflected by the crude airflow of the aging aircraft. It blew into Sloane's eyes and he had to squint painfully to see. He flew as low over the camp as he dared. At this altitude something could rear up and surprise him at any second, like that ridge he remembered from his last visit. It was just east of the road, but where was the road?

The camp seemed smaller from the air, a trampled patch of mud they could just make out during the split second they were over it and then the jungle thickened again and all trace was gone.

He had the Prince doing the reconnaissance so that he could concentrate on his flying. At a glance the low fires that had guided them here looked to be cook fires, formed up in a square in the center of the clearing, where they had burned down to their coals. The refugees of Nong Kai were nowhere in sight.

"Well?" His throat was sore from shouting over the noise of the engine.

The ridge was coming up and Sloane banked away to buzz the camp again. The floodplain was uneven at this point, its shape governed by the course of the deep river and the outcropping of rock that had held their own against its monsoon crest. As they flew up the river they found the trees pressing in on either side; as the plane passed over the camp again the landscape opened but only for a moment or two. Then it closed half a mile to the north where the river branched and ran off toward the Mekong watershed.

"Nobody there," the Prince shouted to Sloane.

"You've got to be kidding. There's supposed to be fifteen hundred people in that camp," Sloane said. "All right, let's get on with it. I'm going to take her up and start a low run down this way from that southwest end. You've got to lay a line of surface flares as tight as you can as we go over."

The Prince reached into the gunnysack he had between his knees and began pulling out the short waxed sticks and piling them in his lap like a bundle of dynamite. His face in the dim glow of the instruments was radiant with nervous glee. He was ready for anything.

Sloane climbed steeply and leveled off at less than a thousand feet. Now that he knew where to look he could just make out the massive bell shape of the stupa and its lofty tower against the stars. He aligned himself with it as best he could and then turned back on his course, settled to tree level, and began his run.

"Wait'll we're past this bend, here . . ." he yelled. *"Now."*

The Prince ripped the striker from the head of the first flare and threw it over the side. Nothing happened. He looked around at Sloane in panic.

"Again! Try it again."

The Prince tore back another striker and this time held it until it was sputtering and spitting bits of fire around the cockpit.

"Throw it, throw it!"

The flare was barely out of the cabin door when it went off with a hissing "s-s-s-fop!" and flowered into a brilliant burst of phosphorous that showered down onto the water.

"Again!" Sloane was yelling. "Another one, quick."

Now the Prince was tossing flares over the side as fast as he could. Not all of them went off but at the end of the run, when they were out of room and had to climb hard to get over the upriver trees, Sloane was able to look back and see a ragged line of flares down on the water to light the way for him to land. They were anti-submarine flares and would burn on the surface, bobbing along with the slow current for five minutes or so and by then Sloane had better have the aircraft down. A blind landing on unknown water would be suicidal.

Again he lifted the ancient aircraft, pulling it almost physically into a sharp climb while it groaned and rattled its wings in protest. Then he lined up on the stupa as he swooped back toward the river but this time at least the way ahead was delineated by the line of brilliant red flares.

"You'd better pray there's nothing in that water we don't want to run into."

There was a crosswind above the trees, Sloane could see it in the rising smoke of the flares as he eased back on the throttle and lowered the last few notches of flaps and side slipped to use up some airspeed. Their rate of descent increased sharply as they passed over the first few markers. There was a shift to the right in the river and then the last of the flares could be seen.

They were running out of space in a hurry so Sloane had to punch the throttle down and rely on the stick to keep the nose up. The aircraft dropped like a stone, hitting the water flat and bouncing hard, its pontoons splaying out like they were on rubber struts and then flopping back into the water again. Their forward motion was checked so abruptly that the Prince banged his head against the control panel.

Even as the craft was settled into its second element, Sloane was ruddering it around toward the dim lights of the camp. He goosed the throttle to get steerage against the current and swept into the shadows nearer the shore.

Enough noise, he was thinking, to raise the dead.

When he cut the engine the quiet was deafening. Even the jungle seemed quiet after the roar of the engine as if the air was too sluggish to carry tales. The starlight made for sharp contrasts in the terrain around them. The brightness was stark and unreal and the dark was as black as ink. While the Prince tied a line to the pontoon cleat Sloane slipped into the water to wade ashore, slopping through the sucking mud of the riverbank until he found a stump in the nearby hardwood thicket to tie off to. The Prince stayed behind to guard the plane.

The camp lay a couple hundred yards in from the water across uncertain ground. Sloane moved from cover to cover, ashamed of his caution at first, but then as the stark strangeness of the empty scene became apparent he forgot his appearance and took to darting short distances and dropping to the ground to survey the next bit of open stretch he would have to cross before committing himself.

There was a graveyard look to the place that made the hackles rise on the back of his neck. It reminded him of one of the war's early disasters, a village in the Fortified Hamlet Program, overrun and left for dead. The smoke from the dying cook fires hung low over the ground and hid the details of the local terrain. He didn't like this at all. The place looked abandoned.

He darted from a small stand of bamboo to a mound of loose dirt and fell into a trench that had been dug behind it. The place smelled like a garbage dump.

"Damn." He had banged his shin in the fall and was rubbing it when, out of the corner of his eye, he saw something move at the far end of the trench.

He didn't know which to do. Move toward it? It might be one of the inmates of the camp. Or move away. Everybody was hiding from something. He stayed where he was but stuck his head up for a peek over the top of the trench. There was somebody in the trench beyond the nearest fire.

Then he caught a glimpse of a small group of figures just as they disappeared into the trees beyond the administration building. There was an excited whisper from the left and then all was quiet again.

Sloane decided to make his way toward the voices. He followed the trench to the left until it ended beneath a pile of sandbags. He climbed over the top and shimmied along the ground toward the spot where the figures seemed to have come from. Another couple surprised him by rising out of the earth ahead of them and slipping off into the trees.

Sloane ducked instinctively and then tried another look. A few feet ahead lay a double row of shallow trenches that appeared to ring the perimeter of the encampment inside the row of posts that were as yet unstrung with barbed wire. Some, like the one they had just left, had a few layers of sandbags piled up in front.

He crawled twenty yards farther, past the hospital tent, until he came to another trench where a small dark figure rose in front of him and stuck the muzzle of an assault rifle in his face.

"Un-n!" He couldn't move. He looked around with only his eyes. "Hold on, now. Take it easy . . ."

"Quiet!" somebody ordered from the dark. It was a hoarse

whisper and it was hard to tell where it came from. "What are you doing here, anyway?"

Sloane put a finger gingerly to the barrel of the weapon and turned it aside. He squinted into the shadows in time to see a mop of pale blond hair.

"Alice?" he said in a stage whisper. "Is that you?"

Alice was working her way down a row of refugees who were huddled in the bottom of the trench. "What are you doing here?" She was angry. She said something to the young boy with the gun, who settled back into his position again, no change in his look of cruel calm.

Sloane edged his way over the brink and rolled into the trench beside the youngster. There were seven or eight of the camp's inmates squatting in the dark, two of them had weapons. Beside Alice was a woman sheltering a baby in the folds of her checkered kramar and a little girl with that same lost, almost passive look of the child whom Sloane had found waiting at the feet of her dying mother—could it have been only a couple of weeks ago?

"What in heaven's name are you doing here?" Alice demanded. "Don't we have enough trouble without you dive-bombing the place?"

While Alice had his attention the little girl crept closer, the instincts that had saved her so far, perhaps, seeking hope in a stranger.

"What's going on?" Sloane demanded. "Why's it so quiet?"

"We've been on alert since seven o'clock this evening. The Khmer Rouge crossed the river on both sides of the camp about an hour before you showed up."

"What are they up to?"

"Who knows? Supplies, slave labor. They overran a camp just south of here a few months ago and took all the surviving men back with them. We've managed to keep out of it until now but something must have stirred them up."

"What about calling in the border patrol?"

"This is an illegal camp, remember? We exist by keeping a low profile and not allowing any official military presence. I don't know what they're up to tonight, though, and we're not sticking around to find out. We're evacuating the camp."

"Evacuating? To where?"

"The woods," Alice said. "The jungle to the west and south of camp. We're slipping away a few at a time to hide there."

By now the little girl had taken one of Sloane's fingers, tentatively, and was holding on to it.

"And what are the Khmer Rouge doing all this time?"

"I don't know. They were just sitting out there as if they're waiting for something. They don't seem interested in us particularly. At least they didn't until you came roaring in like gangbusters, dropping bombs out there. . . ."

"Flares."

"Alright then, flares."

"So we could land."

Alice wasn't listening. "God knows what they'll do now."

"Maybe we've scared them away."

"And maybe you'll have them down on our heads. What more do you want from me, anyhow? You and your friends."

"The Prince is here."

"The Prince?"

"Out on the river with the plane. We've come to get you out of here."

"You! Get me out?"

"S-s-s-s." The woman crouching in the trench nearby tugged at her shirtsleeve. "S-s-s-"

"Janus's up here someplace," Sloane tried to explain.

"Is he? Well, that's not my problem, is it," Alice said, trying hard to keep her voice down. "I've had enough of that kind of world. This is where I belong." She nodded toward the others in the trench.

"Shhh."

"That's not how it works, dammit," Sloane said. "You don't select your problems, you don't dip your toes in and decide the water's too cold. You chose to get mixed up with Pete just like I did, now we've both got to deal with it. This creep is after you, it doesn't matter why, and we've still got to get you the hell out of here."

"But me? Why me?"

"Look . . . look. Okay." Sloane was looking around as if he didn't understand any of it either. "Look, I'll explain all that later."

"Oh, sure," Alice told him. "Fine. And maybe you can explain to those Khmer Rouge out there. And what do we tell these people? 'Well, folks, things are a little tough right now so we're going to hop into our airplane and go bye-bye.' "

"Listen to me. Janus's an animal, a hired assassin, and he's on his way here to get you. He crippled Somsak, he killed Chappy, and now he's killed Jake and you wanna stay here so he can . . ."

"Jake?" Alice said. "Jake's dead?"

"Everything's gotten out of hand. Everything's haywire and there's nothing we can do but get you out of here."

Alice hesitated. She looked around at the others in the trench. All eyes were on her. "We'll see," she said. "When we finish the evacuation we'll see."

The boy with the gun poked his head up to check out the open ground on either side and the deep grass bordering the eastern perimeter. He gave a quick downward motion with the palm of his hand and another couple left the trench. They made their move so quickly that in spite of the glow from the nearby coals of the cook fires they seemed to be swallowed up almost immediately by the dense forest beyond the tents.

"Come on, we're next," Sloane told her.

"Not yet," Alice said, relaying the signal for another few refugees to try for the trees.

Sloane had been watching something in the undergrowth beyond the far end of the camp. The light from the rising moon was enough to make out something rustling through the elephant grass there. "Any of your people in those trenches over there?"

"No. They were the first to go."

"Uh-huh." Sloane sat up watching for a moment while he waited for another sign of movement, his mouth was sour with the tinny taste of fear. "Well, there's somebody in them now."

A low murmur of voices began from somewhere in the tall clumps of grass. A mumble that rose until it became a part of the hidden threat.

"Oh, m'God!" Alice said.

"Sh-h-h."

"What are they saying?"

The voices were like the deep, monotonous drone of a priestly chant, a practiced word uttered over and over from all around the perimeter of the camp. "Pe-tah . . . Pe-tah . . . Pe-tah."

"Peter!" Alice whispered. "Peter? Is that what they're saying?"

"That's it. It's time to get the hell out of here."

"Why Peter?"

"C'mon. That's it." He signaled others in the trench. "Now gimme that kid and let's go." And he scooped up the little girl.

"Petah Woss," someone called from the trees. "Come ou', Petah Woss."

"That way." Alice pointed to the heavily wooded southwest end of the camp as they all rose to a half-crouch and began their run. It was as if the raiders had been waiting for just such a move. Somebody out in the underbrush began yelling orders and a squad of sinister figures emerged from the shadows of the tree line in black pajamas and checkered *kramar* scarves wrapped loosely around their heads. Their bandoliers of bullets glinted in the crimson light of the dying coals.

"Pe-tah . . . Pe-tah . . ."

The raiders began shooting up the place as soon as they had a clear field of fire, and when they did the few remaining refugees in other trenches broke for the woods. Eight or ten of them scattered as the confused fire cut off their line of escape across the muddy field. Bullets followed a young couple as they scrambled out from under the administration hut but they were close to the edge of the camp and made it into the jungle.

The young sentry with the gun and two others who had been covering the retreat jumped out of their holes, firing their captured Kalashnikovs as they ran for the nearby hedge grove. But that's where the bulk of the raiders were waiting and the boys were shot to pieces from the lines deeper in.

Alice screamed and tried to turn back but Sloane switched the little girl to the other arm and used the free hand to grab Alice by the wrist, yank her back on course, and force her to follow his lead. Shots were spattering in the dirt all around them even when they'd reached the cover of the tree line and found a culvert there deep enough to dive into.

The shooting had caught Janus by surprise. He'd been pissing against a tree when it started and wet his shoe. He'd been watching the camp from several points of vantage over the last few hours and he'd seen the Khmer Rouge raiders watching from their leafy cover. They hadn't seen him, though. He moved among them easily, he had the stealth of a cat. He even toyed with the danger of their proximity, using it to enhance the pleasurable stirring in his loins as he stalked the yellow-haired girl.

He'd seen the raiders begin their move as if on signal when the airplane landed but he hadn't expected the shooting. He zipped himself up and crept closer, keeping to a low culvert that ran parallel to his side of the encampment. He saw the foreigners running his way and decided he could intercept them where they'd be most vulnerable, just inside the tree line. He still had a chance at the girl. They'd be blind in the darkness there long enough for him to cut her out in the confusion. But the shooting followed them there and when the bullets began splitting the air just over his head he changed his mind.

He whirled to head back down the gully when the first of the survivors showed up. The woman with the baby pitched herself over the brink and landed on him, knocking him off his feet and rolling with him, screaming baby and all, into the mud. The woman was grateful enough to have found cover. She lay like dead weight where she was while Janus hissed and squirmed trapped in the mud under her.

No sooner had he freed himself than the others came over the top and landed with a splash. Janus barely had time to scramble away before the foliage above them was shattered by a general fusillade. Leaves and twigs blasted from their stems hailed down on them while bullets slapped into the trees and spattered clots of red mud all around. The woman snatched up her baby and began inching herself backward away from the foreigners, for by now it was obvious that they were the center of attention.

The attackers approached at an almost leisurely pace, marauders used to easy killing. They were joking, adolescent boys with greasy noses accustomed to methodically killing whatever they could. Sloane tightened his hold on the little girl and gave Alice a shove to get her going. "That way."

When the Prince heard gunfire he climbed onto the wing to see if he could figure out what was going on. More shooting! It was a real battle. He had never been in a battle zone before but it occurred to him that turning off the engine may have been somewhat shortsighted. Perhaps he could somehow crank it over by himself and have it ready when the others returned.

He reached in and flipped the ignition a few times to make sure it was off and then climbed down backward, to the pontoon. When he got to the end he checked the line. The current had it pulled tight so the aircraft was angled upriver.

He took hold of the propeller and was pulling at it, testing the compression, when he saw a squad of men running toward him down the shoreline. The pistol was in his pocket, perhaps it would be best to hold it at the ready.

He hesitated, hanging from the propeller while he waited for something to happen. Nothing did. Not right away. The men on the shore seemed to be disoriented and more concerned with what sounded like an inland firefight. They ran off again without harming the plane. Perhaps without even seeing it, for the river curved there and the shore behind him was very black against the luster of the starlit sky.

The Prince abandoned his plans to start the engine by himself and moved carefully back along the float to where he couldn't readily be seen. There he took his pistol out and waited for the others to return.

The gunfire was beginning to subside. A good sign? Bad? He didn't know what to make of it so he got to his feet and stepped up onto the stirrup for a better look over the lower wing.

He heard a great deal of thrashing about in the scrub nearby and then Sloane emerged onto the muddy bank with the little girl under his arm and Alice close behind.

That was the moment the squad of raiders chose to return. Everybody saw them, they made enough noise for a regiment, trading shouts and orders while they broke up into groups of twos and threes. This time they saw the airplane.

What nobody saw was Janus. He had escaped the thicket between the two groups and stopped dead when he saw what was happening. On his right were Sloane and the girl, on his left the Khmer Rouge. The only escape was the old plane waiting out there on the water, but how to get himself aboard? He faded back into the shadows to wait his chance.

"Here." Sloane handed the little girl over to Alice. "Tell the Prince to get the plane out of here. Quick. I'll get the rope." And he went splashing off toward the thicket where the airplane was tied off. It would be a close race with the converging party of raiders.

He lunged heavily through the water with his heart pounding and his lungs straining for air. He could make it, but get back to the plane . . . ? The sudden appearance of Janus stepping out of the shadows beside the tethered line brought him to an abrupt halt.

"Huh?" Behind him the raiders were rounding the muddy point and heading their way.

"Ysyryddr flytt," Janus said, keeping well out of reach. His eyes were glittering in the dark.

"Out'a my way," Sloane warned.

"Ysyryddr, flytt," he rasped, glancing back at the Khmer Rouge bearing down on them.

"Get away from me." Sloane shoved past Janus to get to the rope. Janus took out his blackjack but there wasn't much he could do with it.

Upstream, one of the raiders finally took a shot at the plane and the Prince, in reply, held his pistol out in front of him with both hands and fired the first and only shot of his life. The results were disappointing. Just a little "phap," hardly the sound of battle, but it was enough.

The raider he'd shot at looked down at the dark wet spot growing on his shirt and then, as he turned to show it to his comrades, dropped his weapon and fell dead.

The remaining raiders hadn't seen the Prince, just the plane. They were frightened by the mysterious death of their comrade and began firing at the plane and at the sounds coming from the forest and at everything else they didn't understand. Almost immediately they were trading fire with their fellows back in the trees, who thought they were under attack.

Sloane was having a hard time loosening the knot while Janus, in a state of desperation and yet at a loss over what to do, wrung his hands, wet his lips with his long tongue, and tried in his unintelligible way to make Sloane understand. The shooting was getting closer, bullets ripping through the trees and splashing in the water. Time was short.

"Nyt fsyr flytt," Janus warned, waving his ball-tipped blackjack in Sloane's face.

"So you're scared, too, huh?" Sloane didn't even look at him. "Going to get left behind, aren't you?"

Everybody seemed to be shooting something at everybody else by now. Grenades were going off, an automatic rifle began pumping rounds into the night, and the squad of raiders from the camp who'd come plunging out into the open after sweeping the undergrowth for the foreigners took half a minute of concentrated fire before their own shooting ceased.

Out on the water the Prince had the plane's engine coughing and trying to kick over. Another try got it off with a roar. Now everybody onshore had something real to shoot at. Sloane watched as the aircraft, straining against its leash, swung out toward the river in the moonlight. He could see the guns blazing only yards away from him as he tore at the restraining knot.

Janus didn't know what to do. He had to duck the close shots while trying to make himself understood. He threatened, he pleaded, he even waded into the water, ready to make a swim for the plane, but even that idea was thwarted when the knot at last came free and the rope went tearing through Sloane's palms after the escaping aircraft.

"Oh, lord." Sloane grabbed the rope painfully and was yanked from his feet into the water. Janus tried to intercept him but was simply run over as Sloane's big body torpedoed past. "Hey . . . hey . . . !" Sloane was yelling, choking on the river water rushing at him as the aircraft lumbered out into the open.

By now the shots from shore were kicking up a storm of geysers all around and Sloane began pulling himself hand over hand toward the davit on the starboard pontoon. The swirling water sucked at him but he was gaining ground when he chanced a look back. He had the idea that the only danger was behind them now but it wasn't. There was a spark above the trees upriver along their course. Just a spark and then a mortar shell came whooshing in and the water behind him blew up with a roar. The plane was rocked forward and before it could recover there was a second blast on the other side and water came gushing over the wings.

The plane turned downriver away from the shelling and as it did the rope pinioned around from its pontoon to follow the straightest line to the moving davit. It slowed as the aircraft turned until the course between the aircraft and the rope intersected a low rock jetty the local fishermen must have built to cast their nets from.

"Hey!" Sloane shouted, gasping for air and spitting out river water. "Hey, look where you're going."

He waved and the Prince, who saw him from the open cockpit, grinned and waved back. Sloane was kicking away and could do nothing about the figure in the water slipping out from the rocks to intercept him.

He didn't see the figure as a person, nothing human, just some thing in the water to keep away from. He was closing on it quickly and when he was right on top of it, dark in the dark water, he gave it a shove with his foot. Only then did he see what it was. There was a snap, a flurry in the water, and Janus was on him like a leech.

Sloane gasped and fought to keep on the surface. They rolled over and over as Sloane pulled himself desperately along the line. He stopped pulling to try punching at Janus. He shoved and wrestled but he had to break off to haul himself up over the side of the float so he'd have both hands free to get a hold of the davit.

"Let go," he was shouting as he kicked and struggled. "Let me go, goddamit. You'll kill us both."

Alice saw that something was wrong. She climbed down from the doorway and crept out along the bulky aluminum cylinder stretching out to keep her hold on the strut.

"Back inside! Get back inside!" Sloane tried for the davit and missed, his face was pulled under the racing water as the weight of the three of them upset the float's planing angle. The Prince was picking up speed.

How could this maniac hold on, surely he would be washed away. But instead the grip around Sloane only tightened until it was like a vise. Finally, to save himself from the force of the rushing water, Sloane had to let Alice hook an arm through his. It was enough to help him twist both himself and his burden over onto the float.

"Get back inside," Sloane shouted. "The weight's got us circling around." And while Alice felt her way back toward the door of the cockpit, Sloane tried with all his strength to maneuver himself forward for a handhold on the strut that Alice had just left but Janus still clung to him and his weight was just too much.

The plane was picking up speed. More shells were falling but they were well behind them now and the wake of the floats, fluorescent in the moonlight, sprayed out from either side in a wide *v*. The engine noise was deafening, at this speed the prop-wash tore at them like a hurricane. Alice hung from the door trying to get hold of Sloane's arm again while the water blown back by the prop lashed at her back.

Janus had Sloane around the waist and his loose weight, as Sloane reached for the float strut, was worse than a drag. It wobbled behind in the wind, yanking him this way and that as if Janus were purposely trying to pull them both over the side.

The balance of the aircraft had changed. Sloane could feel it in the pit of his stomach. The tail was lifting. My God, he thought. The Prince has her up on the step. She's going to fly!

Alice reached back from the cabin and with a last lunge Sloane managed to grab her outstretched hand. Her strength and Sloane's were enough to drag Janus along with him until Sloane was close enough to anchor his arm into the doorjamb. He couldn't fight Janus's weight much longer, he would last only as long as his grip.

Alice was ready to try anything. She swung at Janus but he was out of reach. She threw things out at him: a wrench, a fire extinguisher. There must be something else. She found a leftover flare but didn't know how to use it so she threw it at him, too. She tried to haul Sloane into the cockpit but that was beyond hope. The plane was almost airborne by now, bouncing on the water in long, bone-crushing leaps, and it was all Sloane could do to just hang on.

The little girl was in the back and Alice kept her there, feeling around for her, now and then, to make sure she was still there while she shouted things out of the doorway that couldn't be heard. The Prince was talking to himself. His eyes were as wide as saucers as he fought the stick. He didn't know how to compensate for the weight and the drag of the two men outside. And there were no flares ahead to light the way.

Well, nothing to be done. He pulled back hard on the stick and to his amazement they were lifted into the air. The nose pointed up and the water fell away but almost at once the sound of the engine changed and the controls all turned to mush in his hands. The trees were coming at them again and the bottom of his stomach seemed to drop away. Somebody was screaming at him and when he turned to look he realized it was David.

". . . *Stalling. You're stalling.*"

Yes, of course. The Prince pitched forward and when the nose fell he tried to lift it again. By then they were too low and the black branches of the trees along the banks of the river were whipping past in the dark.

Janus shifted his grip. With his face distorted like a rubber mask by the howling wind, he wedged his body between Sloane's and the fuselage and pried at him with an elbow in the face, trying to get past him and into the cabin.

Sloane was losing it, his fingers were slipping, and he could almost hear the scream forming on his lips when a shape began to take form out ahead. It was as if the darkness itself had substance. Some massive part of the sky that dazzled them with the silvery glory of the night all around and then, like a mirror turned away, was black again.

"*Up, up!*" Sloane screamed. "*For God's sake, the stupa!*"

The Prince gaped at the mammoth tower for a moment too long. He hauled back on the stick but against the bulk coming at them the plane hardly seemed to rise at all. It just tilted upward, churning at the hot monsoon air in a desperate bid for altitude, and as it did the pontoon foothold of the two outside began tilting, too. Sloane had a hold on the doorsill but for Janus there was nothing. He used one hand to claw at the skin of the fuselage but that wasn't enough, and the strut was out of reach. So he threw his arms around Sloane's legs and held on for dear life.

The ground was far below him now and his feet could only dangle in midair. Janus thrashed his legs around desperately until he managed to hook the pontoon with his heel. The climb continued to shift the angle but at last he was able to get his legs around the big metal cylinder and ride it like a bucking bronco.

Up and up they climbed with the Prince frozen to the stick and babbling prayers as the windscreen turned skyward and the dome of the stupa slipped beneath the cowling. Still the spire loomed high before them.

"*TURN, TURN,*" Sloane yelled. "*DO SOMETHING! ANYTHING!*"

He managed to get one arm well inside as the angle changed. He had a grip on the frame of the seat. Alice had him by the jacket but none of it mattered. They were going to crash.

Through the spinning propeller he could see the tall temple spire closing in. Then the surface glittered like a cosmic wink as the silver tip came rushing down at them from above. Janus saw what was going to happen. His eyes bulged and he opened his mouth in protest as the conical spire came ripping through the struts and spars, crushing the pontoon he was clinging to and tearing the whole assembly off with an earsplitting crash.

The plane was sent cartwheeling through space but Janus was left behind. The impact of his body against that slender column of silver and stone must have been like swatting a fly. It scattered his remains over most of the temple grounds below.

CHAPTER
18

Kiri didn't have enough money. The night train to Cheng Mai was two hundred and thirty baht and she had barely two hundred. She stood at the window for a long time, unable to focus her mind on the bills folded neatly in her hand. The Krung Thep train station seemed like a huge cavern full of faraway noises and demanding ticket clerks and the grief that hung heavily on her mind.

The line of people behind her urged its way forward, nagging, insistent, until she drew aside. One hundred eighty-three, one hundred eighty-four . . . a big clock chimed somewhere and an announcement nobody could understand came over the loudspeakers. What time was it? She hadn't been counting. One hundred eighty . . . Is he there? Could the Khmer have . . . She lost count. Two hundred . . . She would start crying again if she stayed there a moment longer. Could he be dead?

She grabbed her flight bag and ran for the door past the wall-sized map of the country. Aranyaprathet. She pushed out into the drive, a circle that opened onto Rama IV Road where it crossed the Krung Kasem canal into the old city.

There were lights all around from the pushcarts of the street hawkers and the noisy crush of taxis and tuk-tuks vying for fares among the crowd of recent arrivals. They beeped their horns at her: here I am, need a ride? But she rushed on toward the wide girder bridge over the klong, brushing roughly at the tears that clouded her eyes. Where was she to go, what was she to do . . . ?

She found herself out on the road, defying the tide of traffic as she crossed. A taxi almost hit her and several motorcycles, coming upon her suddenly, had to swerve into the oncoming lane to avoid her.

Then a long white car slowed beside her. She had to stop, it was between her and the safety of the sidewalk. The back door swung open and a young sailor stepped out. She hadn't time to resist, she couldn't bolt back into traffic, so it took him only a firm push to land her in the plush backseat beside Park Sung Dai.

The aircraft wallowed across the indigo sky, yawing wildly to the right while the wind howled through its mangled spars and torn fabric. Its loose pieces rained down on the rooftops of Nong Kai. Alice's eyes were clamped shut in terror but she kept her grip on Sloane while the plane waffled and shook him like a dog worrying an old boot. The Prince fought manfully at the controls but, with no instinct for flight, he could rely only on his lessons and these he was reciting like a rosary at the top of his lungs.

"Airspeed," he was yelling. "Airspeed equals control. Nose down. Power. Turn. *Turn* . . ." He shoved on the rudder pedal with all his might as the tired old ship began luffing into a flat spin.

The aircraft was badly damaged. The belly had been torn out of it and every move scattered more debris out behind. One strut of the missing pontoon was sticking downward like a broken crutch while the other was flapping loose at the end of a strip of ripped sheet metal. The Prince pointed the nose down and prayed for enough airspeed to fight the centrifugal force of the spin. A few seconds, that's all he needed. Just long enough for the aircraft's forward motion and its oversized tail plane to prevail.

Slowly the dive brought the tail into line and with only a few feet to spare the Prince found enough air to lift the nose and carve a ragged slipstream out over the moonlit trees.

The broken strut, shearing away from the lower wing, was slapping Sloane painfully across the small of his back and the violence of the collision had broken his grip on the doorjamb, but by then Alice had jammed her knee up against the seat frame and locked an arm under his armpit so now they were both struggling against the force of the gale. His legs, which had been thrust out perpendicular to the fuselage during the spin, were trailing out behind now that the aircraft had righted itself again.

"H-hold on!"

He tried digging his feet into the fabric in the side behind the doorway, but with nothing to brace his weight against his maneuvering only made things worse. He made a try for the stirrup at the base of the wing fairing, only to find himself kicking frantically at empty space. Janus was gone but so was the aluminum float, the only support he'd had under him.

"Hold on." His voice was too small to be heard against the roar. Terror loosened his bowels. "For God's sake, hold on, Alice!"

"I've got you," Alice lied. "Don't worry, I've got you." If she did she was slipping over the sill with him. His strength was gone. He couldn't fight the tearing wind any longer, but if he didn't Alice's grip on him was likely to pull her out after him.

"I can't . . . I can't . . ."

He wormed his loose arm up under the seat brace until he had ahold of the frame deeper inside. With the doorsill as a fulcrum he was able to twist himself an inch or two over it and the feel of something substantial under his chest gave him an instant of hope. The move was enough to shift his weight inboard but not enough to escape the clawing wind.

"Pull, pull," Alice was screaming. She'd never let him go, she couldn't if she wanted to. By now they were knotted up like a pair of wrestlers. One more try, that's all the strength he had left, but it was enough to seesaw over the threshhold. He had to change handholds for better leverage but most of him was aboard now and the next heave combined with an unexpected leap of the aircraft brought him piling into the back on top of Alice and the little girl.

Alice held onto him as if he were still outside, clinging to him fiercely until she had convinced herself that he was safe. Sloane lay where he'd fallen, holding both her and the child in the same grateful embrace, weeping and gasping for air while the Prince went on bouncing the crippled aircraft around the sky.

"Oh, my goodness," he was shouting. "Oh . . . oh, my goodness."

"Prince?"

"Oh, my . . ."

"How are we doing, Prince?"

"Doing? My goodness, we are sure to crash ourselves if we go on this way."

Sloane wiped his eyes and gave the little girl an encouraging squeeze. "Let me take it."

"Please."

"Here. I'll just . . ." It was all he could do to get himself to the controls, for the plane was swerving and gyrating so wildly that as he climbed over the seat into the front he was almost thrown out the door again.

When he was strapped in and had the stick, it still took a few minutes to figure out the new feel of the wounded aircraft.

Oh, my lord, he was thinking, but to the Prince he just said, "You did good."

He looked out at the control surfaces. The starboard lower wing drooped at midpoint where one of the struts had been attached and was flapping like a bird against every sudden move the plane made. God only knew what was holding it together. The whole aircraft was out of alignment and doglegging its way south at the mercy of every current of air and every happenstance of its mechanical distress.

The hot motor made the cockpit smell like they were downwind of a junkyard. It was unbelievable the thing was still in the air.

"Yeah," he yelled to the Prince over the roar of the wind. "Yeah, you did pretty damned good."

The Prince gave up the controls to him and took a moment to grin out at the stars.

The little girl clung to Alice, terrified but too young to know what was happening. She was shivering violently and Alice wrapped her in the blanket Sloane had aboard for something to dry engine parts on. Was the child all right? She never made a sound.

The tiny lights below were scattered more thinly now, it was very late. They gleamed against the darkness of the forest like mysterious sea creatures deep down on the floor of the ocean. They made Sloane think about the medieval village life going on below and the plague of modern war. He thought about Jake and Voss and men at their computers on the other side of the world.

A growing vibration and the chattering of steel against steel brought Sloane back to their predicament.

276 . . .

"See if you can find that flashlight," he yelled to the Prince. "Under the seat . . . No? All right, try the map pouch over there."

When the Prince had found it Sloane played the bright beam along the damaged wing outside. Fabric was streaming out behind and the structural strain of the flapping was beginning to unseat the upper wing, too. Still, it somehow held together and they continued stretching each moment in the air into another moment and then another hour—the shaking, the noise, the endless drone of the water-cooled engine . . .

At last a glow appeared on the horizon ahead of them. Slowly it slid toward them. The lights of Bangkok, shimmering like treasure in a pirate's chest. Sloane was not impressed. He knew what they were up against, putting this broken old bird down on one float.

As the outskirts of the city approached the sky grew less clear and the stars lost their distinction in the haze. Sloane followed Petchaburi in from the east and then turned south over the spotlighted Victory monument, losing altitude as quickly as he dared until their course intersected that of the wide river.

The battered aircraft came in low over the Grand Palace, exposed itself for a second in the searchlights trained on the towers of Wat Pra Keo, and then groaned as Sloane banked slowly to the left and headed toward Arun and the wide Phra Buddha Bridge, the last obstacle the plane would have to hurdle before a long enough straightaway presented itself down on the waterway. Now the lights were racing past as the ground came rushing up at them.

"What's happening?" Alice asked from the back. "What are we doing?"

"Buckle up," Sloane yelled back at her. "Buckle everything up. The kid, too. Put her in the seat beside you and strap her down."

"We're going to crash, aren't we?"

"Of course we're going to crash. How else are we going to get this thing down?"

He banked too sharply and the loose wing was pulling away as he lowered in over the water. It was very late but there was still some traffic below. Some barges were making their way upstream and a ferry crossed their approach as Sloane lined up with the Thai/Tech dock downriver. He was counting on his familiarity with this stretch of waterway and the fact that it was the longest straightaway available.

. . . Or it would have been if the Korean's white trawler hadn't found a fresh anchorage off the company pier.

"Son of a bitch," Sloane muttered. "What's he doing there?"

The Korean's yacht cut the landing space short but there wasn't a choice anymore. Sloane didn't dare strain the wing by trying to climb out of his approach. He came in low, almost brushing the corrugated steel covers of a cement barge, in hopes of dipping his remaining pontoon into the water soon enough to eat up their forward motion in open water.

He throttled down as much as possible and tilted the aircraft to the left as the ripples of glimmering water came racing up at them faster and faster. The roar of the engine against the surface below grew louder. Sloane jerked at the stick to hop over a speeding *hangyao* that came up out of nowhere and then let the pontoon touch the water.

He felt a split second of drag through the stick and then the aircraft jumped free. It touched again, just skimming like a pelican testing the water, and then the drag began sucking at it. The tilt became a wild yaw to the left as the pontoon took the weight of the aircraft and plunged through the surface. Sloane was fighting to keep the nose up in a losing attempt at dissipating his forward motion before the crash came.

For a moment it looked like it might work, but then the bottom right wing broke away at the midpoint. The sudden change in weight caused the opposite wing to dip into the water and after that there was nothing anybody could do. The aircraft somersaulted, crushing and folding the fuselage at its wound behind the cabin and then slapping it into the water behind them like a wet towel. The wreckage sheared through the water for another fifty yards, throwing up an explosion of spray before coming to a rest.

There was a long moment while the water they'd piled into came cascading back down around them and then the left wings began to settle beneath the waves. By a miracle the cabin was still whole and as the wings went under their weight tipped the rest of the wreckage upward, buoyed up on the remaining pontoon.

"Out! Out!" Everybody seemed stunned except Sloane. "Everybody out!" he was shouting as the plane settled. "C'mon, everybody jump for it . . ." As soon as he had his belt off he reached over the back of the seat and freed the little girl. "Alice?"

"Please," the Prince sputtered as the black water came swirling through the door. "You first . . ."

"Get out-a here. Here, take the kid." He passed him the little girl as the rushing water pushed him past and out into the river. "Alice?"

"Something's wrong." She seemed dazed. "Something's stuck." Sloane felt around frantically, losing his grip in the inrushing water, finding her again and yanking at her belt buckle as the wreckage tipped skyward and settled deeper into the river.

The hissing water was already closing over their heads when Sloane felt the buckle release and Alice was floating free. He grabbed her hand and felt his way out of the ensnaring wreckage but by then she slipped away. He held onto a broken spar for as long as he could and felt blindly for her as the wreckage dragged him down. But his breath was gone. His chest was heaving for air and he had to let go.

Alice, he thought in a panic. I've lost Alice. Then, as he rose through the water, he felt her brush by him. She was free and kicking toward the air. He surfaced right behind her and found the Prince nearby treading water. He was holding the little girl as best he could while she thrashed about gagging on the dirty water and struggling against his hold in her panic.

"You okay, Alice?"

"You're hurt."

"What?"

"She's right, David. You are bleeding from your head."

He touched his forehead and found a lump there over the eye. "It's nothing," he said. "How's the little girl?"

"Fine, I think." The Prince wasn't much of a swimmer, that was plain. It seemed all he could do to keep his charge's face above water. "She . . . she won't say anything." He swallowed some water and spat it out. "Maybe . . . maybe she can't."

Behind them the big tail of the broken aircraft lifted in a farewell salute and then went under. Sloane took the child and followed with Alice as the Prince went dogpaddling off in the direction of the Thai/Tech pier.

The current was taking them swiftly downriver. It swept them past the big white yacht where a small knot of witnesses on the stern were peering into the darkness in the direction of the spot where the aircraft had gone down. They were talking excitedly among themselves in several languages.

The current was treacherous, shifting and swirling among the docks and derelicts that littered this industrial section of the river, but the swimmers made steady progress and soon found themselves beneath the pier, a strange closed world among the pilings with the dock looming huge overhead. The air was close and smelled of briny fish renderings and of the creatures that fed upon them.

Worklights from the *nam pla* barge danced on the surface of the water all around, leaving the exhausted swimmers bedazzled and confused.

"*Chuai lua!*" the Prince shouted up at the dock. "*Thi-ni, chuai lua!*"

"Hey!" Sloane yelled. "Hey, somebody!"

"*Chuai lua!*"

"Anybody up there?"

No one answered. Where was the night crew? The barge was in, the fleet was back. "Where is everybody?" Sloane wanted to know. "Didn't they see what happened?"

There was a ladder here someplace, that stairway up from the landing where the *hangyaos* used to collect them for the short trip to the airplanes' mooring. Where was it? They had to hold up for a moment to get their bearings, clinging to the spongy growth at the waterline of the heavy timbers and splashing away the thin clinging scum, and then the Prince paddled off to find the way up to safety.

He was gone for several minutes and the others were ready to press on without him when they heard: "Pssst." In the forest of pilings the sound might have come from anywhere.

"Prince?" Alice called. "Prince, is that you?"

"Sh-h-h."

"Over that way," Sloane said and started off again. The little girl was easier to deal with now and clung to the arm he held her with without struggling. The river had risen with the rains and when at last they found the stairs they found the platform below it was awash. The wooden slats were slippery with slime, the edges rotten and full of splinters but the Prince was there to help.

"Here . . . here, now." He was whispering. "Here, give me the little one."

Sloane wiped the blood from his eye and tried to give Alice some help. "You okay?"

"I hurt all over." Alice groaned. "And what's everybody whispering for?"

Sloane lay where he'd landed, the filthy water lapping at his ears. "Yeah," he said at last. "We're safe. We made it. So how come the big secret?"

"Something is wrong," the Prince confided. "Terribly wrong."

"Yeah? What?"

"Sh-h-h." The Prince nodded in the direction of the inshore end of the landing. "Over there."

"What?"

"Go look."

"Yeah, okay." Sloane got painfully to his feet and padded over the slimy platform for a look, the cuffs of his wet jeans slopping at his ankles.

He almost missed it. It was out of the immediate line of sight, but there was just enough spill from the worklights up on top to catch the glitter of brass in the water past the end of the platform. Sloane squinted. He climbed a few steps for a better look and there, near the first of the empty moored fishing boats was the upturned bow of the submerged white launch. The surface scum had not yet closed over it so it wasn't difficult to see the brass searchlight and the body of a sailor caught beneath it still grasping it in both hands and gawking upward as if on eternal vigil.

"Huh?" It was a startling sight, like coming upon an open grave. He turned to the Prince for an explanation but he only pointed up the steps.

"Something is happening up on top," he said.

"I'll go take a look," Sloane told him.

"And I," said the Prince. "Miss Alice can look after the child."

So together they made their way up to the surface of the pier where they waited for an anxious few moments for a clue to what was going on. They could hear the machinery on the far side of the pier but there was no sign of the men of the swing shift who were supposed to be working. There was a whooping siren out on the water someplace, a patrol boat from the Suriwong police docks heading for the crash site.

Then, from somewhere near the barge, they heard somebody yelling. No wonder the Prince had everybody whispering, it was a very weird scene.

"What's the shouting all about?"

The Prince shrugged. "It's over by the work lights, over there. Some kind of a crazy man, it sounds like."

"Great," Sloane said, shedding his whisper. "C'mon. Let's go see."

He stepped out into the open but the sharp crack of a pistol shot sent them both running for cover.

"Get back. Get back. Leave me alone."

He couldn't mean them, they were too far away. For the moment they left him alone, though. They just stood there behind a trash bin dripping and shivering and wondering what to do next. Then the Prince spotted a group of workers, the shift foreman and two women laborers in their loose, indigo workshirts, having a quiet but animated discussion behind a nearby outbuilding. The Prince signaled Sloane to stay where he was and darted off to see to their situation.

With the Prince gone, Sloane was free to make a run toward the tall work lights where the voice was coming from.

He was nearly there, keeping to the dark behind the stack of crated machine parts, when he came upon a familiar form huddling behind a packing case and peeking around at the lighted area.

"Pete?"

"Nah!" Voss jumped as if he'd been kicked in the seat of his pants. "Jesus Christ, man. Y'wanna get us killed?"

"What's going on?"

"Get down, dammit."

"What the hell's going on," Sloane crouched beside him. "Who's that yelling out there?"

"Sung Dai," Voss told him. "Take a look. *Care*ful. He'll take a shot at you, next."

"I can't see from here. What's he up to?"

"H-he's played his last card, that's what he's up to. And it's the wrong one."

"What's that supposed to mean?"

Voss was frightened and jumpy as a cat. "H-he's been shooting—" He stammered. "Blasting away at everything that moves. And he's got Kiri."

"Kiri!" Sloane turned him around roughly. "Where? C'mon. Show me."

"Over there," Voss said, keeping his head down.

"Come on."

Voss peered around the corner of the crate. "Okay. All right." He hesitated and then led Sloane in a dash along the line of boxes keeping to the shadows beyond the reach of the work lights. Sloane followed, dodging the old truck and sprinting barefoot across a few yards of open deck to the cover of a pile of cable spools.

"See?" Voss said, taking a quick look over the top of the pile toward the river end of the pier.

Sloane raised his head carefully and was greeted with one of the strangest sights he had ever witnessed. The Korean had Kiri, all right. He was backing her along beneath the battery of lights that burned from the top of a leaning steel tower. He had her arm locked behind her back, bending it sharply to keep her in line. Kiri must have been in agony but she fought him every step of the way.

The Korean had his heavy pistol in his free hand. He was raving like a madman and waving it around as if at any moment he might start blasting away at the shadows around him.

"Get away from me!" He had the gun, he had the girl, yet it was he who was terrorized. Like a man pursued by devils, he wanted to run but had no place to run to. The work lights had turned his skin to a ghastly pale green and his voice was reduced to a flat croaking noise but he went on trying to shout.

"We can still make a deal. This trollop, eh? You want her, you may have her. Show yourself, we can make a deal, eh?" He waited for an answer, jumping at every stray sound and waving the gun as he continued backing through the circles of light. "It is Peter I want; then I'll let her go. I will. Just *leave me alone!*"

The Korean turned, startled by a sound somewhere out on the water, and in the shadows behind him a figure passed against the backlight of the barge and then was gone, as silent as death. The hunter had become the hunted. It was the Kid.

CHAPTER
19

"The rest of his crew has run off, I guess," Voss said. "Not a sign of them after what the Kid did to the guy in the launch."

"You've got to stop this."

"Stop it? Stop it how, man? I mean, just look at him out there. There's no reasoning with him, he's scared out of his mind."

"But why? You and Kiri . . ."

"Not me." Voss grabbed him by his wet shirt. He was shaking with frustration. "Not me. The Kid."

"Oh, no."

"See? The worst move he could make and now he knows it. He figured if he grabbed Kiri he could make the Kid come along, too, and he knew I'd do anything for the Kid. Now it's like he's caught in a monkey trap. He can't get away 'cause he can't let go."

"A big mistake," Sloane said. "Trying to make a deal with a psychotic. Look! There he is again."

They could see the Kid move from behind a box beyond the far edge of the light to another in the dark beyond.

"Do something," Sloane demanded.

"Shit, man." Voss looked sick. He was trembling and chewing painfully at the stitches in his lip. "And Kiri! Oh shit, what am I gonna do?"

Out under the light the Korean was circling slowly, trying to zero in on any sound he could pick up. He had Kiri bent over his hip, whimpering as he turned to sweep the area in front of him with his gun.

"I tell you . . ." He wiped his face quickly with his sleeve. "I tell you I am your brother's friend. Do you hear? Are you listening? Peter is my partner. He must have told you, eh? He could deal with me and so can you. Do you hear me? *Do you hear?*"

Sloane saw the Kid again, or thought he did. A glimpse of khaki pantleg, a movement high in the piled crates in the darkness behind the worklights. The Kid sprang easily between stacks and then it was like he had never been there.

There were lights out on the river where the plane had gone under and shouts that carried over the water.

"Show yourself," the Korean cried. "Where are you?" It was like a piece of theater played in the round under stark white stage lights.

"Somebody's going to get killed," Sloane whispered. "It's the only way this can end unless we do something."

"I know."

"And do it now."

"Wait a minute," Voss protested. "Just . . . now just wait a minute." He hunkered down against the boxes, wracking his brain for a stratagem, a scheme, a cheap trick. Anything.

"Now, Pete."

"Shhh. Hold on a sec. Let me think."

"There's no time," Sloane said, making a move to stand up. "All right, then, somebody's got to . . ."

"Wait a minute." Voss tried to wrestle him back against the cardboard boxes but Sloane just pushed him away and got to his feet. Voss had little choice but to rise with him.

"All right. Okay," he told him, keeping his eyes on the Korean. "You're right, I guess. You're always right. I really hate your guts sometimes, y'know that?" He made a poor show of a grin and gave his friend a poke in the ribs.

Park Sung Dai heard them—or at least he heard something above Kiri's protests. "Shut up." He shook her. "Shut up, I said."

"Leave her alone, asshole."

"Petah!"

"So!" The Korean turned sharply and Kiri cried out as he twisted her arm to make her turn with him. He was searching the shadows with his puffy eyes when Voss stepped out into the light. For a moment he regarded Voss as if he'd been expecting him all along. "So you've decided to join us."

"What's this going to get you?"

"Your timing was faulty, Peter. But the results were as you

predicted. The Russians are suspicious already. I know they are. And Hanoi . . . well, my only hope is to head them off before they figure it out."

"You're crazy, Sung Dai. They can't have it figured out yet."

"They know, I tell you! There is nothing to be done but hand you over to them immediately. Tonight. Take you out to the yacht and make you tell them that this trick was none of my doing. That I had nothing to do with any money stolen from their accounts and put into mine. Immediately, do you understand me? Your lunatic brother will just have to do as I say."

"Will he?" Voss looked out into the darkness.

"I have the girl."

"Now that's dumb, man. Really dumb."

The Korean scowled. "But here you are, isn't it?"

There was a sound on the dock behind him. It might have been anything; the breeze stirring the tarps, a scuffling rat—or it might have been the Kid. It was enough to remind the Korean of his vulnerability.

"What is he up to, your brother?" he demanded. "What will he do?" He looked around quickly as if there might be a concerted plan at work here, and then began backing with Kiri toward the barge. Voss moved with him carefully, matching him step for step.

The Korean was scouring the shadows as he retreated, startled by one shadow and then the next. "Stop him, Peter," he demanded. "Stop him, I say. Or is this another of your tricks?"

"No more tricks," Voss told him. "I haven't got any left."

"Where is that maniac? What is he up to?"

"He's gonna kill you, man. What the hell do you think he's up to?"

"I offered him a deal."

"You can't deal with him, he's crazy," Voss told him. "You can deal with me, that's all. Got it? So here's the deal. First thing y'do is let the girl go. Everything will be okay if you let her go."

"Ho! You think I am a fool? She is all I have. Everyone else is gone. You are out to kill me too, is that it?" The Korean raised his gun and aimed down the barrel at Voss's chest.

"Don't." Voss winced and held up his hands as if to shield himself, but when the shot didn't come he said, "Honest t'God, Sung Dai. The only chance you've got is to let her go."

Park Sung Dai seemed to take heart from this brief show of fear. From a frightened, hunted animal he became a man with a chance. After all, he had the gun.

"No," he said. "Oh, no, my friend. She is coming with me and so are you. There are people waiting for you on board my yacht and this time your tricks will amuse no one."

"No . . ." Kiri protested, wiggling painfully in the Korean's grasp. "No, Petah."

"Don't! Okay. Yeah, I'll go with you. Just let her go."

"No, Petah," she cried, fighting the Korean's grip. "Not fo' me. If you only knew what I have done. . . ."

"Done? Oh, you'll do much more," the Korean said. "Much more, indeed. You will keep me alive and make your boyfriend do what I tell him to do. Isn't it so, Peter? Though why your brother should pay so much attention to a cheap little whore . . ."

It was all too much for Kiri. She bent suddenly and kicked back hard at her captor's shin. The Korean yelped with surprise. She lunged and writhed against his grip so that he had to lock his gun arm around her, then, in spite of her pain, she bent her knees and shoved herself forward.

The move had caught the Korean off balance, and to keep from falling he had to let go with his gun hand and use it to prop himself against her back—and when he did so the gun went off.

The shot at such close range was like an explosion. The young girl was pitched forward into Voss's arms, where she slumped against him. She moved her lips but had no breath for words. Voss clutched her to himself.

"*Kiri!*" he cried, but he knew she was dead.

The Korean stared at the body with his mouth open, the gun smoking in his hand. Before he could say anything there came a cry from the dark, an unearthly wail of such anguish that both men were riveted to the spot.

And then, nothing. There was no other sound nor any sign of the Kid. Now the Korean understood what he had done and fell into a state of mortal terror.

"Come out! Come out here, you!" He was in a palsy of fear, "You . . . you . . ." He lurched around like a marionette and waved the heavy pistol. He turned as if to run and then thought the better of it. He waited for something to tell him what to do, a target rushing at him or even just a sound that would tell him to shoot. But the only sound that came was the steady grind of the barge's machinery behind him.

"Bastard." Voss knelt with Kiri's body, lowering it gently to the dock where he closed her lifeless eyes. "You bastard. I should'a . . ."

"There he is!" the Korean cried, whirling on a sound behind him and firing into the shadows, where an enraged Sloane was charging across the heavy planks.

"It's him! It's him!"

Before the Korean could shoot again Voss had jumped up and grabbed him around the waist as if they were having a schoolyard tussle. The Korean rolled with the assault and fired a shot that ricocheted off the plank in front of Sloane, who dodged and dived behind a crate. From there he could see Voss and the Korean at the edge of the circle of light, wrestling each other in a slow-motion tango for control of the gun.

"Gimme that."

"It's him! It's him." The Korean was fighting with the strength of a madman, clubbing away at him with his free hand until he had to duck away and then using the heavy barreled pistol to deliver a sharp crack on the side of his head.

"It's him!"

And as Voss reeled away, dazed, the Korean fired blindly in Sloane's direction. Sloane made a jump for a coil of heavy rope a few feet to his left. The Korean saw the movement and the next shot almost blinded him with a blast of shredded hemp.

"Kid!" Voss was holding his head. Blood was trickling down his face as he scanned the cluttered pier for another sign of what he thought was his brother. "Don't do it, Kid. Leave him to me, I'll take care of it. I'll take care of everything."

Sloane was too enraged to think straight. He didn't realize that both of them now mistook his movements for those of the Kid. He just rubbed his eyes until he could see well enough to make a break for the end of the dock and the cover of the forklift parked behind them.

The Korean got off another shot and Sloane found himself caught in the open. His only chance was to jump for cover to the stern of the *nam pla* barge, but when he tried for it he slipped on the spillings of the conveyor belt.

When he hit the edge of the barge's deck his leg went out from under him and he landed on it with a loud snap.

"Yah!"

"I've hit him, heh-heh-heh. I've hit him."

"*Kid!*" Voss was yelling. "*Kid! Kid!*"

"I've hit him. I've hit him." The Korean stepped over Kiri's body. "I've got him now," he said, and he started for the gangplank of the barge where the machinery was still grinding away by itself.

"Run, Kid." Voss struggled to his feet and went after the Korean. "Run for it. He knows where you are." He intercepted him at the gangplank, holding the two handrails to block his way.

The Korean came at him swinging, forcing him back onto the gangplank, where their combined weight split away the uprights of one of the flimsy rails. Voss made his stand there, grappling with the Korean until he had him wrestled out over the gap of water between the dock and the barge.

"Run for it, Kid." Voss had gotten hold of the Korean's necktie and was holding his head, up trying to punch at it with his fist. The gangplank was tipping them toward the dockside slime a dozen feet below. The Korean was mad with fear. There was only one way out of this. He stuck his pistol into Voss's ribcage and fired.

Sloane saw the blast from where he lay. He didn't hear it above the machinery but there was a flash between the two figures and then his friend seemed to just fold up. He staggered backwards and flattened himself against the cabin bulkhead where he settled almost reluctantly to the deck. His eyes were open.

Sloane rolled to his side and tried to crawl toward him past the stinking open hold. The machinery was still running all around and, without the workers to guide the conveyor belt, the fish renderings spilling down from the cannery were missing the hold and splashing over the deck, making it too slippery to move ahead even on his hands and knees. Sloane had only managed a few feet when the Korean got to him by doubling around from the starboard side.

His lumpy face was fouled by grimy sweat and a bloody nose that dribbled down his chin to his jacket. He was slipping around on the deck like a drunk on skates.

When he saw who it was he couldn't seem to believe it. "You!" he said.

Sloane tried to look up at him. He raised a hand to shade his eyes from the blazing lights overhead and saw a shadow fall from the rigging. The Korean didn't see it. He was bewildered by this turn of events.

"You . . . ?"

And then, like a sprung trap, a thick forearm clamped around the Korean's and he was lifted into the air from behind. The Kid had him.

The Korean clawed at the Kid's arm. He waved and scratched and beat ineffectually at him with his pistol. He shook himself and kicked into the air. The more he struggled the darker his face grew.

He wiggled and pitched and grabbed at everything in reach. He punched at the Kid's head and kicked at his crotch but the Kid hardly moved. Thick blue veins bulged on the Korean's forehead and his eyes popped like a devil mask. He fired his gun into the air. He fired at their feet, blowing fat holes through the hardwood deck, then he twisted his arm backward under his armpit, bending sideways until the muzzle was snug against solid flesh—and fired again. The Kid staggered.

The Korean knew at once that he'd struck home. The Kid hunched his huge body forward and the Korean, seeing his chance, fired again. The Kid swung around on one heel and took a step.

The Korean's eyes rolled down, the grip on his throat was weakening but still no breath would come to him, for it was plain, now, where the Kid was taking him. There was no squirming free. Another step brought them to the brink and yet they lingered.

Sloane was yelling at the top of his lungs but he'd never remember what he said. He tried to reach out for them but his strength was gone and they toppled past him, still locked in their macabre embrace, into the churning maw of the hold.

The screaming was terrible but by the time Sloane managed to crawl to the edge of the hatch he found that the screams were his alone. Below him the Kid was already gone and of the Korean there was only a pair of legs left dancing in the air. The rest had been drawn under by the whirling blades of the worm gears and blended into the swill.

* * *

A fresh sea breeze from the Gulf blew the thin trailing edge of the afternoon rainclouds inland from the Gulf and lifted for a moment the closeness of the early evening air. The clear blue sky cheered the holiday crowd at the Lotus Garden Inn.

There was no lotus garden in the Lotus Garden Inn—the fragrance surrounding the place was from the red zinnias along the walkway and the bougainvillea blossoming from the trellis shading the tables around the patio.

Everyone was tired of the monsoon by now but the evenings were always bright and clear this time of the year and the Thais used any excuse they could think of to go out and enjoy themselves.

"She's a bottomless pit," Alice said as she heaped some more *lon ghai* over the rice in the little Cambodian girl's bowl. Her right arm was still in a cast and she wasn't very good at using her left. "She's probably been running and hiding for most of her life, so she's learned to eat everything she gets a chance at."

It was the evening of the festival of lights and they were celebrating it away from the crowds of Bangkok in the downriver village of Ban Sikhorn. The Lotus Garden Inn overlooked the stretch of waterway where the Chao Phraya begins to spread out to meet the sea. Later there would be crowds lining the banks setting thousands of candles adrift in tiny paper rafts. The Prince had reserved a side table and had the owner move things around to accommodate the cast that had Sloane's leg sticking out in everybody's way.

Sloane watched the child in amazement. They had guessed her age at four, maybe four and a half. Poorly nourished, but better than many who had been on the move so long. She was a sturdy kid. She'd lost her mother and God knows how many other members of her family—the only survivor, perhaps. She'd taken the rigors of the escape and the crash landing in stride and a few weeks in Thomasat University Hospital made her the darling of the pediatrics ward.

But she didn't talk. She never said a word, not a sound. They had her examined, they tested her in all the dialects that might have been hers, but she never said a word.

The owner of the inn was a long-time friend of both Sloane and the Prince. A friendly fellow with a smile as wide as his ample girth, he came sweeping through the crowded tables with a fresh pot of tea and a glass of milk.

"Thanks, Mr. B.," Sloane said. "I hope we've left you enough food for the rest of your customers?"

"Ah yes, Mr. David," he said. "You just enjoy. Plenty more for everybody." As he spoke there was a change in the ambience of the holiday gathering. Everyone fell silent as if an unexpected rain cloud was blowing in to spoil their evening. Even Mr. B. let his happy face fade as he raised his eyes to the river beyond.

A steam tug trailing black smoke was passing by out in the main channel, making its way slowly against the current with another decrepit hull in tow. There was a crew on the afterdeck of the tug but no sign of life from the boat behind.

"More of them," the Prince said as the patrons went back to their eating.

"What are we to do with them all?" said Mr. B. Then, as if his mind had only strayed for a moment, he nodded to Alice and Sloane and headed off to his kitchen again.

"Well, perhaps we can start with this one," the Prince suggested.

"Good idea," Sloane said. "What are we going to do with her?"

Alice sighed. She rested her chin in her hand and watched while the little girl devoured the ball of ice cream Alice had made her wait for. "She has to go back," she said.

"Back?" Sloane was surprised. "Back to that pest hole?"

"Or one like it," she said. "It's the law."

"When did you start worrying about the law? C'mon. You could do it. You must have some pull."

"It's not *my* idea."

"Mm." The Prince was fidgeting with his napkin. "If you will excuse me for a moment, I will see what's keeping my coffee."

"We can't fit her into any of the quotas," Alice continued, hardly noticing the Prince's departure. "Not unless she's under the administration of one of the camps."

Sloane took a deep breath and shook his head. "I don't know how you can do it."

"Do what?"

"Well, there you go again with your rules and . . . and your excuses. You're starting to sound like your Dr. Jorgenson."

"My Dr. Jorgenson? *My* Dr. Jorgenson."

"You're starting to think too much about the rules and not enough about the people you're trying to help."

"How can you say that, David?"

"All right, all right. What are we going to do about this one? Just this one little kid right here?"

"Oh, she's such a cutie." They watched her paint her face with her ice cream spoon. "I'll find a way to look after her myself until we can process her case. Something will turn up."

"Is that what you have to do? 'Process her case'?"

"Please, David. You know how it works. And all that money Peter gave us makes it even more important that we play by the rules. The other agencies are looking for any excuse they can to tie us down."

" 'Quotas,' 'play by the rules,' 'tie us down.' Damn, you and your squabbles. Sometimes it sounds like the good guys have the same mentality as the bad guys." He headed off a major drip on the little girl's chin with the dab of his napkin.

Alice didn't answer. She was looking out over the river where the smoke from the tug still hung in the air, the water was as green as jade. Sloane changed the subject.

"So Pete ended up doing something worthwhile after all."

"I knew he would, didn't you?" She had turned back to him and was watching him with wide blue eyes, a color that the flyer in him had often mistaken for clear weather.

"Yeah, sure." Sloane had been toying with a cigarette for some time and now he tapped the filter on his lighter and lit it, careful to blow the smoke away from their young guest. "Did you love him?" he suddenly asked.

"I must have, I guess," she said. "There was a fascination, a kind of crazyness to it all . . . or maybe I thought I could change him. I wish I could make you understand. You must hate him."

"Nope."

"Well, maybe it's me you should hate."

"What for?"

"For being such a fool."

He suddenly grinned at her. "Crazy Alice," he said. It took her by surprise and she turned red around her nose the way she always did when she blushed.

"I'm serious, David."

"We've all been fools." He shook his head, blowing his cigarette smoke over the dirty dishes. "You know what Jake told me once, a long time ago? He said, 'More than anything else, we are victims of our own expectations.' "

"What's that supposed to mean?"

Sloane shrugged. "Pete thought he could get all the wealth and power in the world because his technological rules were the only ones that counted," he said. "And you thought you could save the soul of a man when you couldn't even understand him."

"And you?"

"Me? I came here wishing that life was simpler," he told her. "Now I wish *I* was."